DONALD E. WESTLAKE

HIGH ADVENTURE

TOR

A TOM DOHERTY ASSOCIATES BOOK

HIGH ADVENTURE

Copyright © 1985 by Donald E. Westlake

"Hey, Dad, This Is Belize!" by Emory King
Copyright © 1977, Emory King
Tropical Books, Belize City, Belize
used by permission of the author.

Bela Lamb, by Zee Edgell
Copyright © 1982, Zee Edgell
Heinemann Educational Books, Ltd, London
used by permission of the author and Heinemann Educational Books.

Reprinted by arrangement with The Mysterious Press

First Tor printing: July 1986

A TOR Book

Published by Tom Doherty Associates
49 West 24 Street
New York, N.Y. 10010

Interior drawings by Sean Westlake

ISBN: 0-812-51056-9
CAN. ED.: 0-812-51057-7

Library of Congress Catalog Card Number: 84-62912

Printed in the United States

0 9 8 7 6 5 4 3 2 1

EVERYTHING WAS
OUT OF CONTROL

There was no way to buy this woman off, or force her silence, except . . .

Vernon put the candle down. "I have to get back," he said.

The skinny black man nodded at the locked door. "Do I take care of that?"

"Well, of course, man, you brought her here, didn't you?"

The skinny black man leveled on Vernon a cold and impatient gaze, and waited.

Unwillingly, Vernon said, "We can't have her walking around the streets now, can we?"

"Say it out, Vernon. Say what you want."

There was to be no escape from responsibility. Vernon looked aside, out the doorway at trees, brush, vines, heavy greenery turning black in the orange light. He shook his head. "She has to die," he muttered, and hurried away.

HIGH ADVENTURE

Look for all these TOR books by Donald E. Westlake

HIGH ADVENTURE
KAHAWA
LEVINE
WHY ME

*This rumpus is for
Emory and Elisa King, and for
Stewart and Lita Krohn, and for
Compton Fairweather, all of whom
may recognize a tree or two in passing;
and for Abby Adams,
who walked this line.*

TABLE OF CONTENTS

PART ONE:
THE FAMOUS PLANE

PART TWO:
TINGS BRUK DOWN

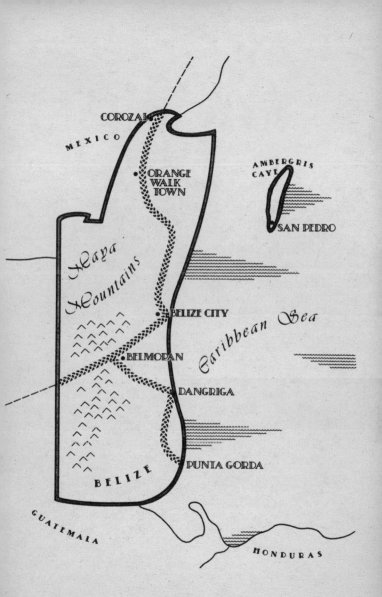

from HEY, DAD, THIS IS BELIZE!
by Emory King (abridged)

The Atayde Brothers Circus visited Belize in the late
twenties. It was around the same time Lindbergh flew into
Belize City with his famous plane. They set up their tent
near Memorial Park, and when the people of Belize saw
what was inside they rushed the place by the thousands.

Animals! Boys, there were elephants, camels, show
horses, polar bears, lions, tigers from India, and even
giraffes. On the 10th of September the circus band marched
through the streets and we almost had a riot.

And a regular band it was too. All the members had
uniforms with gold braid and wore high hats and marched
like soldiers. The leader of the band was a Mexican Army
Major named Ismael G. Amaton. He was on the wrong
side in some revolution in Mexico in those days and had
been forced to run away and join the circus to keep from
being killed.

Every weekend people came from all over to see the
circus. There were clowns, performing horses, acrobats
from El Salvador, trapeze artists, beautiful German girls
dressed all in spangles and tights, who rode bicycles. It
was a sight for the people of Belize.

Well boys, the circus stayed around Belize City for about
two months, giving shows every weekend to packed audi-
ences. But a funny thing happened. The circus went broke.

Nobody knows why. Maybe someone ran off with the
cash. But the circus did not have the money to move on.
Little by little, a few of the circus people left. Some went
to Honduras and Guatemala. Some went back to Mexico.
A few stayed on in Belize.

When there was only about 50 people left, with all the

1

animals and equipment, they decided to sell what they could and rent a boat to take them to Progresso.

A storm came up when the boat, which looked like Noah's Ark, got as far as Caye Caulker's northern point. They could not go out to sea, so they came up to San Pedro and landed.

Well, if you ever saw a circus it was that day. The boat got as close to shore as possible, and they put the poor beasts into the sea to get ashore as best they could.

It was a downhearted bunch of people and a sad bunch of animals. Imagine giraffes and elephants, and dancing horses on the beach.

Of course, we villagers did everything we could to help. Water and meat and food for the animals soon put the town in trouble, but somehow we fixed them up alright. The circus people were nice, and put on a couple of shows for us in the main park.

Oh those were the days, boys. Ever since then, whenever we Belizeans hear of a big project that is going to do great things in the country, we say: Bigger circus than this come to Belize and broke up.

PART ONE

THE FAMOUS PLANE

1

THE CRESCENT EMPIRE

The girl was a real pest. "I think it's terrible," she said.

Kirby Galway nodded. "I think so, too," he murmured, jiggling ice cubes in his glass. Around them the party brisked along, intense meaningless conversation on all sides, mammoth paintings of house parts—a keyhole, a windowsill—visible above and between all those talking heads. In the middle distance, receding ever farther from Kirby's grasp, was his target of opportunity for this evening, one Whitman Lemuel, assistant curator of the Duluth Museum of Pre-Columbian Art, here in New York on a buying expedition, here at this Soho gallery party as a

5

form of relaxation and a story to tell the home folks in Duluth.

Kirby had just this morning learned of Lemuel's presence in New York, had burrowed out Lemuel's evening plans by late this afternoon, and had come down through the snowy city to crash the party early, so as to be ready when his mark arrived. Tall and handsome and self-assured, proud of his luxuriant ginger moustache, dressed with casual impeccability, Kirby was yet to find the party he couldn't crash. And in Soho? He could have come here straight from the jungle, in his hiking boots and oil-stained khakis and battered bush hat, and still they would have swept him right on in, assuming he was either an artist or an artist's boyfriend.

He was neither. He was a salesman, and his customer this evening was one Whitman Lemuel.

Or was to have been; things were looking decidedly worse. Was it the door Lemuel now angled toward?

It had begun well. Kirby had introduced himself in tried-and-true fashion, by actually introducing the other fellow: "Aren't you Whitman Lemuel?"

Non-famous people are always delighted to be recognized by strangers. "Why, yes, I am," said the round-faced Lemuel, eyes benign behind round glasses, broad mouth smiling over polka-dot bow tie.

"I want you to know," Kirby said, "I was really impressed by that upper Amazon show you put together a while back."

"Oh, yes?" The smile grew broader, the eyes more benign, the bow tie brighter. "Did you see it in Duluth?"

"Unfortunately not. In Houston. It traveled very well."

"Yes, it did, really," Lemuel agreed, nodding, but his expression very faintly clouded. "Still, there were parts of it that couldn't leave the museum, simply not. I'm afraid you didn't get the full effect."

"What I saw was definitely impressive. I'm Kirby Galway, by the way."

As they shook hands, Lemuel said, "Are you connected with the Houston museum?"

"No, no, I'm merely an amateur, an enthusiast. I live in Belize now, you see, and—"

"Ah, Belize!" Lemuel said, brightening even more.

"You know it?" Kirby asked, with an innocent smile. "Most people've never heard of the place."

"Oh, my dear fellow," Lemuel said. "Belize. Formerly British Honduras, independent, now, I believe—"

"Very."

"But, I tell you, Mister, umm . . ."

"Galway. Kirby Galway."

"Mister Galway," Lemuel said, excitement making him bob slightly on the balls of his feet, "I tell you, Belize is *fascinating*. To me, to someone in my position, fascinating."

"Oh, really?" Kirby said. His smile said, *fancy that*.

"It's the very *center*," Lemuel said, gesturing, slopping his drink on his wrist, not noticing, "the very *center* of the ancient Mayan world."

"Oh, it can't be," Kirby said, frowning. "I thought Mexico was—"

"Aztecs, Aztecs," Lemuel said, brushing those Johnny-come-latelys aside. "Olmecs, Toltecs," he grudgingly acknowledged, "but comparatively little Mayan."

"Guatemala, then," Kirby suggested. "There's that place, what is it, Tikal, where they—"

"Of course, of course." Lemuel's impatience was on the wax. "Until very recently, we thought those were the primary Mayan sites, that's true enough, true enough. But that's because no one had *studied* Belize, no one knew what was in those jungles."

"Now they do?"

"We're beginning to," Lemuel said. "Now we know the Mayan civilization covered a great crescent shape, extending from Mexico south and west into Guatemala. But do you know where the very *center* of that crescent is?''

''Belize?'' hazarded Kirby.

''Precisely! Coming up out of Belize now, there are pre-Columbian artifacts, jade figures, carvings, gold jewelry, that are just astonishing. Wonderful. Unbelievable.''

''Well, now, I wonder,'' Kirby said thoughtfully, baiting the hook. ''On *my* land down in Belize there's—''

''Mayan?'' said an assertive female voice. ''Did I hear someone say Mayan?''

It was the girl, introducing herself, inserting herself, spoiling Kirby's aim just as he was releasing the arrow. Damn pest. As annoyed as any fisherman at the arrival of a loud and careless intruder, Kirby turned to see an unusually tall young woman in her middle 20s, perhaps only two or three inches shorter than Kirby's six feet two. She was attractive, if sharp-featured, with a long oval face and straight hair-colored hair and eyes that flashed with commitment. Her paisley blouse and long abundant skirt and brown leather boots all seemed just a few years out of date, but Kirby could see that the heavy figured-silver chain around her neck was Mexican and the large loop earrings she wore were Central American, probably Guatemalan, native handicraft. He sensed trouble. Damn and hell, he thought.

Whitman Lemuel, obviously finding the presence of a good-looking young woman taller than himself an even more exciting prospect than the thought of long-dead Mayans, was welcoming her happily into their enclave, saying, ''Yes, are you interested in that culture? We were just talking about Belize.''

''I haven't been there yet,'' she said. ''I want to go. I did my postgraduate work at the Royal Museum at Vancouver, classifying materials from Guyana.''

"You're an anthropologist, then?" Lemuel asked, while Kirby silently fretted.

"Archaeologist," the pest answered.

"Slim pickings from Guyana, I should think," Lemuel commented. "But, ah, Belize now—"

"Despoliation!" she said, eyes shooting sparks.

Kirby had never heard anyone use that word in conversation before. He gazed at her with new respect and redoubled loathing.

Lemuel had blinked at the word, as well he might. Then he said, doubtfully, "I'm not really sure I . . ."

"Do you know what they're *doing* down there in Belize?" demanded the pest. "All those Mayan cities, ancient sites, completely unprotected there in the jungle—"

"For a thousand years or more," Kirby said gently.

"But *now*," the pest said, "the things buried in them are suddenly valuable. Thugs, graverobbers, are going in there, tearing structures apart—"

This was the worst. Kirby couldn't believe such bad luck, to have *this* conversation at such a moment. "Oh, it isn't that bad," he said, determinedly interrupting her, and attempted to veer them all away in another direction by introducing what ought to be a sure-fire new topic of conversation: "What worries *me* down there is the war in El Salvador. The way things are going—"

But she wasn't to be that easy to deflect. "Oh, that," she said, dismissing it all with a colt-like shake of her head. "The *war*. That'll be over in one or two generations, but the destruction of irreplaceable Mayan sites is *forever*. The Belizean government does what it can, but they lack staff and funds. And meanwhile, unscrupulous dealers and museum directors in the United States—"

Oh, God. Please make her stop, God.

But it was too late. Lemuel, looking like a man who's just had a bug fly into his mouth, stood fiddling with his bow tie and shifting from foot to foot. "Well, my drink, umm," he said. "My glass seems to be empty. You'll both excuse me?"

Now, that was unfair. The girl wasn't Kirby's fault, and it was really very bad of Lemuel to lump them together like that and march off. It meant Kirby had no polite choice but to stay, at least for a minute or two, and if he did manage to make contact with Lemuel again this evening it would be more difficult to get to the point of his sales pitch in a natural way.

Meanwhile, the girl seemed just as content to deliver her diatribe to an audience of one. "My name is Valerie Greene," she said. She extended a slim long-fingered hand for Kirby to either bite or shake.

He shook the damn thing. "Kirby Galway," he said. "It's been very—"

"Did I hear you say you live in Belize now?"

"That's right."

"And are you an archaeologist, by any chance?"

"No, I'm afraid not." Then, because Valerie Greene's bright-bird eyes kept looking expectantly at him, he was forced to go on and explain himself: "I'm a rancher. Or, that is, I will be. I'm accumulating land down there. At the moment, I'm a charter pilot."

"What company do you work for?"

"I have my own plane."

"Then you must be aware," she said, "of the pillaging that is taking place on archaeological sites in Belize."

"I've seen some things in the paper," he acknowledged.

"I think it's terrible," she said.

"I think so, too," he murmured, watching Whitman Lemuel recede not toward the bar but toward the door.

Terrible. But not fatal, he consoled himself, not necessarily fatal. In fact, Lemuel's obvious unease when artifact theft was mentioned simply confirmed Kirby's belief that the man was a definite prospect. If Kirby failed to hook him tonight, there would always be another time, in New

York or in Duluth or somewhere. Today was January 10th, so there were still almost three weeks before he was due to return to Belize; plenty of time to find two or three Whitman Lemuels. And in any event, he already had a couple of fish on the line.

"The people who do that sort of thing," Valerie Greene was saying, continuing doggedly and blindly to plow her own narrow field, "have no sense of shame."

"Oh, I agree," Kirby said, watching the white-painted fire door close behind Whitman Lemuel's back. "I couldn't agree more. Well, goodbye," he said, smiled with sheathed hatred, and walked away.

Pest.

2

FLIGHT 306

On a bright sunny afternoon in early February, the temperature 82 degrees on the Fahrenheit scale, a man named Innocent St. Michael drove out from Belize City to Belize International Airport to watch the plane from Miami land. His lunch—with a fellow civil servant and a sugar farmer from up Orange Walk way and a chap interested in starting a television station—sat easily under his ribs, eased down with Belikin beer and a good cigar. The air conditioning in his dark green Ford LTD breathed its icy breath on his happy round face. His white shirt was open at the throat, his tan cotton suit was not very wrinkled yet at all, and in the cool of the car he could still smell the sweet tangs of both his aftershave and his pomade. How nice life is, how nice.

Innocent had been graced by God with 57 years of this nice life so far, and no immediate end in sight. A man who loved food and drink, adored women, wallowed in ease and luxury, he was barrel-bodied but in wonderful physical condition, with a heart that could have powered a steamship. The efforts of assorted Mayan Indians, Spanish conquistadores, African ex-slaves, and shipwrecked Irish sailors had been combined in his creation, and most of them might have been pleased at the result of their labors. His hair was African, his mocha skin Mayan, his courage Irish, and the deviousness of his brain was all Spanish. He was also—and this is far from insignificant—both Deputy Director of Land Allocation in the Belizean government and an active real estate agent. Very nice.

The road out from Belize City to the International Airport is somewhat better maintained than most of the thoroughfares in that nation, and Innocent sprawled comfortably on the seat, two thick fingers resting negligently on the steering wheel. He honked as he drove past the whorehouse, and the girls at the clothesline waved, recognizing the car. A moment later he turned left onto the airport road.

Air Base Camp was to his right, the British military installation, where two Harrier jet fighters crouched like giant black insects beneath their camouflage nets, dreaming of prey. Perhaps they were among those which had gone south not long ago to play in the Falklands war. They were here as part of a 1,600-man British peacekeeping force, the last true colonial link, made necessary by neighboring Guatemala's claim that Belize was in fact its own long-lost colony, which it had threatened to reabsorb by force of arms.

However, since the world recently had seen the result of Argentina's belligerence in its own similar territorial dispute with Great Britain, Guatemalan rhetoric had begun to ease of late, and a settlement might yet be found. This prospect Innocent approved; although war itself is good for business, threats of war sour the entrepreneurial climate. Innocent St. Michael had lots of land he wished to unload on eager North Americans, and it was only the possibility of war with Guatemala that had so far delayed the land rush.

Belize International Airport is a single runway in front of a small, two-story, cream-colored, concrete-block building without glass in its first-floor windows. Taxis and their drivers make a dusty clutter around the building, sun glinting painfully from battered chrome and cracked windshields. Innocent steered around them and parked in the grassy area marked with a rough-hewn sign: VISITORS. He slid the LTD near the only other vehicle there, a crumbling maroon pickup he thought he knew. So Kirby Galway was back, was he? Innocent smiled in anticipation of their meeting.

Kirby himself was around on the shady side of the building, hunkered down like a careless native boy but dressed for business: short-sleeved white shirt, red and black striped necktie, khaki slacks, tan hiking boots. "Welcome home!" Innocent said, approaching, hand outstretched, beaming in honest pleasure. Seeing Kirby reminded Innocent of his own wit, intelligence, guile; the thought of how he had snookered Kirby Galway could always make him happy. "I was afraid you were gone forever," he said, squeezing Kirby's hand hard, pumping it up and down.

Kirby squeezed back; the young fellow was surprisingly strong. With his own smile, he said, "You know me, Innocent. The bad penny always turns up."

If there was one thing that even slightly marred Innocent's pleasure in having clipped Kirby, it was that for some reason Kirby never seemed to mind. Where was the resentment, the grievance, the sense of humiliation? Just to remind him, Innocent said, "Well, you know me, Kirby. Good or bad, if there's a penny around I want some of it."

"Oh, you've had enough from me," Kirby said, with an easy laugh. One more shared squeeze and they released one another's hands. "Selling any more land?" Kirby asked.

"Oh, here and there, here and there. You back in the market?"

"Not yet."

"You be sure to let me know."

"Yes," Kirby said, with a slight edge in his voice, and looked up.

The plane from Miami? Innocent couldn't yet hear it, nor could he see anything when he gazed skyward, but Kirby apparently could. "Right on time," he said.

"Meeting someone?"

"Just a couple of fellows from the States," Kirby said. Moving off, he said, "Nice to chat with you, Innocent."

"And you, Kirby." The fact is, Innocent thought in happy surprise, we do like each other, Kirby and I.

There was the plane. Innocent could see it now, and a moment later hear it, making a great easy purring loop in the sky, like some cheerful iceskater just fooling around. Then all at once it turned businesslike, pointing its no-nonsense nose at the runway, seeming to accelerate as it neared the ground, the big blue-and-white plane surely far too large for this tiny airport, these little scratches in the dirt surrounded by the lushness of the forest a month after the end of the rainy season.

The plane growled as it touched down and raced past the building toward the far end of the runway. Then it roared quite loudly, decelerating, as though warning lesser creatures that the king of the skies was come.

Innocent was not here to meet anyone in particular; he just liked to know who had both the money and the need to travel by air. Absentmindedly grooming with his gold toothpick, he stood in the shade of the building and watched the plane trundle back, a tamed tabby now, an outsized toy. It stopped, and 15 or so passengers got off, to be herded toward the building by Immigration officials in odds and ends of uniform.

Innocent classified the arrivals as they went by: several North American tourists, heading most likely to Ambergris Caye and the offshore barrier reef, where those who like that sort of thing said the scuba diving was unparalleled. Innocent himself wouldn't know; the largest body of water in which he ever intended to immerse himself was his swimming pool, in which he could be sure he was the only shark.

Three serious young men in suits and ties and white shirts were local boys, continuing their studies in the States. The University of Miami is now as important as any British school in turning out lawyers for the Caribbean basin. A couple of slightly older fellows in neat but casual clothing would be expatriates, gone north for the advantages of American wage scales, home on a visit to show off their solvency, and incidentally to get some relief from the horrible winters of Brooklyn, where so many expatriate Belizeans made their home.

A pair of white Americans in sports jackets, carrying attaché cases, but not apparently traveling together, would be either businessmen or functionaries at the embassy; in the former case, they might eventually be of interest to Innocent. And the pair of pansy-boys were undoubtedly the "fellows" Kirby was here to meet.

Definite pansy-boys. They were both in their 40s, quite tall and almost painfully thin, and both unsuccessfully trying to hide an intense nervousness. The one in designer jeans and an alligator'd shirt apparently had grown that absolute forest of a pepper-and-salt moustache to make up for the fact that he was completely bald on top, with thick curly hair standing out only around the sides, resting on his ears like a stole. The other had a slightly less imposing moustache, russet in color, but the top of his head luxuriated in long wavy orangey hair, atop which perched sunglasses. He was got up in a safari shirt and khaki British Army shorts and cowboy boots decorated with stitched bucking broncos. He carried a small olive-drab canvas shoulderbag that tried to look like some sort of military accoutrement, but which was in fact a purse.

Those were the ones, all right. But what did Kirby want with them? And what was making them so excessively nervous? Money is going to change hands, Innocent told himself. He wanted to know all about it.

Remaining outside the building, he glanced through its glassless windows, seeing the sheeplike processing of the arrivals. Out on the runway, luggage extracted, doors shut, the plane snarled and turned aside, at once hurrying back up some invisible ramp into the sky, busily on the way to its next stop, Tegucigalpa, capital of Honduras.

Innocent watched Kirby, inside the building, watch the pansy-boys clear through Immigration, then watched him shake their hands, one after the other. No squeezing hard with those two. They collected their luggage—Louis Vuitton for the bald one, a large black vinyl thing with many zippers for the other—and Kirby escorted them out to the sunlight and over to his pickup.

He would be taking them to his plane, yes? Perhaps a hotel first, but then his plane. Even though Belize is a very small country, and even though Belize City is no longer its capital, it is a city possessing two airports. Commercial international flights moved through this one here, but the charter planes and the small locally-owned craft were all back in town, at the Municipal Airport built on landfill beside the bay. Kirby would take them there, and fly the plane . . . Where?

These were not marijuana buyers. And if they were, they would meet Kirby in Florida, not here.

Pocketing his toothpick, Innocent went inside to chat with the Immigration man who'd checked the pansy-boys' passports. They were named Alan Witcher and Gerrold Feldspan, they lived at the same address on Christopher Street in New York City, and each listed his occupation as "antique dealer."

Innocent went back outside, frowning slightly, feeling a bubble of gas in his stomach. The pickup was gone. He wished he could fly. Not with a plane or a helicopter, but just by himself, like Superman. Except that he wouldn't like that foolish posture with the arms over one's head, as though diving. Arms folded, perhaps, or hands casually in jacket pockets, he would like to be able to lift into the sky like an airship, like a dirigible, and float along behind Kirby, unknown, unseen.

What was Kirby's business with those two? Where was he taking them? To his land? "There's nothing *there*," Innocent grumbled aloud.

He should know.

3

FER-DE-LANCE

"Sweeeeeeeettt," said the tinamou.

"Kackle-icker-*caw*," said the toucan.

"Bibble bibble ibble bibble bibble," said the black howler monkey.

"Ssssssss, sss," said the coral snake.

"This way, gentlemen," said Kirby. "Watch out for snakes." He thumped his machete on a fallen tree trunk, which said *throk*. "The noise keeps them in their holes," he explained.

Witcher and Feldspan, having long since abandoned their earlier pretense at heterosexuality, had been nervously holding one another's hands since before Kirby's little six-seater Cessna had landed. Now, at talk of snakes, they pressed shoulders together and gazed round-eyed at the deceptively peaceful green. Well, it gave them something other than the law to be nervous about.

"I bought this land as an investment," Kirby explained, which was true enough. "Good potential for grazing, as you can see."

Witcher and Feldspan obediently looked about themselves, but were clearly still thinking more about snakes than about grazing land. (A fer-de-lance slithered by, unnoticed.) Nevertheless, at the moment, at this particular moment, the land was very plausible indeed. It began on the east with the fairly level grassy field where Kirby had landed, the slowing plane shushing through knee-deep grasses and clover, the whole area just crying out for a herd of beef cattle. Westward toward the Maya Mountains was the jungly upper parcel into which he was now leading them; at the moment it was rather too overgrown with trees and vines and shrubbery, but a person with vision could imagine it cleared, could visualize the trees themselves being used to build a barn just over *there,* could just see the white sprawling manor at the top of the ridge, like something out of a Civil War novel, commanding a view of all this rich grazing land below.

It had been just this time of year when Innocent St. Michael had shown Kirby this land, and when Kirby had scraped together every penny he could find or borrow to buy it. Just this time of year, two years ago, and Kirby was still struggling to get out from under the mess he'd made of things. But he'd do it, he'd make it. He had the system now.

A self-assured and easygoing fellow of 31, who made his living mostly by flying marijuana bales from northern Belize to southern Florida, Kirby had always thought of himself as pretty sharp. In Belize he had seen the growing influx of American immigrants, attracted by the good climate, the stable government, the cheap and plentiful land. In Texas, where he had worked for a while flying bales of feed to cattle on a ranch which was itself rather larger than the entire state of Delaware, he had seen how the combination of good grazing land and herds of beef cattle could provide its owners incredible wealth.

Texas land, of course, had all been gobbled up well over a century ago. But here was Belize, and here was Kirby in on the ground floor, and the vision of himself as a cattle baron was a pleasing one. (Satin shirts; he'd learn to ride a horse.) Not bad for a boy from Troy, New York, who had been taught to be a pilot by the United States Air Force, but who was of too independent a mind either to stay with the military or work for one of the commercial airlines. His Cessna, which he had named Cynthia, had been bought used from a dealer in Teterboro, in New Jersey, and flown south in easy stages, Kirby finding different temporary jobs along the way. He had met some sharpies, and had dealt with tough guys on both sides of the law, and had never been stung. He was a sharp bright boy, and proud of it.

And then he met Innocent St. Michael.

"A lot of Americans are coming down here," he told Witcher and Feldspan, leading them deeper into the jungle, "because there's just so much available land. Here we are in a country the size and shape of New Jersey, and there's a hundred fifty thousand people here. Do you know how many people there are in New Jersey?"

"No one *I* know," said Witcher. He was recovering from the thought of snakes.

"I had an aunt in New Jersey once," said Feldspan, "but she went to Florida and died."

"There are seven million people in New Jersey," Kirby said. "And only a hundred fifty thousand here." He *throkked* another tree bole, to punish them for being flip, then chopped his way through some dangling vines. There was a well-worn path he and the Indians used, but the customers found it more dramatic if Kirby hacked a fresh path for them through the jungle to the site. And the customer is always right.

"This *is* awfully wild country, isn't it?" Witcher said, clutching Feldspan's elbow with his free hand.

"Just unpopulated," Kirby said. "Human beings haven't lived here since— Well, you're about to see it, aren't you?"

"Are we?" They looked around again at the increasingly dense flora, seeing nothing but shiny green leaves and ropy vines and tree trunks still garbed in their green rainy-season mold. Kirby had led them the long way around through the thickest part of his personal jungle, and now he pointed the machete ahead and slightly to the left, saying, "Just through there. Wait; let me clear some of this stuff out of the way."

Chop; slash; whack. Vines and branches fell away, creating a window in the bumpy wall of green, through which the partly cleared hilltop could be seen, rising steeply upward another 60 feet or more from where they stood. Stippled with a stubble of grasses and brush and a few twisted dwarf trees, the slope ended at a bare conical top. "There," Kirby said, stepped back, smiled, and let the boys have a look.

They looked. They stared. All thought of snakes was forgotten, all thought of the laws they were here to break was swept clean out of their heads. Hushed, Feldspan said, "Is that it?"

Kirby pointed again with the machete. "You see there on the right, about halfway up?"

They saw; they had to. "Steps," breathed Feldspan.

"The temple," breathed Witcher.

"Let's have a closer look," said Kirby.

"Oh, *do* let's!"

Kirby laid about himself with the machete, enthusiastically clearing a path up through the thicket to the clearer part, where he paused, *tinked* an artfully casual foot-square stone with the machete tip, and waited for the city boys, a bit out of breath, to catch up. "Like I told you in New York," he said, "I'm no archaeologist, I don't know much about this kind of thing, but what I *guess* is, the temple probably starts right around here."

Feldspan was the first to notice the stone. "Look!" he cried, excitement quivering in his voice. "A paving block! This has been *shaped*!"

Kirby nodded in thoughtful agreement. "It was seeing a few of those blocks around that first got to me. Then I went down to Belmopan and talked to the government people there, and everybody said there's just no Mayan cities or temples or anything at all like that in this area. They said it's all been studied and checked out, and there's just nothing here."

"They're *wrong*," breathed Witcher. The paving stone must have weighed 40 pounds, but he had picked it up anyway, stood tilted forward a bit, gazing at the stone, turning it slowly and awkwardly in his hands.

Feldspan said, "What's the name of this place?"

"Probably nobody for a thousand years has known the name of this temple," Kirby told him. "The Indians around here call this hill Lava Sxir Yt." (He pronounced it "Lava Shkeer Eat," and then spelled it.)

"Lava Sxir Yt," Feldspan echoed, reverently, as though the words were an incantation to call up an ancient savage Mayan priest.

Kirby said, "Let's go on up."

Witcher carefully replaced the stone, and they continued up the slope, soon coming to partly cleared steps, obviously part of the temple's outer wall. Witcher and Feldspan chattered happily over that discovery, until Kirby shepherded them on upward. Near the top, where they could already look back over the jungle canopy to the tiny blue-and-white plane parked toylike in the field below, they came upon what at first appeared to be a low tombstone, perhaps two feet wide and six inches thick, jutting less than a foot from the ground, tilted slightly forward. The top and sides had been squared off by rough chisel-work, and some sort of scratches were etched deeply into the forward side.

This *really* got to Witcher and Feldspan, who fell to their knees in front of the stone, Feldspan spitting on it and spreading the wet with his fingertips, the better to see the etched-in scratches, while Witcher clawed away at the loose dry soil at the thing's base, revealing more of it. "Jaguar," breathed Feldspan, tracing the lines. There it was; the topmost portion of a typical stylized Mayan drawing of a jaguar's head. The lines continued down into the area Witcher had cleared, and presumably some distance below.

"Scorpion," said Kirby mildly.

They both jumped backward, scrabbling in panic on the weed-grown steps, struggling to their feet. "Where?" cried Witcher.

"No, no," Kirby said. "I just meant to look out for them. *I* wouldn't dig barehanded around here, believe me."

"Oh, I see," said Feldspan, beginning to recover his poise. "You're absolutely right."

"This stela," Witcher said, pointing at the stone, "could be *very* valuable. Depending on the condition of the rest of it."

"There's a bunch of them here," Kirby said casually, watching Witcher and Feldspan exchange a quick hungry look. "Let's go on."

This time they continued all the way to the top, where they found a mostly flat weedy area about 12 feet square. In one corner the old paving stones were completely uncovered. Walking back and forth, alternately staring down at the paving stones and out at the view of jungle and clearings and, in the western distance, the bluish hulking shapes of the Maya Mountains, Witcher and Feldspan were clearly caught up in the myth and the magic of it all; here were they, two New Yorkers, sophisticates, antique dealers, used to the ways of the most modern of civilizations, and they had traveled in the course of one day more than a thousand years into the past. The blood of human sacrifice must have soaked these paving stones. The few visible steps in the overgrown sides of the temple would have been lined with savage worshipers in their bright cloaks and feathers. Here—*here*—the priest would have waited, the rough stone knife held high over his head.

"The temples," Witcher said, and was overcome by emotion, and started again: "The temples were painted red. In the old times, when the Mayans were here. Imagine; from miles and miles away in the jungle you could see the great red temple rearing up into the sky."

"Fantastic," breathed Feldspan.

"Must have been something," Kirby agreed. His job was to be slightly the rube, to their greater sophistication, just as he was meant to be a bit less honorable than they and a bit more dangerous. He enjoyed all parts of the game, including this one.

You take a man out of the world he knows, you sing him your song, you tell him about the mermaids, you put on your shadow show, and if you do it all well enough he believes the whole thing. And then you make your sale.

Witcher said, "When can we begin?"

"We'll have to wait a few weeks," Kirby told him. "The ground back toward the coast is still too wet for the bulldozer, and there aren't any roads around here."

Looking around, Feldspan's expression grew pensive. "It's too bad, really," he said.

"I know what you're thinking," Kirby told him, as well he did; he'd helped the occasional customer through pangs of conscience before. "What we're standing on here isn't merely treasure," he said, "not just gold and jade and valuable carvings. It's the heritage of a people."

"That's true," Feldspan said. (Witcher too was now looking a bit abashed.) "You phrased that very well, Mister Galway," Feldspan said.

Why not; he'd had enough practice. "I have the same feelings you do," Kirby said, "and I wish there was some better way to handle things. If I had the money— Listen, I feel I know you two guys well enough now, I can level with you."

Witcher and Feldspan looked alert, ready—depending on the revelation—to be amused, sympathetic, outraged on his behalf, or generally male-bondive. Kirby gazed out over his private jungle and said, "When we met last month, I told you I was a charter pilot, and I am, but there aren't that many jobs for a private pilot down here. Not legal ones, anyway."

"Ah," said Feldspan, though it wasn't clear what he thought he saw.

"What I mostly fly in that plane down there," Kirby said, nodding at it, "is marijuana."

Witcher nodded. "I'd suspected as much," he said.

"There was a certain faint . . . aroma," Feldspan added.

"I wouldn't do it if I could afford anything else," Kirby said. "I have expenses. Mortgage on this land," he lied, "payments on the plane," he lied, "various other expenses. That's the only reason I make those runs."

"Of course," murmured Feldspan.

"And it's the only reason," Kirby went on, "I'd even consider selling this Mayan stuff." Permitting himself to sound defensive, he said, "I *did* go to the government first, but they wouldn't listen. Nobody's paying *me* to preserve all this."

"That's true enough," said Witcher.

"That's why I was glad to run into you fellows, back in New York," Kirby said. "I knew you were decent guys, well-connected with people who would really *care* about these Mayan things.''

"Oh, absolutely!" said Feldspan, flushing with pleasure at being thought both decent and well-connected.

"It's not like we're destroying it all," Kirby said.

"Certainly not!" Witcher agreed.

"Of course," Kirby said, "there's no way to do it without *some* destruction."

Both dealers looked troubled. Kirby sighed. Witcher, looking about, said, "But nothing that's really valuable."

"The site itself," Kirby told him. "That's why we have to be absolutely sure we can trust one another. We're taking a big risk here, and I don't know about you two, but I don't have any real desire to see the inside of a Belizean jail."

Witcher appeared to consider the idea briefly, but Feldspan was appalled: "Jail! Certainly not!"

"Let me tell you what's going to happen here," Kirby said. "As soon as the ground to the east is dry enough, a friend of mine from Belize City will bring his bulldozer in. He's an old pal, we can trust him."

They both looked relieved.

"What he'll do is," Kirby said, pointing to the base of the hill, "he'll doze around from the bottom, just knocking the temple steps out of the way so we can get at what's underneath; tombs, carvings, all the rest of it. When he comes to big stelae like that jaguar down there, he'll scoop the whole thing out in one piece."

Witcher said, "Will he really be able to work that far up the side of the temple?"

"I don't think you get the picture," Kirby told him. "What he's going to do is, he's going to knock the temple *down*. You come back a year from now, this'll be just a jumble of rocks and dirt."

"Oh," said Witcher. They both had the grace to look embarrassed.

Kirby said, *"That's* why we have to be able to trust one another. They aren't tough about much in this country, but destruction of a Mayan temple is one of the few things that can make them really mad."

"Yes," Feldspan said, "I suppose it would."

"None of us can ever say a word about this temple," Kirby said. "Not here, and not in New York, and not anywhere. All you can tell your customers is, they're getting guaranteed pre-Columbian pieces from Mayan ruins. That's *it.*"

Feldspan nodded solemnly. Witcher said, "You have our word, Mister Galway."

This was the critical point, every time, with all the customers. He had to make them understand the seriousness of the laws they were about to break, and the totality of the destruction he planned on their behalf, and then he had to make them accept their shared responsibility for that destruction. Once they agreed, they were guilty in their hearts, and they knew it. They would never talk, partly out of fear of the law, partly out of fear of *him,* and partly out of shame.

"Okay," Kirby said, his song done. "Seen enough?"

"I feel as though I could stand here forever," Witcher said, gazing around at the day and the jungle and the temple, "but yes, you're right, we should go."

As they turned to retrace their steps, Kirby looked down the far slope and saw peeking out at him from the jungle growth down there a face that would have looked at home in these parts a thousand years ago, when all the temples were red and all the people short, mocha-colored, flat-faced, and utterly unknowable. A Mayan Indian face, male, possibly 30 years old, peering bright-eyed up the slope. The wide mouth grinned, like an imp. The right eye winked.

Behind his back, so Witcher and Feldspan wouldn't see, Kirby gestured for the face to disappear. Queering the deal for jokes! The face stuck out its tongue, then faded from view.

As the trio made their way down-slope toward the plane, Feldspan said, with his own impish smile, "I suppose you must have access to some pretty good pot yourself down here, Mister Galway."

"When we get back to Belize City," Kirby promised him, "I will blow your head right off your shoulders."

Feldspan giggled.

4

NEW YORK MONEY

"I'll sit up front with you,"
Valerie said.

The cabdriver, finished stowing her luggage in the trunk,
seemed pleased by that idea. "Oh, sure," he said. "Sure
ting, Miss." Running around his big rusty green Chevrolet,
he opened the right front door and giggled with embarrassment, saying, "I just clear some junk first, just some
no-count junk." He tried to shield the girlie magazines
with his body, throwing them and the plastic coffee cups
and the beer bottles and the wads of crumpled wax paper
and the sun-yellowed newspapers with their thick black
headlines—FARM MINISTER CALLED "IGNORANT"!
—over the seatback in a shower of trash onto the rear seat

and floor. Behind them, on the other side of the airport building, the plane from New Orleans roared as it flew away.

"All okay now, Miss," the driver said, stepping back, holding the door open. His round face beamed with happiness in the late afternoon as his eyes swiveled toward his envious colleagues clustered around the other taxis, shooting him dark looks. A great big six-footer American woman with nipple bumps on her shirt, and she's going to ride *up front*. Probably perform fellatio on the way to town.

Valerie, only faintly aware of the stir she was causing, and blessedly not suspecting the deep depravity in the minds all about her, lowered herself onto the fairly clean sagging seat and lifted her long blue-jeaned legs in, placing her Adidas on the suburb of trash on the floor. Her attaché case she laid on her lap. The driver, fat and soft-bodied, beaming, perspiring, carefully closed her door, trotted around to his own side, clambered in behind the wheel, and said, "Okay, now. All set now."

"Fort George Hotel, please," Valerie said.

"Oh, sure." He started the engine, which coughed and cleared its throat and wheezed pitiably, while the car shook all over. He turned the wheel several times this way and that before actually shifting into Drive to force the laboring engine to do some real work, and then they bumped and sagged away from the airport building and out onto a blacktop road with jungle on the right and what looked like an army base on the left.

"It's hot," Valerie said.

"Oh, yes," the driver said, nodding, keeping his eye on the absolutely empty road ahead. "Hotter before. When de Miami plane came, very hot. Cooler now."

So that was another reason in favor of her having taken the later plane, connecting through New Orleans. Not only had she given herself an extra two hours in New York to finish squaring things away, and not only was her appointment with Mr. Innocent St. Michael not until tomorrow morning, but she had also avoided the hottest part of the day in Belize. The temperature in New York had been 27 when she'd left.

Nevertheless, it was still quite hot here, probably nearly 80. Pointing to the controls on the dashboard, Valerie said, "Maybe we should have the air-conditioning."

"Oh, I'm sorry," he said, sounding sorry, "but dat's broken. Completely entirely not functioning. Not even de little fan." Then he looked at her with such intense sincerity that even Valerie understood he was about to tell a lie. "We're waiting for a part," he said.

"I see," she said.

They drove in warm and fairly companionable silence for a while—a sluggish *Tom Sawyer*-like river now on the right, jungle alternating with shacks in clearings on the left—and then the driver said, "You goin' on to Ambergris Caye?"

"No, I'm not," she said. "What's there?"

He seemed surprised. "You don't know our barrier reef? Beautiful reef, beautiful water. We get many people come down to Belize *just* to go to dat reef."

"I didn't know that."

"Photography, you know? Beautiful fishes dere. Scuba diving. We get lots of people. And sailboats!" he added, as though it were the clincher in an argument.

"Sounds lovely," Valerie said, to be polite. "If I have time, maybe I'll visit."

He gave her a quick glint-eyed look and away, then said, "You'd be very good, uh, diving. Good long legs."

"I suppose so, yes," said Valerie.

"Good long strong legs," the cabdriver said, nodding, staring through the windshield at some vision of his own. "Very good in diving. I like a woman witt good long strong legs."

Feeling the conversation was moving into murky areas

beyond her comprehension, Valerie said, "Actually, I'm an archaeologist."

He brightened right up. "Oh! De Mayans!"

"That's right," she said, smiling, pleased that he was pleased.

"Dat's me, you know," he said, his simple good humor returning. Leaning a bit toward her, smiling, he patted his chest. "Mayan."

"Oh, really?" She said, *"Anzan kayalki hec malanalam."*

He gawped at her, then straightened, returned his hand to the wheel, looked at the road, looked at her: "What's dat?"

"Kekchi," she told him.

He frowned: "You mean, like a song?"

It was her turn to be confused. "A song?"

"People say, 'Dat song, dat's catchy.' "

"No, no," she said, laughing. "It's the Mayan *language,* the principal Mayan tribal tongue in this area. Kekchi."

"Ohhh," he said, getting it. *"Indian* talk. No, I'm not, I'm not *all* Mayan." Grinning at her, this time he patted his kinky hair, saying, "Creole. I gotta lotta Creole, too. Dat's what I talk. English and Creole."

"I see," she said, not seeing at all.

He said, "You going out to de ruins, huh? Lamanai, maybe?"

"No," she said. "Actually, what I'm doing is rather exciting."

He looked interested, potentially excited, potentially impressed: "Oh, yes?"

"I think," Valerie said, unconsciously spreading her palms atop the attaché case containing her documents and maps, "I think there is a significantly important Mayan site that has never been discovered!"

"Up in de jungle, you mean," he said, and nodded sympathetically. "Oh, it's very hard to get up in dere."

"That's just it," she said. "Belize is still so primitive, so largely unmapped—"

"Oh, now, Miss," he interrupted. "We ain't *primitive,* now. We got movie houses, radio, we gonna get television most any day—"

"No, I'm sorry," Valerie said, "I do beg your pardon, I didn't mean primitive like *that.* I mean so much of the country is still virgin jungle."

"Virgin," he said, as though it too were a Kekchi word. Then he gave her a quick sharp look and nodded faintly to himself.

"What I did at UCLA," Valerie explained, "I got the statisticians interested. There are so many Mayan sites discovered, new ones still being found; what if we did a statistical analysis of site locations, with dates of original settlement and final abandonment? Would that show us where new sites *should be*?"

"Oh, yeah," the driver said, nodding like a metronome. "Dat's pretty impressive stuff."

"Well, we ran it through the computer," Valerie said, smiling in remembered joy, "with a lot of other statistical data, too, of course, rainfall and elevation and all that, and the computer said we were right!"

"Smart computer," the driver said.

"It showed an area that has been missed by just everybody! So I went to New York—"

"It's in New York? De Mayans?" The driver had thought he was more or less keeping up, but this latest turn in the story had thrown him.

"No, no," Valerie said. "The *money's* in New York."

"Lots of money in New York," the driver said, grateful to be on solid ground again. "My brudder's in Brooklyn. He works for Union Gas."

"Well, I spent almost three months in New York," Valerie said, "and I finally interested two foundations, and they are funding me to come to Belize and test my theory! So that's why I'm here.''

"Well, dat's pretty good," the driver acknowledged. "You gonna need a driver while you're here?"

"Oh, thank you, but no. Where I'm going, there won't be any roads. I have a contact in the Belizean government, he'll supply me with whatever I need." I hope, she added silently.

They were coming into Belize City now, a small picturesque port town, somewhat dilapidated, with small scenic bridges over narrow canals used in lieu of a sewer system; prettier to look at than to smell. Most of the buildings were low, almost all wood-framed, with sweet touches of latticework and carpenter Gothic. Built along both sides of the mouth of Haulover Creek where it enters the Caribbean Sea, and extending both north and south along the shore, Belize City looks as perhaps New Orleans did when Andrew Jackson was defending it from the British in the War of 1812, or as any number of pirate towns around the Caribbean basin looked in the eighteenth and nineteenth centuries. The concrete or stucco buildings of downtown, with their clothing shops and supermarkets, seemed to be the anachronisms, rather than the fanciful cupolas Valerie saw, or the large airy porches, or the potholed plowed-field streets. Her cab jounced and creaked and complained along these streets, where most of the vehicles around them looked just as dusty and battered, except for a British Army jeep, dark gray, efficient-looking, containing a couple of red-faced soldiers wearing shorts.

Ahead of them after a while was a beat-up maroon pickup truck with three men visible inside, all bouncing up and down together as the pickup struggled along what had become more of an obstacle course than a thoroughfare. But then, with the pickup still ahead, they passed through downtown and came to a better-maintained street that ran along the north side of Haulover Creek. The water was to their right, while larger, well-painted wooden residences were to their left; they were coming, evidently, to the better part of town.

"Fort George Hotel," announced the driver, and Valerie looked out at a modern but rather shabby building, three stories high, motel style, but with an elaborate curving entranceway.

Unfortunately, the pickup pulled in ahead of them and stopped in front of the steps to the main door, causing a delay. All three men got out, the driver on one side and the passengers on the other. The driver walked around the front of the pickup to shake hands with his passengers, both of whom were very tall and thin. The driver, who seemed more robust, exchanged a word or two with them, and then the passengers went into the hotel while the driver trotted back around his pickup, waved an apology for the delay at Valerie's cabdriver, and climbed up into his vehicle.

I know that man, Valerie thought suddenly. The face, the smile, the easygoing manner, the being rather too sure of himself. She *knew* she'd met him somewhere, but couldn't think where. As the cab pulled forward and the green-jacketed bellboy came out to open Valerie's door, she frowned at the departing pickup and the vagrant memory. Somewhere, somewhere. She got out of the cab, holding her attaché case, and turned to watch the pickup drive away, back toward the center of town.

All she could remember was that she had seen that face before, and that she felt . . . she felt . . .

Trouble.

5

MEETING AT FORT GEORGE

Kirby circled while they took in the laundry, far below. Watching, waiting to land, lightly touching Cynthia's controls, he repeatedly yawned.

It had been a long day, now rushing toward sunset; the shadows of the Cruz family and their wind-flapping laundry stretched long and black over the stubbly pasture. Bright purple or orange sheets; red, black, or green shirts; modest white underpants; the ubiquitous blue jeans; and finally the line itself was unstrung. The smallest Cruz children had meanwhile chivvied the goats into their log pen, and at last Kirby's earphones spoke in Manuel Cruz's Spanish-accented voice: "Sorry, Kirby. All set now."

"Thanks, Manny."

The Cruz kids always loved a little acrobatics, so Kirby turned Cynthia up and over on her left wingtip, power-dived directly at the eastern end of the pasture—the laundry having told him the wind was out of the west—brought the nose up at the last possible instant, and walked Cynthia like a bride across the bumpy pasture to the grove of sapodilla.

There were only five Cruz children, but at moments like this they seemed like 50, swarming around the plane, chirping with excitement, asking a million questions, demanding the right to carry some package from the plane to the house. "But I don't *have* anything," Kirby kept telling them, elbow-deep in kids. "Your goddam old man brought it all out in the truck."

The pickup truck, in fact, was parked in its shed beside the chicken house, with the dishwasher still in it. The other boxes were gone, however, and Kirby was not surprised, on entering the house, to find Manny listing slightly, a happy smile on his face and a glass of red liquid in his hand.

Manny Cruz did love Danish Marys. Whenever Kirby was gone for a while to the States, he would bring back, along with clothing and toys and appliances and cookbooks for Estelle, a few bottles of aquavit for Manny. To mix with it, Estelle grew tomatoes year-round in the kitchen garden, and the necessary spices were for sale eight miles away in Orange Walk.

Four years ago, when Kirby had first met Manny, the skinny little man with the happy smile and the brightly shining eyes was one of life's more cheerful losers. A subsistence farmer on rough land that had been stripped in the nineteenth century by the lumber industry, he was—like most of the other rural people in this corner of Belize—also a marijuana farmer in a very small way, tending his little field, turning over the occasional bale of really fine sinsemilla for some really fine greenbacks. To Kirby, then, Manny had been simply another Spanish/Indian local supplier in tórn workpants, with gaps between his teeth, the only difference being that Manny Cruz tended to smile more than most people, so his tooth-gaps were more memorable.

But then the DEA, the Drug Enforcement Administration from the United States, in one of its doomed, humorless, arrogant, sporadic efforts to force the Belizean government to dry up the finest source of foreign exchange in the whole country, compelled the local authorities at least to make a *gesture*, arrest *somebody*, destroy *some* patch of marijuana plants, and poor Manny turned out to be the last one standing when the music stopped. The next thing anybody knew, his pot crop (and part of Estelle's corn crop as well) had been burned, his 18-year-old International Harvester step-in van (still reading *Lady Betty* on the side, under all the newer coats of paint) had been confiscated by the law as having been involved in the transportation of drugs, and Manny was sentenced to 20 years in Lynam Prison down by Dangriga.

Well, the whole thing was a shock to everybody in the area. The taking of the truck, the Cruz family's only means of travel to and from civilization, seemed as Draconian to most people as the removal of Manny from his children for a term longer than their childhoods. They would all be *married* by the time he got out.

A kind of unofficial Cruz family welfare program started up among the other farmers in the area, as well as some of the merchants from around Orange Walk and some of the middlemen in the marijuana trade and even a few of the North American pilots who fly the stuff out, including Kirby. At that time, Kirby had been around the scene only about five months, and was still settling in. He had an unsatisfactory relationship going with a legal secretary in Homestead, he was beginning to be interested in Belize as a place rather than merely a cargo stop, and he saw a way he might both help the Cruz family and introduce a little stability into his own life.

Estelle Cruz, as short and skinny and brown and gnarled as a cigarillo, had at first thought Kirby was suggesting a sexual relationship between them during the term of her husband's incarceration, and she was edging toward the machete before he managed to make his proposition clear. What it came down to was, he wanted a home.

There was a pasture in front of the Cruz house that could serve as a landing strip for Cynthia—better than some of the jungle strips he normally used—and a good grove of trees at one end in which to park her. A mule shed on one side of the house could be enclosed for a separate apartment for himself. Estelle could cook and clean for him, the children already knew better than to tell their business to strangers, and Kirby would have a real base of operations at the Belize end of his route.

What he offered in exchange was, in effect, the twentieth century. The Cruz family homestead was too far off the beaten track to tap into the public power lines, and they'd never been able to afford their own gasoline-powered electric generator. Kirby promised to supply electricity, and the appliances to be run by it. No actual cash would change hands between himself and the Cruzes, but he would provide them with *things* and they would provide him with a home.

It was a fine deal for everyone. While some Cruz and Vasquez (Estelle's family) relatives built the addition onto the house, complete with a concrete floor and glass in the windows, Kirby brought in load after load of matériel. His southern flights had always been cargoless—except for wads of greenbacks, with which to pay for the northbound cargos—and money at that time seemed no problem (he hadn't yet met Innocent St. Michael), so down came two composting toilets, an electricity-generating windmill, four solar panels, a gasoline-driven generator for emergencies,

a washing machine, a television set, a refrigerator, three
air conditioners, four blue-light bug zappers, assorted lamps,
and a Cuisinart. And from a dealer in Belize City came the
used pickup, which Estelle could use whenever Kirby
didn't need it, replacing the confiscated van.

Even without the Cuisinart, Estelle had been a wonderful
cook, and modern appliances simply made her output more
lavish. In Belize, Kirby ate better than ever before in his
life, and when he looked out his window he could see the
spot where his food had been growing until earlier that
same day. The Cruz family was company without being
intrusive (he was gradually learning rudimentary Spanish
and Kekchi from the kids), his quarters and clothing were
kept scrupulously clean, and during those extended inter-
vals when he was up north he knew his goods were safe.

When, in the middle of all this, the Belizean authorities
released Manuel Cruz from prison after less than nine
months of his term—the DEA apparently at last looking
the other way—it changed nothing. Kirby and Manny hit it
off very well, Kirby teaching Manny cribbage while learning from Manny an Indian game involving small stones
and a number of cups, and Manny sometimes helped out in
small ways.

Bringing the pickup truck to town today, Manny had
carried a shopping list from Estelle—cloth and thread for
the girls' school dresses, salt, filters for Mr. Coffee—so
he'd spent the afternoon downtown while Kirby was off
showing the temple. After dropping Witcher and Feldspan
at their hotel, Kirby had given the pickup to Manny and
gone to see a fellow about a shipment to be taken north on
Friday. For security's sake, they'd had their conversation
in the fellow's Toyota, driving around and about for a
while, there being some disagreement about money. Finally, consensus having been reached, the fellow dropped
Kirby at the Municipal Airport, from which Manny and

the pickup and the dishwasher and the other goods had long since departed.

Feeling weary from his long day, and a bit cranky because of arguing about money with a man in an air-conditioned Toyota, Kirby had flown north and west, less than 60 miles, and when the familiar design of the Cruz homestead had spread out below he had smiled and relaxed, not even caring that Manny hadn't yet had the pasture cleared.

Estelle, who was very short, always looked up at Kirby with adoration glistening in her eyes. For a while he'd been awkward with her, thinking her feelings toward him were sexual, but everything became all right once he understood her passion was religious. On the surface a rational modern woman, who enjoyed the Guatemalan and Mexican television stations as much as the kids did and who frequently talked back at the announcers during news broadcasts, somewhere in her deepest soul Estelle was still a pre-Columbian artifact herself, an unreconstructed Maya. Kirby was the creature who dropped out of the sky, bringing electricity and magic, bringing comfort and riches. What was the name of such a creature? Exactly.

Now, with the usual light in her eyes, Estelle approached Kirby with a bottle of Belikin beer in one hand and a piece of notepaper in the other. "Cora brought it home after school," she said, extending the paper. Since there was no telephone line out here, Cora, the eldest, picked up Kirby's few messages at the store in Orange Walk.

Kirby took the beer with more pleasure than the message, which must have shown on his face, because Estelle said, "You look tired, Kirby."

"I'm very tired."

"I hope you got a good appetite."

"I've always got an appetite, Estelle," Kirby said, and swigged beer, and looked at his message.

Shit and damn! Whitman goddam Lemuel!

Last month, three days after the disaster at the Soho gallery, when that irritating pest had queered his pitch, Kirby had run into Lemuel unexpectedly at another party—this one on Park Avenue in the 90s, in the apartment of a rich and avid collector of pre-Columbian art—and on that second try he had succeeded at last in landing his fish. Yes, Whitman Lemuel was interested in previously unknown Mayan artifacts. Yes, his museum had the funds to support that interest. *Yes,* they were prepared to be casual about the provenance and prior ownership of items they bought. YES, he would come to Belize to look at an undiscovered Mayan temple!

Next week, next Thursday. It had all been arranged, with an exchange of phone numbers and a writing down of dates. And now here was a message from Whitman Lemuel, bland as could be, saying he would arrive tomorrow! "Know you'll understand my impatience. Wouldn't want anyone else to beat us. Will be on afternoon Miami plane. Fort George Hotel reservation confirmed."

No; it's not possible. On Friday, day after tomorrow, Kirby had another shipment to fly north, the very topic of his discussion this afternoon with the man in the Toyota. But that problem paled next to the *real* worry: Tomorrow Witcher and Feldspan would still be here, also at the Fort George.

Estelle looked worried on Kirby's behalf, saying, "Kirby? Bad news?"

"Bad news," Kirby agreed. "I'm sorry, Estelle, maybe I don't have such a good appetite after all."

Witcher and Feldspan. Whitman Lemuel. It was not acceptable that they meet.

6

THE MISSING LAKE

When the driver steered his cab into a cemetery, Valerie was certain some sort of mistake had been made. "But I want to go to Belmopan," she said.

"Oh, sure," said the driver. "This is the road."

It was the road. Cemetery flanked them on both sides of the meandering two-lane blacktop; very white stones, very red ribbons wrapped around bright sprays of flowers or around gaunt remnant clusters of sticks. Off to the left two sinewy black men, stripped to the waist, dug a grave in the heavy red clay. At one point, the road bifurcated, making an island of thick-trunked short trees intermixed with more grave markers; tree roots had pushed up through the black-

44

top, forcing the cab to slow to five miles an hour as they jounced by.

It's like the beginning of a horror movie, Valerie thought, except that it wasn't, really. The sun was too bright, the sky too large and beautiful and blue, and the cemetery itself too cheerful and festive. And the air coming through the taxi windows—apparently, the air conditioning in *all* Belizean taxis awaits a part—was too soft and languid, too full of the sweet scents of life.

Most of the world was still theoretical to Valerie Greene, who was painfully aware of how many places she hadn't been. Her pursuit of Mayan sites through the computers of UCLA and the foundation grantors of New York had been spurred—beyond her natural enthusiasm as a scholar—by her need to travel, to get out into what her colleagues called "the field," to get out into the *world*! It was time, Valerie thought, that she and the world got to know one another.

Her father, Robert Edward Greene IV, was a minister in southern Illinois, a fact Valerie found embarrassing without knowing exactly why. Her older brother, R. E. Greene V, was an English teacher in a high school 11 miles from their father's church, and it was Valerie's considered opinion that Robby would *never* travel. Nor marry. Nor do anything. An R.E.G. VI seemed exceedingly unlikely. And, in truth, unnecessary. Redundant. Even otiose.

It was to be different for Valerie. Archaeology was endlessly fascinating to her, and not only because of the travels to remote corners of the globe that the discipline implied. In her mind, she traveled as well into the past, the remote and unreachable past, in which the people and the cities and the civilizations were so *different* from southern Illinois. If asked, as she rarely was, what had led her to archaeology in the first place, she invariably answered, "I've *always* loved it!" since she herself had forgotten how profoundly she had been influenced, at the age of nine, by *Green Mansions*. (Rima the bird girl! Rima! Rima!)

After the cemetery, Belize City was left behind, and the Western Highway settled down to being an ordinary two-lane bumpy potholed country road. It was 52 miles to the new capital at Belmopan, all of it ranging very gradually uphill, and within just a few miles of the coast the broad-leaf tropical greenery gave way to scrub forest, intermixed with weedy fields and intense patches of cultivation. Small unpainted shacks housed families, usually with many children.

There was little traffic on the road: the occasional lumbering large truck (sometimes with Mexican license plates); the small farm truck with half-naked men standing in the back, sometimes waving or making other gestures to Valerie; and every once in a while a chrome-gleaming horn-honking high-speeding closed-windowed big American car with Belize plates, transporting some government official between the nation's capital and the nation's city.

Certainly the nation's capital was no city, when they reached it an hour and a half later. Invented in self-defense in the 1960s, after one hurricane too many had leveled the original capital, Belmopan has so far failed to become very real. Official efforts to force-breed a city tend to be more official than human, and that's what happened in Belmopan. Whenever buildings remind you irresistibly of the artist's rendering, something has gone wrong somewhere.

The driver, who had been very uninterested in conversation (Valerie eventually having become quite nostalgic for yesterday's chatterbox), also had no idea where Innocent St. Michael's office might be found. "Maybe there," he said, pointing vaguely either to the structure that looked like a prison camp's administration building or possibly at the outsized World War II pillbox beside it.

The pillbox was too intimidating; in the other building Valerie found many people, some typing, some talking,

some reading, some chewing thoughtfully on various kinds
of food, all in many small offices to both sides of a central
corridor. A woman darning with tiny stitches a boy's white
school shirt, the shirt almost completely covering the type-
writer on the desk in front of her, said, "Oh, Mister St.
Michael, that's Land Allocation, that's upstairs."

Upstairs another woman, this one leafing through a
recent issue of *Queen,* directed Valerie to an office where
a slender young black man stood up from behind his desk
and said, "Oh, yes, Miss Greene, you have an appointment with the Deputy Director."

"Yes, I have."

Glancing at his quartz watch—perhaps flashing it a bit
more than necessary—the young man said, "I'm afraid
you're a bit early."

"Actually," Valerie said, looking at the large white-
faced clock on the wall, "I'm three minutes late."

"Yes, well," the young man said, with a here-and-gone
smile. "The Deputy Director isn't quite here yet."

"Oh," said Valerie.

The young man looked bright-eyed, saying, "I'm the
Deputy's deputy, as it were, his Senior Secretary. Vernon
is my name; perhaps I could be of help?"

Wondering if Vernon were his first or last name, Valerie
said, "Well, I did want to talk to Mr. St. Michael about
exploring some land."

"Oh, yes, Mayan temples," Vernon said, nodding, pat-
ting his palms together, silently applauding one or the
other of them, perhaps both. "I recall replying to one of
your letters. Fascinating things, computers. I have a great
interest in them myself."

"It's mostly the Mayan temples I care about," Valerie
said.

"Yes. If you could tell me the area of your interest, I
could have the proper surveys, maps, whatever you'll

need, out of the files and on tap when the Deputy Director arrives.''

"Oh, that's fine," Valerie said. Opening her attaché case on his desk, she brought out her own maps, first the large one of the general area, then the smaller one with the specific target site. She pointed, describing this and that, and he nodded, frowning, moving the maps slightly by grasping their very edges between the tips of thumb and finger. "Right *there*," she said at last, pinning down the putative temple beneath her thumb.

"Oh, yes, I see where you are," he said. When she lifted her thumb he moved the map again, infinitesimally, raising his head to look down across his cheekbones, pursing his lips. "But that's," he said, shaking his head. "No, no, that's no good."

"It's there, I mean," Valerie said, poking the map once more.

"Yes, I see that, I see what you have in mind," he said, "but it's not possible. You won't find any temples *there*."

"Oh, I'm certain I shall," Valerie said, becoming more formal in the face of opposition, wondering why this fellow was making trouble. She had heard that some Third-World people wouldn't cooperate unless they were given a bribe or a tip; did this Vernon want money? Theoretically she understood the concept, didn't even have any true objection, but in real life she had never actually bribed anyone, and she found herself now too embarrassed to make the attempt. "I'm certain it's there," she insisted, thinking that Mr. St. Michael, when he arrived, would be above such petty money schemes.

"But it can't be, Miss Greene, I'm sorry," Vernon said. Moving across the room, he gestured to her to follow, pointing at a large map on the side wall and saying, "Let me show you on this topographical map."

A bit reluctantly, she crossed to stand beside him and watch his slender fingers move across the map. "Here is your site," he said. "You see how the higher land is around your land on three sides?"

"The mountains, yes," Valerie said. "It's just where the mountains *start* that we'll find our settlement."

"No, I'm sorry," he said, blinking at her somewhat owlishly, looking far too earnest to be interested in bribes. "Something the map does *not* show," he said, his fingers moving, "is an underground fault that runs along just about here, under your site and east, coming out in these two streams down here and this one over here. Now, the situation is," he said, taking a professorial stance, nodding at her, "all of these first lines of mountains here drain down through your parcel of land, all of them. It is the narrow end of the funnel, you see, the bottleneck in the watershed."

"I don't see what you're getting at," Valerie confessed. (She had now come to the conclusion that he was, however misguided, essentially serious.)

"What I'm getting at is," he said, "in the rainy season, in the wet six months of the year, this is all swamp through here, bog, simply impassable. There's no way to change it, not the sluice at the bottom of an entire watershed." Then, chuckling a bit, his pointing fingers making an arc westward of her site, he said, "Oh, I suppose a billion dollars to put a dam across here between these mountains might help a little, but even so it wouldn't work, you'd still have ground seepage, all these other mountains draining. So you see the difficulty; for six months of the year, total swamp."

"But the Mayans *specialized* in clearing swamp," Valerie objected. "Along the coast, there are evidences of *milpa* farming two thousand years ago where now it's all swamp again."

"The Mayans never tried to divert the runoff from eleven mountains," Vernon said drily. "But even so, there's the other problem, the underground fault. Without it, your site would be perfectly fine, it would contain perhaps Belize's only lake, but as things are the land can't retain the water, it all just runs right through, to these two streams and that one. So, for the dry six months of the year, the swamp becomes almost a desert. No lake, no water, nothing will grow, nothing at all can exist there.'' Tapping the map with his hard fingernails, he said, ''No, I'm sorry, Miss Greene, this is the one parcel of land in all Belize where not even the Mayans ever lived.''

Valerie, despite herself, was a bit daunted by what he had said, but she did have the computer results to buoy her, and the faith of the two New York foundations, and the results of her own study, so she said, ''I'm sorry, um''—not knowing whether to call him *Vernon* or *Mister Vernon*, therefore calling him *um* instead of either—''but I really want to go see the place for myself.''

''Of course, that's your privilege,'' Vernon said, smiling at her to show it was no skin off *his* nose. ''In fact,'' he said, ''if you were to go there now, just today, the area would look very nice indeed. The rainy season ended a few weeks ago and the water is still draining away, so the vegetation hasn't all died yet but the ground is dry.''

''I *would* like to see the place,'' Valerie said firmly, aware of the office door opening behind her, ''and as soon as possible.''

''Ah, here's the Deputy Director now,'' Vernon said, smiling, gesturing for Valerie to turn about and look.

The man she saw was an inch or two shorter than herself, barrel-bodied, older than 50, with tightly curled black hair, skin the color of milk chocolate, eyes and teeth that flashed with pleasure at the sight of her, and a strong aura of self-confidence, mastery. Without being offensive about it, he would dominate any room he entered.

As he dominated this one, approaching Valerie, thick-fingered hand out to be shaken as Vernon performed the introductions: "Deputy Director St. Michael, this is Miss Valerie Greene, an archaeologist from the United States."

"Delighted," St. Michael said, closing her hand briefly in both of his. (His hands were warm, not unpleasantly so.)

"You recall, Deputy Director," Vernon was saying, "the correspondence concerning undiscovered Mayan ruins, possibly to be traced by computers at the University of California at Los Angeles."

"Yes, of course." St. Michael beamed at her, as though he'd just this minute invented her. "Miss Greene, of course. And how is Los Angeles?"

"Actually," Valerie said, "I came here from New York."

"Ah, New York! I love that town." St. Michael's beam turned reminiscent, then waggish. "Cold up there right now," he said, "but give me a New York restaurant any day. Even in January. Has Vernon been helpful?" (Which didn't help much in the first-name-last-name question.)

"Very," she said. "Though he has been trying to discourage me."

"Oh, I hope not." St. Michael waggled a finger at Vernon, saying, "Never discourage our friends from the north."

"I don't think Miss Greene can *be* discouraged," Vernon said. "She showed me the area where she expects to find the temple, and I had to tell her the problems."

"Problems?" Even this St. Michael reacted to with an undercurrent of waggish humor. Valerie was surprised to realize the man was—despite all the obvious differences—reminding her of Orson Welles in "The Third Man." She half-expected him to call her Holly.

"Well, here, sir," Vernon was saying, pointing to the topographical map again, "you *know* this piece of land, you'll see the difficulty right away."

"I do?" St. Michael strode over to the map, he and Vernon consulted for a few seconds, and then St. Michael thumped his finger against the map, saying, "Here, you mean?"

"Right there, yes, sir."

"I see." St. Michael brooded at the map, suddenly very thoughtful. Valerie took a step closer.

Vernon said, "I did explain about the drainage problem, the underground fault—"

"Yes, yes, Vernon, of course," St. Michael said, still thoughtful, still brooding at the map. But then, his good humor regained, he smiled roguishly at Vernon, saying, "But the Mayans had minds of their own, didn't they? No telling *what* the buggers might do."

"But, sir," Vernon protested, pointing at the map, "no one could possibly—"

"Abandoned their own cities," St. Michael said, overriding his assistant, plowing blandly on, "going off into the jungles for no rhyme or reason." Turning to Valerie, he said, "Isn't that right, Miss Greene?"

"That's the great unsolved mystery of the Mayan civilization," Valerie agreed.

"Exactly," St. Michael said. To Vernon he said, "Disease didn't get them. Not war, not famine. They were healthy, civilized, doing very well for themselves, then one day, up they got and marched off into the jungle, and a thousand years later most of them still haven't come back. Just walked right out of their cities."

"Not all at once, though," Valerie pointed out. "It happened in different places at different times, over hundreds of years."

"But sooner or later," St. Michael prompted.

"Oh, yes," she agreed. "Eventually, they turned their backs on their entire civilization."

"You see?" St. Michael opened his arms in triumph, smiling at his assistant. "If those people would *leave* a city for no good reason, who's to say where they wouldn't build one?"

Vernon was clearly not entirely convinced by this logic, but an assistant knows when to retire and leave the field to his number one. "You might be right, sir," he said, with only the slightest visible reluctance.

"Or I could be wrong," St. Michael cheerfully replied. "I expect Miss Greene will soon be able to tell us." He smiled again at the map, thinking about something or other, then turned to Valerie, saying, "I do know that piece of land, though not well. I know its owner."

"Oh, yes?"

"He's a compatriot of yours, named Kirby Galway."

The name meant nothing to Valerie. She said, "Would he object to my going out there?"

"Now, why would he? As a matter of fact, Miss Greene," he said, moving away from the map at last, coming over to stand just a bit too close to Valerie, looking for a quick instant at her breasts before gazing her frankly and openly in the eye, "as a matter of fact, it's possible we could be of help to one another."

Valerie thought, Why does he make me nervous? She said, "Of course, if I can."

"I've been interested for some time," St. Michael said, "in what Kirby Galway plans to do with that land. In my position here, you can see I would be."

"Ye-ess."

"But also because of my position," St. Michael said, shrugging slightly, smiling at himself, "I can't really ask him the Question Direct. He might be afraid of government interference, red tape, that sort of thing. I don't want to pester people, I *want* development of our Belizean land. My department wants it. This is just a . . . personal curiosity. Do you see what I mean?"

"I think so," Valerie said.

"You could go in there," St. Michael said, "no official connection, no interest in anything but Mayan ruins, and when you came back, you could tell me what else you saw.''

"Do you mean," Valerie (who read the newspapers) said, "marijuana?"

St. Michael seemed honestly startled, then amused. "Oh, Miss Greene, not at all! Oh, no, the conditions there would be completely wrong."

"As I said," Vernon put in quietly.

"No, I'll tell you what I have in mind." St. Michael reached out to lightly touch her forearm. "Nothing criminal, nothing like that at all. Miss Greene—Valerie, is it?"

"Yes."

"May I call you Valerie? And you must call me Innocent."

What an idea. Valerie stared at him, speechless.

"We have here in Belmopan," Innocent St. Michael said, squeezing her arm gently, "just one excellent restaurant, called the Bullfrog. Not up to New York standards, but very nice. Please permit me to treat you to lunch at the Bullfrog, where I will tell you exactly how I hope you will be able to help me."

In the background, Vernon looked knowing. In the foreground, Valerie felt confused. "Thank you very much," she heard herself saying. "That sounds nice."

7

TO LIVE FOREVER

From the air, Kirby could see the wheel marks of yesterday's landing; scuffed paler streaks through the grass and clover of the field. And here he was, about to make a second set of the same stripes. Another irritation; somehow, all those lines would have to be obliterated by tomorrow.

He flew on, up and over the hill—from the air, his temple wasn't visible at all—and buzzed the Indian village in the cleft beyond, to let the boys know he wanted to see them. Bare-assed kids between the low brown huts waved at him as he circled overhead. He waggled his wings in reply, then flew back to the field and landed.

He had already walked partway up the cleared temple

side—about at the spot where Witcher and Feldspan had
yesterday discovered the jaguar carving—when the group
appeared above him, rising up onto the flattened temple
top. They were half a dozen short, chunky men in rope-
soled shoes or barefoot, wearing old work pants and home-
dyed shirts. Four carried machetes loosely at their sides.
They had the flat, blunt, enigmatic faces of Maya Indians,
and they waited in silence for Kirby to climb the rest of the
way to the top.

"Well, Tommy," Kirby said, when he reached the top.
"Hiya, guys. Let me catch my breath."

Tommy, whose shirt was several shades of green, said,
"Something wrong, Kimosabe?" His joke.

"Nothing we can't handle," Kirby told him. "Not us
guys."

Luz—red shirt, badly torn—said to Tommy, "He means
us guys."

Kirby grinned and looked out over his mousetrap. It *was*
better, and the world *was* beating a path to his door. His
temple door.

This is where he'd been standing, just under two years
ago, when he'd first met Tommy and the others, and when
their unusual alliance had begun. Of course, the top hadn't
been cleared then; there was no temple.

Kirby stood panting atop the low scrubby hill in hot
sunshine and gazed out in disgust over his land. *His* land.
"Innocent St. Michael," he muttered, looking out over the
blasted heath and his blasted hopes. He had never felt so
low.

In the six weeks he had owned it, this land had under-
gone a ghastly transformation, like a vampire left out in
the sun. The grassy field down there on which he had first

landed was now a cracked dry moonscape, pale tan, as lined and creased as W. H. Auden's face. Even the corpses of the grass so recently growing there had dried to ash and blown away.

The upper slopes of his land were, in their way, even more terrible, having become a landscape from Hieronymus Bosch. Gnarled and twisted trunks produced leathery sharp-edged leaves. Yellowish grass in long razor-sharp clumps stubbled the rise. Nasty fork-tongued creatures that only a luggage maker could love moved in and out across a landscape of rocks and boulders and scaly dry dirt. Birds cawed in derision as they flew westward, toward the verdant hills, the blue shapes of the Maya Mountains, lush with rich dark soil, fecund with greenery. "Fuck you," Kirby told the birds.

They went on, their laughter fading, and in the silence he could almost hear the land as it dried, as new seams and cracks opened in the dead skin of his ranch. Cynthia, baking in the sunglare down below, looked ready to fall into one of those lesions and disappear into the baked dry bowels of the earth. Kirby was of half a mind to join her.

Movement attracted his attention down the opposite slope, where he saw half a dozen wiry-haired Indians making their slow way up toward him, little dust-puffs rising from each step. Good, he thought, now I'm gonna get killed for my watch.

He put his watch in his pocket. Too bad he couldn't put his boots in his pocket. Put his whole self in his pocket. Maybe he could trade them; they'd let him go, and he'd give them Innocent St. Michael. They could rend him down for a lifetime supply of lard.

The Indians, squat tough-looking men with hooded eyes and gleaming machetes, reached the hilltop and stood gazing at him. One said, "Hello."

"Hello," said Kirby.

"Nice day."

"If you say so," said Kirby.

"Cigarette?"

"No, thanks," said Kirby.

"I meant for me," the Indian said.

"Oh. Sorry, I don't smoke."

The Indian looked disgusted. Turning, he spoke to his friends in some other language, and then they all looked disgusted. Shaking his head at Kirby, the spokesman said, "It used to be, the one thing you could count on from Americans was a couple of cigarettes. Now you all quit smoking."

"They want to live forever," suggested one of the other Indians.

Was that a veiled threat? Kirby said, "I've got some gage in the plane, if you're interested."

"Now, you're talking," said the spokesman. The one who'd made the possible threat translated for the others, who all managed to perk up while remaining essentially stoic; it was like seeing trees smile. Meanwhile, the spokesman told Kirby, "We've got some home-brew back in the village. Make a dynamite combo."

"Where is this village?" Kirby asked. He was thinking, maybe they're on my land, maybe I could charge rent.

"Back that way," the spokesman said, negligently waving his machete, not quite decapitating any of his friends.

"How much shit you got?" asked the perhaps threatener.

Kirby said, "How big's your village?"

"Eleven households," the man said seriously, as though Kirby were a census taker.

"Then I've got enough," Kirby said.

The spokesman smiled, showing a lot of square white teeth. "I'm Tommy Watson," he said, extending the hand without the machete.

"Kirby Galway," Kirby said, taking the hand.

Nodding at the alleged threatener, Tommy Watson said, "And this is my cousin, Luz Coco."

"How you doing?"

"Sure," said Luz Coco. "Let's go get your stash."

They all walked down the hill together, and Kirby got the two Glad Bags out of the pocket in his door. "I don't have enough papers for everybody."

"That's okay," Tommy said. "We'll get some toilet paper from the mission." He spoke to his friends again, and a disagreement took place. Hefting the Glad Bags in his palms, Kirby leaned against his plane and waited it out. What the hell, there was no hope anyway.

Kekchi is a language containing a lot of clicks and gutturals and harshnesses even when people are being friendly with one another; when they're arguing about who has to go over to the mission for toilet paper and therefore miss the beginning of the party it can sound pretty hairy. But eventually two of the group acknowledged defeat and went sloping away, glancing mulishly back from time to time as they went, and Kirby joined the rest of them in a walk over his sun-bleached hill and halfway up the next slope and around into a green and cheerful declivity in which the 11 wood-and-frond huts were placed higgletypigglety on both sides of a swift-moving, clear, cold, bubbling stream. "You bastards even have water," Kirby said. They were by now well away from his land.

Tommy looked at him in wonder. "Jesus God," he said. "So that's what you're hanging around for. You *bought* that swamp."

"Desert, you mean," Kirby said.

"You haven't seen it in the rainy season."

"Hell and damn," Kirby said.

But there was little time for self-pity. Kirby had to be introduced to all the villagers—fewer than a hundred people, none of whom had more than a smattering of English—and the party had to be gotten under way. The home-brew, which came out in a variety of recycled bottles and jars, was a kind of cross between beer and cleaning fluid, which in fact went very well with pot.

Tommy said the village was called South Abilene, and maybe it was. Most of its residents were actually very shy, prepared to accept Kirby's presence—and his donation—but otherwise staying well within their stoic dignity, though they did express amusement when their two friends came back from the mission all out of breath, carrying rolls of toilet paper and pamphlets explaining the Trinity.

These were the descendants of the people who had built the temples. Their relationship with the world had narrowed since those glory days; now, they were farmers, jungle dwellers with only a tangential connection to the modern age. Small villages like this were scattered through the Central American plains and jungles, their Indian residents clinging to a simple self-sufficiency, almost totally separate from the technological civilization swirling around them. They had given up both temple building and war; they neither fought nor praised, nor even very much hoped; they subsisted, and survived.

Tommy Watson and Luz Coco were the only South Abilenians fluent in English and, so far as Kirby could tell, the only sophisticates in the crowd, whose conversation and manner betrayed a wider knowledge of civilization. With their half-mocking existential hip form of the traditional Indian fatalism, they were like a couple of Marx brothers wandering through a Robert Flaherty documentary. They were so total a contrast, in fact, that Kirby would have loved to know their story, but they insisted he tell them first how it happened that he had bought the farm.

"It looked great when I saw it," Kirby said. "St. Michael was just representing the real owner, some big aristocrat up in Mexico. The aristocrat couldn't take back a mortgage on account of taxes, so the price was right because I could pay all cash."

"Fat man?" Tommy asked. "Happy with himself?"

"That's Innocent St. Michael," Kirby agreed.

"It was his land," Tommy said. "He's been looking for a first-class fish for years."

"I appreciate that information, Tommy," Kirby said.

"So you're a rich man, right?" said Luz. "You can afford a mistake."

"Rich men," Kirby told him, "don't risk their ass and twenty years in jail flying pot to the States. That's how I got the money. Oh, Jesus," he said, remembering.

Tommy swigged home-brew and puffed pot and said, "Something else, huh?"

Kirby swigged and puffed and swigged and puffed and said, "I just gave the rest of my money to a guy in Texas for some cows."

Luz laughed. Tommy tried to look sympathetic, but he was grinning. Kirby swigged and puffed, and then he too laughed. "Well," he said, "I guess I'm not as smart as I think I am."

"Nobody is," Tommy said. "But what the hell, we can still enjoy ourselves."

They enjoyed themselves. Various anonymous foods—some animal, some vegetable—were consumed, all liberally laced with hot peppers and other explosive devices. The home-brew cooled the throat while the marijuana cooled the brain. A plastic radio picked up a salsa station from Guatemala, fading in and out while the sun went down and the breeze whispered funny stories among the leaves in the upper branches, to which the stream chuckled and giggled below. Various people showed what they looked like dancing on uneven ground while both drunk and stoned. Night fell, and so did many of the villagers. Fires were started; in the orangey-red light, black ghosts whipped by, and people spoke to them in their native tongue.

Kirby lay on the cooling ground, head propped on an empty inverted clay stewpot, half-empty jug in one hand

and faintly smoldering joint in the other, as he watched the moon come up over his mountain. Seated cross-legged beside him, dark face stony and rough-sculpted in the moonlight, Luz Coco told his story: "I was a kid," he said, "my Mama took up with an oilman."

"Rich oilman?"

"That's what *he* said." Luz spat at the fire, which spat back. "Just a ragged-ass geologist, is all, wanted somebody with him in his sleeping bag. Looks for oil in these hills around here, works for Esso. They called it Esso then."

"There's oil here?" Kirby was trying to find his mouth with the unlit end of the joint.

"Lotta good it does," Luz said. "Oil's got to be in lakes, down underground, or it's no use. This limestone around here, the oil's just in millions of little bubbles, not worth shit. Cost too much to pull it up."

"You know all that, huh?"

"I grew up with it," Luz said. "That's the story. The village threw my Mama out, we went to Houston."

"Back up a little bit," Kirby said. "I don't think you touched all the bases."

"These assholes around here," Luz said, waving an arm to indicate each and every resident of South Abilene, "they're very strict, man. Specially about sex. You fuck around the wrong place, you're in *trouble*."

"I get it," Kirby said. "Your mother was sleeping with this geologist—"

"And my Daddy wasn't dead yet," Luz pointed out.

"So the tribe threw her out."

"The *village* threw her out."

"Okay," Kirby said. "I buy that."

"She took us kids along," Luz said, "mostly because she was pissed off. I was nine, Rosita was one."

"Rosita?"

"My sister. You met her before."

"Okay."

"So we went to Houston, and Cary'd forgot— Did I tell you? His name was Cary Smith."

"Really?"

"He was *John* Smith," Luz said, "my Mama'd never found him. But she got him. We went up through Mexico, wet-backed into the States, got to Houston, and old Cary'd forgot to mention *Mrs.* Smith."

"Whoops," said Kirby. "So then what?"

"Mama signed on as the maid. Lois didn't give a shit."

"That was Mrs. Smith?"

"She was okay," Luz said. "Had three kids of her own, older than us. We all grew up together, big fucked-up family. Tommy come to visit a couple of times—"

"Wait a minute. Tommy Watson?"

"Yeah, he's my cousin."

"He came up from South Abilene to *visit*?"

"Naw," Luz said, "South Abilene didn't want to *know* about us. Tommy was in Madison, Wisconsin."

"Wait a minute," Kirby said. Surging to his feet, he reeled away into the darkness. He propped himself against a tree for a while, listening to the splash, then found another jar of home-brew and came back and fell on the ground again beside Luz. "Madison, Wisconsin," he said.

"You from there? Cold, man."

"*Tommy* was there."

"Sure," Luz said. "His old man was with the college, the scientists took him up. He knew all that carving stuff, you know, the old arts and crafts baloney from the old days, he taught it and, uh . . . What do you call it when you say this thing's okay, this thing's a piece of shit?"

"Validate?"

"That's cars."

"Authenticate," Kirby decided. "Say if it's real or fake."

"That's it. Tommy's old man did that. Tommy could do

it, too, but he's like me. We've *seen* the world, man, you can have it.''

"How'd you both wind up back here?"

"Tommy's old man died, is how with him," Luz said. "Tommy brought the body back, he was nineteen, he felt relaxed here, he never did like that snow shit, he was home again.''

"Same with you?"

"Naw. I'm sixteen, Rosita's eight, Mama gets mad at Cary, we go off to L.A., get into some very *weird* scenes. Mama's dealing, we're into all this heaviness, Chinamen, Colombians, I took it three years, I said, I got to get *out* of this. I got in the car, head south, turns out Rosita's hiding in the trunk, she can't stand that shit either. So we go down to San Diego, sell the car, come on down south.''

"Where's your Mama now?"

"Alderson, West Virginia.''

"That's a funny place to be.''

"Not that funny. It's the Federal pen for women.''

"Oh," said Kirby. He thought a few seconds, and then he said, "Luz?"

"Present.''

"If these people here are so moral . . .''

Some time went by. Luz said, "Yeah?"

Kirby woke up: "What?"

"So what's the question?" Luz said. "If these people here are so moral, what?"

"Well," Kirby said, taking a hit as an aid to thought, "to begin with, how about all this pot?"

"What's immoral about pot?" Luz wanted to know.

"Good point," Kirby said.

"You go on south," Luz told him, "you got people down there, all these mushrooms, these button things, they got peyote coming outa their *pores*, man. You got people down there, nobody's seen their eyes in *years*.''

"Okay," Kirby said. "Okay.''

"Pot and brew, now, you just relax. *Sex*, now, that's family, it's property, people's feelings, it's, uh, it's, uh, it's *politeness*."

"Got it," Kirby said. "Sexually conservative, makes sense."

"So your question is," said Luz, "how come these simple, conservative, primitive assholes put up with spoiled goods like Tommy and Rosita and me. Right?"

"I guess so," Kirby said.

"Everybody's cousins," Luz said. "That's number one. And our Mama, Tommy's daddy, they took us away, and on our own we came back, that's number two."

"Okay."

"Everybody knows we're different, cause we were out *there*, but we're still family."

"That's nice."

"We just lay back," Luz said. "Tommy and Rosita and me, we just coast with it."

"Go with the flow," Kirby suggested.

"You got it. Where else we gonna do that? Play by our own rules and they *accept* us, man. Listen, I'll be right back." Luz rolled over, and left. On all fours.

Kirby slept, or maybe not. Maybe those weren't dreams. The white moon rolled slowly across the blacktop sky. Then a form slid between him and the moon, and collapsed in a flutter of skirts. "Hello," she said.

This was the sister of Luz, Kirby remembered that now, and if the moon weren't revolving in those slow circles up there he'd probably even remember her name. "Harya," he said.

"Rosita," she said.

"You're right. You're absolutely right." He remembered her now. She was as short as the rest of them, but skinnier, with the wiry spareness of the born neurotic. Her eyes were large and liquid brown, cheekbones strong,

mouth broad and sensual, skin like warm cocoa. She
moved like a puma.

While Kirby watched the way moonlight silvered her
earlobe, she took the joint from his fingers, made inhaling
sounds, put the joint back where she'd found it, leaned
down over him, kissed him, and exhaled smoke into his
mouth.

It took a major effort of will neither to throw up nor bite
her tongue in half, but he managed, and when he obediently inhaled while she exhaled, then exhaled while she
inhaled, it turned out the moon was making those slow
revolutions inside his head.

After a while, she lifted up and said, "You sleep out
here all night, the bugs gonna bite you to death."

"True. True." It was a sad thought.

"So come inside," Rosita said.

So they went inside, and soon it was morning and his
body and brain were in terrible difficulties. He had a rash
like poison ivy on the surface of his brain, he knew it, he
could tell. He felt as though he were being digested, his
whole self shriven and melted by the gastric juices inside
the whale that had eaten him.

He crawled out to a sun that had approached much
closer to Earth overnight, was now about 11 feet from the
ground. He peered around and was not surprised to see
that the rest of the human race was as stricken as he. Was
there hope for mankind?

Some. Coffee, bacon, more coffee, tortillas, more coffee, a joint, and a brief retirement with Rosita all helped.
The villagers doctored themselves in similar fashion, and
in the afternoon the party started again. Rosita explained to
Kirby how she'd always felt maybe she'd left the States a
little too soon, before she'd really experienced the place,
given it a chance. She was just a kid, really, when she
came back. She'd always thought, she told Kirby, it might
be nice to go back there some time, spend a while; with

the right companion, you know. "Uh huh," Kirby said, and went off to wander around town.

He found Luz and Tommy together, and joined them, and that was when the conversation turned to the heritage of the Maya Indians, and the mystery of their past. "At least," Tommy said, "you fucked your own self—"

"With Innocent St. Michael's help," Kirby said.

"Still, you were there. *We* were screwed out of our rights by our ancestors. A thousand years ago, our people lived in some really class cities. Duded themselves up with gold and jade and all that stuff."

"Human sacrifice," Luz said, and grinned like a wolf.

"Then our people left," Tommy said. "Property values went to hell. You got to *maintain* a temple, or pretty soon it's just a pile of rocks."

"Especially in the jungle," Kirby said.

"That's right. The dirt piles up, things grow, die, rot, more dirt, more things grow. Rain eats out the mortar between the stones, the whole thing goes to hell. Used to be a temple, now it's just a hill, you can't even *see* it any more."

"Listen," Kirby said, "you guys both used to live in cities, you gave all that up, remember?"

"Madison," Tommy said, with curled lip. "Houston. I'm talking about *our* cities. Lamanai. Tikal. Colorful places."

"Colorful ceremonies," Luz said, with that grin again.

"I don't know," Kirby said. "Not to insult your ancestors, but I don't think I'd like to live in places where they do human sacrifice."

Luz frowned at him: "Why not?"

"I'm a human."

"Hmmmm," Luz said, and they grew quiet for a while, silently contemplating the various functions of spectator and participant.

The next day, Kirby sobered himself up and kissed

Rosita and flew away to become a cargo pilot again and start to dig himself out of the hole Innocent St. Michael had walked him into. And two weeks later, eyes shining, he had flown back to his dried-out land and carried two more Glad Bags up into South Abilene, and told Tommy and Luz his scheme.

"Rosita says hello," Tommy said, tired of waiting for Kirby to catch his breath. "She says is your wife any better," he added solemnly.

"Alas, no," said Kirby. "She had two more violent spells, they had to put her in the strait jacket again. It's looking pretty bad."

"I'll tell Rosita," Luz said, straight-faced. "She's very interested in the condition of your wife."

"Yes, I know."

Tommy said, "Those two customers from yesterday; they making trouble?"

"No, no," Kirby said. "They bought the story all right. I'll see them this afternoon, make the final arrangements. The problem is the next guy."

"Yeah?"

"I got a message yesterday. He isn't due till next week, but all of a sudden he's coming in *today*."

Tommy translated this for the others, and everybody looked distressed. Luz said, "Asshole."

"Exactly," Kirby said. "But it's too late to stop him, he's on his way. So I've got to stall him somehow in Belize City, and keep him from meeting the other two, and then bring him up here tomorrow. So you've got to get the place ready by then."

"Not much to do," Tommy said. "The last guys didn't

dig around a lot, like some of your people. Just the jaguar stela, basically.''

Luz said, ''They didn't even find the stone whistle.''

''The main problem is the field,'' Kirby said. ''The place shouldn't look as though it gets a lot of traffic, but you can really see Cynthia's landing tracks there.''

''So we'll mush them up a little,'' Tommy said.

''Right.'' Kirby looked serious. ''And, Tommy,'' he said, ''don't do your little peeking-out-of-the-bushes number any more, okay? If one of those guys had seen you yesterday, he'd have had a heart attack right there. It's bad business to kill the customers.''

''I never have any fun,'' Tommy said.

8

THE QUESTION

"Do you like the conch?" Innocent asked, pronouncing it *conk*, as in *conk on the head*, and Valerie said, "Very much." Innocent smiled. "I take all my girlfriends here," he said. "Before sex, after sex. They always like the conch. They like it better after sex."

Valerie didn't quite know how to answer that, nor did it seem possible to eat the firm white conch immediately after such a remark, nor drink some more of the Italian white wine, so she filled her mouth with salad instead.

Delicious salad. Very nice restaurant at the back of a private house, more outside than in, the widely spaced white tables surrounded by the flowers and plants of a nursery, that being the proprietors' other business. Hanging plants, lengths of tall picket fence, moist dirt floor beyond the tiled part, areas roofed with sheets of translucent plastic.

Tropical flowers are so much more *blatant* than the flowers of southern Illinois. In southern Illinois, the flowers aren't all in hot, hot oranges and yellows and reds, and they don't all look like human genitalia. Idealized male and female parts hung in the air and protruded from clay pots and peeked with false modesty out of veils of shiny green leaves.

The waitress came over to see how they were doing, and Innocent put an arm around her hips, his hand caressing her leg. "So you're working here now, huh?" he said.

"Just for a little while." She was short, plumpish in a jolly way, with a very pretty face and reddish-brown flesh. She seemed not to mind Innocent's hand on her leg. "I got tired being cooped up in an office all day," she said. "Maybe I'll go back to Belize."

They were, of course, already in Belize, and it took Valerie a minute to realize the girl meant Belize City. (In just the same way, people in Mexico say they're going to Mexico, not Mexico City, and people in New York State say they're going to New York, not New York City.)

Innocent grinned at Valerie. "Susie liked the conch after the sex." Squeezing her leg, he said, "Didn't you, baby?"

Susie giggled. Innocent winked at Valerie. "But she liked the sex better."

Susie gave Valerie an arch look, woman to woman. "These men," she said. "They all think they're the best, right?" Imitating a little boy, pressing one fingertip to her cheek, she said, "Wasn't I great, honey? Ain't I the best you ever had, honey? Don't I beat all the other fellas, honey?" Then she became a schoolmarmish sort of woman, humoring the little boy: "Oh, you were wonderful, dear.

Such a great *big* thing.'' As Innocent guffawed, she held up her hands, palms facing each other, like a fisherman describing an extremely small fish.

Valerie had to laugh. She also had to eat conch. The question was, did she have to go to bed with Innocent St. Michael?

Not *have* to, that wasn't the word. It wasn't as though sex would be his kind of bribe, the gift to the Third Worlder to gain cooperation. That wouldn't be Innocent's way. Valerie wasn't too awfully wise in the ways of the world, but she did understand that Innocent was merely permitting the subject of sex to float in the air all around them, giving her the opportunity to decide whether or not to go to bed with him, and suggesting without too much blatancy the reasons why she should.

Generally speaking, Valerie was confused about sex. The gropings and kissings and sweaty fumblings of her early teenage years had seemed somehow off the mark, irrelevant to the hunger that certainly did exist. The idea that these nervous jackrabbit boys might have the solution to the problem, might be able to guide her into understanding and contentment, was absurd on the face of it. And when, at 16, she had finally ''done it'' on the floor of a living room where she was babysitting, the boy had been so nervous, so overly eager, so inexperienced and gawky, that in some ways it had been worse than learning to dance.

Her experiences since then had been infrequent, but varied. Most of the time, she hardly thought about sex, and on those occasions when it did become a part of the agenda she mostly just tried to retain some dignity. She did learn something nearly every time, but many of the lessons were depressing. She now knew there *were* self-confident and capable young men in the world, who could stop thinking about themselves long enough to think about the girls they were with, but there were darn few of them.

On the other hand, older men could sometimes be just as jumpy and inept as any callow youth. It was impossible, doggone it, to tell what a man was going to be like in bed just by looking at him.

Or was it? Here was Innocent St. Michael, deliberately and smoothly filling her head with thoughts of sex, then actually bringing out a previous girlfriend to give him a reference; which she had done, too, even though in a backhanded way. He would not be the first dark-skinned person she'd gone to bed with—if the previously unthinkable were actually to occur—but he would probably be the oldest. And maybe the heaviest; would that matter much?

He has me *considering* the idea, Valerie thought, astonished at herself. And he knows it, too; look at him there, smirking and winking across the table, smacking Susie's behind, telling the girl, "You just want to keep me for yourself, that's all."

"Keep you?" Susie slithered out of his grasp; moving away toward the kitchen, she said, "I caught you once, and threw you back."

He can be kidded about sex, Valerie thought as she drank more wine, because he's so very sure of himself.

Innocent beamed at her. "You like the conch, Valerie?"

She giggled, like one of his women.

9

THE BLACK FREIGHTER

"This stela," Witcher said, while the skinny black man looked out the hotel room window, "could be very valuable. Depending on the condition of the rest of it."

Directly below the window was the hotel's swimming pool, in which no one was swimming. Just out of sight to the pool's left were the large ocean-facing windows of the dining room. From where he stood, the skinny black man could not quite see the dining-room windows, but he knew who was there.

"There's a bunch of them here," Kirby said casually, while the two cassette tapes turned, steady and unroman-

74

tic. "Let's go on." The voices stopped, to be replaced by the panting and rustling sounds of hill-climbing.

The skinny black man glanced over at the dresser top, where the linked cassette players squatly sat, each with its own red eye. Then he looked down again, vaguely regretting that he couldn't quite see into the dining room where at this moment Kirby, Witcher, and Feldspan were having lunch and continuing their discussion. Were Witcher and Feldspan taping this meeting, too? Would he be sent back to copy another conversation?

If so, he would hear Kirby say, "The deal is, then, I'll get the stuff out of the country, whatever we find inside the temple. You guys sell it through your contacts, and we split fifty-fifty."

"You'll have to trust us," Witcher pointed out. "Though I suppose you know the general value of such things."

"Fairly well," Kirby said, shrugging the problem away. "Besides, we have to trust one another, don't we? You have to trust me not to give you fakes."

Feldspan looked surprised, but Witcher, merely amused, saying, "For Heaven's sake, why would you? There's a whole temple of *real* things there, probably encugh to make us all rich; why jeopardize the relationship?"

"Exactly," Kirby said. "And you fellas have the same motive to give me a straight count."

"Of course."

Feldspan said, "The only problem, really, is getting the material out of the country."

"I have my methods," Kirby said, and stopped, because the waitress was bringing them their main courses. Silence reigned at the table until she was done, the three men looking out the window at the empty swimming pool and, beyond it, the open sea. Out there, a black freighter stood at anchor; some nosy British Coast Guard people had grabbed it a few weeks ago, north of here, finding it full of marijuana. They'd impounded it (like Manny Cruz's step-in van), and now it was waiting to be auctioned by the Belize government.

Upstairs, the cassette on the dresser said, in Kirby's voice, "None of us can ever say a word about this temple. Not here, and not in New York, and not anywhere."

The waitress left at last, and Witcher said, "Americans *have* been caught, you know, trying to get out of Belize with carvings or whatnot. Caught and jailed."

"That's why," Kirby said, "in this operation, you're dealing with the right man."

Feldspan said, almost timidly, "I don't suppose you could tell us your smuggling method."

"Why not?" Kirby grinned. "Truthfully, I'm proud of it. You see, there isn't just one smuggling business out of Belize, there's two. There's Mayan antiques, that's one, and the other one is marijuana."

Feldspan smiled reminiscently, and Witcher said, "You're involved in both, aren't you?"

"I've *combined* them both," Kirby told him. "The government comes down hard on the artifact smuggling, as you know. In fact, they'll probably search your luggage on the way out, since your passports say you're antique dealers."

"Oh, dear," said Feldspan. He and Witcher exchanged a troubled glance.

"It's only pre-Columbian stuff they care about," Kirby assured them. "As for the marijuana trade, the British and the Americans make a little trouble if they can, but locally nobody gives a damn. It brings in a lot of U.S. cash, it's all on a small-time basis and a lot cleaner and less violent than Colombia or Bolivia with their cocaine industries, and it makes a good back-up crop for the sugar farmers up around Orange Walk. I've flown a lot of bales of pot out of this country, and nobody's ever looked at me twice. In fact, after lunch I have to see a fellow about that side of it."

Witcher and Feldspan both looked agog. Leaning forward, speaking much more confidentially than when they'd been discussing the smuggling of valuable Mayan artifacts, Feldspan said, "You mean a dealer?"

"A middleman," Kirby told him. "An American, he's coming in on the plane this afternoon." Then, as though afraid he'd said too much, he too leaned forward and dropped his voice, saying, "Listen, this is a very bad man up north. If he thought I was talking about him, we'd *all* be in trouble."

"We wouldn't breathe a *word*," Witcher breathed.

"If you see me with him," Kirby said, "just pretend you don't know me."

"Absolutely," said Witcher, nodding solemnly, a co-conspirator.

"Okay," Kirby said. "Here's my little stunt. I get in my plane, I fill it up with bales of pot, everybody knows what I'm doing, nobody gives a damn, off I go to Florida." Leaning forward, winking, he said, "Now, what if there's Mayan antiques *inside* the bales?"

"When we get back to Belize City," the cassette with Kirby's voice told the other cassette, "I will blow your head right off your shoulders." Then it giggled with Feldspan's voice, and its red light clicked off. The skinny black man yawned, stretched, walked away from the window, and punched the buttons to rewind both cassettes.

"Brilliant!" breathed Feldspan.

Kirby smiled, nodding, appreciating their appreciation.

"I'm stealing wheelbarrows," Witcher said.

"Exactly," Kirby said.

Feldspan said, "The Purloined Letter. The Trojan Horse."

"I never said I was original," Kirby said, getting a trifle nettled.

Witcher said, "And when you get to Florida, out they come!"

"Right," said Kirby. "Now, that brings up another

question. When I reach the other end, will it be you two meeting me, or somebody else?''

"In Florida, you mean?'' They looked at one another, and Witcher said, "I think we have to do it ourselves.''

"Yes,'' said Feldspan. "You just let us know where and when.''

"Okay,'' Kirby said. "Then I won't deal with anybody else. In fact, I won't even get out of the plane unless I see one of you guys.''

"I suppose you have to be very careful,'' Feldspan said. "In your business.''

"Careful is my middle name,'' Kirby told him.

The skinny black man put the talking cassette player back where he'd found it, pocketed the listening cassette player, and let himself quietly out of Witcher and Feldspan's room.

10

OUT OF THE PAST

Whitman Lemuel obediently fastened his seatbelt, then pressed his right temple to the cool lucite window and looked down past the wing at Belize. Far away to the west were lavender mountains, blurry and faded, blending and tumbling into greener hills, smoothing down toward a pale band of beach on which a white foam line ran and spread and vanished and ran again. Blue-green water, as clear and gleaming as new stained glass, spread out from the shore, the color deepening into blue, then breaking at a broad white irregular gash running parallel to the coast, a few hundred yards off shore; the barrier reef, second longest in the world, running for 175 miles north and south, separating the Belizean coast from the Caribbean deeps.

Ahead, where a blue scribble of river cut through the greenery to the coast, a clustered, cluttered, colorful town had grown. The harbor was full of small boats, and a black freighter stood off shore.

Lemuel's eyes moved away from the town, back toward the jumbled greenness of the nearer mountains. Somewhere in there was Kirby Galway's temple. He stared, unaware of the lucite's vibration against his brow.

The stewardess distributed landing cards to be filled out, and Lemuel wrote, without hesitation, "teacher" and "vacation." He had been a teacher in the past, and technically his current job with the museum could also be described that way. Knowing the Belizean government's parochial attitude concerning antiquities, he saw no reason to call attention to himself by putting down his actual job title, and he *certainly* wouldn't describe his true reason for being here: "to save irreplaceable Mayan artifacts."

The Mayan sites, except for the few largest, were not being properly cared for. Much had already been lost forever, and much more would soon be gone. Even if Third-World governments like that in Belize had the will to save what had not yet been destroyed, they would never have the money or knowledge or resources for the job. Frequently, as well, in these parts of the world, there was corruption among the very officials charged with the task of preservation.

Governments like Belize's should *welcome* men like Whitman Lemuel, scholars, historians, restorers, men selflessly devoted to preserving the best of the past, in carefully controlled environments with prescribed public access, allowing the people of today to experience for themselves the mystery and wonder of the long-ago. It was only ignorance and naiveté, combined with backward peoples' inevitable jealousy of the better-educated and the better-off, that made it necessary for Whitman Lemuel, who knew himself to be a decent and honorable and law-abiding and well-educated and intelligent and reasonable man, to *sneak* into Belize as though he were a thief, as though he were planning to do something *wrong*.

Take this fellow Kirby Galway. On the surface a plausible chap, an American, but underneath the glib exterior what was the fellow but a smooth thug? It had been a very fortunate accident that Lemuel had met him again, that second time, and they'd had their little talk, very fortunate indeed, because there was no question in Lemuel's mind that Galway would be prepared to sell the objects from his temple to anybody, just *anybody*. Galway was the sort of person the Belizean government *ought* to concentrate on, not honest scholars like Whitman Lemuel.

But if he was to be honest about it—and Whitman Lemuel was rigidly honest—he had to admit there were Americans too who completely misunderstood the situation, as though scholars like himself were here for *profit*, as though they were somehow stealing something that belonged to someone else rather than preserving the past— which belongs to all mankind—to be handed on, selflessly, properly catalogued and annotated, to generations yet unborn. He remembered with particular distaste that tall young woman who had interrupted his first conversation with Galway, squawking words like "despoliation." Such individuals, unhampered by facts, took on moral positions just for the good feeling that comes from being holier-than-thou.

Outside the window, the turning earth approached, red roofs stood out among the colors of the town, individual trees waved to him, and in a sudden rush and jolt the plane was on the ground, hurtling past the tiny airport building, reluctantly slowing, then turning, coming back.

Lemuel was among the few passengers getting off. He always felt a little nervous when he entered a basically primitive country; who knew what ideas these people might get in their heads? Shuffling slowly through Customs & Immigration, he kept craning his neck, looking for Galway, but didn't see him. His bow tie constricted his neck in this unaccustomed heat, but he wouldn't remove it. All clothing is a uniform, and Lemuel's uniform made clear his status: American, college-educated, nonviolent, intellectual. Nevertheless, he was ordered to open both his suitcases, and the black Customs inspector fingered his Brut aftershave as though he would simply confiscate it. In the end, he merely made an annoying long scrawl of white chalk on each suitcase lid, and sent Lemuel on his way.

Outside, blinking in the dusty sunshine, still not seeing Galway anywhere—he wouldn't have reneged at the last second, would he?—Lemuel fought off the persistent taxi offerers with just as persistent head shakes, until he realized one of the men was calling him by name: "Mister Lemuel? May I take your bags, Mister Lemuel?"

Lemuel frowned at him, seeing a short and skinny Indian type, with bright black eyes and a big smile showing gaps between his teeth. "You know me?" he said.

"I am from Kirby Galway." The man had an accent that was nearly Hispanic, but not quite. "I am Manuel Cruz."

"I expected Mister Galway himself," Lemuel said, prepared to be irked.

"There were little problems," Manuel Cruz told him, more confidentially, flashing looks left and right as though afraid to be overheard. "I'll tell you in the truck."

"Truck?" But he permitted Cruz to carry both his suitcases and to lead the way over to an incredibly filthy, battered, rusty pickup truck. When the suitcases were thrown in back, onto all that rust and dirt, the Customs chalkmarks became irrelevant.

The interior of the pickup was at least roomy and fairly comfortable. Cruz was a bit too short for the controls, which only increased his childlike aura; also, he drove in sudden jolts and hesitations, his feet playing the floor pedals like a pianist, hands struggling the wheel back and forth, back and forth.

Out on the empty blacktop road, Cruz settled down to a less fitful driving method, and explained, "Kirby, he had to see some other men. You know about the gage?"

Lemuel didn't. "Gauge?"

"Pot," said Cruz. "Weed. Tea. Smoke."

"Oh, *marijuana*!"

"That's it," Cruz said, happily nodding.

"He smuggles it into America," Lemuel said, with some distaste. "Yes, I know about that."

"Okay. Now, some men come down from up there," Cruz said. "Kirby, he didn't know they were coming, you know? But these kinda men, they come down, they say, 'We gotta talk,' you say, 'Okay, sir, yes, sir.'"

"Ah," said Lemuel, nodding at this glimpse of what was under the rock.

"So Kirby, he sent me down, pick you up, say he sorry."

"I see," said Lemuel.

"I take you to the hotel. Kirby, he call you later, he take you out there tomorrow."

"Tomorrow? Not today?" One of the reasons Lemuel had decided to come down to Belize a week early—in addition to the honest excitement and anticipation he'd cited in his message—was the fact that he didn't entirely trust Kirby Galway. He didn't know what sort of scheme Galway might be able to perpetrate against him, but perhaps if he were to show up a week early it might keep the man off balance and give Lemuel some advantage. But now Galway was begging off until tomorrow; was that significant? Was there anything Lemuel could do about it?

Probably not. Still, it was worth a try. "My schedule is pretty tight," he said. "Perhaps I should talk to Galway right now."

"Oh, no," Cruz said, looking a bit frightened. "Kirby, he told me, 'Don't let Mister Lemuel come talk to me when I'm with these men. Tell Mister Lemuel to pretend he don't even know me.' That's what Kirby said."

"Why?"

"These are very bad men," Cruz said. "They got—whatchu call it—*front*, some kinda legitimate life up in the States, they don't want nobody know what their business is. They kill a man if they got to."

Lemuel, of course, had heard of such people, as who of us has not? The drug world quite naturally drew them, and yes they would kill rather than have the seamy truth exposed to their families and neighbors. "I see," he said.

"If you go to Kirby with those men," Cruz went on, "if you say, 'Hi, Kirby,' then you and Kirby and me, we all in terrible trouble. If those men know you know Kirby, and they got to know you from the States just to look at you, then they figure you know Kirby's in the gage business—you know, the marijuana—"

"Yes yes," Lemuel said. "Gauge. I do remember."

"Well," Cruz said, as they drove down the torn streets of Belize City, "they got to protect their lives, you see? Their *front*."

"So if I see Galway with any Americans," Lemuel said, a bit amused at the cloak-and-dagger aspects of the situation, "I should just pretend I don't know him."

"Oh, you'll probably see him," Cruz said. "Kirby, he's with those men at the hotel right now."

"Oh, is he?" Lemuel hoped he *would* see Galway and his mobster friends; curiosity and a faint prickle of danger made his eyes light up, and he rode the rest of the way trying to imagine what the "very bad men" would look like.

The hotel itself was decent enough, the staff competent, the room large and cool and pleasant. Lemuel undertipped the bellboy, then removed the constricting bow tie, opened his shirt, strolled over to the window, and looked down at the swimming pool, wondering idly why no one was in it. He had brought a bathing suit; perhaps, after he'd unpacked, he would go for a dip himself.

An el of the building was to the left, with large windows on the first floor through which he could see the dining room, where he would undoubtedly be eating tonight. At one of the window tables sat three—

Galway!

Lemuel pressed close to the louvered window, looking down. Galway and two men, just finishing their lunch. The other two were hard to make out, at this angle and from this far away, but they were certainly white men, undoubtedly Americans.

The three stood, pushing back their chairs. Galway said something and laughed. All three men wore moustaches; a change in male style that Lemuel had failed to notice just as thoroughly as he'd missed the demise of the bow tie.

What could he make of Galway's companions? They didn't look like mobsters out of a George Raft movie, but of course they wouldn't. These were drug dealers, a new breed of criminal, used to working with huge amounts of cash, trading with rich and influential people. They were dressed a bit flamboyantly, but not too much so, and Lemuel remembered what the man Cruz had said about them being men with a *front* back in America. Record company producers, perhaps, or with a business in commercial real estate.

Galway shook their hands; first one, then the other. A few more words were exchanged, rather sinister smiles formed under the moustaches, and then Galway left. The other two remained standing a moment longer beside the table, murmuring together, one with his hand on the other's elbow. Menace seemed to hover about them. They both turned to look out the window, and Lemuel flinched back, suddenly afraid.

Had they seen him?

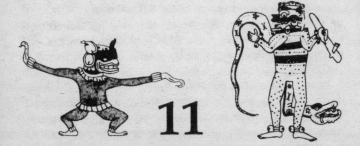

11

THE WARNING

What a lot of different positions he likes, Valerie thought as she rested on knees and shoulders and left cheek. If she lifted her head slightly to look down her own length, the parts of Innocent St. Michael that she could see framed by her arched legs dangled comically, but the feelings he was inducing through her body were not comical at all. "Again?" she asked, surprised, and the answer came in a rush.

This time, Innocent joined her, and after a brief spell of intense thrashing they lay beached together on the sheet, companionably side by side, catching their breath. Above, a slowly turning fan made absolutely no difference.

Shortly, Innocent heaved himself up off the bed and

padded out of the room. Perspiration slowly drying on her body, Valerie rolled onto her back and stretched, long and luxurious, from her down-pointing left big toe through her happily achy body to her upthrust right wrist, her knuckles brushing the rough stucco wall.

They were in one of the small houses in Belmopan's sterile residential area. At the restaurant, Innocent had excused himself to make a phone call, then had driven her here in his large green Ford LTD with the icy air conditioning. "I know there's nobody home," he'd said. "Belongs to a friend of mine." The bedroom was small, filled by its double bed, the perimeter cluttered with laundry and books and magazines.

Marcia Ettinger, an older woman at the Royal Museum at Vancouver, had warned her about this, she really had. "You want to be careful," she'd said. "There's something that happens to young single women the first time they're in a really *foreign* place all by themselves. It's as though all restraints are gone, none of the rules matter any more, and you find yourself going to bed with the first man who asks you." Valerie had pooh-poohed that, of course: "I'm my own person," she'd said. "I make my own decisions."

Had she made this decision? Smiling, stretching the other way—right toe through arching waist to left wrist— she told herself the decision had been a good one, no matter who had made it. At the very least, she would endorse it.

Innocent came back, water beads sparkling coolly in his hair. He was smiling—he was always smiling, wasn't he?—and when he sat on the bed he bent over to kiss her left nipple. "What a big girl you are," he said.

"I was always tall." She knew her capability for small talk was minimal, and hoped she would improve with time and experience.

Experience.

"Unfortunately," Innocent said, "we can't stay here forever."

"No." Valerie sat up, looking around. "I suppose the person who lives here will come back after a while."

"Not with my car in the driveway," Innocent said.

The encounter suddenly took on an unpleasant public aspect. "I'll get dressed," she decided, rising from the bed.

He patted her rump. "Tomorrow morning, very early," he said, "I'll have a Land Rover and a driver pick you up at your hotel back in Belize and drive you out to that land you want to see."

"Thank you." Sudden doubt, insecurity, awkwardness, made her say, "He—the driver. He won't know about *this*, will he?"

Alarmed, concerned, almost shocked, Innocent bounded to his feet with a surprising agility. "Valerie, Valerie!" he cried, holding her elbows, his manner totally serious for the first time since she had met him. "We aren't enemies! I would never embarrass you, humiliate you!"

"But you tell everybody everything, don't you?"

Releasing her, he said, "You mean Susie, at the restaurant?" He grinned, relaxing, a happy bear, shaking his head. "When I have lunch there with a businessman," he said, "or someone from the government, do you think I tell him, a *man*, 'I had that waitress?' What would Susie do to me?"

"Pour your lunch on your head," Valerie suggested.

Innocent laughed. "You misunderstand Susie," he said. "She would stick a knife in my neck."

Valerie believed him. He would preen in front of women, but not in front of other men. It made him somehow more likeable, and at the same time more juvenile. "All right," she said.

While Valerie visited the tiny rust-spotted bathroom, Innocent dressed and went out to start the car, so that when Valerie was ready to leave she entered a vehicle already well chilled. Innocent got behind the wheel, patted her knee in fond familiarity, and said, "If you can wait half an hour, I'll drive you back to Belize."

"But my taxi is waiting."

"Oh, I already paid him off and sent him away." Steering toward the clumped government buildings, he said, "Now, tomorrow, you pay good close attention to everything you see, and I'll be in Belize when you get back."

"All right."

Again he patted her knee. "Good rooms at the Fort George," he said. "Air-conditioned. Very nice."

12

THE BLUE MIRROR

"Oh, dear," Gerry said. "Oh, dear, oh, dear, oh, dear."

Alan had spread the blue trunks and the silver-and-red trunks on the bed, side by side, and stood back, knuckles under chin, trying to decide which to wear for their dip in the pool. Now he looked over at Gerry, who was frowning into his open dresser drawer. "Lose something?"

"The recorder was moved."

"You put it in there yourself," Alan said, misunderstanding. "I saw you."

"I put it under the leather vest," Gerry said. "I very specifically remember doing that, because the black case of the recorder would be less noticeable under black leather."

Alan, a faint vertical frown line forming between his brows, came over to stand beside Gerry and also look into the open drawer. Both men were naked; in the blue-tinted wide mirror above the dresser they looked like a rather crude parody of Greek temple sculpture. Alan said, "Are you sure?"

"*Al*-an," Gerry said, which was what he always said when he felt Alan was insulting his intelligence, which was what he felt rather frequently. "I already *told* you."

The leather vest was folded neatly on the left. Gerry had turned back the little stack of ironed white T-shirts, and there was his recorder. Alan said, his voice a little scared, "Is anything missing?"

"My jewelry's still here." Picking up the recorder, Gerry turned it around and said, "The tape's still in it."

"The same tape?"

"Oh, my gosh." Gerry pushed PLAY. After an interminable period of faint shushing sounds, Kirby Galway's voice said, "This way, gentlemen. Watch out for snakes." Sighing with relief, Gerry pushed OFF and then REWIND.

Alan looked over at his own recorder, on the bed with his crumpled lunchtime clothes. "We'll have to find a better hiding place," he said.

"But they didn't *take* anything," Gerry said, putting the recorder under the leather vest. He looked fretful.

"The maid, maybe," Alan suggested. "Just interested in something new, to look at it."

"I don't know," Gerry said. "Maybe this isn't such a fun idea, after all."

"We *can't* chicken out now," Alan told him. "Hiram would just simply laugh us to scorn."

"It seemed a lot different in New York," Gerry said, taking out his ecru fishnet trunks and stepping into them. "Here, it's getting scary."

"Well, we did promise," Alan said. "And we've started,

we're here, so we might as well go ahead and finish. You ready for the pool?''

Gerry said, *''I'm* not the one with his little thingies hanging out.''

So Alan chose the silver-and-red trunks and put them on, while Gerry went over to look out the window to see if the pool were still unoccupied. ''Alan!'' he said, a shrill whisper.

''Now what?''

Alan joined him at the window, and they looked down through the louvers at the pool, beside which two men were standing; Kirby, fully dressed, as they'd last seen him at lunch, and a man in a very large yellow boxer-type swimsuit. This man was middle-aged and round-shouldered, very pale in the tropical sun, with a round pot belly, a round balding head, and very large round dark sunglasses. He stood with hands on hips; despite being older, and physically out of shape, and a bit foolish-looking in those great ballooning trunks, he gave off an aura of self-assurance and command. There seemed to be a vague echo down there of old movie scenes of Italian mobsters conferring in the local steambath; not Gerry and Alan's kind of steambath, the other kind.

''The drug dealer!'' Gerry whispered.

They watched Kirby and the man confer, both of them intent and serious. The drug dealer seemed irritated by something, Kirby placating and reassuring him. The awareness that this was a man who could order a murder with a snap of his fingers seemed to send a ripple of chill breeze across the blue pool water.

Kirby and the man shook hands, Kirby left, and the man walked around to the shallow end of the pool, where he went down the steps slowly, wincingly, as though entering ice water. Ribcage deep, he rested his back against the side, then abruptly looked up, the huge dark sunglasses staring directly at them.

They both flinched; they couldn't help it. "He saw us!" Gerry said.

Alan recovered first. "He has no idea who we are," he pointed out. "Come on, let's go down, I want a better look at him. Shall I bring my recorder?"

"*Al*-an, are you crazy?" Gerry glanced down again at the pool and the enigmatic man behind his black sunglasses. "We can't fool around with the likes of *him*," he said.

13

WANTED!

Kirby awoke when the pickup left the road. "Jesus!" he cried, as trees plunged past the windshield. Grabbing dashboard and windowsill for support, he straightened in the passenger seat, glared at Manny, and said, "Give me a little warning, will ya?"

"It's okay," Manny told him, grinning, flashing his tooth-gaps. "All under control."

All under control. The Northern Road was behind them, already obscured by trees and shrubbery. The dirt path corkscrewed ahead, twisting deeper and deeper into wilderness, so that you could never see more than twenty feet before the next sharp curve presented a wall of green. Already the trail was so narrow that dusty leaves touched

94

the fenders on both sides as they pushed through, and Manny couldn't steer around the larger stones and deeper ruts but had to plow right over them. He grinned broadly as he drove, and every once in a while, when they crashed against some particularly large obstruction, Kirby could hear the *clack* as Manny's remaining teeth cracked together.

All under control. Back in Belize, at the Fort George, were two customers at the same time, one individual and one team, and Kirby could only hope they wouldn't happen to get into conversation. If only there were another first class hotel in Belize City, one with air conditioning and reliable hot water, he would have managed somehow to switch Lemuel over to it, lessening the danger; but there was not.

Well, at least it was only for the one night. Tomorrow morning, he would put Witcher and Feldspan on the Miami plane. Tomorrow afternoon, Lemuel would be shown the temple. By sometime tomorrow, if Kirby's luck held, everything actually *would* be all under control.

But what would happen, what *could* happen, if his customers chanced to get into conversation tonight? The odds were against it, and even further against any of them talking about a contemplated grand larceny with a stranger, but say it happened, say everything fell out wrong. What was the worst-case scenario? The scheme would be destroyed, of course, permanently killed. Could Kirby himself go to jail? Probably so, probably in more than one country. Belize and the U.S. might very well vie with one another for the pleasure of putting Kirby Galway away.

How nice to be wanted.

At a seemingly impassable spot in the surrounding wilderness, Manny swung the wheel hard left and the pickup veered away from the diminishing dirt track, made a tight turn around a thick, scarred tree trunk, and bumped and skidded down a long brush-covered slope to a narrow muddy stream, where Manny pumped the brakes—his short

legs stretching and stretching, sandaled toes pointing down—
until they slued to a stop. Kirby climbed out, slid the two
long planks out from under a lot of bushes and vines, and
dropped them into position across the stream. Manny drove
on over, the planks sagging down into the water, then
accelerated up the other side, the pickup throwing mud
clots out behind it like a bucking bronco. Kirby, to avoid
the hurled mud, waited on the near side until the truck was
some distance away, then trotted across on one of the
boards, hid them both in their places on this side, and
made his way up to where Manny was waiting, the pickup's engine gasping like an overworked beast of burden.

There was one other stream to cross, somewhat larger,
but here the locals had long ago made a porous causeway
of logs and stones, which the pickup could cross with a lot
of side-slipping and potential disaster. After that, it was
merely the impossibility of the hilly jungle-covered terrain
that slowed them, until at last they came out in the clearing
behind the Cruzes' house, next to the kitchen garden. Home.

(There was an easier route down from Orange Walk,
which they took whenever carrying anything large or delicate, but that meant driving all the way north to Orange
Walk first, then doubling back south, which could add
almost an hour to the journey. It was better to be knocked
about a bit harder, but for a shorter period of time.)

Estelle would be cooking now, while the kids and the
dogs watched television, so when Kirby climbed awkwardly out of the pickup, feeling stiff and tired, he went
around to his own entrance. The combination lock on the
door was meant primarily to thwart the curiosity of children, since Manny and Estelle both knew the sequence.
Yawning, stretching, Kirby spun the dial, opened the door,
entered the living room, and switched on his air conditioner.

Kirby's apartment was two rooms and three closets. His
living room was small and square, with windows in two
walls, reed mats over the concrete floor, a rough home-

made table in the center where he and Manny played
games, several mismatched small chairs, a few lamps, and
one big, comfortable easy chair. On a shelf mounted on
the wall opposite the easy chair were a TV set and a
Betamax; the videotapes were in a rickety bookcase
underneath.

The other room, which was smaller, contained his bed
and two large wooden trunks and another rickety bookcase, this one half filled with books. A few air charts—
sections of Burma, Madagascar, the Aleutians—were on
the walls for decoration. The three closets were all off this
room; the first was for clothing, the second for a shower
stall, the third for the composting toilet.

Kirby, still yawning as he removed his shirt, entered the
bedroom, kicked off the rest of his clothing and stood in
the shower awhile, until he no longer felt like a horse that
had just been sold for glue.

Twenty minutes later, happy in crisp clean clothes and
old moccasins, Kirby went back around to the Cruz side of
the house, where he and Manny played cribbage while
Estelle ran the Cuisinart and the kids and the dogs watched
"Rio Grande" on TV, dubbed into Spanish. ("Rio Grande"
in Spanish is "Rio Grande.") At one point, when John
Wayne made a rather spectacular leap from a running
horse, Kirby nodded over at the set and said, mildly,
"That's my father."

Manny looked up, in mild surprise. "John Wayne?" He
turned to look at the set.

"No," Kirby said. "My father did that jump off the
horse."

Estelle had come over from the Cuisinart to frown at the
TV, where a close-up of John Wayne now showed. In
Spanish, John Wayne had the deep gruff voice of an old
man missing some teeth. "He *looks* like John Wayne,"
she said dubiously.

"Not there," Kirby said. "Only in the long shots, doing the stunts."

"A stunt man!" Manny said, pleased at knowing such esoteric English.

"That's right," Kirby said.

"Very brave, stunt men."

"Kind of foolhardy," Kirby said, and shrugged.

"You grew up around the movies, huh?" Manny was bright-eyed from more than Danish Marys; Kirby didn't often open up about his background.

"I would have," Kirby said, "only things went wrong." He looked at his cards, not liking them very much, then glanced up to see Manny and Estelle both watching him, expectant. "Oh, well," he said. "It was one of those things. My father was a stunt man, my mother was an actress."

"A big star?" Manny asked, and Estelle told him, "Hush."

"No, just an actress," Kirby said.

Estelle, hesitant, nodded shyly toward the TV. "Is she in this 'Rio Grande' movie?"

"No. They always wanted to work together, but they never did. Then they had a chance to, on a circus movie, in Spain. What they called a runaway production. I was only two, so I don't really remember it."

"You went with them, in Spain?"

"Sure." Kirby sighed, and dropped the cards on the table. Might as well go ahead and tell it. "They only had one scene together," he said, "on a rollercoaster. It was supposed to be safe, but it wasn't."

Hushed, Estelle said, "They were killed?"

"Yeah. I got shipped home to my aunt in upstate New York."

Manny said, "So you didn't know them, like."

"Not really," Kirby said, but in his mind's eye he could see the pictures of his father and mother all over his

Aunt Cathy's house. Old-maid Aunt Cathy, his mother's sister, had had a lifelong crush on Kirby's father and had transferred it to Kirby. From the time he could first remember, Aunt Cathy was saying things like, "Oh, you'll be a devil with the girls," and, "You've got your father's wildness. I can see it in your eyes." He'd been spoiled rotten, and he knew it.

Manny maybe had some inkling of Kirby's thoughts. He said, "You think you're like him, your old man?"

"Some ways, some ways." Kirby shrugged. "I think I've got more interest in a real home somewhere; they never much cared where they lived. The other thing is"— Kirby picked up his cards again, studied them, seemed reconciled—"I stay away from rollercoasters."

14

THE UNKNOWN LAND

"We must drive the corrupt profiteers out of government," Vernon said, as he changed the sheets on his bed, "or *we'll* never get the profit." Above, a slowly turning fan made absolutely no difference.

"Hush," said the skinny black man, holding up the cassette recorder. "Listen to this part."

"I don't think you get the picture," Kirby's voice told Vernon, as he tossed the rumpled sheets into the hall and snapped the clean lower sheet into the air, holding it by his fingertips; gently, the sheet settled onto the bed, guided by Vernon's hands. "What he's going to do is," Kirby said, "he's going to knock the temple *down*. You come back a year from now, this'll be just a jumble of rocks and dirt."

"What do you think of *that*?" the skinny black man asked.

"Greedy bastards," Vernon said. "Most of the tomb robbers just burrow a hole in, they don't knock the son of a bitch down."

Vernon finished making the bed while Kirby and his customers talked about the destruction of the temple. Then he carried the dirty sheets to the back of the house, the skinny black man following, holding up the recorder. After tossing the sheets in the big laundry sink, Vernon went to the kitchen, got two bottles of beer, and he and the skinny black man went to the living room to sit and listen to the rest of the tape. At last Feldspan giggled his giggle, the skinny black man pushed OFF and REWIND, and Vernon said, "Jail."

"For somebody," the skinny black man agreed.

"St. Michael," Vernon said, with savage hope.

"I don't see it yet," the skinny black man told him.

"St. Michael's a crook," Vernon said.

"The sun rises in the east," the skinny black man said.

"He's in my way. He stands between me and, and, and . . ."

"The pot of gold."

"Do you have to give him that?" Vernon asked, pointing at the cassette.

"You know I do. I can *play* it for you, in here, nobody knows about it, but now I gotta go *give* it to St. Michael."

"Maybe the tape got loused up some way," Vernon suggested.

The skinny black man shook his head. "You don't want me to lose my job," he said. "Think about it."

"I need to hear it again," Vernon said, making a fist, punching his own knee in his frustration. "If I could have a *copy*."

The skinny black man looked around at the underfurnished

tiny living room. "You don't have anything to make it with," he said. "Or play it on."

Vernon stared furiously around his room, blinking; with every blink, he was seeing something else he didn't own. "I want," he said, through clenched teeth, "I want . . ."

"Yeah, man," the skinny black man said. "So do I." He got to his feet. "I got to go, man, I'm taking too long as it is."

"Wait a minute," Vernon said. "Tell me about these guys, the ones on the tape. Who are they?"

"They're what they say," the skinny black man said, shrugging. "Antique dealers from New York City."

"They couldn't be federal agents?"

"No. Federal agents don't travel with K-Y jelly."

"Then *why* are they taping Galway?"

"I don't know, man. Maybe they're just afraid they'll get cheated, they want some kind of record."

"To go to court with? *That*?" Pointing at the cassette.

"I got no answer," the skinny black man said. "Vernon, I got to go."

"Wait," Vernon said, jumping to his feet. "It's St. Michael and Galway, isn't it? We're agreed on that, right?"

"Seems that way."

"They're in on something together," Vernon said, "only they don't trust each other."

The skinny black man laughed. "Why should they?"

"So St. Michael has you search those guys' room, and you come up with the tape, and St. Michael gives you the machine, says make a copy."

"And now I got to go give it to him."

"I need to *hear* it again," Vernon said. "Maybe there's a clue."

"To who the guys are? Why they made the tape?"

"Not so much that. *Where* they were when they made it."

The skinny black man was surprised. "Galway's land, isn't it?"

"No, that's the goddam point. I've *been* there, with St. Michael, back when he still owned it. There's nothing there."

"Maybe it was all overgrown. You know the way those temples get."

"I'd have seen it," Vernon insisted. "*St. Michael* would have seen it. Do you think that man—or me either—do you think we could have walked around on a mountain of gold and jade and precious stones and not *know* it? Do you think St. Michael's going to sell that land without he already squeezed it with those big hands of his, just to see what comes out?"

The skinny black man frowned at the cassette player in his hand. "Then I don't get it," he said.

"That's the *point*," Vernon said, and then more quietly, as though in a conscious effort to calm himself, "that's the whole point. Galway goes off like it's to his own land, but it isn't. Somewhere up in those mountains, don't ask me how, maybe he saw something from the air, just lucked on it, who knows, but somewhere up in those goddam fucking mountains Kirby Galway has found a *Mayan temple*! A brand new undiscovered temple, nobody knows about it!"

"Jesus," breathed the skinny black man, and looked at the cassette player with new respect. "So that's the news I'm taking to St. Michael," he said.

"God *damn* it, I don't want that bloated son of a bitch to know!" Vernon stomped around his tiny living room, driven mad by frustration and poverty and greed and spite. Anybody he'd have bitten at that moment would have *died*.

"An unknown temple," the skinny black man said. Belizean dollar signs danced in his eyes. "Riches," he said. "Beyond the dreams of whatchamacallit."

"Not beyond *my* dreams," Vernon assured him. "This

is what I hate about this," he said. "I got to get the goods on St. Michael, I got to expose his corruption and get him thrown out and put in jail and *me* to replace him. But the closest thing I got to proof right now is that goddam record you're gonna—"

"Cassette."

"*Record*, goddamit!" Vernon's eyes were big round circles. "But if I get rid of St. Michael by using this temple, then *I* lose the temple!"

"Ouch," agreed the skinny black man. "But if we could get there first—"

"That's just it," Vernon said, pacing the room, punching his own thighs and shoulders. "Where *is* the goddam thing?"

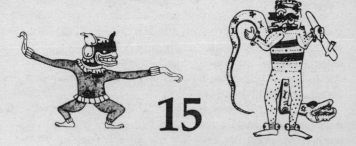

15

WARRIORS AND MERCHANTS: A PRELUDE TO DISASTER

At night, tall ivory-colored curtains are closed over the dining room windows at the Fort George Hotel, eliminating the featureless, dark, infinite, eternal, perhaps unsettling view of the nighttime sea. The lights are dimmer, the tablecloths are thick and soft, and the chunky waitresses in dark green move silently on the carpeted floor. The room is no more than half full, conversations are muted. Tourists smile at one table, businessmen look serious at another, the occasional solitary traveler reads a magazine while spooning his soup.

Whitman Lemuel looked up from his magazine and his soup when Valerie Greene entered the dining room, and his first lightning-quick thought process, almost too fast for memory, involved a series of rapid vignettes: "We're both alone. Why don't we eat together?" "I don't want to be mysterious, heh, heh, but I really can't talk about what I'm doing down here in Belize." "But why is a beautiful woman like *you* alone in such an out-of-the-way place?" "Oh, my dear, I *am* sorry, it must have been dreadful for you." "Don't cry, here's my handkerchief." "I do have some vodka in my room." There then followed an amber-toned scene, which crumbled and liquefied when, as Valerie followed the hostess past Lemuel to a table in another corner, recognition came.

My God! *Her!* "Despoliation!" "Unscrupulous museum directors!" He didn't remember her name, but he was unlikely to forget her face. *Or* her voice. Slopping soup onto the snowy tablecloth, Lemuel raised his magazine up in front of his face, showing all the world that he was a reader of *Harper's*.

Unaware that the stir she had caused was anything other than the normal erotic ripple that followed her everywhere and which no longer very much impinged on her conscious attention, Valerie took her seat, glanced toward the draped windows with a slight passing regret for the lack of a sea view—the limitless ocean at night, heaving away, held no terrors for Valerie—accepted the large menu, and answered the hostess's question with, "Just water, thanks."

Behind his magazine, Lemuel gulped his vodka sour.

Witcher and Feldspan, arriving then, obediently waited by the lectern for the hostess to finish with Valerie. They glanced around at the lack of imagination displayed in the conversion of this large rectangular room from a warehouse *manqué* to a restaurant, and then Feldspan gasped and whispered, "Alan!"

"What now?"

"It's him! Behind the magazine!"

"Oh, my Lord," Witcher said. "You're right. Don't look at him!"

"I'm not looking at him. Don't *you* look at him."

Witcher was always the first to recover. "Well, why wouldn't he eat here?" he said. "He's *staying* here, the same as us."

"But who's he hiding from?" Feldspan asked. "Surely his type doesn't actually *read Harper's.*"

"Well, maybe he does," Witcher said, becoming a little testy at Feldspan's nervousness. "He has to read something, doesn't he? And I really doubt there's a *Drug Dealer's Digest* published anywhere."

"Hush!" Feldspan said, because the hostess was approaching, a smile on her face, her arms full of menus.

The hostess led them to a table along the right side wall. She was a good hostess, who didn't believe in crowding the customers together in one area of the room for the convenience of the help, but who believed in spreading the customers out as much as possible for their own convenience and privacy and enjoyment of their meals. Therefore, once she had placed Witcher and Feldspan, the situation was this:

Among a scattering of other patrons, Witcher and Feldspan were a short way into the room, against the right wall. Lemuel was midway down the room, one table in from the left wall. Valerie was most of the way down the right side, one table in from the side, one back from the non-view. In this triangle, Valerie and Lemuel were seated so as to face one another directly, while Witcher and Feldspan, opposite one another with the wall beside them, were situated out of Valerie's line of sight but so that Feldspan offered Lemuel a three-quarter profile and Witcher gave him a view of his right ear and the back of his head.

Lemuel simply couldn't stand it. Every time he peeked over the top of his magazine, there *she* was, across an uncrowded room, *facing* him. And he daren't let her see him, dare *not*.

She would know, she would have to. He had identified

himself to her at that party back in New York as a museum curator. They had spoken about Belize; the subject of antiquity theft had come up, had most certainly and emphatically come up. She would see him, and she would immediately know what he was doing in Belize.

Then what? Given her vehemence in New York, Lemuel knew exactly what would happen next; she would inform the police. Most likely, she would leap to her feet right here in this public restaurant, point a finger rigid with virtue, and denounce him to diners and help alike.

What could he do? His main course hadn't even arrived yet; to get up and flee the restaurant now would merely call attention to himself. But to sit directly in that woman's line of sight was simply not possible; he couldn't hold *Harper's* up in front of his face indefinitely.

He peeked over the magazine's top, to see that *she* was holding the large menu up in front of herself much as he was holding *Harper's*. If he were to do anything, improve the situation in any way, it would have to be *now*.

What if he were to face in the opposite direction? But to stand, walk around the table, move everything with him to the opposite side, all of that would *also* attract too much attention. Besides, there wasn't even a chair over there. The only other chair at this table was to his left.

Well, a partial move would certainly help. Quickly but smoothly, while Valerie continued to study the menu, Lemuel slid from his chair and, without rising, made it into the chair to his left. He drew the soup, the silverware, the bread plate and the glasses over with him, and laid the magazine on the table to the right of his setting. In reading the magazine now, his head would quite naturally be averted from Valerie, showing her much less than a profile. With the dim lighting, and at this distance, she was most unlikely to recognize him. Feeling much better, he looked up, and found himself staring directly into the eyes of one of Kirby Galway's drug dealers.

The waitress asked Valerie if she were ready to order, and she said yes.

"He's staring at me," Feldspan said. There were little white spots under his eyes, and he spoke in a harsh whisper, not moving his lips. "My God, Alan, he moved around at the table so he could *stare* at me."

Lemuel, seeing the drug dealer glare at him while muttering to his partner without moving his lips, looked down in fright and gazed unseeing at *Harper's*.

Valerie ordered the shrimp cocktail and the chicken parmigiana.

Witcher, as though suddenly interested in the non-view, turned to gaze at the curtains at the far end of the room. His eyes swiveled to look at Lemuel, who was reading his magazine and not staring at anybody at all. Witcher's mouth curled in the expression of contempt he was about to show Feldspan.

Lemuel looked up, and they were *both* glaring at him, *grimacing* at him.

Valerie thought she might have a glass of white wine as well. But no more; she'd had too much to drink, really, at lunch.

The waitress, in asking Lemuel if he were done with the soup, interposed herself between him and the table containing Witcher and Feldspan. "Yes!" said Lemuel. "Could you hurry the duckling, please, I have to leave soon."

"The chef is working on it, sir. You can't really hurry a duckling."

Witcher and Feldspan looked at one another. Witcher said, "It doesn't mean a thing, Gerry."

"*Al*-an, he *moved*! He was sitting the other way, and he moved around that way so he could *stare* at me! He *knows*!"

"For Heaven's sake, Gerry, *what* does he know?"

"He saw us looking at him," Feldspan said, "when he was out by the pool with Galway."

"It's a public place," Witcher pointed out. "And he was still there when we went for a swim; he didn't act like anything was wrong then."

"He left right after we got there."

"A few minutes later."

"*Al*-an," Feldspan said, leaning forward, "why did he *move*?"

The waitress having departed, Lemuel could see the one drug dealer leaning forward to speak tensely and grimly to the other one. Were they talking about *him*? They'd come down to the pool this afternoon, decadent creatures, reeking of crime and unholy knowledge. Drug dealers tended to be addicts themselves, didn't they? Those two weren't like oldtime mobsters at all, they were like the criminals in recent French films; civilized in a sneering way, secure in their power, spouting philosophy, utterly cold and emotionless. Lemuel had waited just a minute or two after their arrival, not to call attention to himself, and then had hurried back to his room.

The waitress asked Feldspan and Witcher if they were ready to order. "I don't think I can eat," Feldspan said.

"You should take Lomotil," the waitress told him.

Witcher said, meaningfully, "Gerry, don't call attention to yourself." To the waitress, he said, "We would both like a very dry Tanqueray Gibson on the rocks, please."

"I don't think that'll help," the waitress said.

Lemuel, at a loss for what to do, turned his head, gazed this way and that, and found himself staring directly into the eyes of Valerie Greene. A small involuntary moan escaped him.

I know that man, Valerie thought. Isn't that odd; the short time I've been here, and I've already seen two men I think I've met before. First the driver of that pickup truck outside the hotel, and now this man. It's probably just that people look like other people; or maybe this man was on the same plane coming down, though I don't seem to remember him from then.

I'm going to die, Lemuel told himself, and the thought was not entirely unpleasant. He stared at a page in *Harper's* in which the art department had decided to snazz things up a bit by tilting the illustration at an angle; down to the left and up to the right, to indicate happiness. (The reverse tilt indicates mental imbalance.) Unconsciously, Lemuel tilted his head to match the illustration, and stuck a breadstick into his cheek.

Witcher ordered food for himself and Feldspan, who had been unable to concentrate on the menu. "You know you like shrimp," Witcher said, after the waitress departed.

"I won't taste a thing," Feldspan said.

Valerie took from her purse a paperback edition of *Maya: The Riddle And Rediscovery Of A Lost Civilization*, by Charles Gallenkamp, and began to read chapter 13, "Warriors And Merchants: A Prelude To Disaster."

Feldspan gulped his Gibson.

As one waitress brought Valerie her shrimp cocktail and glass of white wine, the other brought Lemuel his duckling. "And a glass of red wine," he said. "No, wait! Never mind." I dare not get drunk, he thought.

Feldspan gulped Witcher's Gibson.

"Gerry," Witcher said, "get hold of yourself."

While reading her book, Valerie ate her shrimp cocktail with her fingers, licking her fingers after each shrimp. Two businessmen at a nearby table watched her intently, all talk of tractor tires forgotten.

Lemuel tried to call the waitress without attracting attention to himself.

The other waitress brought two more Gibsons to Witcher and Feldspan, saying, "Feeling better?"

"Not yet," Feldspan said.

The waitresses passed one another. "Some really weird ones tonight," said the one. "Mm-*mm*," said the other.

Then, seeing Lemuel's hand waving discreetly next to his ear, she veered away in that direction: "Sir?"

"On second thought," Lemuel said, "I believe I'll have another vodka sour. No, wait a minute, make it a vodka on the rocks."

"Water on the side?"

"Yes."

"He could be bribing the waitress," Feldspan said. "They're awfully chummy over there."

"Bribe her to do what?"

Feldspan leaned forward. Three Gibsons on an empty stomach had turned his eyes into cocktail onions. "*Poison us*," he whispered.

"Gerry, *please*."

Valerie finished the last shrimp. For the last time, she inserted a finger into her mouth, pursed her lips around it, and drew the finger slowly out, freed of red sauce. She read her book. The businessmen discussed tractor tires.

In his nervousness, Lemuel crunched duckling bones, eating the little wings entire.

"He's eating *bones*," Feldspan said.

"Gerry, stop *looking* at him."

Feldspan blinked. He wanted Witcher's Gibson, but Witcher kept holding it. He said, "He looks like Meyer Lansky."

"He does not," Witcher said, though he didn't turn around to look. "Meyer Lansky was about a hundred, and Jewish."

"He could be Jewish."

"Gerry."

"Meyer Lansky wasn't *always* a hundred. It's just like *The Godfather*; they almost look like normal people, but they have dead eyes. It's because their souls are so black."

Valerie looked up from her book, and her face suddenly suffused with a bright red blush. The waitress, removing the empty shrimp cocktail goblet, glanced at the blush and at the book and went away, shaking her head.

But it wasn't the book that had done it; there's nothing in *Maya: The Riddle And Rediscovery Of A Lost Civilization* to make any damsel blush. Valerie had just remembered where she'd seen Lemuel before.

Lemuel, peeking around his own left shoulder, looked off toward Valerie and found her staring directly at him, wide-eyed. "She's recognized me!" Hunching down, shielding his face with his shoulder and arm, he ate frantically, hurriedly gnawing at his dinner, trying to finish it and get out of here.

"He eats like an *animal*," Feldspan said.

"Gerry, will you please eat your nice shrimps, and stop looking at that man?"

Maybe she isn't absolutely sure it's me, Lemuel thought. If I can just get out of here— He picked up his fresh vodka with greasy fingers, and drained half.

It all came back to Valerie in a rush of mortification. She'd had a little bit too much to drink that time, too, and she'd gotten on that hobby horse of hers about stolen antiquities. Of *course* it was a problem, world-wide, ranging from the current Greek demand that the British return the Elgin marbles to the recent pillaging-under-cover-of-warfare at Angkor Wat. But still Valerie knew she tended to take it all a bit too personally, and that she could very easily become a bore on the subject, and loud as well. Particularly at parties.

She could always tell when she was behaving badly in that fashion; men walked away from her. In the normal course of events, men walked *toward* her, but when she was carrying on about her crusade they walked away from her. That night in New York, at that party— Why, that poor man had probably thought she was accusing *him* of stealing ancient treasures!

Oh, she thought, I do hope he doesn't recognize me.

"Miss," Feldspan said, to the passing waitress, "may I have another Gibson, please?"

"Certainly, sir."

"Gerry, are you *crazy*?"

Valerie's chicken was placed in front of her. She ducked her head to eat it, hoping the man across the way was too absorbed in his magazine to look around and recognize her.

Lemuel, wiping his messy hands, waved the napkin at the wrong waitress, who sent him the right waitress. "Check, please."

"No dessert? We have ice cream, cheesecake—"

"No, please, just the check."

"Nice tropical fruit, very—"

"Just the check, please."

"No coffee?"

"Check!"

"Certainly, sir."

"Alan, give me the room key."

"Why?"

"Because I'm going to throw up."

"Gerry, you're just too emotional."

Lemuel, blinking, watched one of the drug dealers leave the restaurant and the other one stay. It's a pincer movement, he thought. One is in front of me now, and the other behind me. His mind filled with visions of what might happen when he opened his room door. Why hadn't he asked for his check earlier, or just simply left the restaurant at the beginning, no matter *what* they thought?

"Miss, my friend and I were wondering if we could buy you an after-dinner drink?"

Valerie looked up at the tractor-tire salesman and smiled. She had seen Lemuel ask for his check, and she knew her ordeal would soon be over. "No, thank you," she said. "But I do appreciate the thought."

The waitress brought Feldspan's last Gibson, and looked

at the empty chair. "I knew these things wouldn't help," she said.

"That's all right," Witcher told her. "Just leave it, I'll find something to do with it."

"Will your friend be back?"

"I trust not."

She picked up the plate of barely-touched shrimp. "Shall I put these in a bag for you?"

"Good God, no."

Lemuel signed his check. I can't go to the room, he thought, not by myself. I'll tell the desk clerk I'm having trouble with the air conditioner and insist on a bellboy to come with me and look at it. If no one's there, I'll just lock myself in for the night. And I'll stay in the room until Galway comes to pick me up tomorrow to take me to the temple. And now I know I never should have involved myself with a man like that in the first place.

Valerie was so pleased to see Lemuel get up to leave that she almost changed her mind and said yes to the tractor-tire salesman after all.

Witcher watched Lemuel go by, noticing the grim set to the mobster's jaw. Most likely, the man did suspect something, and he'd moved to that other chair to warn them to mind their own business. Well, they certainly *would* mind their own business, wouldn't they? And tomorrow morning they would get on the plane and *leave* this place.

Lemuel felt Witcher's eyes burning into his back as he left the room.

Valerie asked for tropical fruit for dessert.

Witcher, knowing that Feldspan would have disgustingly passed out in the room by now, dawdled over the final Gibson, but eventually he signed the check and departed.

"Thank you," Valerie said to the waitress as she left. "It was a lovely dinner."

16

SUNRISE

When the sun rose, Innocent St. Michael stepped nude from his house, smiled, stretched, walked across the cool dew-damp lawn (emerald green, aglisten in the orange birth of day), and then over the cool terracotta tiles to the pool's edge. There was only the faintest of breezes, turning the water into pale blue-green brushed chrome. "Nice," Innocent murmured, and dove like a dolphin into the water, swimming strongly beneath the surface to the far end, where he burst up into the air like a walrus blowing, releasing breath with an exuberant, "PAH!" and shaking water drops from his hair in a great fan around his head.

Ten laps in the pool; rest a while, floating; ten more

laps. Meantime, the sun rose higher in the eastern sky, the vault of heaven lightened from charcoal gray through smudged ivory to palest blue, and the St. Michael house began to stir with activity.

It was a large house, though not as large as its model, Monticello. Three stories high, broad, white, pillared, the house stood on a broad knob of hill, facing north. The pool behind the house was in sun all day, though shade trees were handy to both sides. Within the house were Innocent's wife Francesca and their four daughters: Elizabeth, Margaret, Catherine, and Patricia. All now in their teens, they were a lot of little prigs, raving feminists who utterly disapproved of their father. Well, he had wanted respectability, and the detestation of one's children was apparently one of the prices to be paid.

The house also contained several servants, one of whom— the stout motherly sort that Francesca preferred—came out as he was finishing his laps. She laid a snowy white terrycloth towel and a clean fluffy terrycloth robe of Virgin Mary blue on one of the wrought iron white chairs beside the pool. "Good morning, sir," she said to Innocent's passing churning form in the water, and returned to the house.

Innocent ate with a good appetite, under the censorious glares of Margaret and Patricia, then dressed in seersucker and a wide-collared white shirt, kissed short, fat Francesca goodby, spoke cheerfully to a sullen Catherine, and went whistling to his car, which had been buffed clean since he'd last driven it yesterday. His house, on a private road north of the Western Highway, between the ranches of Beaver Dam and Never Delay, gave ready access to both Belmopan to the west and Belize City to the east. This morning, he turned east.

He listened to the tape for the third time on the drive to Belize, occasionally stopping the recorder, running it back, listening to a sentence again, sometimes listening to one bit several times. For instance, the point early on where Kirby said, "I bought this land as an investment. Good potential for grazing, as you can see." *Good potential for grazing* was word for word what Innocent had said to Kirby when selling him that parcel. And what other land did Kirby own? None. So it *had* to be the same.

But on the other hand, it couldn't be. Innocent knew damn well what was and wasn't there, and it didn't include any goddam Mayan temple. Another sentence he listened to a lot was Feldspan's, "Look! A paving block! This has been *shaped*!" Then Kirby says that nonsense about checking with the government—he never had, of course—adding, "everybody said there's just no Mayan cities or temples or anything at all like that in this area. They said it's all been studied and checked out, and there's just nothing here."

Well, if the conversation were taking place on the land Innocent had sold to Kirby, "everybody" was absolutely right. But Kirby's statement was immediately followed by Witcher's breathed, heartfelt, awed, "They're *wrong*."

Then the next bit was also a problem. Feldspan: "What's the name of this place?" Kirby: "Probably nobody for a thousand years has known the name of this temple. The Indians around here call this hill Lava Sxir Yt." Then he carefully spelled it.

Lava Sxir Yt? There was no such place. Innocent would have some friends check among the up-country Indians, but he doubted they'd find anything. It was just some goddam exotic-sounding name Kirby had made up, that's all. His own personal private Shangri-la.

So what were the possibilities here? One: Kirby had found an entire Mayan temple on the land Innocent had sold him, even though Innocent knew every inch of that land and it contained *no* temple.

Two: Kirby, possibly while flying over the terrain or one time when he landed in the jungle to pick up a load of marijuana, had found an undiscovered Mayan temple, and was lying to his customers, telling them it was his land when it was not.

Three: Kirby and the two pansy-boys were involved in a complex con game—possibly aimed at Innocent himself, but more likely at someone else—in which they just walked around some dumb piece of bush somewhere and read from a script; there *was* no temple, in other words. (Which would also explain why the pansy-boys had made this infuriating tape in the first place.)

Of the possibilities, Number Two seemed the likeliest, though Number Three also suited what Innocent thought of as Kirby's character and style. As for Number One, Innocent just found that impossible to believe, but if it were true it raised a fresh problem, and that problem was Valerie Greene.

Let us say, let us just say for argument's sake, that Innocent St. Michael at one time owned a Mayan temple without noticing the fact. Let us further say that Innocent innocently sold this land to one Kirby Galway, who managed to see something there that Innocent had not. Clearly, with shaped stones and jaguar stelae lying about in plain sight (according to this damn tape), Kirby has done some preliminary excavation here, just enough to see what he's got.

So, when Valerie Greene, an archaeologist and a girl of undoubted honesty and probity—and a sweet ass, but that's another story—goes to this land today she will *see* the temple. This sight will vindicate her theory, which is all well and good for her, but it will also *make public* the temple. Kirby will no longer be able to rape it at will, and Innocent will no longer have the possibility of cutting himself in on the action.

On the other hand, if he didn't send *somebody* to Kirby's land, there never would be a way to prove or disprove possibility Number One. Besides which, he'd already promised Valerie cooperation; his driver would be picking her up at her hotel this very morning, before Innocent reached the city. Presumably, Innocent could still stop Valerie from going out there this morning, but if he did so it might look bad later, if and when the whole story came out. And Valerie, a determined girl if he was any judge, would manage to get to the site with his cooperation or without.

No, there were other and better ways to deal with the problem, which was one of the reasons Innocent was driving to Belize this morning. His first stop would be at the law office of his good friend, sometime partner, and old crony, Sidney Belfrage, where the preliminary steps would be taken to prove that the original sale of land to Kirby Galway had been invalid; a lawyer with Sidney's brains and experience would have no trouble finding grounds. No real legal action would be taken as yet, but the first steps would be put in train, so that, if indeed there *was* a temple on that land, Innocent would be able to demonstrate that he had, in all good faith, been attempting to correct a legal wrong for its own sake, starting when he still thought the land was worthless, *before* the temple was discovered.

So that was to be his first stop today, but not the only stop, because there was a second problem created by the existence of this tape, and the second problem was *the tape*. Done by the pansy-boys. Whoever and whatever they turned out to be, and whatever their reason for making the tape, those two would have to be neutralized, wouldn't they?

It was an odd position Innocent found himself in; he smiled as he thought of it, speeding toward Belize, listening to the tape. In order to keep some control over the situation while finding out exactly what was going on, he had no choice but to protect Kirby Galway.

17

HASTE TO BE RICH

**He that maketh haste to be rich
shall not be innocent.**
Proverbs, XXVIII, 1

At Georgeville, 15 miles west of Belmopan and 12 miles before the Guatemalan border, the Western Highway crosses two tiny roads. The northbound road winds just a few miles into the scrub before it stops at the hamlet of Spanish Lookout—the English-speaking people of Belize have anticipated trouble from the Spanish-speaking nation to their west for a long long time—while the southern road climbs steadily into the Maya Mountains, toward the Vaca Plateau, twisting and turning past San Antonio and Hidden

Valley Falls and on past the small airfield and forest station at Augustin. For mile after mile the road continues on, chopped out of a pine and mahogany forest, over gorges and around the shoulders of mountains, ending at last at Millionario, 19 miles south of the Western Highway as the crow flies, more than twice that by road.

Vernon wasn't traveling that far. A few miles south of Augustin he turned his coughing orange Honda Civic right onto a logging road that might have led him eventually to Chapayal or Valentin Camp, except that he stopped at a place where it was possible to park to one side of the twin-rutted track.

Driving out from Belmopan, Vernon had been dressed as though for the office, in white short-sleeved guayabera shirt and dark gray slacks and black oxfords, but now he stood beside the car and changed completely, putting on baggy green army fatigue pants, tall hiking boots, a M*A*S*H T-shirt, a lightweight gray-green windbreaker and a camouflage-design billed cap which he'd bought in a five and dime in Belize City. On branches above and around him, toucans and macaws watched with round rolling eyes, skeptical and amused but still astonished. The squeals and squawks of the jungle ricocheted from high branches through angled pillars of sunlight. It was 9:30 in the morning and the air was damp, not yet too hot. Vernon moved methodically, rigidly, his face expressionless, as though firmly repressing all doubt, all second thoughts. Locking the Honda, staring around one last time at a teeming world in which he was the only human being, he turned away and set off along the narrow spongy trail through the jungle toward the place where he intended to sell out his country.

The jungle grows quickly, and its leaves retain the night's moisture. As Vernon strode along, brushing dangled branches aside, his head and arms and windbreaker became increasingly wet, so that he glistened as he passed through sunny patches. He had brought no machete, but this trail was in frequent use and was never overgrown to the point where he had to make a detour. From time to time he passed evidence of recent logging, and twice he heard the sounds of human activity from elsewhere in the forest: once, the faraway buzz of a chain saw, and the other time an abrupt laugh from somewhere off to his right.

He froze at the laugh. The one danger here was to be discovered by a British patrol. Because Guatemala claimed the entire nation of Belize as its own long-lost province, stolen from it by the British in the nineteenth century, and because various Guatemalan leaders over the years had vowed to reclaim their property by force, one strange element of Belize's independence was that 1,600 British troops (plus two Harrier jets) remained for what the British-Belizean agreement called "an appropriate period" on Belizean soil, guarding the 150-mile Guatemalan border. Patrols through the mountains and jungles were mostly carried out by Gurkha troops, tough chunky little Asian soldiers from the mountains of Nepal, with a reputation for ruthlessness and bravery.

Vernon did not want to be found here by a British patrol, whether of Gurkhas or not. They wouldn't let him go until he had identified himself, and he could provide no convincing reason for his presence on this remote trail. It would all get back to St. Michael, who would not be satisfied until he found out what his assistant had been up to. Vernon hunkered down on the trail, listening, as wide-eyed but not as brightly colored as the jungle birds overhead, but the laugh was not repeated, and after a while he straightened, and cautiously moved on.

After half an hour's walk, he crossed an invisible line on the Earth and was no longer in Belize. He couldn't tell precisely where that point was, but eventually he knew he was safely in Guatemala and away from possible discovery—

except for the return trip, of course—and 20 minutes later he came out to a dirt road, not far from the Guatemalan town of Alta Gracia. To his right, a tall stocky man in high-ranking military uniform stood pissing on the left rear tire of a dusty black Daimler. The man's head turned, he gazed through extremely dark sunglasses at Vernon, and he nodded a hello as he went on with his tire wash.

Vernon waited quite a long while, watching the Colonel piss. He was aware of two people in the car—a soldier-chauffeur in the separate driver's compartment in front, and a woman with a mass of black hair in back—but the Colonel was the only one who mattered.

This was Colonel Mario Nettisto Vajino, of the Army of Guatemala, until recently a vice minister of defense in the last government but one. The Guatemalan political system alternates rigged elections with American-sponsored coups, but no matter the route of accession the man at the top is always an Army man, always a general, and usually a previous minister of defense. Colonel Nettisto Vajino could reasonably expect to become minister of defense (and a general) in some future government, if he weren't assassinated along the way.

This was not the colonel who had once publicly said that Guatemala would deal with the large black population of Belize by "expanding the cemetery," nor was he the colonel who had dealt with the problem of peasant Indian sit-in strikers in the Spanish embassy in Guatemala City on February 1st, 1980, by sending the police and army to firebomb the embassy, killing 38 people inside, peasants and employees and visitors alike, everybody but the Spanish ambassador himself, who got out with his clothes on fire and left for Spain as soon as he could. This was a different colonel, but not very different.

The Colonel shook himself, paused briefly to admire himself, tucked himself away in his trousers, zipped up, and approached Vernon, saying, "You're a bit late."

Reflecting how lucky it was that the Colonel didn't regard him as an equal, and would therefore not offer to shake hands, Vernon said, "I thought I heard a patrol."

Nettisto Vajino grimaced, unwillingly looking eastward, toward the lost province. There were no colonels of his sort over there. There was no such thing as a Belizean army as such, only the rather casual Belizean Defense Force, the BDF—known locally as the Bloody Damn Fools—a mere 300 strong. There were policemen as well in Belize, but they didn't carry guns. In Guatemala, on the other hand, there was the ordinary Army, plus various unofficial private armies, plus three police forces, every one of them armed to the teeth. The busy death squads in their woolen masks and army-issue boots were also well equipped with guns. But when Nettisto Vajino looked eastward, what his mind's eye had to see was the British peacekeeping force and the Gurkha patrols and the Harrier jets and the memory of the Falkland Islands, and no wonder he grimaced. How Guatemala would love to spread its culture and democracy to Belize!

Nettisto Vajino shook his head, returning his attention to Vernon, saying, "You've brought me something?"

"Yes." From a long pocket in the left leg of his fatigue pants, Vernon took a map, which he opened out to a square almost three feet on a side. "I circled the camps in red," he said.

"Mm." Nettisto Vajino carried the map back to the Daimler, where he spread it on the large curved trunk and pursed his lips as he studied it. Vernon, standing beside him, was extremely aware of the woman in the car looking through the rear window at him. She was exotic looking, like Rita Hayworth in "Gilda," but wilder. She never looked toward the Colonel at all.

Vernon was also acutely aware of the large Colt .45 in its holster on the Colonel's right side. It had been his fear—one of his fears—since the beginning of this relationship, that the Colonel would some day pull that gun and simply shoot Vernon dead, as a way of ending the association. Once his usefulness was over.

Well, his usefulness wasn't over yet. And when the time came, Vernon was determined that he would resign in his own way. He'd be very quick about it, too.

Nettisto Vajino tapped his knuckles on the map. "These are all new settlements?"

"Within the last six months," Vernon assured him. "That's what you asked for."

The Colonel grunted, continuing to brood at the map, his mind working in some slow and labyrinthine way. Vernon wished he knew what the Colonel's scheme was, but he didn't dare ask about it directly. *Out* would come the Colt, no question.

What Vernon had brought the Colonel today was a large topographical map of Cayo District, one of Belize's six districts, one of the three next to Guatemala. The new capital of Belmopan is in Cayo and so was all of Vernon's trip today until he'd crossed the border. In recent years, refugees from Central American bloodshed, mostly from Guatemala and El Salvador, have made their way in the thousands to Belize, where they have been offered land free for the tilling and have started tiny new communities, mostly in the southern half of the country. The Department of Land Allocation, in which Innocent St. Michael was Deputy Director, was of course involved with this aspect of the immigration, so it hadn't been hard for Vernon to collect the data on the most recent arrivals.

"Very good," the Colonel said, though noncommittally, as though it were merely a polite kind of cough he'd learned. Folding the map, his hooded eyes unreadable behind the dark glasses, he said, "And the pictures?"

"Oh, yes, certainly."

From a shirt pocket Vernon removed a roll of Kodacolor film, in its gray-capped black plastic canister, which he placed in Nettisto Vajino's waiting palm without a word. Why the Colonel wanted photos of Gurkha soldiers and Gurkha patrols, with details of uniform and equipment, Vernon neither knew nor cared. Sufficient that the pay was good, and that by pretending to be a tourist he had received the amused cooperation of his subjects.

The fact was, Vernon, like most Belizeans, was convinced the Guatemalan claim was just nonsense, old history. The Belizeans wouldn't permit Britain to give their land away, and the British wouldn't permit the Guatemalans to just come in and grab it, so that was that. So if some crazy Guatemalan Colonel shows up with money in his hand, willing to pay for a lot of dumb things like maps and photographs, why not take his money? Vernon *knew* what was going on here was a simple con job, himself giving worthless trash for real cash, but he also realized that to an outsider it could possibly look like, give the impression of, even appear to be . . .

. . . well, treason.

Expressionless, the Colonel closed his hand around the film roll, making a casual fist. "Wait there," he said, and turned away, returning to his car. When he opened the right rear door of the Daimler, Vernon caught a glimpse of long bare legs against the black plush. His heart ached in his breast. He wanted to live in a country where he could be a colonel. Maybe the crazy Guatemalans would pull this off after all, and he . . .

No. That wasn't a future he could think about.

The driver's door of the Daimler opened and the blank-faced soldier came around the rear of the car with a white envelope in his hand. He gave it to Vernon, turned about, and went back to his place in the car, while Vernon lifted the flap and looked at the sheaf of U.S. greenbacks inside. He couldn't count it now, not with them still here. Lifting his eyes, he saw the woman looking at him again out the back window. She didn't gaze with normal curiosity, as one human being looks at another, but with a flat and feral expression, as though she were an animal staring out of its cage. Or was *he* the animal, and she among the humans?

The Daimler backed in a half circle, then drove away. Vernon stuffed the envelope into the pocket that had contained the map, and started the long walk back. The sun was higher, the day hotter, the jungle smells stronger. The money was heavy in his pocket.

18

WINDING TRAILS

Parking in the forecourt of the Fort George Hotel, Kirby stepped out of the pickup and nimbly dodged a peach-colored topless Land Rover with official license plates, which had rushed in the EXIT side of the hotel's circular driveway and now slammed to a stop at the entrance. Its driver, a skinny black man, hopped out and strode briskly inside, and a moment later Kirby followed, strolling into the cool dim lobby and seeing the driver in converse with the desk clerk.

The house phones were around to the side. Kirby called Lemuel first, let it ring six times, and was about to give up when there was a click and Lemuel's voice, hushed, suspicious, frightened, said in a half whisper, "Yes?"

Kirby was used to his customers being a little spooked, since they weren't used to the criminal's life, but Lemuel was overdoing it. His manner as soothing as possible, Kirby said, "It's Kirby Galway, Mister Lemuel."

"Galway!" Lemuel managed to sound both relieved and aggrieved. "Where are you?"

"In the lobby. I just have to take, um, those people . . . You know?"

"I certainly do."

"To the airport. Then we're done with them."

"Good!"

"You might as well wait in the room until—"

"Believe me, I will!"

Smiling, pleasantly surprised at how well his drug-dealer yarn had gone over with this one, Kirby said, "We'll *both* breathe easier once they're gone. I'll give you a call when I get back, we'll have lunch in the hotel before we go out to the site."

"I'll wait right here," Lemuel promised.

Kirby broke the connection and was about to dial Witcher and Feldspan's number when he was briefly distracted by seeing, out of the corner of his eye, the passage through the lobby of what appeared to be a good-looking woman. He turned his head, but she was already past, striding rapidly in the wake of the skinny black man from the Land Rover; so she was his passenger. There was only time to register that she was tall, with brown hair under a large floppy-brimmed hat, and that she was dressed for hiking, in khaki shirt and new blue jeans and tall lace-up boots. She carried a gray attaché case in her left hand, and a large and apparently heavy canvas shoulder bag bumped along on her right haunch. Then she was gone, and Kirby dialed the other room number, and Witcher answered on the first ring: "Alan Witcher here."

"And Kirby Galway here."

"Oh, good! We're all set, we'll be right down." There

were mutters in the background; sounding annoyed, Witcher said, "Would you hold on, please? Just one second."

"Sure," said Kirby, and spent the next several seconds listening to muffled conversation and a repeated *thumb-thumb*. Oh, of course; Witcher had covered the mouthpiece by pressing it to his chest, and Kirby was listening to his heart.

Then his voice: "*Gerry* wants to know," Witcher said, with worlds of meaning, "if your friend is anywhere down there."

Kirby grinned. Got them both, by God! "No," he said. "He's gone away up-country. There's a fella up there he says is cheating him. He took a couple local boys and left first thing this morning."

"Oh." Witcher didn't seem to know what to do with all that information. "Just so he's not in the lobby."

"You're safe," Kirby assured him.

"I'll tell Gerry," Witcher said, putting the charge of cowardice back where it belonged.

Hanging up, Kirby went over to the broad front doorway and looked out at the peach-colored Land Rover, which was just leaving via the ENTRANCE. The girl, in front beside the driver, was slipping sunglasses on. The floppy-brimmed hat, a very sensible defense against the tropic sun, kept him from seeing much of her face. Her jaw was perhaps a little too strong. Then the Land Rover was gone, and a stir in the lobby recalled him to business.

Kirby helped the bellboy load luggage into the back of the pickup while Witcher and Feldspan checked out, and then they came outside, both behind large-lensed dark glasses. Witcher looked irritable, Feldspan hung over. Good mornings and handshakes were exchanged, and Feldspan said, "We'll make the plane, won't we?" His voice was shaky; behind the dark glasses, his eyes asked for pity.

"Plenty of time," Kirby assured him.

"Of course there is," said Witcher. "Get hold of yourself, Gerry."

Gerry didn't; nevertheless, they all got into the pickup, jounced away from the hotel, and made their way back through the sunny town. Once on the road out to the airport, Kirby took a folded sheet of paper from his breast pocket, handed it across Feldspan to Witcher, and said, "This is the place we'll meet."

Opening the paper, Witcher read aloud: "Trump Glade, Florida. Route 216 south eight point four miles from movie house. Left at sign reading Potchaw 12. Dirt road. Fifteen point two miles to red ribbon on barbed wire fence." Witcher nodded. "And that's where you'll be, I take it."

"Rent a car," Kirby told him. "Don't take a cab."

"Certainly not."

"And it's just you two there," Kirby said, "or I don't get out of the plane."

"We understand," Witcher said. Between them, in the middle of the seat, Feldspan lowered his head, raised a quaking hand to his brow, and faintly moaned.

"When I've got something to deliver," Kirby said, "I'll cable you in New York and give you a day and a time."

Witcher said, "What if you have something too large to bring out that way? The jaguar stela, for instance. That could be eight or ten feet tall, and it would weigh a *ton*."

"We'd have to do that by ship," Kirby told him. "There's places up the coast where we can bring in a small boat at night. It's expensive, and a lot trickier, but if we're careful it'll be okay. I tell you what; if I have anything too big to fly out, I'll take Polaroids of it, give them to you guys, and once you have a buyer we'll arrange to get it out by boat."

"Fine," Witcher said.

"I think I'm going to be sick," Feldspan said.

"*Gerry*," Witcher said, through clenched teeth.

Kirby angled across the empty road and parked on the left verge, beside the easygoing Belize River. "Better here than in the plane," he said.

So Witcher, disapproval etched in every line of his being, got out of the pickup, and helped Feldspan out and walked with him down to the river bank. Kirby whistled quietly to himself and looked out at the pleasant day. If he were a man who fished, he'd want to fish right now.

A horn honked. Kirby looked over as Innocent St. Michael went by in his dark green Ford LTD, heading toward the airport, waving at Kirby from his air-conditioned luxury. Kirby grinned and waved back. Innocent sure did like to visit the airport.

When Feldspan returned, he was paler but somehow better. "I'm sorry," he said.

"Happens to us all," Kirby assured him. The line of Witcher's mouth said it didn't happen to *him*.

There were no more events till they reached the airport, where Witcher insisted on unzipping his bag atop the pickup's tailgate, so he could remove two Sony Walkmans from it, one of which he extended toward Feldspan, saying, "You *know* this will make you feel better, Gerry."

Feldspan looked with repugnance at the Walkman before him, then seemed to remember something. "Oh," he said. "Oh, yes." He flashed Kirby a guilty glance through his dark glasses as he accepted the Walkman, hooked it onto his belt, and put the earphones in place on his head. Now he looked like something from *The Wizard of Oz*.

Kirby grinned at him, amused. So these boys were smuggling something out of Belize in their Walkmans, were they? And they didn't want their pal Kirby to know about it. Idly, he wondered what they'd found, idly decided it was probably marijuana.

Extending a hand, Witcher said, "We'll hope to hear from you." His earphones were draped around his neck.

"Two or three weeks," Kirby promised, shaking his hand. Then he shook Feldspan's. "Have a nice flight," he said. Feldspan smiled gamely.

"Come along, Gerry," Witcher said, hefting his bag. His earphones were now in place on his ears.

Kirby stood by the pickup and watched them walk to the small terminal building. Witcher was swaying and snapping his fingers and just slightly boogalooing to the sounds coming into his ears. After several steps Feldspan started to do the same, in pale and shaky imitation.

In a shaded spot at the corner of the building, working on his molars with his slender gold toothpick, stood Innocent St. Michael, also watching Witcher and Feldspan. His eyes looked very interested. It was hard to be sure with his hand up in front of his mouth that way, but he might have been very faintly smiling.

Hmmmmmm, thought Kirby.

19

SATISFACTION

                  Gerry plodded manfully along,
carrying his heavy bag, snapping the fingers of his free
hand in some sort of rhythm, nodding his head metronomi-
cally to the sound of Kirby Galway, in his earphones,
saying, "A lot of Americans are coming down here, because there's just so much available land."

The worst part of travel is travel. To get out of Belize,
there was so much red tape to overcome: forms to fill out,
lines to stand in with other passengers, documents to
display, questions to answer. And all taking place without
benefit of air conditioning, among bodies that could only
have been improved by a flash flood. Gerry just suffered
through it all, remembering to nod his head and tap his

toes, following Alan's lead as he listened to his own voice say in his ears, "I had an aunt in New Jersey once, but she went to Florida and died." We're going to Florida now, he thought. What does it all mean?

As Kirby Galway had suggested might happen, their luggage was given a *quite* extensive search by a large and menacing Customs person, who made them put their Walkmans on the counter with their suitcases and then took a positively unhealthy interest in the contents of their luggage. Some of the more stylish garments produced from this individual various grunts and snarls absolutely out of a *zoo*. "What you call dis?" the fellow demanded at one point, holding up an object from Gerry's bag between thumb and finger.

The indignity of it. "It's called sachet," Gerry said, enunciating carefully, reminding himself it's best to be gentle with the lower orders. "It's to keep the bag sweet-smelling, you know."

The Customs man held the small sealed packet to his nose and noisily sniffed. "Could be dope," he said.

"Certainly *not*." Stomach churning, mind rattled, Gerry struggled to remember the contents of sachet, saying, "It's—oh, rose petals, cloves, lavender . . ."

"Passports," said a sudden harsh voice from a new and unexpected quarter; that is, from behind them. Gerry and Alan turned, in some surprise, to see a short impatient scowling woman standing there, holding out her hand for their passports.

Was this right? While Alan briskly turned over his own passport, Gerry had to search himself like a policeman frisking a suspect, having no idea what he'd done with his passport, not expecting to need it at just this juncture . . .

The roar of the descending plane was heard. The woman was actually snapping her fingers. Gerry, third time through his shirt pocket, found the passport and handed it over. In lieu of a *thank you*, the woman said, "Tickets."

Well, *that* was all right; Alan had them both. He turned them over to the woman, who barely glanced at them before shaking her head, saying, "Not this flight."

"What?" Gerry thought he would die, he actually thought he would die.

But not, apparently, Alan, who did some barking of his own, telling the woman, "Of course it's this flight."

"SAHSA flight," the woman said.

"That's right," Alan told her. "SAHSA is exactly what it says on those tickets."

"Not today."

"Oh, *really*," Alan said. "It is our flight, it is this airline, it is today."

Gerry moaned faintly, hoping no one would hear. The plane was waiting outside. Passengers behind them on line were getting upset. Off to one side, a stout man being disgusting with what seemed to be a gold toothpick appeared to enjoy the show.

Then, all at once, it was over. With one last firm nod, as though she'd solved a knotty problem for them at last, the woman handed the passports and tickets back to Alan and said, "You can go now."

"I can *go* now? After you've—"

"The plane is waiting," the woman said, with urgent shooing gestures. "Hurry, hurry."

The plane was waiting. The other passengers were waiting. The Customs man had finished pawing through their personal possessions and sent their luggage on to be loaded. Their Walkmans and carry-on bags awaited them on his wooden counter. Over by the door to the plane, a uniformed man gestured urgently at them, repeating the impatient woman's "Hurry, hurry."

They hurried, out of the building and into the blinding sunlight, Alan jogging ahead across the tarmac. Jouncing along in his wake, head and stomach both terribly upset, Gerry couldn't get the Walkman back on his belt until they were actually going up the steps and into the plane. The stewardess pointed Alan toward their seats, and Gerry followed, adjusting the earphones and fiddling with the Walkman's controls as he trailed Alan down the aisle. Ahead, Alan was also still setting up his Walkman.

Then abruptly Alan stopped, and Gerry almost ran into him. Alan turned about as though to run back off the plane; he stared wide-eyed at Gerry, his mouth open in shock. The aisle behind them was full of boarding passengers. The stewardess was closing the door. It was too late.

Gerry also at last had turned on his Walkman, and now he returned Alan's horrified stare as, "I can't get no," Mick Jagger wailed in his ears, "no no no."

20

THE LOST CITY

"The map is not the terrain," the skinny black man said.

"Oh, yes, it is," Valerie said. With her right hand she tapped the map on the attaché case on her lap, while waving with her left at the hilly green unpopulated countryside bucketing by: "*This* map is *that* terrain."

"It is a quote," the skinny black man said, steering almost around a pothole. "It means, there are always differences between reality and the descriptions of reality."

"Nevertheless," Valerie said, holding on amid the bumps, "we should have turned left back there."

"What your map does not show," the skinny black man told her, "is that the floods in December washed away a part of that road. I see the floods didn't affect your map.''

Valerie was finding this driver very difficult. He had a mind of his own, and an almost total disregard for Valerie's opinions. He drove rapidly and rather recklessly, and from the beginning he had disdained Valerie's maps and charts and directions and suggestions and *everything*. He wasn't her driver so much as she was his passenger, the excuse for him to take his Land Rover out for a spin.

He wouldn't even tell her his name. "Hi, I'm Valerie Greene," she had greeted him back in the lobby of the Fort George. "I'm your driver," he'd responded, then had turned on his heel and marched outside, leaving her to follow as best she could, carrying all her own gear. Hurrying after him, she'd been aware of some man over by the house phones staring at her, probably thinking she must be a very silly woman to let her driver—her *servant*, technically, provided by the Belizean government itself—treat her like that.

The vehicle, this peach-colored topless Land Rover, was a perfect match for the driver. It too was all hard edges and businesslike bluntness. What the driver lacked in politesse, the Land Rover lacked in springs. The driver's absence of small talk and common courtesy was echoed in the Land Rover's uncushioned gray metal seats. The driver's skinniness and blackness found their counterpart in the Land Rover's metal and tubing, painted the colors of an aircraft carrier's corridor. Peach and gray, heavily rusted, rough to the touch.

Valerie felt unwanted emotion rising within her. She wasn't exactly sure why it was that girls weren't supposed to do things "like a girl"—throw a ball like a girl, cry at every little thing like a girl—but she did know that was the rule, and so she fought down the tremulousness that frustration had built within her. Only the tiniest bit of it showed when she said, "I thought we could stop for lunch along that road. There's supposed to be a really beautiful little stream there."

"That's what flooded," the driver said. "Besides, there's no stores down that way."

"I have food." Valerie gestured back at her canvas bag, now bounding around like a basketball in the storage well. "I had the hotel make some sandwiches," she explained. "Plenty for both of us."

"You still have to buy beer."

"I don't want beer," Valerie said.

"I do."

Valerie stared at him, while several sentences crowded into her brain, beginning, *Well, I never*— and, *Of all the*— and, *If your superiors*— What kept all those sentences incomplete and unspoken was the driver's absolute self-assurance. He wasn't being calculatedly arrogant, or deliberately hostile toward her, or playing testing games with her, or actually behaving toward *her* at all. He was merely being himself, which Valerie understood, unfortunately, and which kept her from wasting breath trying to get him to be somebody else. You might as well tell a cat to turn around and walk the other way.

And this was who she'd picnic with; what a waste.

They rode on in bumpy silence, Valerie thinking about all the reasons she had left southern Illinois in the first place, all the vague hopes and dreams inspired by her determination to see the great world, and the unpleasant contrast between all that and this reality. Here she was, flopping about in this hard-edged biscuit tin beside a self-absorbed and utterly unappealing man, and not even going to have the *picnic* she'd planned.

So far, in fact, the great world really wasn't showing Valerie Greene very much. Yesterday's encounter with Innocent St. Michael had certainly been enjoyable, but there'd been very little of the romantic in it; the mode of that scene had been mostly comic. And this driver today was as much a washout as (according to him) the road they weren't taking.

All her hopes now were pinned on the lost Mayan city. It would be there, it *must* be there, where she and the computers had decreed (and despite the nay-saying of Innocent's man Vernon), and from the instant of her discovery of it everything in her life would change. Archaeologists would write her respectful letters, asking for details of her methodology. Reporters would gather for news conferences. Governments would take her seriously. She herself would lead the expedition to clear away a millennium of jungle and free the ancient city to thrust its towers once again into the air.

A buzzing sound caused her to lift her head. A small blue-and-white plane was flying by, rather low, not much faster than they, and heading in the same direction. Probably it was actually following the same road, there being very few landmarks in the jungle. Valerie found herself eyeing that plane wistfully, envying whoever was in it, no matter what their purpose or destination. *There* was romance, soaring above the jungle, sailing through the sunlight.

An airstrip beside the lost city spread its scythed green carpet in her mind, and she smiled after the plane. But then, before it was out of sight, she was recalled to earth by the driver abruptly braking hard, the Land Rover bucking to a stop.

Valerie lowered her gaze and looked around, as the dust of their passage caught up with them, making a gray-tan haze in the air. They had stopped at an intersection, where their oiled gravel "highway" crossed a meandering dirt road. To their right, a small building was covered with tin soft drink signs. "Coca Cola," said one, and beneath that in Creole, "quench yu tus."

The driver switched off the engine. In the sudden silence, dust slowly settled. Valerie said, "What's this?"

"You can get the beer in there," he said.

"*I* get the beer?"

Pointing to the left, he said, "Then we take that road. There's a place to stop and eat down a few miles."

"In a swamp, no doubt," she said, becoming irked.

He looked at her with mild surprise but calm willingness: "You wish to eat in a swamp?"

"No, no." Even sarcasm was lost on this creature. Looking at her map, as an excuse to regain her poise, she said, "I can't tell where we are."

"That's all right," he said. "I know the way."

Valerie sighed, realized how inevitable that answer had been. Acknowledging defeat, she opened the attaché case and stowed her map in it, then put the case back in the storage well with her canvas bag. Beer, she thought in fatalistic irritation, as she clambered out of the car. And she might as well get beer for herself, too; this place wouldn't have white wine.

21

REUNION

Lemuel found the whistle. "Now, this *is* something!" he said, holding it at arm's length, staring at it.

Kirby was just as pleased as Lemuel about the discovery. He never prodded his customers, never directed, always permitted them to make their own way across the terrain, and as a result only about half found the whistle. Which was a pity, because it was a beauty.

About eight inches high, made of limestone carved with primitive stone tools, it was the figure of a priest in a high headdress, with arms straight out at his sides and a long skirt over slightly spread feet. A hole bored through from the top of the headdress to the bottom of the skirt between

144

the feet had originally made the whistle, but when Lemuel now tried to blow through it nothing happened. "No, it wouldn't," he said, wiping his mouth. "It's too old."

"To do what?" Kirby asked, parading his ignorance.

"This is a whistle," Lemuel explained, his amiability lightly sheathing his condescension. Lemuel was a changed man now that the dread drug dealers were gone. During lunch, over a vodka and tonic, he had reconstructed his academic armor, had got himself back under control, and during the flight out had even discoursed on his few encounters with marijuana, reminiscences occasioned by Kirby having pointed out cultivated fields of the stuff down below, orderly rows of fuzzy light green among the jumbled thousand greens of the jungle.

Lemuel, in fact, had become so thoroughly the academic and the expert that he'd even shown some early indications of skepticism as Kirby had led him up the side of his extravaganza. "Hmmmmm," he'd said, when he'd come to the shaped building block, and, "Odd this should be out here in plain sight like this."

"It was farther up when I found it," Kirby told him. "I did some digging here and there, test-boring for a septic system, and that thing rolled down."

"Hmmmm," Lemuel repeated, and when Kirby pointed out the silhouette of temple steps against the sky on the right side of the hill Lemuel had said, slowly, "Possible, possible. Could be a natural formation, or it might mean something."

But all skepticism had vanished once Lemuel's foot, in poking into the hillside in search of purchase, had dislodged the whistle. Brushing dirt away, turning it around and around, even trying to blow through it, Lemuel had to know that what he was holding was the real thing.

Real, but not particularly valuable. There were certainly hundreds, possibly thousands of similar whistles legally for sale among antique dealers and curio shops around the

world, most of them priced at less than $200. The one
Lemuel was turning this way and that way in his hands had
most recently sold for $160 U.S.

But value here wasn't the point. This small artifact was
real, it was honest-to-God one thousand and two hundred
years old, the lips of priests had encircled that blowhole,
the hands of real-life ancient Mayans had held that whistle
just as Lemuel was holding it right now. The whistle was
legit, and Lemuel had to know it.

He did. "A whistle," he repeated. "Late Classical
Period, I would say, prior to 900 AD."

"You know a lot more about it than I do," Kirby
assured him.

Lemuel held the whistle up so the little priest faced
Kirby, arms spread wide, like an infant recognizing its
father. "This would have been used in religious ceremonies," he explained, and then frowned past Kirby, saying,
"What's that?"

Kirby turned. They were just high enough so they could
look over the intervening jungle at the meadow—visibly
drier today, by the way—where the plane waited and
where now a coiling column of brown dust spread out and
away from behind an approaching vehicle. "Hey, wait a
minute," Kirby said.

Lemuel's nervousness had shot back into existence, and
in full flower. Stepping back a pace, his eyes getting
rounder and rounder behind his round glasses, he looked
from Kirby to the oncoming car and back to Kirby, saying,
"What is this? What's going on here?"

"I don't know," Kirby said, "but I'll damn well find
out." This remote place didn't get *visitors*. Below, the
vehicle had paused at his plane, but had not stopped, and
now came rapidly on, bounding and bumping over the
rough dry land, moving at an angle that would take it
around to the easier slope, the one Kirby and the Indians

used but which he never showed the customers. "You wait here," Kirby said. "This is *my* land, goddammit."

Lemuel's one sartorial concession to a trek in the wilderness had been to wear Adidas sneakers with his usual gray slacks and pale blue shirt and light cotton sports jacket. Till now, his garb had merely made him look slightly foolish but, with fright blotching his face and agitating his limbs, he looked exactly like the victim in some sadistic tale of a city man strayed among brutes; possibly by Paul Bowles. Staring fixedly at the machete held loosely in Kirby's right hand, "I *demand* to know what's going on," he cried, spoiling the effect when his voice broke on the word *demand*.

"So do I," Kirby told him. He knew nothing about that onrushing car except it was none of his doing and was therefore trouble. "Wait here," he repeated. "Play with the goddam whistle while I get rid of—whoever they are."

He *hated* having to take the easier path in full view of the client, but there was no choice if he were to stop the interlopers before they actually reached the base of the temple. Running diagonally down the hill, around to the right side, he kept catching glimpses of the car between vines and tree branches, and be God-damned if it wasn't the peach-colored Land Rover from the hotel this morning! That, or one exactly like it.

This morning's Land Rover had had government licence plates.

"Hell and damn," Kirby muttered, running harder. Innocent has something to do with this, he told himself, but he was moving too fast to think about the question.

A knot of vines was in his way. He swung the machete with both hands, teeth gritted, wishing it were Innocent's neck. The vines fell away, grudging him a foot or two at every swipe, until all at once the hole was open, the Land Rover was dead ahead, and Kirby hurtled out and down onto the barren flat, waving the machete over his head and yelling, "Stop! Stop!"

The Land Rover veered. There were two people in it, the driver black and male, the passenger white and female. They were the people he'd seen at the hotel this morning. He saw them, the driver blank-faced and the woman yelling something, as the Land Rover angled around him, not even slackening speed.

What were they up to? Kirby turned, panting, the machete sagging at his side, and saw the Land Rover's brake lights go on as it suddenly jolted to a stop. The woman was waving her arms, now yelling at her companion. The back-up lights flashed as the Land Rover came sluing and sliding backward, slamming to a stop beside Kirby, where the woman glared at him through her large sunglasses from under her floppy-brimmed hat and yelled, "*Who* are *you*?"

"Who am I? Lady, what the hell are you—"

"There's a *temple* here!" she cried, astonishingly, horribly. Kirby gaped as she clambered out of the Land Rover, some sort of map or chart flapping in her left hand. Behind her, the driver sat immobile, taking no part.

"Oh, no, there isn't," Kirby said. "No, no. No way."

"But there *is*! There must be!" Waving the map at him, she insisted, "It's all worked out! All I have to do—" She started around him, headed for the slope.

"Wait! Wait!" Kirby ran to get in front, to stop her. "You can't just— You can't— This is trespassing!"

"I have authority from the Belizean government!" She stood even taller than her normal six feet when she said this, and her eyes flashed.

Innocent. *Has* to be Innocent. Damn, damn, damn the man, what was he up to and *why*? Kirby said, "This is private land, this is my land and you can't—"

But now she bent almost double, looking upward past Kirby's right elbow, whipping off her hat so she could see better. "*There*!" she cried.

Oh, God. Kirby reluctantly turned, also crouching a bit, and right there, through the hole he'd just this minute himself cut through the vines, was framed the top fraction of the temple. Steps, stela, flattened platform at the top. It was like a picture from a textbook. "No," Kirby said.

"The temple," breathed this miserable pest of a woman, and Lemuel appeared in the opening, carrying the whistle.

Shit. Kirby came around again to stand close in front of the woman, trying to block her vision, praying Lemuel would have the sense to stay away. "Cut this *out* now," he insisted. "This is my land, this is private property, you can't just barge—"

"I *know* you," she said, staring at him, and all of a sudden he knew her, too. Oh, this is impossible, he thought, this is unfair, this is beyond anything. This pain in the ass can't queer my pitch with Lemuel *twice*.

Yes. Lemuel did not have the sense to keep out of it, because here he came, carrying the goddam whistle, looking frightened and suspicious and determined and fatuous, saying, "Galway, I have to know what's going on here, I have a reputation to—"

"You!" cried the woman. The pest. Valerie Greene; the name returned unbidden to Kirby's mind. Valerie Greene, twice in one lifetime.

Lemuel also recognized her, if belatedly. His jaw dropped. "Oh, no," he said.

She saw the whistle in his hand. She pointed at it, rising up taller than ever, seven feet tall maybe, eight feet, nine. "DESPOLIATION!" she cried.

Now everybody acted at once. Valerie Greene thundered into her historical-preservation speech, Kirby yelled uselessly for everybody to shut up and go away, and Lemuel backtracked, flinging the whistle away backhanded, like a small boy caught smoking. "I won't— This isn't—" Lemuel sputtered, "I can't— Kirby, you have to—" And he turned and ran pell-mell toward the plane.

"National treasures— Priceless antiquities— Irreplaceable artifacts—" Valerie Greene was in full cry now, orating to a stadium of 60,000.

Kirby held the machete up in front of this virago's face. His eyes were on her throat. "One," he said.

22

HALF A LEAGUE

"Two," said the crazy man.

Valerie backed away. Was he counting to ten . . . or to three?

The crazy man's face was very red. Veins stood out on his neck, reminding Valerie irrelevantly of Michelangelo sculptures, and he raised the machete even more menacingly, like Reggie Jackson seeing a fat one come across the plate. He didn't say *three*.

"I—" Valerie said, back-pedaling. "You—"

She hadn't realized the Land Rover's engine was off until she heard, behind her, the driver switch it back on. *Nrnrnrnr, cough,* CHUG.

Would he leave without her? Would the one in front

chop off her head? *Men!* Valerie turned about and scampered to the Land Rover, leaping in as the skinny black man shifted into low; so she would never know if he'd been waiting for her or if she'd just made it. The Land Rover jolted forward, the driver spun the wheel in a hard right which took them in a loop around the crazy man, and from the safety of the moving vehicle Valerie yelled at him, "I'll report you! I'll tell Mister St. *Michael!*"

Something, probably the threat, possibly the name, drove the crazy man over the edge. With a mighty oath, he flung his machete to the ground, where it bounced in a sudden jump of pebbles and flutter of dust. Tearing his bush hat from his head, he hurled that atop the machete, then jumped on the hat with both feet.

Twisting around in the metal bucket seat as the Land Rover sped back the way they'd come, Valerie saw the crazy man jumping up and down on his hat and machete, then pausing to pant and cough in all the dust he'd raised, then shaking his fist after Valerie, then shaking both fists at heaven. All at once, he stooped, picked up a handful of pebbles, and threw them after the Land Rover, though they were far out of range by now.

Valerie looked up, and there it was, serene, silent against the blue sky, indomitable: the temple, looking like nothing more than a hill from this distance. Covered by a millennia of jungle growth, a thousand years of accumulated earth, growing plants, rotting flora and fauna, nature's heavy veneer disguising the works of man. "Do you know what that is?"

The driver looked in his rearview mirror: "A very angry man."

"No," Valerie said. "The *temple*. I was right!"

The driver veered, jolting Valerie almost out onto the hard dry ground covered with dead and dying grass. She faced front, and saw they were angling around the airplane, where Whitman Lemuel—oh, she remembered *him*—

stood holding his jacket up over his head like arrested numbers runners in newspaper photographs. "I know *you*!" Valerie yelled, shaking her finger at him on the way by.

And to think, to *think*, she'd been embarrassed at dinner last night, afraid *he* would notice *her*!

The driver leaned forward, squinting at the rearview mirror. "That hill?" he said. "That's really a temple?"

"Over a thousand years old," Valerie told him, awed by its existence, its reality, her own astonishing brilliance in rescuing it from oblivion. "A Mayan temple."

"Well, that's pretty good," the driver said. "And nobody knew it was there."

"The *world* is going to know, just as soon as I get back to Belmopan," said Valerie.

"Uh huh," said the driver.

23

CURRENTS OF PASSION

"Not back yet?" Innocent shook his head, smiling at the desk clerk. "Women," he said. "Never on time anywhere."

The desk clerk answered the smile; he and Innocent St. Michael had known one another a long time, in a limited but satisfactory way. "But what could we do without them, eh?" he said.

"Bugger all," said Innocent. Before the desk clerk could decide whether that had been idiomatic or literal his switchboard lit up and he had to excuse himself, being the only person on duty at the desk at this time.

Innocent studied his watch: a Rolex, a birthday gift from his wife, selected and paid for by himself, gift-wrapped by the girl in the store. Two minutes to five, it said; by the time he got to the bar, the sun would definitely be over the yardarm.

"Yes yes," the desk clerk was saying. "I'm doin' the best I *can*, Mister Lemuel, but it just may not be possible. Oh, yes, sir, I'll go on trying." Hanging up, he turned back to Innocent, shaking his head and saying, "It always be Americans. Impossible."

Innocent had heard the name *Lemuel* and his ears had pricked up, because he knew who that was. Another of Kirby's strange visitors from the States; a teacher on vacation, he claimed. "What's this one want?" he asked.

"The Earth and all," the desk clerk said. "He registered here for two more days, but now in a rush his plans all different. He run in here an hour ago like the end of the world, had to be on a plane *today*, had to be out of Belize this very minute, sudden urgent message from home. Foo," commented the desk clerk. "If this man got any sudden urgent message from home, I'd *know* it, wouldn't I? I'd *hand* it him, wouldn't I?"

"Of course you would," Innocent said, thinking, Hmmmmmm. "Sounds like he picked up the running shits," he said.

"I don't know what that man's problem be," said the desk clerk. "I done all I can. I told him, there's no more flights out to the States today, so then he wants a charter, he won't spend another night in Belize. I told him, he already got to pay for tonight at the hotel, it way too late to check out, he don't care 'bout that. I tell him, any charter out of the country, there's all kinds of paperwork, Customs clearance, police, all that, now he'll take a flight anywhere, he don't care. Honduras, El Salvador, Jamaica, all the same to him. Now, you *know* there's nothin' I can do 'bout that."

"So he'll spend the night," Innocent said, "and go out in the mornin'."

"Complainin', complainin'," commented the desk clerk. "Well, I go off at six."

"Let's hope my little lady's back by then," Innocent said. "I'll be in the bar."

"I be sure to let you know," the desk clerk promised.

On his way back to the bar, Innocent paused at the public phone booths to make three calls. In the first, he said, "There's a man at the Fort George called Whitman Lemuel. Just a couple minutes after six, you call him, tell him you hear he's looking for a charter flight, tell him to meet you at the Municipal Airport right away to make the arrangements, you'll get him right out tonight. No, you don't have to go to the airport."

In the second call, he said, "There's an American fella named Whitman Lemuel gonna be out to the Municipal Airport around six-thirty, looking for some charter flight. Arrest him on twenty or thirty technical charges. No, no, you won't have to defend them."

In the third call, he said, "There's an American name of Whitman Lemuel gonna be comin in around seven. He'll be spendin the night. Don't hurt him, but do scare him. I'll be comin down in the morning to rescue him, and I'm hopin to see a grateful man."

Smiling, well pleased with himself, Innocent went on to the bar, where he ordered a gin and tonic and sat on one of the low broad swivel chairs, looking out at the view over the tame swimming pool at the feral sea. The pool, in the hotel's late afternoon shadow, looked cold, but the sea, glistening in amber sunlight, looked warm. The impounded black freighter still stood in the offing, awaiting auction. White sails far out moved toward the barrier reef.

White sails. Valerie's round white behind. Innocent smiled, content to wait.

24

WHEN, IN THE MIDDLE OF THE AIR

When, in the middle of the air, Kirby saw his land and temple again, it was just five o'clock, and he'd been flying into the sun for half an hour. As though he weren't annoyed and irritated and angry and irked and furious enough already.

Lemuel had been absolutely unsoothable on the flight back to Belize City, had refused to talk rationally, had alternated between moaning about his lost reputation and bitterly accusing Kirby of being responsible for blighting his career. At the Municipal Airport, he'd flung himself from the plane the instant it stopped rolling and went galloping off toward the operations building, yelling, "Taxi! Taxi!"

And now Kirby was back to his mousetrap, the sun in his eyes and ashes in his mouth. Skimming the temple top, he flashed down the other side, buzzed the Indian village low enough to cool soup, rotated Cynthia on her left wingtip, snarled over the hill again, hurled the plane to the ground as though he hated her, and stomped up the slope to the temple roof, where Tommy and Luz and the others were grouped about, gazing at him wide-eyed. "That was pretty close, Kimosabe," Tommy said.

"You don't know what close is," Kirby told him, disgusted. "There was a goddam archaeologist here a little while ago. She's on her way to report she has just found a previously unknown Mayan temple."

"Shit," said Luz.

Tommy said, "On her way where?"

"We can't stop her," Kirby said, "and it doesn't matter who in particular she talks to, what matters is that this goddam pestiferous woman is *honest*."

"Ugh," said Luz.

"I *hope* she can't bring back reinforcements tonight," Kirby said, looking over his shoulder at his blasted plain. "But she'll certainly be back tomorrow. She thinks I'm here to *despoil* the temple."

Luz said, "Do what?"

"Steal," Tommy explained. To Kirby he said, "So what do we do? Hold them off?"

"We're not talking about General Custer," Kirby told him. "We're talking about policemen, reporters, photographers, archaeologists, government officials—"

"The whole shmeer," Tommy finished. "Too bad; Custer we could have handled."

Kirby looked about, shaking his head. "I hate this," he said, "but we've got to dismantle it."

"Shit," said Luz.

Everybody looked concerned. Tommy said, "Forever?"

"Christ, I hope not." Kirby sighed, gazing upon his

masterpiece. "But at least until the fuss dies down. She'll come back here with a lot of people, she'll point, but there's nothing here. With luck, everybody says she's crazy."

"It's her period," Luz suggested.

"Exactly," Kirby said. "We wait a while, it blows over, we start up again."

"Maybe," said Tommy.

Adversity made Kirby philosophical. "*Maybe's* the best we can hope for in this sad world, boys," he said.

25

THE SAPODILLA NARRATIVE

"The alternative," the skinny black man said reasonably, "was to let her tell everybody about the temple."

"So you brought her *here?*" Vernon demanded.

Here was a small loggers' cabin above the Sibun Gorge, a deep narrow winding groove through the Maya Mountains, gouged out over the millennia by the busy Sibun River. The cabin itself, low and slant-roofed, like a lean-to, was 30 years old or more, rank with mildew and the sweet smell of rotting things. Dirt-floored, lacking any furniture, it was built of horizontal pine-slabs nailed to upright posts pounded into the ground. Apparently it had once been half its present size, just one room, but then a second room was added, making the original front wall a dividing wall. There were no windows in either room, but plenty of air circulated through the uneven cracks between slabs. From the outside the place looked like the log cabin on a maple syrup label, but inside it looked like the attic in your grandmother's house after she moved out. The logcutters who had built this rough shelter had long ago departed, on to other parts of the forest, and in the intervening years it had been occupied only rarely, by hunters or fugitives or lovers. And now by kidnappers and their victim.

"Where else?" the skinny black man demanded, giving Vernon a challenging look. Clearly, he had expected praise for his initiative, not all this carping. "Not to *my* house," he went on. "Should I have taken her to your place?"

"She can identify you anyway," Vernon pointed out.

"Not if she never sees me again. I can just disappear for a while, it's happened before."

"Well, I can't," Vernon said. "I have a job to protect."

"Tied down by things," the skinny black man commented, with the smug superiority of the ne'er-do-well.

"All right, all right," Vernon said, struggling to subdue his fury. The thing to do was accept the situation, he told himself, as he paced back and forth past the open doorway, where gnats and dust motes practiced football plays in a shaft of orange sunlight. Lord, give me the strength to change that which can be changed, he thought, the patience to live with that which cannot be changed, and the wisdom to tell the difference. Lord, he thought, I'm up to my ass in *shit*, Lord!

Too many things going on, too much happening. Now he was somehow responsible for the kidnapping of an American woman, which would probably become an international incident, with the Sixth Fleet making a show of strength off St. Georges Caye and U.S. Marines walking around Belize City giving people chewing gum.

(Earlier in this century, after the world market in mahogany faltered, chicle, being the latex sap of the sapodilla tree, used in the making of chewing gum, became for a while Belize's primary export to the United States.)

There was no furniture in this place, no objects but an unlit candle stuck in a beer bottle in one corner, nothing to kick but the pine-slab walls. Punching his own thighs, Vernon paced back and forth, thinking many different thoughts, until the skinny black man said, easily, "If you're that worried about her, we can always . . ." He drew a line with his finger across his throat.

That was it, *that* was the thought Vernon had been avoiding and denying, circling around and around. In his mind and in his heart, he had committed many, many murders over the years, both of individuals and of groups, but out on the griddle of reality he had never even hit anybody very hard. Was this what a decisive man would do at this juncture? Just shoot the woman right off the—

He didn't have a gun.

All right, stab her just as quick as—

He didn't have a knife with him, either, except his imitation Swiss Army knife (imitation! how that galled!), which might eventually do the job, but not with one clean quick *slice*.

All right, all right, strangle the goddam . . .

He looked down at his hands. He imagined a face between them, gargling. The eyes get bigger and bigger, red veins standing out on the whites. The tongue protrudes from the begging mouth, growing thicker, flopping like a red fish. The feeble fingers grope in agony at his hands. Drool pours from the mouth, snot oozes from the nostrils, the eyes bulge as though they would explode like grapes, the flesh turns mottled, purple . . .

Vernon thought he might be sick.

"Well?" said the skinny black man.

Vernon swallowed, looking out the open doorway at the

heavy jungle and the fading day. "Uhhhh," he said.
"We'll decide that later. First I have to question her."

"About what?"

"About the *temple*!" Vernon spun around, furious again.
"Was that really and truly Galway's land?"

"Looked that way on the map. *She* seemed to think it
was. And the temple was there."

"You saw it. You saw the temple."

"I told you already, I saw a hill with some rocks on it.
Come on, man, make a decision."

The loneliness of command. Vernon bit his cheeks, he
punched his knuckles together. All at once, it occurred to
him, like a light shining from heaven, that he wouldn't
actually himself have to do the, uh, crime personally.
Leaving here tonight, he could simply say (out of the
corner of his mouth), "Take care of her," and his partner,
untroubled by conscience, unaffected by imagination, un-
thinking of consequence, would do the dirty deed.

"What do you *want*, Vernon?"

Vernon looked at the closed door to the inner room. The
partition having originally been an exterior wall, it was
still covered with bark, and the pine-slab door itself was
thick and solid. It opened inward, but there was a rusty old
hasp lock fixed in place with a broken-off piece of branch.
"I'd better go question her now," he decided, and sighed.

Taking the pillowcase from his pocket, he slowly and
deliberately unfolded it, then slipped it over his head. It
was a yellow pillowcase with a large sunny flower design;
the eyeholes so he could see had been cut into the center of
two daisies.

"Take the candle," the skinny black man advised. "It's
dark in there."

So Vernon lit the candle in the beer bottle, the skinny
black man undid the hasp and opened the door—a scurry-
ing sound came from within—and Vernon stepped through
into the other room, peering through the damn eyeholes,

stumbling a bit because he couldn't see his feet. Behind him, the door was closed, the hasp lock rasped.

Valerie Greene stood tall—very tall—against the rear wall, arms at her sides, chin up in a posture of defiance. "You won't get away with this!" she cried.

"I've already gotten away with it," Vernon told her, sneering a bit. (He'd seen the same movies.)

"When I get out of here—"

"*If* you get out of here," he said, and was gratified to see her blanch a bit, one hand lifting, fingers curled, the knuckles just touching her chin. "All you have to do," he told her, "is cooperate."

Her eyes flashed. "What does *that* mean?"

"Oh, don't worry," he said, scornful and superior, "I have no designs on your maidenly virtue. I know how important that is to you Americans."

"You do?" In the flickering candlelight her expression was difficult to read.

"I am here," he said, "to talk about the temple."

"Despoliation!" She took an aggressive step forward, almost as though to launch herself at him. "You, a Belizean, and you don't care *what* happens to your own *heritage*!"

"What makes you think I'm a Belizean?" he asked, trying on a Texas accent.

"Oh, don't be silly," she said. "I know who you are."

"You may *think* you know—"

"There is one thing I wish you'd tell me," she said.

This interview was getting out of control—now *she* was questioning *him*—but there seemed no way to get back to the original path: "Yes?"

"Is Vernon your first name or your last?"

Behind the door, someone snickered. She heard us talking! Dammit, dammit, through all these cracks in the wall. Vernon said, in a stage-Irish accent, "It is none of me names. You can't see me face, you can't identify me voice, you can't prove a thing."

"We'll see about that," she said, and folded her arms beneath her proud bosom.

"Listen," he said, stepping closer, "you talk about heritage, but what do you think Kirby Galway's doing up there? He's *selling* stuff!"

"That makes you no better."

"All right," Vernon said. "I'll tell you the truth. I am Belizean."

"Of course you are, I know that."

"I want to rescue the temple from Kirby Galway," Vernon went on, looking guiltless and pure-minded under the pillowcase, "so I can protect it for my people."

"Oh, no, you don't," she said, "or you wouldn't lock me up in here. You and *Innocent* St. Michael. Boy! Was I ever taken in by your boss!"

Oh, ho, Vernon thought, she thinks St. Michael's part of this scheme. That's good; somehow or other, it's good. He said, "Never mind all that. The point is, that *was* Galway's land you went to, is that right?"

"Of course it was," she said. "The temple's just where I said it was, all along, and *you* were wrong with your drainage and faults and all that."

Vernon resisted the bait: *I am not Vernon*, he reminded himself, and said, "Is it valuable? Rich things there?"

She gave him the exasperated look of the professional faced with the amateur. "How am I supposed to know *that*? I haven't investigated the site, that man drove me off with a sword!"

"A sword?"

She made swishing gestures, saying, "You know, that thing, *you* know."

"Machete," said the skinny black man from the other room.

"You keep out of this!" Vernon yelled. With his free hand, he punched his hipbone. Inside the pillowcase, his head was getting hotter and hotter, in more ways than one.

Everything was out of control. There was no way to buy this woman off, or force her silence, except . . .

Ohhhhh, ohhhhhh. *How* had he gotten into this? "That's all for now," he said, backing away to the door. He thought, I'll go to the land, I don't know how we all missed the temple, but it must be there, I'll go there, I'll hunt around right now, tonight, if I'm lucky I'll find some jade, maybe some gold, a couple hundred thousand worth (U.S.), I'll skip the country *tomorrow*. Start all over again somewhere else, where nobody knows me, change my name, do things right this time. At the same time, he knew he wouldn't. He wouldn't go there tonight, and even if he did he wouldn't find anything useful by stumbling around in the dark, and even if by some insane chance he did happen upon something valuable he still wouldn't flee Belize.

Where would he go? What would he do there? Who would he know there?

"Leave me the candle," Valerie Greene said.

"What?" he asked, disturbed from his reverie.

"It's dark in here. I need the candle."

"Oh, no," he said. He'd seen *that* movie, too. "You'll set fire to the place and escape."

"I just wanted some light."

"You don't need light," he said ominously, holding the candle closer to himself, not quite igniting the pillowcase. He pushed on the door, and nothing happened. His partner had locked it. So much for his exit line; hating the sense that he was somehow becoming a figure of fun, Vernon resignedly knocked on the door.

"Who goes there?"

"Oh, open the goddam door!"

The hasp rasped, the door swung open, and Vernon glared back through the pillowcase eyes at Valerie Greene: "I'll see *you* later," he said, and this time made his exit.

"I have to go to the bathroom!"

The skinny black man shut and locked the door. The sun would soon be setting; orange rays crossed almost horizontally from the doorway to soften the roughness of the dividing wall. Vernon put the candle down in its corner, still burning. "I have to get back," he said.

The skinny black man nodded at the locked door. "Do I take care of that?"

"Well, of course, man, you brought her here, didn't you?"

The skinny black man leveled on Vernon a cold and impatient gaze, and waited.

Vernon dithered. Unwillingly, he said, "We can't have her walking around the streets now, can we?"

"Say it out, Vernon. Say what you want."

There was to be no escape from responsibility. Vernon looked aside, out the doorway at trees, brush, vines, heavy greenery turning black in the orange light. He shook his head. "She has to die," he muttered, and hurried away.

26

THROUGH THE LOOKING GLASS

Home.

An accumulation of mail. No burglaries, thank God. The cats and plants *had* been taken care of after all by Richie from across the hall; what a relief. Sour milk in the refrigerator, but otherwise fine in there. Seltzer gone flat, so the homecoming Cutty Sarks had to be splashed with water from the kitchen sink. And among the messages on the answering machine was the hearty robust cheerful voice of Hiram: "Hanging by my thumbs down here, can't wait to hear all. Give a buzz the *instant* you get in."

"Oh, dear," Gerry said. "I'm not sure I can face him."

Back on home ground, Alan was less judgmental, more

compassionate. "I know what you mean," he said, "but we might as well get it over."

"Can't I at least shower first? We just walked in, we haven't even unpacked."

"You go shower," Alan told him. "I'll call Hiram and tell him to give us half an hour, and then *I'll* unpack." (Alan was feeling a bit guilty at the memory of his tension-caused snappishness down there in Belize.)

"Oh, I do appreciate that," Gerry said. "Thank you, Alan." The Scotch had made him feel better already, and so had Alan's supportive mood, and so had the very fact of being home, here among the things he loved.

Before showering, and while Alan made the call to Hiram's apartment three floors below, Gerry went back to the living room simply to drink in the atmosphere for a moment; the reassurance of one's own nest. Coming in from Kennedy in the cab through the evening rush, smears of wet dirty snow beside the roadway, Gerry had *yearned* to be home, and now at last here he was, in his own living room.

On a basic motif of French Empire gilded furniture, Gerry and Alan had overlaid an eclectic mix of other items, all a little outrageous, and yet all coming wonderfully together, like a perfect little ragout. The nineteenth century English rhinoceros horn chair, for instance, made a blunt masculine statement that eased somewhat the overly pompous and delicate Napoleonic pieces, while the heavy window treatments of fringed green velvet against the slightly darker green of the lacquered walls created an interiority, a *hereness* saved from claustrophobia by the leopard skin casually thrown on the Aubusson rug. The dark Coromandel screen in the corner served as a focus for the room's *objets*; teakwood Balinese demons grinning at brass many-armed Indian goddesses under the baleful gaze of English cathedral stone gargoyles and medieval icons, lit by Tiffany lamps.

Home!

Actually smiling, for the first time in who knows how long, Gerry went on through to the bedroom, hearing the murmur of Alan on the phone in the office, and if the eclectic living room had soothed him the bedroom, designed for comfort and solace, made him almost weep with pleasure. The pattern here was English pastel flowered chintzes, basically in soft pinks and blues on a setting of cream. The king-size bed stated the motif, with a chintz spread tossed with lacy pillows, each in its own patterned cover reflected elsewhere in the room. The walls were sheathed in the softest and most delicate of cloth, with a slightly stronger statement made by the thick chintz window draperies sweeping the floor, backed by lacy sheers. The only strong note in the ensemble was a brass-legged glass table, flanked by low broad armchairs, very overstuffed beneath their chintz covers, soft and squishy and wonderfully comforting to sit on.

Gerry and Alan hadn't gotten around to doing the bathroom yet, unfortunately—they wanted to get it exactly *right* before calling in the workmen—so it still reflected the taste (for lack of a better word) of the landlord. Still, the shower was as wonderful and restorative as anticipated.

Thirty minutes later, wearing a black muumuu decorated with dragons, and carrying a fresh Scotch and water in a wide, heavy-based glass, Gerry answered the doorbell to let in Hiram Farley, a tall barrel-chested balding happy man, an important local magazine editor, which means a man who found it impossible to take life seriously. "Gerry, my darling, you're *tanned*!" Hiram said, grabbing Gerry by both cheeks and tilting his face down so he could be kissed on his tanned brow. "How beautiful you are," Hiram said, "and how beautiful that drink looks."

"No soda, I'm afraid. Plain water all right?"

"Fish fuck in it," Hiram said, "but on the other hand birds fuck in midair."

"Hiram," Gerry said, "was that a yes?"

"The day I say no to a drink," Hiram said, "*any* drink, that's the day for you to arrange for the six black horses, and the six good men well-hung and true."

Hiram's words generally went by Gerry like traffic; in the pauses, he crossed the conversational street: "I'll make your drink."

"Thank you, sweetness."

They bifurcated, Gerry moving kitchenward, Hiram toward the living room, Gerry saying, "Alan will be right in, he's just finished his shower."

When Gerry returned to the living room, in fact, carrying Hiram's drink as well as his own, Alan was already there, dressed in his black-sashed white kimono and seated crosslegged on a white-and-gold chair. Hiram had, as usual, settled his bulk onto the chair framed in rhinoceros horn, which made him look like the white villain in a Tarzan movie. Gerry's spot was the Madame Recamier.

"To your happy return," Hiram said, raising the glass Gerry had handed him.

"Here, here," said Alan, and everybody took a ritual sip.

Hiram smiled hopefully at his hosts. "And to a successful trip?"

"Not entirely," Alan said.

"Not at *all*," Gerry said. "In fact, a disaster."

"Oh, I wouldn't go that far," Alan said. "We know a lot more about how it's done. You're too pessimistic, Gerry."

"The tapes are *gone*!"

"Hold on," Hiram said. "Do what the King of Hearts told Alice to do, and what *I* tell writers every blessed day, ink-stained wretches, prose from amateurs, talentless bastards."

Gerry blinked. "Pros from amateurs?"

Hiram leaned forward, assuming a pedantic yet royal

posture. " 'Begin at the beginning,' " he quoted, gravely, " 'and go on till you come to the end: then stop.' "

Alan said, "Everything seemed fine until the very end."

"And then it *wasn't*," Gerry said.

"No, no," Hiram said. "Listen more carefully this time. 'Begin at the beginning—' "

"Oh, *Hiram!*" Gerry said, at wit's end. "The tapes are *gone*, okay?"

Alan said, "Wait a minute, Gerry. Hiram's right." Turning to Hiram he said, "From the beginning, then," and went on to give a mostly coherent account of their time in Belize, fictionalizing only their reaction to the presence of the mobster at their hotel, and finishing, "Now, obviously somebody *knew* we'd made those tapes, and guessed we'd try to sneak them out in our Walkmans."

Hiram nodded, thinking about it. "Galway, do you think?"

"I just don't know," Alan said. "There wasn't the slightest hint of such a thing, he doesn't seem the type to be able to dissemble that well, and yet, who knows, really?"

"Oh, it was Galway, all right," Gerry said. "He's very *devious*, that one."

"Well," Hiram said, "if Galway has those tapes, that's that."

Alan said, "Must it be? We remember exactly what he told us, the whole method to smuggle everything out and all that, what he's going to do to that poor temple—"

Gerry said, "I was a bit tempted, I must say. Just go ahead and do it; we could make a *lot* of money."

Alan gave him an arch look. "Yes, I could tell what you were thinking."

"Well," Gerry said, "after all, we *could*, couldn't we? I mean, we're not police, are we?"

"You're good citizens," Hiram told him. "Remember

how sickened you were when I showed you those pictures of the looted graves?''

Gerry laughed, with a negative hand-wave. "Oh, I don't mean I was *seriously* tempted," he said. "Just a little bit."

"Anyway," Alan said, "we still have the facts, even if we don't have the tapes. Wouldn't that be enough?"

Hiram shook his head. "Your unsupported word," he said. "Even if the lawyers would let us publish, *I* wouldn't. It's just hearsay, puffed up. If we don't nail a villain, we don't have a story."

"It's too bad, really," Alan said. "I was rather enjoying being a spy."

Hiram looked as wistful as a large heavyset bald man can: "An exposé of illegal art smuggling, leading right here to New York. What a nice change of pace that would have been. I can't tell you guys how tired of it all I get. The fifty-seven best pizza parlors in the Hamptons; your guide to a chiropractor on the West Side; questions raised about real estate developers. And here we had something *real* for once: antiquities, villains, airplanes, clandestine meetings in cornfields—"

"I think it's some kind of ranch," Alan said.

"Same idea," Hiram told him. "Trickier footing, of course. Well, it's all over now." He sighed, and swigged half his drink. "You'll never hear from Kirby Galway again."

27

THE BEACON AND THE VOICE

I can still call those two guys in New York, Kirby thought, as he lifted the too-full Cynthia over the mountains in a great looping half circle. Just so that damn woman's story doesn't hit the wire services, I can still call them in three or four weeks and start making deliveries, whether I have a temple set up down here or not.

Around and behind him the marijuana bales made small squeaking and scraping sounds as Cynthia labored through the moonlit night. The first few trips with this sort of cargo, Kirby had thought the grass was infested with bugs, but then he came to realize it was just the bales shifting and adjusting as air currents toyed with the plane.

The only way to make a living at all carrying this sort of bulky cargo in this small plane was to overload it and hope you were as good a pilot as you thought you were. More than once, waddling along some bumpy pasture or a pot-holed secondary road toward a line of trees dead ahead in the darkness, Kirby had thought he'd overdone it this time—and wouldn't that be a penny-ante way to die—but so far luck and skill and vagrant breezes had conspired to help him rise above all those trees and his own foolhardi-ness as well.

But now that he had the temple scam, he was doubling the risk. Having loaded the plane, having said farewell to the contact here at the Belizean end, he struggled Cynthia into the sky, set off northward and, once securely out of sight and sound of the men to whom he'd just waved goodbye, turned around in a long ungainly loop, hugging the treetops, Cynthia straining all the way, all so he could fly back south to his own land for an extra landing and takeoff.

Again tonight. He flew on south, mostly by feel, as clouds rolled in to block the moon. Coming in over the former temple, the world below him unrelieved black, he switched on his landing lights at the last possible instant, to see Luz and a couple of the others scurry out of his path. His land was even dryer than this afternoon, the first cracks appearing among the brown stubble.

Chunk! went Cynthia, hitting hard, the whole plane groaning in complaint. Kirby turned, flashed his landing lights briefly once more to find the Indians, then pushed Cynthia over to where they stood gathered around a couple of large cardboard cartons.

The loading didn't take long; they'd done all this before. Out of the cardboard cartons came smaller or larger parcels wrapped in recent Belizean papers, mostly the *Beacon* and the *Voice*. The smallest parcel was no bigger than a coffee mug, the largest about the size of a table lamp without the shade. "Careful with this one," Tommy said, handing over a medium-sized piece, "it's broken."

"Right," said Kirby, stuffing it gently into one of the marijuana bales.

It was now a little past midnight, and he had nearly 800 miles to travel, most of it over water. Depending on winds and weather, the trip would take between five and seven hours; in any event, it would be before dawn when he landed. Stowing the last parcel, he yawned and said, "You get the temple put away?"

"Oh, yeah," Tommy said. "The hill's a little scuffed up, that's all. You can see there's been digging."

Luz said, "I'm lookin' forward to those assholes. They'll shit when they get here and don't see any temple."

"Just so that ends it," Kirby said, and yawned again. "I'll see you guys next week some time," he said. "When I get back from this trip, I'm just gonna hibernate."

Innocently, Tommy said, "What's hibernate?"

Kirby said, "What bears do in winter."

Tommy said, "What's winter?"

"Oh, fuck you," Kirby said, and flew away with the music of their laughter in his ears.

28

BUT NOT IN COROZAL

Nine A.M. Saturday morning, and the first thing Innocent saw when he walked into his suite of offices in Belmopan was his faithful assistant, Vernon, elbow deep in paperwork. "Well, good morning," Innocent said. "Working on a Saturday?"

Vernon looked up from his graphs and lists: "I had to see the dentist yesterday, so I came in to get caught up." He looked as though he still had the toothache.

"I have some phone calls to make," Innocent said, "then an appointment down in Belize." He grinned, thinking about his appointment. How happy he was going to make Whitman Lemuel, by rescuing him. For a price.

Vernon reached for his phone. "Who do you want to call?"

Good old reliable Vernon. "Transportation," Innocent told him. "I signed out a Land Rover yesterday, I want to know if it's back."

While Vernon made the call, Innocent reflected again on yesterday's unsatisfactory conclusion. Having arranged for the harrying of Whitman Lemuel, he had sat in the bar of the Fort George, one G and T after another in his hand as he'd watched daylight fade over the ocean. In air conditioning, behind glass, he had seen the slowly changing colors of sky and sea as a huge television production, slow but vast, put on particularly for him. Occasionally, a dusty cartop was visible, passing by on the dirt road beyond the hotel property's stone wall. But none of those cars contained Valerie Greene.

Full night turned the windows into mirrors, and the view of himself sprawled on the low dark chair, drink in hand, waiting hour after hour for some woman who never appeared, finally irritated Innocent to the point where, a little after 7:30, he went back out to the phone booths, called a friend in the police, asked one or two guarded questions, and was assured no government vehicle of any kind had been involved today in an accident. (A rare day.) He then called Belize City Hospital, where no female U.S. citizen had been admitted in the last 12 hours. Likewise the Punta Gorda and Belmopan hospitals. He didn't phone the hospitals up in Corozal and Orange Walk because that was the other end of the country; Valerie had been traveling south.

At that point, he could have taken a room at the hotel for himself, and there were any number of women he could have phoned to come join him, but he just didn't feel like it. His appetite had been set for Valerie Greene, and he wanted no substitute. Besides which, he was somewhat surprised to realize, he *liked* that girl, and wanted to be sure she was all right. So he ate alone in the hotel dining room, facing the curtains that close out the night view, and when she still hadn't returned he left a simple message for her with the night clerk: "I'll phone in the morning. Innocent." Whereupon he drove home, took a quick moonlight swim in the pool to get the kinks out of his body, and slept like a baby.

This morning, as promised, he phoned from the house, but Valerie Greene had never returned to the hotel. Her possessions were still in her room, as though she expected to come back, but the girl herself had been neither seen nor heard from.

His first appointment today was to have been with Whitman Lemuel, but the disappearance of Valerie Greene changed all that. The amount and kind of telephoning he had to do would not be possible at home, where he was surrounded by hostile spies with his blood in their veins. So he must first come here to the office in Belmopan.

Where the loyal Vernon immediately took over the dog's body work, making the call, saying, "No, nothing's wrong," hanging up, saying to Innocent, "It's still out."

"Hell," Innocent said.

Vernon looked alert, ready to be of assistance. "Something the matter?"

"That archaeologist woman," Innocent said.

"Oh, yes. Is that the car?"

"She didn't come back."

A cloud passed over Vernon's face; perhaps his tooth twinged him. He said, "Who was the driver?"

Innocent looked and felt uncomfortable; this was the real problem in the affair. "You know that fellow I use," he said, gesturing vaguely.

Vernon looked shocked. *"Him?"*

"I needed someone . . ." Innocent paused, but then went on, since he kept very few secrets from Vernon. "I needed someone to report to *me*," he said. "Someone I could trust to keep his mouth shut."

"Someone you could trust with a woman?" Vernon asked.

"Oh, I don't think he'd . . ." But Innocent's voice trailed away. In his heart, he had to admit he wasn't sure about that part of it.

"Is *he* back?" Vernon asked.

"He isn't on the phone."

"Where does he live?"

"Teakettle," Innocent said, naming a tiny hamlet a few miles away toward the Guatemalan border. "But I have to get down to Belize."

"I'll go out there," Vernon offered, "see if I can find him. You can phone me here later."

"Thank you, Vernon," Innocent said. "I don't know what I'd do without you."

29

IN WHICH IS RECOUNTED LEMUEL'S ARRIVAL IN BELIZE, HIS TRAVELING TO THE TEMPLE WITH GALWAY, THE UNEXPECTED APPEARANCE OF VALERIE GREENE, GALWAY'S ASTONISHING BEHAVIOR THERE-AFTER, AND LEMUEL'S DECISION TO HAVE NOTHING MORE TO DO WITH THE WHOLE DUBIOUS AFFAIR

"Mistah Whitman?"

Lemuel rose from a sweaty unrestful humid sleep, up out of discomfort and nightmare into worse discomfort and much worse reality. Jail. Fetid odors fixed in the dank air like flies in amber. Something dripping far off, against some ancient stone. The night's clamminess just giving way to the day's heat. Jail; a *foreign* jail.

Gray light seeped through the filth on the barred window, illuminating the concrete walls and floor, the bare thin ticking without sheet or mattress in which Lemuel had tossed and turned in sleepless terror all night, only to fall into exhausted unconsciousness at the first hint of dawn. And now he was startled awake by a voice, rasping his name:

"You dere, wake up. You Mistah Whitman?"

Sitting up, dazed with fear and lack of sleep, Lemuel blinked at the silhouette beyond the barred door. "Lemuel," he said. His tongue felt swollen, against his furry teeth. "My name is Lemuel."

"You no Mistah Whitman?" The silhouette wore a uniform of some sort, must be a guard.

"Whitman is my first name." Trying to wake up, trying to collect his scattered wits, Lemuel dug knuckles into his sandy eyes.

"Huh," said the guard, and rattled papers. "Whitman be you *Christian* name?"

"Yes."

"And Lemuel, now. Lemuel be you *family* name?"

"That's right."

The guard chuckled, rattling his papers. "There be many a strange name in this world," he said philosophically. Keys rattled now, clanged in the lock, and the door squeaked open. "Well, Mistah, Mistah *Lemuel*, Mistah *Whitman Lemuel*, you got a visitor."

A visitor? What could it mean? Who knew he was here? After hours last night of struggle and protest, hours of being lied to or intimidated or merely ignored, Lemuel had finally given up hope of ever getting a message through to the American embassy, or the hotel, or anyone anywhere in the world who might be able to help him escape this sudden tropic Kafka. So who could this be, coming to visit him here in this awful place? Lemuel asked the guard: "What visitor?"

"The man who want to see you."

"Who? Who is he?"

"You don't want no visitor this morning?" The door squeaked again, ominously, as though with the idea of closing. "You want me, I tell him you be too busy for visitor this morning."

"No no!" Anything would be better than this verminous cell. Rising too hastily, Lemuel was engulfed in dizziness and had to lean a moment against the wall, under the eye of the impassive guard. Then he moved on, out to a concrete hall being mopped by a small and toothless inmate. The guard led Lemuel toward the front of the building, but veered them into a small side office where a large stout chocolate-colored man in a light gray suit and pale green open-neck shirt stood leafing through a wall calendar from Regent Insurance Company, taking a great deal of interest in the months ahead. Translucent louvers in both windows were slightly open, letting in light and air without permitting a view of what lay outside.

"Mistah St. Michael," said the guard, with some odd combination of deference and jocularity, "this be Mistah Whit-*man Lem*-uel." Shooing Lemuel into the office, the guard snicked the solid door shut with himself on the outside.

Mr. St. Michael dropped the year and turned to brood upon Lemuel, who keenly felt his own griminess, his wrinkled clothing and unwashed body and unshaven face. St. Michael, for such a big man in such a hot climate, was absolutely dapper. A thousand sentences rushed through Lemuel's mind—greetings, queries, demands, supplications—but none seemed precisely suited to the situation, so he remained silent, not even trying to alter the look of desperation and bewilderment and fear he knew to be on his face.

It was St. Michael at last who spoke, in a mellifluous

radio announcer's voice, saying, "Well, Mister Lemuel, I'll say this for you. You don't *look* a crook."

So it was, that was it, his worst fears realized, the Kirby Galway situation, that was it. The terrors that had kept him awake all night were justified; reputation ruined, a dank jail cell his portion forevermore. "Oh, no, sir," Lemuel said, in that moment a broken man, "no, sir, I am *not* a crook."

"We have heard Americans say that before," St. Michael told him.

"It was Galway," Lemuel said, all in a rush. "Kirby Galway, he lied to me, said all he wanted was my expert opinion, there wasn't the slightest *hint* of impropriety until it was too late, I was already there, right there at the temple, the *first* time he made the suggestion, that's the—"

"At the temple?" St. Michael's eyes gleamed; his interest had been captured. A super-detective, that's what he must be, a manhunter thrilling to the chase.

Well, Lemuel wanted no part of it. Let this manhunter chase Kirby Galway, and let Galway *try* to weasel out of it later, try to pin any of the blame on a respectable scholar like Whitman Lemuel, just let him try. "I don't know what the girl told you," he began, "but I was out there *strictly*—"

"The girl? Valerie Greene?"

"Is that her name? Whatever she said, I assure you—"

"Wait, wait, Mister Lemuel," St. Michael said, suddenly accommodating, reassuring. "Sit down here. Begin at the beginning, please."

There was a small mahogany desk in the room, and a pair of armless wooden chairs. Lemuel and St. Michael sat across the desk from one another, and Lemuel told him everything, every single thing from his first meeting in New York with Kirby Galway *and* the girl—Valerie Greene, yes, both there, but they gave no indication they were together *at that time*—through the subsequent meeting with

Galway alone in New York, Lemuel's agreement to come to Belize to inspect Galway's temple, his arrival, their traveling out together, the unexpected appearance of the girl, Galway's astonishing behavior thereafter, and Lemuel's decision to have nothing more to do with the whole dubious affair. He gave St. Michael this entire history, and almost everything he said was the absolute truth. Only in one small detail did he lie; in *his* version of events, Kirby Galway had approached him exclusively as an expert, had asked for an opinion as to the value and authenticity of the material he had found on his land, and had not suggested smuggling or the illegal sale of Mayan antiquities until they were already standing on the temple itself, until, in fact, just before the girl arrived.

"So it's there, in other words," St. Michael said, when Lemuel was done. "The temple is there."

"Well, yes, of course."

St. Michael brooded some more. Did he believe Lemuel? If he didn't, it was still possible that Lemuel was too unimportant to bother with further. Particularly if Lemuel volunteered to be, to do—what was the legal term for selling out your partners? Oh, yes—to give evidence for the prosecution, that was it. "I'll be happy, if necessary," Lemuel said, smiling a bit as man to man, "to give evidence for the prosecution, though of course, with my reputation at stake, I'd prefer to have as little to do with this sorry mess as—"

"Tell me about," St. Michael interrupted, as though he hadn't heard Lemuel talking at all, "tell me about, mmmm—" He withdrew a flat white envelope from his inner jacket pocket and consulted something written on its back: "Witcher and Feldspan."

"Who?"

"Alan Witcher and— Here, see for yourself."

"St. Michael tossed the envelope across the table. It landed face up, and Lemuel had time to see that it was addressed to one Innocent St. Michael at some Belizean government department, and that the printed return address was a bank in the Cayman Islands. But then St. Michael reached out, turned it over, and tapped the pen notations on the back, saying, "That side."

"Yes, of course."

Lemuel drew the envelope closer, to read what was written there: *Alan Witcher, Gerrold Feldspan, 8 Christopher Street, New York, NY 10014.* "Who are these people?"

"That's what I am asking you, Mister Lemuel. Who are they, and *why* did they tape-record their conversation with Kirby Galway?"

"But I have no idea, I've never heard—"

St. Michael's big palm boomed down onto the desktop with a crack of doom, so forceful that everything in the room jumped, including Lemuel, who very nearly went over backwards out of his chair. His large round face all thunderclouds, St. Michael roared, "Do not toy with *me,* Mister Lemuel, or it will go very badly with you, I assure you. You can spend a *month* in that little cell, if you think you'd like it, if you—"

"No, please!" Lemuel leaned forward, gasping for breath, ribcage pressed against the rough edge of the desk. "I'm telling you the truth! I swear I am! I'll tell you anything you want, anything you need to know!"

"Tell me about Witcher and Feldspan, then, and stop wasting my time!"

"But I don't *know* them! Honest to God, oh, God help me, oh, what am I going to do, I should never have, it's all Galway's fault, he kept saying this and saying that, and that *girl,* I don't know what she told you, she's as bad as he is, they're in it together, I know they—"

"Oh, be quiet," St. Michael said, all his fury gone as abruptly as it had arrived, like a summer storm. Shaking his head, he said, "You're telling the truth now, all right. You don't know any more than you just said."

"That's right!"

"So Kirby brings down those pansy boys. And then he brings down you. And he knows Valerie Greene, but he don't like her so much. And when you see her, you get the wind up, you figure you gonna be arrested for what you planned, stealing our antiquities, you try to run—"

"I never, never had any—"

St. Michael pointed a thick finger at Lemuel. "You come down here, at *your* expense, because Kirby's got no money to throw away on strangers, *your* expense, just to play expert, that's all it is. You tell that story, Mister Lemuel," St. Michael said, and smiled a thin and dangerous smile. "You tell that story in a Belize court, Mister Lemuel."

"It's the truth," Lemuel said weakly. But the Belize court loomed in his mind, as foreign as Brobdignag, as implacable as the Inquisition.

"Mister Lemuel," St. Michael said, "I can arrange to have you released now, send you back to the hotel. You take a shower, calm down, check out like anybody else, get on the plane, go back to the States. You can do that, Mister Lemuel."

"Oh, thank God," Lemuel said.

"But, do you know," St. Michael went on, "do you know what you *can't* do, Mister Lemuel?"

"Wha—what?"

"Get within two blocks of the American embassy," St. Michael said. "That you can't do. Don't even *think* about turning your head in that direction."

"Oh, I won't," Lemuel said, in utter sincerity. "Believe me, Mister St. Michael, I've learned my lesson. You'll never—" His voice broke; he started again: "You'll never *ever* hear from me again."

30

BEFORE THE STORM

When the alarm went off, Kirby moaned, thrashed about in the confined space, smacked gummy lips, and reluctantly opened gummy eyes just long enough to find the damn wind-up alarm clock on Cynthia's dashboard and push in the button to stop the awful noise. His sticky eyelids immediately squeezed shut again, but too late; he had seen the clock face, he knew it was 9:30 tomorrow morning, he knew he was awake.

Hell and damn. The smell of marijuana all about him was hot and dry and pungent. Only a part of the plane was under the tree branches, and the metal fuselage had conducted heat forward from the sun-drenched tail section. He hated to sleep in the plane, anyway; there was never enough room for his long rangy body, and he always awoke stiff and sore, with aches that would take hours to fade. Still reluctant to accept consciousness, pawing in his door pocket for his sunglasses, he looked out and around at this little corner of the world.

The Florida Everglades. East of Cape Romano, south of Fort Myers, the Everglades was a flat and soggy confusion of land, some of it still pristine uncleared swamp, some dry scrub covered with dwarf pines and dusty shrubs, some reclaimed into citrus groves, some dried to grazing land, supporting horses or cattle. Kirby was parked at the narrow end of a long paper-airplane-shaped pasture flanked by bog, hemmed in by gnarled trees. Horses used to graze here, unfenced except at the wide farther end, held in by the swampy footing on both sides, but the land had changed ownership a couple of years ago and now it lay deserted.

Or almost deserted. Three young deer, adolescent males, grazed around Cynthia's nose, looking up without much interest when Kirby began to move around inside the plane, but then bounding off into the swamp when he opened his door.

A hot day already, and quite humid. The insect repellent he'd put on three and a half hours ago, when he'd landed here in darkness and set the alarm and tried to get caught up on some of his lost sleep, had faded by now, and he had a few nice fresh bites under his eyes and between his knuckles. Itchy, hungry, irritated, weary, aching all over, he clambered awkwardly out of the plane and down onto the faintly spongy ground, where he held one of Cynthia's struts and did some not-so-very-deep knee bends to limber up.

The bog on the right side of the field was stagnant, but on the left ran a narrow course of moving cool water, in which Kirby washed his face and hands, brushed his teeth with his finger, soaked his hair, and gargled. With water running down his neck and under his shirt, feeling slightly better, he walked back to the plane and ate the food he'd brought along: an apple and a health-food carob candy bar. He was just finishing when he saw the car approach from the wide end of the pasture.

The right car: a white Cadillac Seville with Dade County plates. Nevertheless, Kirby felt the same tension he always did at this point. He was dealing in stolen goods, and in things of great value; at least, that was the perception. People in such occupations sometimes were killed by their partners or their customers. Kirby had tried to be careful in his choice of clients, but one could never be absolutely certain. Not absolutely certain.

There seemed to be one person alone in the car, which was the way it was supposed to be. The Cadillac approached, moving slowly on the soft uneven ground, and Kirby squinted as he looked through the windshield, at last recognizing the driver. His name was Mortmain, he was somewhere the wrong side of 70, and he was dapper and elegant, from his full head of carefully waved white hair over a broad-browed, deeply tanned face set off by humorous blue eyes, through the white ascot and navy blue blazer and white slacks and white shoes which were his habitual costume. He was "retired," Kirby didn't know from what, and he was the go-between for a customer of Kirby's in Los Angeles, an artist/designer/interior decorator/ antique dealer whose clients were mostly celebrities, people for whom smuggled Mayan statuary was not the only illegal material from Latin America to be of more than passing interest.

Kirby walked around to the right side of the Cadillac as it came to a stop. Glancing first into the rear seatwell to be certain no one was hiding there—an automatic reflex by now—he slid into the air conditioned interior. "Morning, Mister Mortmain," he said.

"Good morning, Kirby." Mortmain must have been quite a burly man in his prime, and was still pretty big,

with a deep mellow voice and large-knuckled tanned hands
on which the liver spots could almost have been youthful
freckles. Reaching to his blazer's inside pocket, bringing
out a thick white envelope, he said, "Bobbi apologizes for
the amount. He swears it was the best he could get. The
recession and all that."

"Mm-hm," Kirby said, taking the envelope. As usual it
contained, in addition to his share of the sales, in cash,
Xeroxed copies of Bobbi's customers' checks to Bobbi
(their famous names and signatures discreetly blacked out),
so Kirby would know he was getting a full count. Of
course, there was no reason for Bobbi not to ask his
customers to pay him in *two* checks; he could mention
some vague tax reason, for instance. But that was all right;
Kirby assumed his clients would cheat a little, it was part
of the game.

While Kirby opened the envelope, counted the cash and
looked at the checks, Mortmain carefully backed and filled,
turning the Cadillac around and backing it into Cynthia's
left armpit, where the car's trunk would be nearest the
pilot's door.

"No," Kirby said, shaking his head. "I'm sorry, Mister
Mortmain, but no." This time, Bobbi had gone too far.

Mortmain looked mildly surprised, politely concerned.
"Something wrong?"

"This is *way* too little," Kirby said. "There's another
man I was talking to, he says he can get me a lot better
prices."

"People always make promises, Kirby," Mortmain said.

"Maybe. Or maybe the recession didn't hit as hard in
Chicago."

"Is that where your friend is?"

"I can't give you this shipment," Kirby said.

Now Mortmain *was* surprised. "You'll fly it back with
you?"

"No. I'll leave it with friends in Florida, and call the other guy."

Mortmain sighed. "Well," he said, "that's up to you, of course. I know Bobbi will be very disappointed."

Kirby didn't know the precise relationship between Mortmain and Bobbi, whether Mortmain was merely a messenger, or somehow a partner, or possibly even the brains of the operation. It was hard to negotiate with somebody who might not even be present. Nevertheless, Kirby said, "Bobbi won't be as disappointed as I am right now. I'll tell you what I think, I think Bobbi's getting second checks from people. I thought he was honest, but now I don't know."

Was Mortmain amused? Kirby's occasional displays of naiveté and stupidity were believed precisely because no one could imagine him deliberately painting himself in such colors. Mortmain nodded in perhaps exaggerated solemnity, considering what Kirby had said, and then said, "Kirby, I don't think Bobbi would do a thing like that but, to be honest, I couldn't swear to it."

"I'm sorry," Kirby said, and reached for the door handle. The air conditioning in here was very nice.

"Wait a minute," Mortmain said. "I can't let it end like this. Could you wait for me to go phone Bobbi?"

"I can't," Kirby said. "I still have to deliver that other stuff."

"Of course." Mortmain considered. "I'm going out on a limb here," he said. "I can't really speak for Bobbi, but I think I must. He's done very well from your relationship."

"He sure has," Kirby said, sounding bitter.

"Well, so have you," Mortmain pointed out. Gesturing at the envelope in Kirby's hand, he said, "How much more do you think you should have had?"

"A thousand dollars would just *begin* to cover it."

"Split the difference with me," Mortmain said. "Don't end the relationship now. I promise you I'll talk with

Bobbi, and I'll tell him I guaranteed you another five hundred dollars from the last shipment. And I'll tell him about your friend in Chicago, and say he'd *better* find some more generous customers from now on.''

Kirby would accept this offer, of course, there being no friend in Florida with whom to stash the goods, and the $500 being a bonus he hadn't expected, but he let Mortmain watch him brood about it for a while. Mortmain could see his furrowed brow, could see him gradually overcoming his sense of grievance and deciding to take the offer. ''All right,'' he said at last.

''I'll talk to Bobbi this afternoon,'' Mortmain promised.

''Fine.'' Kirby gave him a frank look: ''I'll tell you the truth, Mister Mortmain, I wish it was *you* I was dealing with.''

Mortmain gave a modest laugh, and Kirby got out of the car.

Prong said the Cadillac's trunk, opening itself as Kirby came around; Mortmain had pushed the button in the glove compartment. Kirby unloaded all the parcels, stowing them carefully in the clean empty trunk of the Cadillac, aware of Mortmain's eyes on him in the rearview mirror. Finished, he slammed the lid and waved to Mortmain through the rear window. Mortmain waved back and the Cadillac rolled slowly away.

From here on, it got easier. Cynthia being almost out of fuel, she was much lighter now, and lifted easily from the pasture. Nine miles and seven minutes later, he was circling over another field, where the two slat-sided farm trucks and the half-dozen men were waiting.

This part of the job was all cut-and-dried, the negotiations having been completed long ago, nobody here but low-level peons. While Cynthia was unloaded and her fuel tank refilled from jerry cans brought out on one of the trucks, Kirby lay in the shade of his baby's wing, and thought about life. It was complicated, he decided, but amusing. All in all, not bad.

A little trouble in Belize right now, of course, with Lemuel getting spooked and the Greene woman making a fuss, but that would sort itself out. Or, it wouldn't; in which case, he would tip his hat and go away. In any event, he wouldn't worry about it now.

The truck engines started up, waking him from a light nap. A few clouds had sailed into view, dark with cargoes of rain. His clothing was stiff and heavy with perspiration. "Take me home, Cynthia," he said, as he climbed back into his seat. "I'm gonna sleep a week."

Time for a breather.

• INTERMISSION •

from BEKA LAMB, by Zee Edgell

"Nothin' lasts here, Beka."
Gran's eyes looked funny. "Tings bruk down."

"Ah wonder why?" Beka asked, bringing the conch and minced habanero peppers to the stove.

Her Gran leaned the fork carefully against the frying pan, pushed the window over the back stairs, and propped it open with a long pole. Then she said,

"I don't know why, Beka. But one time, when I was a young girl like you, a circus came to town. I can't remember where it was from, and don't ask me what happened to it afta. The circus had a fluffy polar bear—a ting Belize people never see befo'. It died up at Barracks Green, Beka. The ice factory broke down the second day the circus was here."

PART TWO

TINGS BRUK DOWN

1

JADE NOR GOLD

It was nice to see Belize City again. Driving in Haulover Road in the battered pickup truck, entering town through the white, bright, flower-strewn cemetery, seeing the little pirate port sagging out ahead of him as ramshackle and unworkable and permanent as ever, Kirby smiled and felt himself relax; it was good to be home.

Time *is* the great healer. Today was Tuesday, the 21st of February (temperature 82 degrees, sky azure, humidity 90 percent, sun blinding). It was just 11 days since Black Friday, that awful day when Valerie Greene had blown his beautiful temple scam; when Whitman Lemuel had panicked and run back to Duluth with his tail between his

201

legs; when Kirby had reluctantly, angrily, but necessarily told the troops to dismantle the temple, while he himself took what might very well be the final shipment of fresh-made antiquities north to market. A furious, weary, and pessimistic Kirby had made that flight, but the Kirby driving into Belize City today, Manny gap-toothed and grinning beside him, was a changed man: happy, content, and hopeful.

What had happened in those 11 days to change him so thoroughly? Very little. In fact, like Conan Doyle's unbarking dog in the night, it was what *hadn't* happened that had most encouraged him.

After the marijuana-and-artifact flight of the weekend before last, Kirby had told himself he should take on a lot more cargo jobs, since the temple business was probably dead, but he just hadn't had the strength of will. For four days, back in his little nest among the Cruzes, he had simply sat and felt sorry for himself and watched video-tapes: Errol Flynn in *Captain Blood,* Burt Lancaster in *The Crimson Pirate,* Clark Gable in *China Seas.* He had eaten Estelle's food, drunk a moderate amount of Belikin beer, played card games and pebble games with Manny, and made no plans. Cynthia sat alone and un-wanted in the shade of her hangar of trees. Messages were neither sent nor delivered. Hope did not put in an appearance.

But then Tommy Watson did, last Friday afternoon. The only one of his Indian co-conspirators from South Abilene who had ever visited Kirby at home, Tommy came saun-tering up the path out of the jungle, next to the tomato patch, strolled over to where Kirby was hunkered in the dirt playing aggies with two of the kids, and said, "How, Kimosabe?"

"Fried." That was Kirby's joke.

"We don't see you around the old joint very much any more."

"There is no old joint any more," Kirby said. "Hush a second." With a greenie nestled in the crook of the first knuckle of the first finger of his right hand, thumb cocked and ready, he took careful aim across a clear patch of packed tan dirt at a beautiful steelie, paused, squinted one eye shut, fired with absolute precision, and missed by a mile.

As the kids crowed and hollered, Kirby sighed, shook his head, and got to his feet, brushing off his knees. "You distracted me," he accused Tommy, and told the kids, "I'll get even with you guys later."

Their jeers echoed around the clearing. Dignified, Kirby turned away and strolled toward the house, Tommy at his side. "What's happening on my land?" he asked, as though it were a casual question.

"Nothing."

"Excitement all over?" That would be a good thing; the sooner ended, the sooner forgotten.

"No excitement at all," Tommy said. "Nobody come out except that turkey sold you the place."

"Innocent?"

"There's a Mom and Dad couldn't read the future."

"Innocent came out? Nobody else? No cops?"

"No. And no firemen, no farmers, no cooks, no sailors, no truckdrivers and no high school girls. In other words, nobody."

"All right, Tommy," Kirby said. "Don't get your back up."

"I'm happy," Tommy said, as Kirby opened the front door and led the way inside. The Betamax stood with its mouth open, ready to entertain. *"I'm* not hibernating," Tommy said, following him in, shutting the door. "I'm out and about."

"All right, all right." Kirby shut the Betamax's mouth, as a hint to Tommy. "Sit down," he said. "You want a beer? You want to tell me about it?"

"Sure, sure, sure."

So they sat, and had a beer together, and Tommy described the inaction out at the former temple. After a whole night and morning of back-breaking labor—Tommy made quite a point of that part of it—untempling the hill, absolutely nobody showed up for the closing. All day Saturday the Indians waited, using all their age-old lore to watch from cunning concealment as no police Land Rovers came across the plain, no vans of reporters and photographers, no truckloads of archaeologists. No reconnaissance planes circled low for aerial photography. Nothing at all, in fact, had occurred. "It was very boring," Tommy said.

"Sometimes it's better to be bored. Then what happened?"

"More of the same."

Sunday had been a repeat of Saturday. By midafternoon they weren't even bothering to keep watch anymore, but merely walked around the hill every once in a while to see if there were any activity, of which there continued to be none.

"They were holding off," Kirby suggested. "Watching from afar, hoping to catch the perpetrators in the act, or on the site, or something."

"We figured it could be that," Tommy said, "so we laid low. Luz went to the mission Sunday afternoon, see was there any news, any gossip, but no. I myself went out almost all the way to Privassion, but there wasn't a thing, man. No vehicles, no stakeouts, nothing."

"That woman was on her way to the law," Kirby said. "Valerie Greene. There's no question in my mind."

"Well, maybe there was questions in *their* minds, because we still don't have any law." Tommy drained his bottle. "You got another?"

"Tell me about Innocent."

"I'm too dry."

Kirby got them a pair of beers, and Tommy said, "That was Monday afternoon. He come out with this other fella, skinny nervous tan fella."

"He's got an assistant like that in Belmopan," Kirby said. "Young guy."

"That's the one. They come out in a nice new pickup, said on the doors it was from the Highways Department."

"And what did they do?"

"Walked," Tommy said, and swigged beer at the memory of what a hot and tiring sight that had been. "They walked all over the hill. Your pal—"

"Call him Innocent, not my pal."

"He isn't *my* pal," Tommy pointed out, "and if I call him Innocent I'll have to confess it in church."

"What did he *do*, Tommy?"

"Marched around. Kicked the ground a lot. Stomped. Looked mad, confused, worried, upset, pissed off. The young guy with him looked scared."

"Scared?"

"It was like a man out with his dog," Tommy said, grinning a bit. "Your pal stomped up and down the hill, while the little guy scurried this way and that, looking behind bushes, over the edges of drop-offs, up and down and back and forth like he's chasing a rabbit."

"Then what did they do?"

"Left," Tommy said simply.

"Come on, Tommy," Kirby said, trying to look and sound dangerous. "Tell me what happened."

"I am telling you. They walked up and down the hill. They stood on the top a while, your pal scratching his head and the other guy making little dashes back and forth, looking under pebbles. We watched them, but we stayed out of sight, and you can't see South Abilene from up there, so there was never any conversation. And after a while they went back down the hill again, your pal pounding his feet down like he was mad at the ground, the other guy rushing back and forth, *smelling* the earth. Then they got back into their Highways Department pickup and left. Your pal was driving.''

"That was Monday?"

"And today is Friday, according to the mission," Tommy said, "and that's the last visitor we had."

"I don't get it," Kirby said.

"It's beginning to look," Tommy said, "as though the coast is maybe clear."

It was beginning to look that way to Kirby, too. Had Valerie Greene simply been too wild-eyed and weird, and had her story therefore been ignored by the authorities? Anybody who knew that parcel of land at all well, of course, would disbelieve Valerie Greene from the outset.

Which raised the problem and question of Innocent. Why, at that time of all times, had Innocent and his office assistant decided to come visit his old land? What had he been looking for? He, of all people, had to *know* there was no Mayan temple there, that Lava Sxir Yt did not exist and had never existed. So what was he after? What garbled story had reached Innocent's ears that had led him to believe there might be something of interest on Kirby's land?

And who had told him the garbled story, whatever it was? Over the weekend, Kirby brooded on those questions, on the absence of official response to Valerie Greene's undoubted report, on the bewildering visit of Innocent St. Michael, and finally he came up with a scenario which seemed to him to fit all the facts:

Valerie Greene, as Kirby well knew, was an hysteric, particularly on the subject of purloined antiquities. Let's just say she went to town, she made a report to the police at the top of her lungs, yelling and hollering and demanding immediate action and send in the troops. What would the police do? They would not want to be around such a crazy person, but just on the off chance she was right they would not want to throw her out of the office either, so they would pass her on to some other authority, who would pass her on to somebody else, and so on and so on, until at last someone would recognize the land in question as having once belonged to Innocent St. Michael. A quick phone call to Innocent in Belmopan would produce his guarantee that no Mayan temple could *possibly* be found out there, and various maps and surveys would support his statement.

In the meantime, of course, Valerie Greene would also have been hollering about Whitman Lemuel, as being part of the scheme. Let's say somebody went to question Lemuel before he boarded his plane. That was exactly the sort of situation Lemuel would know how to deal with; stand on his dignity, show his credentials, denounce Valerie Greene as a dangerous lunatic with delusional ideas. With a member of government (Innocent) assuring everyone the woman's story was impossible, and a distinguished North American scholar (Lemuel) assuring the same everyone that she was crazy, and with Valerie Greene herself ranting and raving in office after office . . .

Yes. It could have worked that way. It was a very probable scenario. The absence of any official response at *all*, not even a quick casual investigation, supported the idea. And if someone *had* checked with Innocent, it would explain his driving out there to find out what if anything was going on. Trust Innocent to leave no stone unturned.

This scenario fit the facts as no other did, so by yesterday Kirby had become convinced of its truth. Valerie Greene had done her worst, and had not been believed. Innocent's curiosity had been aroused, but had not been satisfied. Whatever tempest in a teapot might have occurred in Belmopan or Belize City, it was over now. Lava Sxir Yt could rise again!

There was no reason to even slow down. Tommy and his fellow workers had been busily creating carvings etched in stone, bone utensils, broken terracotta pots with one triangular piece missing. Kirby for his part had two sets of customers, Mr. Mortmain's friend Bobbi and the team of Witcher and Feldspan, who had already seen the temple. It was time to start rolling again by selling Witcher and Feldspan some pre-Columbian artifacts.

Sorry; no jade, no gold. Must have been a temple in a poor neighborhood.

So yesterday Kirby had finally come out of his funk and become decisive again. Last night he'd gone up to Orange Walk and talked to some people, and had come back with a job flying a cargo to Florida this coming Saturday. And this morning Estelle had given Manny a shopping list, and off he and Kirby had gone, jouncing in the pickup the other way to Belize City, where Kirby dropped Manny off by Swing Bridge and went on to Cable & Wireless, where he sent Witcher and Feldspan the good news: See you Sunday, with our first shipment.

Coming out of Cable & Wireless, Kirby ran into the devil himself; that is, Innocent. "Well, well," Innocent said, spying him, "my old friend Kirby. You haven't been around, man." There was more than the usual edge in his voice.

They shook hands in the usual way, though, gripping as hard as they knew how while smiling in one another's faces, but it seemed to Kirby somehow that Innocent's heart wasn't in it. The smile on Innocent's face seemed false, the strength of his grip a fraction off. In that first instant, it seemed to Kirby that Innocent was somehow doing an Innocent *imitation*.

They released one another. "I've been resting," Kirby told him.

"Heavy labors?"

"Man must work," Kirby said. "How about you, Innocent? You up to anything these days?"

"Not much, Kirby." There was something *grumpy* about Innocent, underneath the imitation smile. "Too many schemers around, man," he said, smiling hard at Kirby. "Too many schemes. Too much competition."

Kirby grinned. "Maybe," he said, "maybe, Innocent, you ought to retire."

That put the steel in Innocent's backbone. Rearing up, eyes sparking, Innocent said, "When I retire, Kirby, you'll be the first to know. And when I *don't* retire, you'll be the first to know *that*, too."

2

THE END OF THE WORLD

What a nerve that man has got, Innocent angrily thought, as he watched Kirby swagger away down the street amid the pedestrians and the bicycles and the rump-sprung big American cars and the dusty pickup trucks and the dope dealers' shiny-bodied black-windowed Broncos. To do what he has done, Innocent bitterly thought, and show his face in this town again.

Valerie Greene. A vision of her fine white rump grasped between his two hands came unbidden into his mind, and he sighed. Her guileless big eyes and happy wide smile shone on him like a memory of the sun in the rainy season down south. But this rainy season would never end; the sun was gone for good. There was hardly any doubt in

Innocent's mind any longer that Valerie Greene was dead, and just as little doubt that Kirby Galway had done it.

He himself was also guilty, of course, if only in a small way. He had trusted that poor girl to a very bad man. He had trusted her to him *because* he was a very bad man, but a very bad man whom Innocent believed he could control. And now see what had happened.

Valerie had never returned to her room at the hotel. The Land Rover had never been brought back to its garage. The driver had never showed up at his home in Teakettle.

The Fort George, seven days ago, had packed up Valerie Greene's luggage and stored it away. The day before that, the Transportation Section had reported the Land Rover stolen. Over the last 11 days, Innocent had left messages for the skinny black man at all his usual haunts, and some unusual haunts as well, but no answer had as yet been received. Nor had the stolen Land Rover been found. Nor was there the slightest trace of Valerie Greene, alive or dead.

On Monday, thinking the land might tell him something about Valerie's disappearance, or about whatever the *hell* Kirby's scheme was, Innocent had driven out there, looking fruitlessly all the way for signs that the Land Rover had been in an accident. He'd brought Vernon along, to be a second person in case a witness was needed, or if there was trouble, and that was when he first became aware that Vernon was apparently in the middle of a nervous breakdown.

Another unnecessary complication. Vernon was too conscientious, that was the whole trouble, in a nation where the lackadaisical was the norm. Innocent told him so, on the drive out: "You work too hard, Vernon," he said. "You don't have to prove to me how valuable you are, I already know it. I know you're trustworthy, and I guarantee you'll be sitting in my chair someday. You've got a bright future, Vernon, you've worked hard for it and you deserve it. A man's reputation is everything, and yours is grade A. If you just don't overwork and make yourself sick, man, you've got it made.''

You'd think all that would have perked Vernon up a little, but no, just the reverse. The more Innocent tried to make him feel better, the more jumpy and unhappy and pessimistic Vernon became.

Out at the land, it was even worse. Innocent hadn't told Vernon much about what they were doing there, so the young man could have had no idea what he was looking for, but he spent the whole time running up and down that hill, looking here, looking there, frantic and urgent and searching like a man who just lost the winning lottery ticket.

As for the land, it had been exactly the same, of course, which made Innocent mad at *himself*. What had he expected out there, an entire Mayan temple, one he'd failed somehow to notice all the years he'd owned this parcel?

But if there was no Mayan temple here—*and there was no Mayan temple here*—then what the hell was everybody so excited about? What had that expert Lemuel thought he was looking at? What was that conversation recorded by Witcher and Feldspan all about? And what had *Valerie* seen, when she'd come here?

Valerie. Poor sweet Valerie. Poor sweet dead Valerie. Though Innocent tried to continue to hope against hope, by now, 11 days after she and her driver and her vehicle had all disappeared, what other possibility was there?

All right, it wasn't the end of the world. Well, it was the end of *her* world, obviously, but it wasn't the end of Innocent's. It was time to get back to his own concerns. And if, in dealing with his own concerns, it so happened he could poke a sharp stick into the eye of Valerie's probable murderer, so much the better.

Meaning Kirby Galway.

It all fit. According to Lemuel's story, there had been a

minute or two when Kirby had been with the people at the
Land Rover before Lemuel joined them; he could have
paid the driver then to do the job. Or, after unloading
Lemuel in Belize City—by air, remember, by air—Kirby
could have flown back and intercepted the Land Rover still
on the way.

Which was, of course, why Kirby had been so thoroughly out of sight the last 10 days. Naturally afraid his
plot would fall through, or be exposed, he'd lain low until
he was sure there was no more danger. And now here he
was again, walking the streets of Belize City as big as you
please, cocky and smiling, going so far as to taunt Innocent that he should retire! *Retire!*

Surly, unhappy, unwilling to admit that his confidence
in himself had been shaken, Innocent glowered after the
departing Kirby. "Retire," he muttered. "I'll show *you* a
thing or two about retiring."

His real estate office was over on Regent Street. Walking there, feeling unusually heavy, oddly stiff in his joints,
he went in to find a telephone message from Vernon in
Belmopan. "Hmmm," he said, and went back to his
office, switched on the overhead light and the ceiling fan,
sat down at his mahogany desk, and phoned.

"Oh, Mister St. Michael," Vernon said, sounding terrible, worse than ever, "the police called."

Innocent's eyes widened. He sat upright, hand squeezing the phone. Which of his many many plots and scams
had come unglued? "Yes?"

"They have found that Land Rover," Vernon said. The
man sounded as though he were actually weeping. "You
know the one I mean, the one we—"

"I know the one! They found it?"

"In pieces."

"An *accident*?" Innocent was flabbergasted.

"No no," Vernon whimpered. "Taken apart. Somebody took it apart all last week, down by Punta Gorda.

They sold the parts down there, to different people. The police got onto it Saturday night when there was an accident, and the radiator—''

''Yes, yes, never mind police procedure. Do they have the man?''

''No, sir. They think they got about a quarter of the parts now, they want to know should they go on looking.''

''What do *I* care?'' Innocent yelled, raging. ''Am I their *nanny*?'' He slammed the phone down on Vernon's mewling, and sat glaring at the maps of nation and city decorating the opposite wall.

Punta Gorda. The city at the very southern end of Belize, where eastern and western national borders fold toward one another, meeting at the Bay of Honduras. From Punta Gorda it is no distance at all to the border. From the border it is 30 miles across Guatemala to Honduras. And from there lies the entire world.

The driver was gone. He fled in the Land Rover, disassembled it and sold the parts in Punta Gorda to finance his flight, then left the country. He would never return.

The last dim hope was gone. Valerie Greene was dead.

3

CYNTHIA TAKES IT OFF

Cynthia stood on her left wingtip and looked down through the warm air to the top of Kirby's barren hill. Then Kirby slid her out of the roll, eased down the far flank of the hill, and pushed the knotted face towel out the small side-flap window as he approached South Abilene. Dancing children came scampering up out of the huts, chasing the towel as it tumbled down through the sky. They would bring it to Tommy, who would already know the message inside, but who would carefully undo the knots anyway, open the towel, find the little plastic film canister, pop the top off that, and read the scrawled note on the torn-off piece of manila envelope: "Bring out the goods."

215

Feeling fine, Kirby flew around a little more, watching the clot of children find the towel, fight over it briefly, then race it back en masse to town. Twice he buzzed the huts, not too low, just for the hell of it, but when he saw the Indians start to file out of the village and up the hill, each one carrying a sack or bag or parcel, he angled away, flying high and higher into the pale blue, then dive-bombing his damn property, pulling out of the dive low enough to cause dust-devils on the hill's eastern flank, then landing on the cracked dry plain, creating great billows of tan dust in his wake. He turned Cynthia and she trundled over as close as possible to the base of the hill, her wings jiggling gently over the uneven ground.

The dust had all settled and Kirby was hunkered in the shade of Cynthia's left wing, scratching a picture of a horse in the dry dirt (it looked like a dog, or maybe a frog), when Tommy and the villagers arrived. "Well," Tommy said, "you're feeling pretty good about yourself, huh?"

"Pretty good," Kirby admitted. "We're back in business."

"You mean we get to put the temple back up?"

"Sure. I'll be around Belize City this week, maybe go out to San Pedro, find a live one, or go up to the States for a while. We're full time in business again."

Luz said, "You bring any gage?"

"Not this time. You don't want too much of that anyway, Luz, it'll rob you of ambition."

Tommy turned to look at Luz, squinting, trying to visualize him robbed of ambition.

Kirby had opened the cargo door at the left rear and the passenger door behind the copilot's seat on the right, and the villagers methodically stowed all the packages they were carrying, then each one stolidly headed back to South Abilene. Mostly they didn't look at Kirby at all, but if he did catch somebody's eye that person would give him a shy smile and a nod and that was all. Tommy and Luz were the link between Kirby and the Indians, and nobody ever tried to bridge the gulf.

Kirby wasn't even sure, in fact, why the Indians went along with this scam. They liked the money, obviously—most of it went into colorful clothes and sweet processed foods from town—but he had the impression they could get along just as well without it. It seemed sometimes as though they did it for its own sake, that they found it *fun* to recreate their ancestors' art and artifacts. The shyness linked up with that idea, the modest appreciation of his appreciation of their skills.

Watching as Cynthia was loaded, Kirby said, "I hope you gave me a lot of Zotzes."

"Well," Tommy said reluctantly, "actually, no."

"Not a lot? How many?"

"Well," Tommy said, "actually, none."

Kirby gave him an exasperated look. "Come on, Tommy, you know how they love Zotz in the States."

"Maybe so," Tommy said, "but down here old Zotzilaha is bad news. People don't like to make him."

Luz said, "These are very primitive assholes here, you know. They do Zotz, they figure Zotz maybe gonna get them."

Kirby understood the problem, but it was still a real annoyance. Zotzilaha Chimalman, the bat-god of the ancient Maya, was the most fearsome of the Mayan demons, a grinning evil creature who lived in a gruesome cave surrounded by bats. One of his tasks was to divert the souls of the recently dead from the path leading to Mayan paradise and send them instead to the eternal darkness of hell. In "Popol Vuh," the great Mayan creation myth, Zotzilaha appears as Camazotz, the enemy of man. After less than 400 years of Christianity, the Indians still found their ancient gods potent, and none more so than Zotzilaha Chimalman, the powerful personification of evil, the bat-god who flies, who owns the night and who destroys human beings out of sheer joy in his own viciousness.

It was easy to understand why the villagers didn't like creating images of Zotzilaha, but the problem was that naturally the great demon-god was extremely popular among Kirby's customers. Give a sophisticate a devil to play with any day; heroes are boring.

"Tommy," Kirby said, "I really need some Zotzes."

"I'll talk to my troops," Tommy promised.

"Why don't you do some yourself?"

Tommy looked vague, his eyes wandering away as he shrugged and said, "I've been busy."

"Jesus, Tommy. You, too?"

"You'll get your Zotzes," Tommy said defensively. "Okay?"

"Okay."

Not wanting a fight with Tommy, Kirby made a point of going over to the plane to watch how the loading was coming along. Luz's sister Rosita came over to Kirby and said, "You ain't been around."

"Been busy, been busy."

"How's your wife?" There was some sort of edge in Rosita's voice, some sort of glint in her eye.

Kirby pretended not to notice. "Worse," he said. "She keeps seeing spiders on the wall."

"Maybe there *is* spiders on the wall. Most walls got spiders on them."

"Not these walls," Kirby assured her. "It's a very clean hospital, completely clean."

Rosita nodded, scuffing her filthy toe in the dirt. By daylight she was, paradoxically, less attractive and more interesting. The wild girl tends not to be too interested in personal grooming. "Sheena says—" she said.

"Who?"

"Sheena, Queen of the Jungle."

Oh; a comic book. "Sorry," Kirby said. "What does she say?"

"She says she figures you don't got a wife at all."

Kirby stared. "She what?"

"She says she figures you're some kinda con artist," Rosita said. "Well, that's what you are, huh?"

"Not with you, Rosita."

"Huh." The glint in Rosita's eye was on the increase. "What Sheena says, she says you just don't wanna get married, or maybe you just don't wanna marry *me*, so you make up this wife in the crazy hospital, you can't get a divorce unless she gets sane again."

"That's what Sheena says, is it?" Kirby was beginning to get a little irritated.

"Yeah. That's what she says."

"You talk to Sheena, Queen of the Jungle, and she talks back to you."

"Sure."

"Well, you tell Sheena," Kirby started.

"Tell her yourself. She's over in the village."

What Kirby might have said next he would never know, because Tommy and Luz came over then and Tommy said, "Come on back to the fort, Kimosabe, let's party."

"Can't today," Kirby said. "I've been letting things slide, I've got to get moving again." The truth was, he was too impatient right now for partying. A week and a half sitting around was more than enough.

Luz said, "We got a surprise for you."

Rosita said, "I already told him about it."

They all frowned at her, Kirby in bewilderment, the others in exasperation. "Asshole," her brother Luz commented, and Tommy said, "What did you do *that* for?"

"I don't owe him no favors," Rosita said, and went away with a straight back and a little whip-switch movement of the behind.

They all watched her go. Tommy said, "Kirby, I got the feeling your wife just died."

"Somebody put some ideas in that child's head," Kirby said. Maybe somebody at the mission, he was thinking. He was very bitter. "I really better not come back to town this time."

Tommy and Luz agreed. Cynthia was loaded by now, so Kirby climbed aboard, waved, and waited till the Indians were partway up the hill on their way home before he started the engine, not wanting to strangle them in dust. Then he turned his trusty steed aside, got up to a gallop, and became once again airborne.

He wasn't happy with the way he'd left things; turning down their party invitation, getting static from Rosita and not dealing with it very well. Circling around in the sky like a lazy wasp, he decided to go over and buzz them once more, waggle his wings, let them know everything was still basically okay.

The line of Indians, single file, had crested the hill and started down the other side. Kirby flew east, then came back low, right down on the deck as he crossed the dry plain, leathery snakes ducking their heads, the hill looming up ahead. He ran up the hill, Cynthia's wheels just yards above the scrub, and burst with a roar over the top, suddenly visible and extremely audible to the people on the other side.

The Indians loved it. They fell around laughing, holding their sides, pointing at Cynthia as she circled, waggling her wings. Even the plane seemed to grin.

Kirby rolled over them once more, then headed down and around for South Abilene to give the shut-ins a treat. The cluster of huts came into view and a figure ducked into one of them, out of sight, as Kirby flew over. He gave them some throttle, stood Cynthia on her tail over the village, and heard some of the cargo shift around. Deciding to quit endangering the merchandise, he leveled out and turned north-northeast, toward the Cruzes and home.

Nice day. Nice lot of artifacts aboard to sell to Bobbi and to Witcher and Feldspan. Nice to be in motion again.

A memory tugged at him as he flew along, the many dark greens below, the pale blue high above. The memory of that figure who had run away into one of the huts as he'd come over town. In his memory that figure was awfully *pale*. And had his eyes deceived him, or had the figure been femále?

Sheena?

Queen of the Jungle?

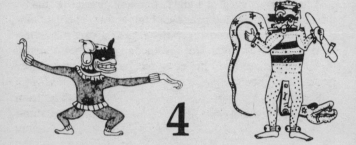

FATHER SULLIVAN DRIVES BY

Valerie stuck her head out the hut door and watched the nasty little plane buzz away at last. "*Him* again!" she said.

The tribespeople were coming back into the village, all laughing and talking and slapping one another's shoulders. They'd *loved* being endangered by that airplane, Valerie could tell. Only Rosita looked less than delighted by it all. Could it be . . .

Valerie went over to Rosita, and pointed toward the now-gone plane. "Him?" she asked. "Is *he* the man you told me about?"

"You bet," Rosita said grimly. "And I just give it to

him straight, what you said to me, and he got *pretty* shifty.
I bet you right all along.''

"I *know* I'm right! *That* man?''

Rosita looked alert. "You know Kirby?''

"Kirby Galway, that's right, that's his name!''

"You *know* him, Sheena?''

Valerie had long since given up trying to get the tribespeople to quit calling her Sheena and call her Valerie.
Even though her hair wasn't blonde, and even though her
remaining rags of clothing bore no resemblance at all to a
tiger skin, and even though she had never swung from
vines in her entire life, nevertheless when she had stumbled into this village a week ago the man called Tommy
Watson had at once dubbed her Sheena, Queen of the
Jungle. And so had everyone else, deeply amused, once
he'd explained that comic book character to them. In fact,
it was during his description of the comic book Sheena, in
Valerie's presence, with some of the comparative details
becoming rather personal, that Valerie had let them all
know she understood Kekchi and wished they wouldn't
talk about her in quite that manner.

"She speaks our language!'' Tommy had cried, in de-
light and wonder. "She *is* Sheena!''

In fact, the variant of Kekchi spoken in this village was
not at all the same as the pure language she had so
doggedly learned, but at least it was similar enough so she
could understand most of what was said to her, unless the
person spoke very fast.

And as to their calling her Sheena, after three days and
nights of wandering through forest and jungle and swamp
and desert Valerie would have agreed to any condition in
return for a full meal and a safe bed. That the only
condition imposed was that she answer to the name of
Sheena was odd, but not difficult. Sheena she became,
Sheena she had been for a week, and Sheena she would go
on being for . . .

. . . who knew how long?

She didn't dare go back to civilization, at least not yet. Who knew how many more of them were in that rotten racket together? Kirby Galway; the driver who had locked Valerie in that filthy hut; the man Vernon who had come to give the driver his orders. And of course Innocent St. Michael must be the ringleader, the brains behind the whole scheme.

She had been foolish to let Vernon know she recognized him, because that was what had tipped the balance at last and made them decide they had to commit murder. Even though that nasty dark room had been very hot and humid, a chill had gone through her when she'd heard the driver say, "Say it out, Vernon. Say what you want," and Vernon answer, "She has to die."

After Vernon left, Valerie stood quaking in the darkness of the inner room, wondering if she had the strength to fight off the driver, knowing she did not. It was so dark in here she couldn't see if there might be a stick or something lying around that might help.

Was there anything in the structure itself that might become a weapon? Valerie made her way to the rear wall and, partly by sight, partly by touch, made out that the slabs were nailed to vertical two-by-fours, a foot and a half apart, with here and there a horizontal two-by-four for extra support. Perhaps one of those horizontal pieces could be worked loose? She tried one, just at eye level, pried it a bit, pushed on it, and the two-by-four with the whole slab behind it, six feet long, simply fell off the building, with a clatter that made Valerie go rigid. Her head turned to stare at the closed door, but nothing happened, so the driver hadn't heard or was possibly out somewhere.

Digging a grave.

It was then just a matter of moments for Valerie to force an opening large enough to eel through, ripping her left sleeve on a nail stuck out of the boards. The sky ahead was completely black, with visible stars. Above, it modulated through bruised-looking blues and sullen reds to become orange on the far side of the shack. So east must be straight ahead, which meant that north—and Belize City—were to her left. Miles and miles and miles away to her left.

Valerie struck off northward, moving as quickly as possible in the uncertain light over the uncertain ground. A half moon shone with increasing brilliance off to her right—giving her a guide to move north by—but its light wasn't really much use.

Half an hour from the shack, Valerie all at once came upon the Land Rover. Her feet, seeking out the path of least resistance, had all unknowing found and stuck with the trail she and the driver had taken up from where the little dirt road had ended. And here she was back again, the Land Rover looking more nautical than ever in the watery moonlight.

Had he left the keys? Certainly not. Frustrated, unhappy, wishing she hadn't had a useless brother like Robert Edward Greene V but a *real* brother who would have taught her how to jump ignitions, Valerie sat in the driver's seat, resting from her exertions and trying to think what she could possibly do next. All at once she heard a racket headed this way, a crashing and muttering as of some ogre in a fairy tale, lumbering through the woods and telling himself about the children he would eat.

The driver!

Valerie hopped out and hurried away into the darkness, tripping over roots and rocks, falling once, skinning her knee, and deciding at last to wait right *here* and not injure herself any more out of panic.

She lay in deep darkness, amid shrubbery and low twisted trees. The Land Rover sat in a moonlit open space. Valerie was close enough to hear what the driver said as he too entered that moonlit space and paused to search himself with quick anger for the keys, and what he said was:

"Oh, no, not *me*, not Fred C! You don't put Fred C. in one of those jails, oh, no, no you don't. She's gone, she's gone, she gonna raise the alarm, everybody can go to jail but not Fred C., no, sir. Fred C. is *gone*! Down to Punta Gorda, sell this damn vehicle, go on down to Colombia, down where they got no law at all. Fred C. is *out* of this story! Where's the damn *keys*? Here they are."

With that, he hopped into the Land Rover, a second later the starter made its grinding noise, the engine caught, and headlights cut the night into the quick and the dead. The Land Rover jolted backward in a half-turn, those bright beams swinging this way, then it roared off, bouncing like a toy down the road, soon out of sight, then out of hearing.

Valerie stood. She had the night to herself. But at least she had that road. By morning, she would be back in her room at the Fort George, enjoying a wonderful shower, and Kirby Galway and Innocent St. Michael and Vernon Vernon would all be in jail, right where they belonged.

If it hadn't been for the headlights, everything would have been all right. Valerie had been walking almost two hours when she saw them slowly advancing, jouncing along, the beams first looking up at the sky then ducking down to stare at the road immediately ahead then snapping up to gaze at the sky again, and her first thought was: *Rescue!*

But her second thought was: *Maybe not.*

She was alone in a strange land. So far, the people she had trusted—Innocent and Vernon and to a lesser extent the driver—had proved false. So she should think very carefully before attracting the attention of whoever was coming this way.

Could this be the driver, panic over, realizing Valerie

wouldn't get far at night on foot, coming back to do the job after all? It could.

Could this be *Vernon*, returning to make sure his orders had been carried out? It very well could.

Could this be some other friend or ally of those people, who would smile at her and promise to take her straight to the police, but who would take her to her death instead? It most definitely could.

The headlights jerked closer. Valerie *wanted* to believe she could just stand here, wave her hand, and be rescued, saved, returned to Belize City. She wanted to believe it, but she turned and hurried away from the road instead, up a rocky slope where she kept feeling too exposed, because of those headlights flashing around all over the place. So she kept going, up over the top, and down into a shallow basin, and waited.

Some sort of truck engine. She couldn't see the lights any more, but she could hear the straining engine, hear it approach, become briefly very loud, then recede, then fade away.

She waited a while longer, mostly because she was very tired, her muscles very sore. Then she made her way back up the slope, and it took much longer than she'd expected to reach the top. When she finally did, there were no headlights to be seen anywhere, so she made her way down the other side and found nothing but a narrow ravine with a little quick stream running through it.

Where was the road? She kept looking around, but in the moonlight every hill and boulder and shrub looked the same. Still, the road had to be very close by.

She never found it again. The moon had risen higher in the sky, giving marginally more light but no longer marking the east. The road was gone. It occurred to her to worry about wild animals.

She remembered from something she had read that the best way to be safe from wild animals in the wilderness was to sleep in a tree, so she chose a rough-barked thick-trunked tree near the crest of a hill and with some difficulty climbed up to a crotch about seven feet from the ground, where she did her best to become reasonably comfortable, and to sleep.

No wild animals found her in the tree, but many mosquitoes did. They kept her awake a long while, until at last nothing in the world could keep her awake any longer, and she slept, crumpled up in the tree crotch, being fed on all night by nasty little flying things.

In the morning she was so stiff, and so hot, and so itchy, and so dry, and so hungry, and so uncomfortable, she thought she would die. She thought it would be more comfortable to die. Twisting around in the tree crotch, every movement an agony, she searched from her vantage point for the road—for *any* road or any other sign of human existence—and saw nothing but woods, forests, jungle growth, high mountains to the west and south, a broken tumbled landscape untouched by man. Sighing, she made her creaky painful way down from the tree and plodded off northward, guided now by the sun.

At first her spirits weren't really low, because she was distracted by her training. Her studies in archaeology and her interest in the ancient Mayans had led her to Belize in the first place, and now here she really was, in conditions as primitive as anything the Mayans ever faced, crossing broken barren ground they had crossed a thousand years ago.

They had survived. She would survive. In the meantime, were there discoveries to be made in this wilderness, finds of archaeological interest and importance? She surveyed every rut and arroyo, frowned at every rock.

And yet, the distraction wasn't total. In the back of her mind, she already knew this wasn't an adventure of the kind she'd dreamed of while half dozing over her textbooks. She had imagined a life of purpose and work with some limited hardships—nothing a sturdy pair of boots couldn't handle—but not all this, this, this . . .

Danger.

Confusion.

Trouble.

She had come out to find the world, knowing she knew nothing about the world, and was this it? A hot and stony place, alone, with no comforts and no certainties. All her old beliefs seemed to flow out of her with her perspiration, leaving her miserable and confused and dizzy. Plodding along, walking because there was nothing else to do, she soon forgot to look at stones for significance, holes in the ground for meaning. Here was the meaning: There was no meaning.

She hadn't wanted to know any of this.

The next three days were terrible. In the middle of the day she would rest in whatever shade she could find, while all morning and all afternoon she walked northward, seeing no one, never finding any road. Each night she slept in another uncomfortable tree. The occasional quick cold stream provided water for bathing and drinking, and on the morning of the third day a brief torrential downpour did her laundry, but she never did find anything to eat. Berries, she thought, but there were no berries. Roots, she thought, but had no idea how to recognize an edible root nor where to dig for it nor what to dig for it with.

I could *die* out here, she thought, getting lightheaded from the sun and the lack of food. The thought was frightening, but what was even more frightening was that the thought was also tempting. To give up the struggle, to lie down and rest, to stop being hungry and itchy and tired and stiff. She fought off that temptation by thinking about Innocent St. Michael, and Kirby Galway, and Vernon, and Fred C. She would *not* die. They would *not* get away with it. She would live through this experience somehow, and *bring those devils to justice!* Thus thinking, while her shoes disintegrated on her feet and her sunburned skin peeled and her empty stomach begged for something more than cold water, Valerie soldiered on.

It was near sundown on the third day when, coming up along another stream, starting to look for tonight's tree, she had stumbled into this little Indian village, where a great fuss had been made of her and where the head man, Tommy Watson, had announced, "It's Sheena, Queen of the Jungle!"

And so that's who she was, and who she had been for a week. The tribespeople had fed her and given her a place to sleep, and the next morning had treated all her many cuts and scratches and abrasions; not with ancient tribal remedies but with mercurochrome and Unguentine and Band-Aids. "From the mission," they told her.

The mission. If she were to go to the mission, surely she would be safe? But then she thought again about the man she was dealing with, Innocent St. Michael, an important government official, a rich and powerful man, and she realized two frightening things: First, he must know she had the evidence to bring him down. Second, he must know his henchman had failed to silence her.

Wouldn't a man like Innocent St. Michael have spies all over the country? Even assuming the absolute probity and integrity of whatever priests or doctors or nurses might be at the mission, wouldn't there be other people there as well, locals who could betray her? And how safe from Innocent St. Michael would she be in a small and isolated mission deep in the jungle?

The same fears kept her from telling the truth to her benefactors, the Indians of South Abilene. At first she claimed to be suffering amnesia, but that piqued their

curiosity too much, so at last she let them understand she
was a rich girl who was running away from a marriage
arranged by her father. She had been flying her own small
plane when an unexpected storm had dashed her against a
jungle mountain. The rest they knew.

They were delighted by that story, and made her tell it
over and over, with more and more details. She added
yachts, a severe limp to the elderly wealthy groom, a
dipsomaniac mother helpless to save her daughter from
being sold to the highest bidder. (Her Kekchi improved
and improved.) They lapped it up, wide-eyed, loving every minute of it, and agreed the best thing she could do
was stay here in South Abilene until her father would be so
amazed and relieved to see her still alive that he would
allow her to call off the wedding.

"And you're a pilot," Tommy Watson said.

"That's right."

"We got a pal who's a pilot. Nice fella. You and him,
you'd get along terrific."

"Wait a minute," said one of the young women, whose
name was Rosita Coco. "Just wait a minute, okay?"

Her brother Luz told her, "Just for friends, that's all."
(Luz and Rosita and Tommy were the only ones who
talked to Valerie in English.)

"That's right," Tommy told Rosita. "They could talk
pilot talk together."

Instead of which, in the days ahead, Valerie and Rosita
talked girl talk together, and when Valerie heard the story
this pilot had told Rosita she was just *outraged*. Wasn't it
like a man, every time? Valerie put Rosita straight on *that*
fellow, and though Rosita didn't want to believe her pilot
was lying, the evidence was pretty clear.

Generally speaking, Valerie got along with all the South
Abilenos, male and female, young and old. They accepted
her at once, shared their small bounty with her, and—
encouraged no doubt by her knowledge of their tongue—

allowed her to enter at least as an observer into their social lives. What an ideal position for an idealistic young archaeologist!

The one fly in the ointment in all this was marijuana. The whole village appeared to be addicted to it, and spent most nights puffing themselves insensible. In order not to appear prudish, Valerie begged off by claiming a respiratory disease that prohibited her from smoking in all its forms. "Poor Sheena," Rosita said, "I make you some pot tortillas some day, blow you right out of the tree." Valerie managed a smile and an expression of gratitude, but so far, thankfully, nothing had come of the offer.

Actually, for Valerie these days marijuana would be superfluous. She was high already, high on just being alive and high on this wonderful village in which she found herself. Her initial fears that she might be sexually mistreated faded rapidly when she saw how thoroughly this was a *family* village; life here was too open and monogamy too ingrained for any hanky-panky. (Had a few of the boys first met Valerie *away* from town it might have been a different story, of which she remained happily ignorant.)

But the point was, these were *Mayas,* true Mayas. Unlike the other archaeologists Valerie had known, her teachers and her contemporaries, she had *gone through* the time barrier, had actually entered into the ancient civilization the other scholars only studied. It is true these people were no longer temple builders, were merely the decayed remnant of a once flourishing culture, but their clothing (apart from the inevitable blue jeans) bore echoes of ancient themes, ancient designs, ancient decoration. The faces of the people were the same as the faces on bowls and stelae a thousand years old.

And they still made the old artifacts! When Valerie first stumbled on their little factory, where stone whistles and bone statues and terracotta bowls were being manufactured by men and women alike, they seemed almost embarrassed at having her know, as though wanting to practice the ancient crafts in secrecy and privacy. But when she extolled their abilities, when she spoke knowledgeably of their sources and their craft—hurriedly inventing an archaeologist boy friend in college, to explain the rich girl's sudden expertise—when she expressed her true admiration, they lit up, smiled together, almost shyly showed her examples of their work.

"But this is wonderful!" she said, over and over.

"Do you really think so?"

"But yes, yes! Why"—turning a bone statuette of a leaping jaguar—"you could put this on display in any museum in the world, and no one would *guess* it was anything but a thousand years old!"

"I'm really glad to hear you say that, Sheena," Tommy said. "That makes us all feel really good."

What charming people. What a delightful simple lifestyle; except, of course, for the addiction to marijuana. Civilization with its medicine and information was as near as the mission, and otherwise their lives were idyllic. I wonder how long I'll stay, Valerie thought from time to time, and every reminder that she must eventually leave this Eden saddened her, made her turn her mind to something else.

But now Kirby Galway had appeared! Out of the blue, quite literally out of the blue.

Earlier today Tommy had come by to say, "Listen, Sheena, there's a guy coming today to pick up some stuff. We make some goods for market, you know, tourist stuff."

Valerie could imagine: glossy mahogany statues of Maya priests, cheap pieces of decorated cloth. The sort of thing primitive people do all around the world, debasing their culture for currency, hard cash.

"Probably," Tommy had gone on, "you ought to stay here in town. You don't want this guy spreading the word there's a white woman hiding out in South Abilene."

"You're absolutely right," Valerie said, and stayed out of sight when the plane first came over. Then some time later she heard it leave, and came out of the hut, and was walking around waiting for everybody to come back when all at once there was the plane again, diving right down at the village! *Into* the nearest hut she had run, the image of the plane burned into her mind, and at *once* she remembered where she'd seen that plane before. It was Galway, Kirby Galway.

Which Rosita confirmed, when she came back: "You know Kirby?" she asked.

"Kirby Galway," Valerie said, excited, "that's right, that's his name!"

Rosita's eyes got very wide. "You *know* him, Sheena?"

Oh-oh. The implications could be very bad, Kirby Galway's relationship with these Indians could be simple and benign—merely flying their tawdry commercial gewgaws to town and no doubt cheating them mercilessly—but nevertheless Galway and the Indians were aligned. Did Valerie at this point dare tell the truth?

No.

Thinking fast, she said, "I certainly do know him, Rosita, and let me tell you, he's a very bad man!"

"Oh, I thought he was," Rosita said. "You bet I did. He rape you one time, did he?"

"No, no," Valerie said, then wished she'd said yes-yes; it would paint him blacker in Rosita's eyes. Instead, she said, "He used to work for Winthrop."

Rosita was impressed. "Wintrop Cartwright?" she asked. "The man your papa gone make you marry?"

"Yes. He worked for Winthrop and cheated Winthrop

very badly. This was a few years ago," she added, not knowing how long the Indians and Galway might have known one another.

"Well, ain't that something," Rosita said, and gazed away sharp-eyed at the empty sky. "Next time he come around here," she said, "I think I give him a spider in his ear."

"You mean a flea in his ear," Valerie said.

"Oh, no, I don't," Rosita said.

5

BOOTS AND SADDLE

It was embarrassing at first, but also rather funny. Gerry winked at a boy in Sheridan Square who then turned out to be a girl, who gave him such a *glare*. Giggling to himself, Gerry walked on through the slushy snow toward home, waving at a friend in the window of the bar called Boots & Saddle, continuing on his way, wishing he could share the funny moment with Alan—"I winked at a very nice hunk in Sheridan Square who turned out to be some awful dike in *full* drag"—but Alan would think the point of the story was his winking rather than the sexual confusion, and there'd just be argument and upset and wild talk about disease, and Gerry just didn't think he could face it, so he decided not to mention it at all.

What he needed, he reflected, not for the first time, was a boyfriend on the side, someone he could really *talk* to.

The sun was shining today, but the wind-chill factor was somewhere down around your ankles. Walking west on Christopher Street, looking at the anemic milky sky over the Hudson River, Gerry found himself thinking again of Belize. That had been rather fun, really, in parts, and God knows it was *warm*. It had been a mistake to play investigative reporter for Hiram, just too nerve-wracking.

If they'd simply gone down there on their owny-own—

To actually deal with Kirby Galway? To actually *buy* smuggled pre-Columbian artifacts for resale?

Well, maybe that wouldn't have been such a bad idea at that.

The more Gerry thought it over, in fact, the more he believed he and Alan had been hasty in talking to Hiram, and in deciding the point of *that* story—like the wink and the dike—was a magazine article exposing the racket rather than the potential of the racket itself. He hadn't quite had the courage yet to broach the subject with Alan, so of course he had no idea if Alan were still content with their having sacrificed themselves for king and country.

Entering the lobby of his home, Gerry sighed, thinking just how difficult it was to understand Alan, to follow his moods, to *cater* to him. We all have our crosses to bear, he thought, and went over to the mailboxes.

The usual bills. A tacky postcard from a friend wintering in New Orleans. And a blue and white envelope containing a cablegram. A cablegram? Gerry went to the elevator, which for once was right here on the first floor, boarded, pushed his button, and ripped the cablegram as the elevator started up.

"*Al*-an!" Gerry called, entering the apartment, waving

the cablegram in front of himself, all thought of the wink-dike story fled from his brain. "Alan, you will simply not *believe* this!"

Alan appeared, covered with flour. So they'd be eating in tonight; good. "All right, Gerry," he said, very testily (he was wonderful in the kitchen, but it was bad for his nerves), "what now? I'm in the middle of things here, I hope this is important, not some *silliness*."

"*Al*-an," Gerry said, aggrieved. "Would I disturb you for nothing at all?"

"You would, and you have. Well? What is it?"

"Oh, you take the heart out of everything," Gerry said. Tossing the cablegram on the nearest table, he said, "Read it for yourself," and went on into the bedroom to sulk.

Well, of course Alan came in three minutes later, flour washed off, black apron removed, cablegram in hand, to say, "Gerry, you're absolutely right. I was abominable."

"It's only because you're cooking," Gerry said, having decided to be magnanimous. "I know what it does to you, but it's perfectly all right, it's worth it, because I know what comes out of your kitchen is just *fabulous*."

"Gerry," Alan said, positively blushing with pleasure, "you are in truth the sweetest person, I don't know what I ever did to deserve you. The good fairy brought you to me."

"I *am* your good fairy," Gerry said, beaming, happy they'd made up. Pointing to the cablegram, he said, "And what do you think of *that?*"

"This." Alan held the cablegram up, frowned at it. "I just don't know," he said.

"*Al*-an, it's from Kirby Galway!"

"I know that."

"He still wants to do business with us!"

"He says so."

"He says so? He says this Sunday, in Florida!"

"I know he does," Alan said. But still he frowned and looked disapproving.

Gerry couldn't understand it at all. "*Al*-an," he said, "this is wonderful news!"

"If true."

"Alan, for heaven's sake, what's the *problem?*"

"Our missing tapes," Alan said.

"Oh, dear," Gerry said, suddenly seeing it all.

"This could be a trap, Gerry. If Kirby Galway is the one who arranged to steal our tapes . . ."

"Oh, dear, oh, dear," Gerry said, and the doorbell rang.

Alan frowned. "That's the *upstairs* bell," he said.

"Then it must be Hiram," Gerry said, starting out of the bedroom. "We can ask *him* what he thinks."

"At this hour?" Alan was finding fault with everything, as usual. "I don't know, Gerry," he called, as Gerry went on through the apartment toward the front door. "That door downstairs has been funny lately, it—"

"Oh, it's bound to be Hiram," Gerry called back.

"Yesterday I saw him going out with *suitcases.*"

"Oh, who else could it *be?*" Gerry called, flung open the door, and found himself staring at the mobster he'd seen with Kirby Galway back in Belize. "My *God!*" he cried.

"My *God!*" cried the mobster, recoiling.

Gerry would have slammed the door in a trice if his own feelings of shock and terror had not been so vividly mirrored on the mobster's face. A mobster displaying shock and terror?

"The drug dealer!"

Oh, dear, oh, dear: Gerry had cried that out, but the mobster had also cried it out, at the same instant, pointing at Gerry, who now said, "But *you're* the drug dealer!"

Wide-eyed, the mobster said, "Kirby Galway told me you—"

"Kirby Galway told us *you*—"

"Gerry, for heaven's sake, who is it?" Alan called, from deeper in the apartment.

"It's— *It's*— I don't *know!*"

"I am Whitman Lemuel," the ex-mobster was saying, extending his card. "I am assistant curator of the Duluth Museum of Pre-Columbian Art."

Gerry took the card. He looked at it with a sense that the world was spinning, the entire Earth flipping on its axis. "I don't understand," he said.

"I think I'm beginning to," said Whitman Lemuel. "I was given a real run-around down there in Belize—"

"Oh, so were *we!*"

"I was told your names, and asked questions about you, by a man named Innocent St. Michael."

"I've never heard of him."

"Consider yourself lucky."

"Oh, my *God!*" Alan cried, putting in an appearance, staring at Whitman Lemuel.

"Alan, Alan, it's all right," Gerry said, clutching at Alan's arm, stopping him from fleeing back to the nearest phone.

"All right? All right?" Alan pointed a trembling finger at Whitman Lemuel. "How can *that* be all right?"

"Kirby Galway lied to us."

"To all of us," Whitman Lemuel said. "After I got back to Duluth, I started to think about things, and it seemed to me maybe I hadn't entirely understood everything that went on down there."

Gerry was showing Whitman Lemuel's card to Alan, saying, "See? Look." Turning back, he said, "Mister Lemuel, I think we all should sit down and have a talk."

"I was thinking the same thing," Lemuel said, and came into the apartment.

"Well, for God's sake," Alan said, staring at Lemuel's card.

"And to *begin* with," Gerry told their guest, "there's a cablegram we just got that you will find *very* interesting reading."

6

SAND AND SAIL

The sun rose out of the Caribbean, pouring blue on the black water, lighter blue on the great vaulted dome of sky. The islands awoke, palm trees nodding good morning, all the way from Trinidad and Tobago in the south up to Anguilla and Saint Maarten in the north. The sudden tropic dawn moved westward toward Jamaica and beyond, out over the flexing waters, winking next at the tiny dots of the Cayman Islands. Hundreds of miles of open sea awoke with yawning mouths until the sun reached the great barrier reef along the Central American coast; nearly 200 north/south miles of coral reef and tiny islands called cayes, just offshore from Belize. Hurrying to that coast, in a rush to get inland and raise the great green hulks of the Maya Mountains, the sun met a tiny plane coming the other way.

Kirby yawned, squinted in the sunshine, and settled himself more comfortably at the controls. Dew dried on Cynthia's wings, removing her jewelry. Eggs and tomato and coffee made themselves comfortable in Kirby's stomach.

Out ahead was the coast. The sea was shallow between here and the reef, the green water so clear as to be invisible from the air, so that you seemed to look down on an exposed world of sand and grass and coral formations all in shades of gleaming green. Only when you flew very low could the surface of the water be made out, as a kind of pebbled glass through which you studied the airborne ballet lessons of the schools of fish.

At the northern end of the great reef lies Ambergris Caye, largest of the islands, 30 miles long and two blocks wide, containing a dozen small hotels and a little fishing village called San Pedro, with a single-runway airstrip. Kirby rolled in there at 7:45, Cynthia's shadow landing on the grass swath beside the strip. He parked her with the half dozen one- or two-engine planes already waiting here, checked in at the office shack, and strolled into town, looking for a live one.

Much of Belize's small tourist industry is centered on Ambergris Caye. Fishing, snorkeling, scuba diving, all are at their best along the barrier reef. The hotel bars boast a mix of local entrepreneurs, sunburned American tourists, tipsily smiling remittance men, crewcutted British soldiers on R&R, whisky-voiced widows, and pale-eyed leathery people who forgot to go home 30 years ago. There are always a few large private boats from Texas or Louisiana tied up at the hotel piers, and up and down the long skinny island are a scattering of the vacation homes of well-off Americans.

Some of these Americans were in business in a small way in Belize, running tourist hotels or exporting mahogany and rosewood or dealing in real estate or owning farms over on the mainland. Every once in a while, one of them could be persuaded to do a deal in pre-Columbian artifacts.

San Pedro starts early and finishes late. Kirby strolled through the bright morning sun to Ramon's Reef Resort and had a cup of coffee at the open-air bar with a couple of fishermen; doctors from St. Louis, not in quite the right league. Their guide and boat arrived, they left, and Kirby wandered down the beach to the Hide-A-Way, had an iced tea there—the day was getting hot—and headed back to town. He had lunch at The Hut with a pilot he knew and a real estate man he was just meeting, heard some gossip, told some lies, heard some lies, told some gossip, and went strolling again.

In the bar at the Paradise, north end of town, most elaborate of the cabana-style hotels, he got into conversation with a Texas girl of about 30, whose daddy's boat was moored at the end of the hotel pier. Three-story-high boat, gleaming white with gold trim, tapering from a wide, comfortable below-deck to a high, teetery-looking bridge. On the stern in golden script was its name and home port: *The Laughing Cow, South Padre Island, Tx.* "There's a cheese called that," Kirby said. "A French cheese, *La Vache Qui Rit.*"

"It's Daddy's favorite cheese spread," she said. She was an ash blonde, tanned the color of human sacrifice, with something just a little vague in her pale eyes and just a little loose around the edges of her generous mouth. She had the look of someone who wants something but can't quite remember what it is, or what it's called. She herself was called Tandy.

Kirby said, "Your daddy named his boat after a cheese? I figured he was a rancher or something."

"Oh, he is," Tandy said. "Up home in Texas, we got a *big* spread. Get it?"

"I guess I do," Kirby said. "Funny thing, I once

named something after that cheese, too. *La Vache Qui Rit.*
Except I spelled it differently."

"You want to see the boat?"

"Sure."

They carried their glasses of rum and grapefruit juice
across the burning sand and out the weathered pier to The
Laughing Cow. It was Daddy that Kirby was most interested in, but he wasn't aboard right now. "He's gone
ashore to raise some supplies," she said. In the bar she'd
been wearing white shorts and a pale blue polo shirt, but
now she put down her drink, stepped out of her clothes,
and revealed a dark blue bikini on the kind of body it was
designed for. "This is the main cabin," she said, pointing
at the main cabin, picking up her drink again.

Tandy took him through the boat, telling him what
everything was: "That's the refrigerator," she'd say,
pointing at the refrigerator. "That's the shower. That's my
bunk."

They made their way by stages to the bridge, where
Tandy finished the tour by pointing at the wheel and
saying, "And that's the wheel."

"And there's the Caribbean Sea," Kirby said, nodding
at it.

"Oh, look at the sailboat!"

Just offshore, a sloop with two white sails slid peacefully northward. Shading his eyes, Kirby said, "Yeah, I
know that boat. It's full of sand."

Tandy looked ready to laugh, just in case there was a
joke somewhere inside there. Kirby looked at her, serious,
and said, "No, no fooling. It's full of sand. On its
way up to one of the construction sites farther up the
island."

Tandy frowned. "Where is this sand *from?*" she asked.

"The mainland, down below Belize City."

Tandy looked back at the Paradise Hotel: a half-circle of

cabanas and other buildings on raked white sand. She looked at Kirby again, and her expression now said she was getting a trifle irritated. "Just why, Kirby," she asked, "would anybody haul sand from Belize City to out *here?*"

"River sand," he explained. "This sand here is coral, it's powdery, they don't like to use it for mixing up cement. So that boat there goes back and forth, usually brings sand, sometimes gravel. All by sailpower, no engines."

"How long does it take?"

"Five to six hours out, four to five back. They'll shovel it out tonight, head back early in the morning, load it up again when they get to the mainland, lay over the night, and head back this way day after tomorrow."

She looked out again at the sloop, now beyond them, making better speed than it looked. "Shit," she said, "and I thought it was romantic."

"It is romantic," Kirby said.

She thought about that. "I see what you mean," she said.

"Just sailing and sailing," Kirby said. "A few hours shoveling at each end, that's not much of a price to pay."

"No price to pay at all," she said, sounding bitter. "When all you got to shovel is *sand*." She knocked back her drink and looked at him. "How about you, Kirby?" she said. "You romantic?"

"Very," Kirby said, and a hoarse voice shouted, "Tandy?"

Daddy was back, with three San Pedrans carrying cardboard cartons. Daddy barked orders and distributed U.S. greenbacks, while Tandy took Kirby's glass and her own and made fresh drinks in the galley. Daddy and the drinks were finished at the same time, and Tandy made introductions: "Daddy, this is Kirby Galway. I just picked him up in the bar there."

If that was supposed to be provocative, Daddy ignored it. Sticking his hand out, staring at Kirby *hard*, he said, "Darryl Pinding, Senior."

"How do you do, sir?" (It seemed to Kirby that Darryl Pinding, Senior, would enjoy hearing "sir" just once from a younger man.)

"I do fine, Kirby. And yourself?"

"I have nothing to complain about," Kirby told him.

"Good. Tandy, did you make me a drink?"

"I will now."

She went off to do so, and Darryl Pinding, Senior, gestured at the blue vinyl, saying, "Sit down, Kirby, take a load off. What business you in?"

It was fun talking with Darryl Pinding, Senior. He was a rich man who thought his money proved he was smart. He knew a lot about three or four things, and thought that meant he knew everything about everything. He liked to spray his imperfect knowledge around like a male lion spraying semen. He was a big man in his 50s, probably a football player in college, now gone very thick but not particularly soft. Sun, sea, high life, and skin cancer had turned him piebald, particularly on his broad high forehead, where Kirby counted patches of four separate shades of color, not counting the liver spots.

Tandy grew grumpy when it became clear that Kirby was not going to cut short the conversation with Daddy. She threatened to leave, then left, while Kirby and Darryl (they were both on first-name terms now) chatted on.

It was established early that strict legality had never been an absolute prerequisite in Darryl's life; a plus. Somewhat later it was made clear that Darryl had *done* a bit of smuggling for profit in his life—a boat like this, why not?—and had enjoyed the raffish self-image as much as the money; another plus. Treading slowly, Kirby established that Darryl did know something about pre-Columbian artifacts, though by no means as much as he thought he knew. Darryl also understood vaguely that the southern governments were trying to stem the flow of antiquities northward, and he thought they were damn fools and pig-ignorant for taking such a position; a major plus.

But then came the down side: "Let me tell you something, Kirby," Darryl said four or five drinks later, hunkering a bit closer on the vinyl. "My son is a faggot. Do you hear what I'm telling you?"

"Uhh, yes."

"I don't know how it happened. God knows he didn't have a domineering mother or an absent father, but there it is. Darryl Junior is gay as a jay."

"Ah," said Kirby.

"He's an *artist*," Darryl said, with an angry sneer in his voice. "Out in San Francisco. Artist. These pre-Columbian things, statues, all this stuff. You know what it all is?"

Kirby looked alert.

"Art," Darryl said. "It's all art."

"I guess it is," Kirby said.

"I hate art." Darryl nodded. "Nuff said?"

"Nuff said," Kirby agreed.

He had dinner at El Tulipan with a girl named Donna who ran one of the gift shops in town. They had drinks after at Fido's, listening to Rick play the piano, Rick announcing to the world at large, "I'm getting drunk, but I never make mistakes." Donna had to retire early, so Kirby roved on, not expecting much, having used up his psychic energy on Darryl Pinding, Senior, just fooling around now.

Back at Fido's around midnight, there was Tandy at the

bar, talking with two American college boys. She left them, carried her glass over to Kirby, and said, "You and Daddy all talked out?"

"Your father's a forceful personality," Kirby said.

"I didn't see you fight him off much," she said.

Kirby looked at her. "Honey," he said, "if *you* haven't got ahead of him in thirty years, how do you expect me to do it in an hour?"

She blinked. She frowned. "Twenty-eight," she said, and knocked back some of her drink.

"My apologies."

"The sun ages you," she said, forgiving him. "Every fucking thing ages you, come to that. Where are you staying?"

"Nowhere yet."

Surprised, she managd to focus on him, saying, "You don't have a hotel room?"

"Not yet."

She laughed, a throaty chuckle that suggested the baritone she would be in 20 years. "You're a damn beach bum!" she said.

"I told you earlier," he patiently explained, "I flew in this morning, thought I might fly out again this afternoon, never got around to it."

"That's right, you're a pilot, I forgot. Come on and sleep on the *Cow*."

He considered that. "Daddy?"

"When Daddy sleeps, Daddy sleeps. That's one place, Kirby, where I will not put up with trouble."

He gave her an admiring grin. "Tandy, you're an interesting woman. You have depths."

"Check it out," she said.

If Daddy slept through all that, his subconscious must have thought they were sailing through a hurricane. Tandy's elegantly cramped quarters were below, a long isosceles triangle beneath the foredeck, while Daddy slept in the convertible sitting lounge above. A small air conditioner competed with the capacity of two active human bodies to generate heat, and lost. Everybody'd had a bit too much to drink, Tandy refused to permit any light at all, and *The Laughing Cow* bobbed and rolled in its mooring in arhythmic sequences that Kirby could never quite adapt to. The whole thing became as much an engineering problem as anything else, but one well worth the solving. Slippery rubbery flesh slid and tumbled, muscles moved beneath the skin, arms and hands reached for purchase and slid away. "I think it goes like this," Kirby said.

"Oh, Jesus. That's the way, that's the way."

Kirby chewed on a nipple that tasted of salt. Breath in his ear sounded like far-off surf. The rhythms of sea and man merged and separated, merged and separated. "God, I'm thirsty!" Tandy cried, and collapsed like a sail, in the calm after a storm. Kirby had never heard a woman say precisely *that* in such a situation before.

A lot of elbows woke him, some of them his own. Cool darkness, the hush of a nearby air conditioner, all these elbows and knees and—ouch—foreheads in this too-small bunk. Memory came to his rescue just as Tandy patted him all over, hoarsely whispering, "Who the fuck are *you*?"

"Kirby Galway," he told her. "I'm the pilot. One of the better guys."

"Shit," she said, "you probably are, at that." She laid her hot dry head on his chest, and he put an arm around her vulnerable thin shoulders. "What a life," she said, and they slept.

7

GLIMPSES

The sun that had greeted Kirby in the sky early that morning had a little later peeked down through the moist layers of leaf and branch and vine and foliage to the jungle floor in the Maya Mountains near the Guatemalan border where it caught glimpses of a hunched hurrying figure in camouflage fatigues, moving west, staring about himself, nervous, flinching from every jungle sound, occasionally staring up in anguish at the watching sun, as though it were a hawk and he a vole.

Vernon panted as he moved, more from fear than exertion. He hadn't expected another summons from the Colonel so soon, nor had he realized before last night just how completely he was in the Colonel's power. He could no longer refuse the man, was no longer his own master. The Colonel could destroy Vernon at any time, not by reaching into his holster for that big Colt .45, but simply by passing on to the British Army or the Belizean government the proof of Vernon's . . .

. . . treason.

"It means *nothing*," Vernon gasped, hurrying to meet his master. Guatemala could never invade, could never capture Belize. Taking the Colonel's money was dishonorable, yes, chicanery at worst, because it was not within Vernon's power, or anyone's power, to sell Belize to Guatemala. And yet, and yet . . .

Everything was coming together at once, in the most terrible way. He had murdered Valerie Greene, yes he had, he had murdered her just as surely as if he had done it himself with his own hand. But he was not cut out to be a murderer; too late he understood that. He wanted to be a man with no conscience at all, and he was riddled with conscience as another man might be riddled with leprosy. The sting of his petty treason was as nothing to the savage burn of his guilt as a murderer.

And just as the Colonel held Vernon's fate and future in the palm of his hand, so did the skinny black man, Vernon's partner in murder. He had disappeared without a word, without a word except for a circular trail of Land Rover parts around Punta Gorda. Presumably he had fled the country; certainly, the police were looking for him. Could it be (astonishing idea) that he too had been unequal to murder, had been unhinged by it, driven to flight? If so, and if he were found, he would surely spill the whole story, *starting* with Vernon's name.

"Too many things," Vernon muttered, thrashing through the undergrowth, the moisture of his face part sweat and part dew and part tears. The wet fronds slapped at him, the ground was soggy and treacherous beneath his feet, and he could never entirely hide from the sun.

The Daimler wasn't yet there. Good; it gave Vernon a chance to get control of himself, calm down, dry his dripping face on his shirttail. He walked back and forth in the clearing, in and out of sunlight, commanding himself to be at peace. The Colonel would not betray him, because he was still too useful. The skinny black man would not be found and would not return. Be calm, he told himself, be tranquil, be at rest.

How he longed to be at rest.

The Daimler came slowly through the jungle, like a whale, like a black puddle. Vernon stood to the side of the dirt track as the Daimler approached, sunlight winking at him from its glass and chrome. The big machine stopped beside him, its passenger compartment window slid smoothly down, and the Colonel appeared in the dark rectangle, leaning forward, eyes hidden by large dark sunglasses. Behind him the feral woman sat reading a French magazine: *Elle*. Vernon, inadequately protected behind his own sunglasses, blinked and blinked.

The Colonel extended a ringed hand out the window, holding a white envelope. "This is for you," he said.

Vernon took the envelope. It was softly thick with currency, a lot of currency. *What does he want from me?* Why did things always have to move so inexorably from the theoretical to the real?

The Colonel had something else for him; a single sheet of paper. Vernon took it, and saw it was a Xerox of a part of one of the maps he'd given the Colonel the last time, a map showing recent refugee settlements. One of these was now circled in red. As he frowned at this map, wondering what it meant, the Colonel said, "On Friday, the day after tomorrow, a group of British journalists will be in Belice."

"Journalists?" Vernon reluctantly looked up from the map. "I don't know anything about that."

"They are coming," the Colonel said. "One of the things they will do in Belice is visit a refugee village, on

Friday afternoon.'' Pointing at the map in Vernon's hands, he said, "You will see to it *that* is the village they visit."

"But— Journalists? That has nothing to do with my department, I don't—"

"You have a driver? Your confederate?"

Shocked that the Colonel knew so much about him, Vernon stammered, "He's—he's gone. Ran away a week ago. No-nobody knows why."

"Someone else then," the Colonel said, dismissing the problem with a flick of his fingers. The woman turned a page of her magazine; this time, she had no interest in Vernon at all. The Colonel, delegating authority, said, "You'll arrange it. The journalists go to *that* village."

"I don't know if I can—"

"It is necessary," the Colonel said. He confronted Vernon, impassive behind his dark glasses, waiting for another objection, prepared to slap it down. It is necessary; that was all his creature needed to know.

I will *not* think about why the Colonel wants all these things, Vernon told himself, his plans are foolishness and vain, nothing can happen, nothing can *change*. "I— I'll try," he said miserably.

"That village," the Colonel said, and the window smoothly rolled up, ending the conversation.

Bewildered, bedeviled, hopelessly entangled, Vernon stood and watched the Daimler drive away, returning the Colonel to his world of certainties. Rest. Tranquility. What was going to happen? Would it never end? What terrible fate was he fashioning for himself?

Nearby, in bright sun, a large parrot on a branch looked at Vernon, spread his wings, and laughed.

8

NORTH GUATEMALA:
ME TAUGHT RON

The Indians of the Central American forests are peasants, farmers who scratch a living and a life from the rich jungle soil. Their ancestors have lived on that soil and been buried in that soil for 2,000 years. They have endured famine and flood, disease and wild animals, fire and enemy tribes; but whatever has happened, the passive Indians have always stayed with the land.

Today, the Indians want no more and no less than what they have always had; a piece of land in the jungles, small interrelated communities, and to be left alone. But today Central America is a part of the great world, and in the great world *no one* is left alone. The Indians cannot fight the death squads armed with submachine guns and the soldiers armed with helicopters. They can expect no mercy from the Ladinos who call them "animals with names." Almost unbelievably, driven beyond endurance, the Indians are leaving their land.

Refugees. After thousands of years, they have become refugees. The Miskito Indians have been in almost constant harried motion through Honduras and Nicaragua for the last three or four years, chivvied and persecuted by "civilized" men, driven to distraction. More truly civilized men and women in private religious groups have been helping Salvadoran and Guatemalan peasants relocate in Canada, and what on Earth shall they think of *Canada?* And some, in tribal and family groups of 10 or 20 or 50, thousands of them by now, have made the terrible, long, dangerous overland journey to the border of Belize, and across it . . . to heaven.

It is the jungle, as at home, but a wonderfully empty jungle, with miles and miles of unclaimed territory in which to scratch out a piece of land and start to live again. No armed masked men rove at night. The only military aircraft is the occasional British Harrier jet, gone almost before it arrives, flashing along the border to remind the Guatemalans of the futility of their dreams.

The refugees arrive, fearful, ignorant, almost without hope. They begin their settlements, hiding as best they can from the world, and in a week or six months or a year they are found and the Belizean government sends its emissary to them; a social worker, perhaps, or an unarmed policeman, or a medical officer. They are told they have been accepted as immigrants; there are no formalities and they shall not be returned to hell. So long as they live on their piece of land, and use it, it is theirs. So long as they mind their own business, they will be left alone. The government is not their enemy, and is not at war with them. It asks only that they send their children to school: "We want to make good Belizeans of them."

The Indians don't entirely understand, nor entirely believe. They build their huts out of the materials available in the jungle, they work their fields, and they keep one eye over their shoulder. But nothing happens. And slowly, over the course of years, they come to realize the truth:

The war is over.

9

A SMALL FORTUNE

Innocent hardly tasted his food at all, and barely glanced at the beautiful sea. Lunching on lobster at the Chateau Caribbean, just up the bayfront from the Fort George, he had smilingly but firmly refused offers to join friends at this or that table, preferring his own gloomy company. Two Belikin beers had not restored him, nor had the sounds of happiness and good fellowship all around him. (At a nearby table, businessman Emory King, an American-born Belizean citizen, was explaining to his group, "How do you wind up with a small fortune in Belize? You start with a large fortune.")

Valerie Greene. He simply could not get her out of his mind. This morning, doing his usual laps in the pool, it

258

had occurred to him that Valerie had never seen his house, had never swum in his pool, and the thought had so dispirited him he'd stopped swimming at once, breaking his morning ritual for the first time in memory, trailing away unhappily to the house to get dressed.

Which was all, of course, ridiculous. *None* of his women had seen his house, nor swum in his pool. Take a girlfriend to *that* wife, *those* four daughters? Not a chance.

And yet, however absurd the idea might be, it still had the power to deflate him. Every thought of Valerie had the power to deflate him, in fact, rob him of happiness and contentment. And the strange thing was, as time went by his thoughts and memories were less and less about sex and more and more about *her*. Her smile, her naiveté, her simple worldliness, her passion for honesty and truth. In his mind, she was becoming a saint.

He avoided the word that would describe his condition. He could acknowledge—to himself—that he was grieving for her, but not even to himself could he face the reason why.

"Innocent St. Michael?"

Innocent looked up from his untouched lobster and unassuaged melancholy to see a white man looming over his table, extending a hand with a card in it. A *very* white man, ashen as a barracuda's belly; just off the plane from the snowy north, no doubt. "Yes?" Innocent said, wanting nothing more than for the man to cease to exist; or at the very least, to go away.

But he wouldn't; waggling his fingers, he said, "My card."

Come along, Innocent, he told himself, *you're* still alive. Here's a man with a *card*. Here's a North American with money in his pockets, probably looking for a little investment, some land to buy or a business to associate himself with, a man wanting to wind up with a small fortune in Belize. Take an interest, Innocent.

He took the man's card, though not really with very much interest. The card told him the man was named Hiram Farley and he was associated with a magazine in New York City called *Trend*. Had Innocent managed to drum up any interest, it would now evaporate: "Reporter, eh?"

"Editor," Hiram Farley said, and uninvited pulled out the chair to Innocent's right. Seating himself, stacking his forearms on Innocent's table, he said, "Mister St. Michael, how familiar are you with your nation's Antiquities Law of 1972?"

Innocent raised an eyebrow. "The act says the Mayan ruins within Belize belong to the nation of Belize," he said, "along with any and all contents, all others to keep bloody hands off. Is that familiar enough for you?"

"Good," Hiram Farley said. "Fine. And since that law was passed, back in 1972, that's been the finish of the trade in smuggled Mayan artifacts, is that right?"

"That's called irony," Innocent told him. "What you just did there." Despite himself, he was becoming involved with this fellow.

Hiram Farley smiled. "Occupational hazard," he explained. "Such a good cheap weapon, irony." Then he switched to a keen look, saying, "Mister St. Michael, some time ago I became aware of a scheme to smuggle pre-Columbian artifacts out of Belize and into the United States."

"Which you promptly reported to the officials of both nations," Innocent suggested.

"Irony; that's good. Mister St. Michael, I had no proof, only a vague rumor. Hoping to get solid documentary evidence, both to turn over to the authorities and to present in an exclusive story in my magazine—"

"Ah, yes, of course."

"It isn't only charity that begins at home, Mister St. Michael."

"I don't know much about charity, Mister Farley,"
Innocent said. "Tell me what you've done."

"I encouraged two friends of mine to come down here
and pursue the suggestion of becoming engaged in the
smuggling operation. Antique dealers from New York."

By God: Witcher and Feldspan! Innocent became so
delighted with this revelation that absolutely nothing showed
on his face. So *this* was the reason for the taping!

And if Innocent hadn't stepped in to remove those tapes,
Kirby and his smuggling operation would right now be
plastered all over the pages of *Trend* magazine!

And Valerie? Would she be alive or dead?

No; *Trend* would not have come out in time to save her.

Kirby . . . Kirby . . . Kirby would already have killed
her, in any event.

Hiram Farley continued, while Innocent's thoughts went
racing. Farley explained about the tape recordings, their
being stolen at the airport, and went on, "My friends—
they're not the sort for intrigues like this, certainly not for
anything dangerous—they've made it clear they don't have
the heart to go on with the investigation, particularly if
those tapes are now in the hands of the smugglers, as they
almost certainly are."

Innocent's mind was full of thoughts of Valerie and
Kirby, but he managed to follow Hiram Farley well enough
to say, "So now you'll do it yourself?"

"Mister St. Michael, I still want that story for *Trend*.
And I imagine you would like to help save your patrimony
from the thieves and smugglers."

"But of course, Mister Farley," Innocent said, thinking, Is this fellow a pansy-boy, too, like his friends? Yes.
More subtle about it, not noticeable at all if you aren't
looking for it, but yes. On the other hand, shrewder than
his friends, tougher. Not an easy fellow to take advantage
of.

Farley was saying, "Mister St. Michael, I'll level with

you. After my friends threw in the towel, I looked around, asked around, trying to find somebody else with a connection in Belize. Do you remember a man named Rodemeyer? William Rodemeyer?''

The name rang a distant bell, no more. Innocent frowned, saying, "I'm not sure . . ."

"This would be several years ago. You sold him a piece of land in Ladyville.''

Ladyville was the little community next to the International Airport. Its future was in fact quite promising for commercial properties, should Belize ever become a considerably larger and more bustling nation than it now was. Innocent had owned different parcels out there over the years . . .

Rodemeyer! It came back to him now, the man with the odd name. "The magazine man!''

"That's right," Farley said. "He wanted to found a weekly business magazine for the English-speaking Caribbean basin.''

"Yes, I remember that man," Innocent said. "He wanted land out by the airport, to build offices and his own printing operation out there, distribute by air through the Caribbean. Very ambitious project.''

"Too ambitious, as it turned out," Farley said.

"Bigger circus than this come to Belize," Innocent told himself.

"Beg pardon?''

"Nothing. Seems to me that man went bust.''

"Yes, he was undercapitalized.''

"That's the big trouble in the Caribbean," Innocent agreed, nodding like a statesman.

"He's back in New York now, Rodemeyer is," Farley said. "Working for *Barron's*.''

"Aristocrats pay pretty good, I hear," Innocent said.

"I understand he sold the land back to you before he left, for rather less than he'd paid for it.''

"Very depressed real estate market, just at that moment," Innocent murmured.

"Yes," agreed Farley. "The point is, Bill Rodemeyer told me he met several people in Belize, but you were the one I should see. He said you were the shrewdest, toughest con man he ever met in his life, but you were important in the government, and if there was something in it for you I could probably get you to work with me on this smuggling story."

"I have never had anything but the nicest remarks to make about Mister Rodemeyer," Innocent said, putting on a faintly insulted air.

Farley laughed. "And why not? You made a pretty penny off him." Becoming more serious, he said, "I'll let you personally break the story in Belize, and I'll feature you prominently in the write-up in *Trend*. We give each other an exclusive. My information plus your local contacts, and we expose these smugglers together."

By now, Innocent's mind was functioning simultaneously on two completely different levels. On the surface, operating out of long practice and engrained habit, he listened to Hiram Farley, heard his ideas, decided how to play this latest fish on his line. But underneath, his mind was full to overflowing with thoughts of Valerie Greene. And where the two thoughtstreams converged was at Kirby Galway.

Kirby the smuggler. And Kirby the murderer.

"So you want to expose these smugglers in your magazine," he said. "You want to catch them in the act, you mean, with photographs and all."

"That would be best," Farley agreed. "I can handle all that part of it myself. What I need from you, if you think it's a good idea, is help on the ground."

"To catch the smugglers," Innocent said, brooding. To catch Kirby the smuggler; yes, that would be a good thing, with this man Farley along to get the evidence that would stick. But what about Kirby the murderer?

Farley said, "Do we have a deal, Mister St. Michael?"

"Let me think about this, Mister Farley," Innocent said. Kirby the murderer is up to me, he thought. Inexorably he was sliding toward a decision that was very unlike him, very out of character. And yet, there it was. And still he hung back from it.

Tomorrow, he promised himself. Tomorrow I'll choose; Farley or Kirby. "I'll get in touch with you by tomorrow afternoon, Mister Farley," he said, "at the Fort George."

Farley was surprised. "How do you know I'm staying at the Fort George?"

Innocent laughed, though his mind was full of Kirby the murderer. "Every American I do business with is at the Fort George, Mister Farley," he said.

10

TOTAL RECOIL

"Seven," said Kirby.

"Fourteen for two," said Manny.

Kirby grinned, and laid down a third seven. "Twenty-one for six," he said, and moved his back peg forward six spaces on the cribbage board. Only then did he look up to see every tooth gap in Manny's head gleaming at him; the man smiled like a tunnel entrance. "No," said Kirby.

"Yes," said Manny, and gently placed the fourth seven on the table. "Twenty-eight for twelve." He leaned forward to study the board. "And the game."

It was true; the 12 points put Manny out. "At least it wasn't a skunk," said Kirby, whose lead peg was 11 spaces from victory.

"What's the score now?"

Kirby turned the board over, where ink checkmarks in groups of five ran in battalions down two strips of masking tape, which were themselves laid over previous strips bearing previous battalions. Making another mark with his ballpoint pen, Kirby said, "You're ahead, as you damn well know."

"How much? How much?"

"Three hundred twenty-nine games to two hundred seventy-eight." Shaking his head, Kirby turned the board over. "I should have taught you checkers instead."

"Teach me now."

"You sound too eager," Kirby told him, and glanced over as a couple of the dogs—who had been peacefully watching Guatemalan television with Estelle and the kids—got up and turned around and looked at the door.

"Somebody coming," Manny said.

"Could be Tommy."

Manny liked Tommy Watson well enough, but Estelle always got purse-lipped when the Indian was around, as she did now, remaining silent but giving Kirby a quick look. "I'll talk to him outside," Kirby promised.

And in fact he had something to tell Tommy. Yesterday's expedition to San Pedro had been a bust, at least from a business point of view, but when he'd flown in here just before noon today—not wanting to miss Estelle's lunch—there had been a message waiting which Cora had brought down from Orange Walk. It was Witcher and Feldspan's answer to his cable, and it assured him Sunday would be just fine for taking delivery on the first shipment. So Kirby's message to Tommy would be, *Produce some Zotzes!* Let's start these new customers off right, with a nice platoon of devil-gods. No more excuses about how everybody's too superstitious and afraid to make the damn things.

Estelle still looked disapproving—she felt Tommy's mere

existence was a bad influence on the children, whom she had dreams of civilizing someday—so Kirby got to his feet and said, "Okay, okay, I'll head him off." While Manny sat shuffling the cards like the scraggliest cardshark in history, grinning faintly to himself, Kirby went out to greet his faithful Indian companion.

Except it wasn't. Squinting in the outer sunlight, Kirby first saw the gray Land Rover over near Cynthia, and then saw it was Innocent St. Michael who was clambering out of it. And not only that, but he was clambering out of the driver's seat; he'd come here alone.

Here? Innocent St. Michael, *here?*

Kirby walked over toward the heavyset man, noticing that Innocent seemed rumpled, troubled, very unlike his usual smooth self-confident self. Innocent saw Kirby approach and reached back into the Land Rover to pick something up off the passenger seat. Kirby was just calling, "What's happening, Innocent?" when Innocent turned around with the gun, pointed it more or less toward Kirby, and started shooting.

The gun was a British-made revolver, the Webley and Scott Mark VI, weighing two pounds six ounces, length eleven and a quarter inches, six-shot capacity, firing a .455 caliber cartridge, and famous in the British Army and in many police forces around the world for a whole *lot* of recoil. Wherever Innocent had gotten this monster, the thing clearly had not come with instructions, nor had he taken it around the block for a few practice spins ahead of time. He clenched his jaw, squeezed the trigger, the gun made a sharp explosive sound flattened in the surrounding air, and the bullet went up over Kirby and over the house and headed out on a rising line toward the coast.

"Hey!" said Kirby.

Innocent's second bullet whizzed up and away southward, climbing into the sky, straining toward a far-off tree just inland from Punta Gorda.

"What the *hell!*" said Kirby.

Innocent's third shot went almost straight up into the empyrean. Some time later, in fact, it landed unnoticed between Kirby and the house.

"Jesus *Christ!*" said Kirby.

Innocent, looking intent, exasperated, determined, flustered, enraged, grieving, and bollixed, grabbed the goddam gun with both hands and wrestled its barrel back down to point at Kirby's nose.

"*Ahhh!*" said Kirby.

The fourth bullet whispered in Kirby's left ear on the way by.

"DON'T!" said Kirby.

Innocent mumbled something and stepped closer, holding the gun out in front of himself with both hands, as though it were an angry cat. The cat spat, and bullet number five made a scratch—but cauterized it immediately—on the skin above Kirby's left clavicle, or collarbone, which is the top of the pectoral arch, extending from the breastbone to the shoulderblade.

All of this was happening very fast, so it wasn't until now that Kirby got around to taking appropriate action, which was to scream and hit the dirt, so that bullet number six passed through the air where the middle of Kirby's head had recently been, then continued on its way to chunk into the door frame just as Manny opened the front door to find out what all that popping was about.

Manny looked at the spot where the bullet had said "thup" going into the wood of the frame. He looked at Innocent with the gun, and Kirby on his face on the ground. He stepped back and closed the door.

Kirby rolled over and looked up. Innocent, closer, stood over him with the expression of a man seating himself for the first time in front of a word processor; he *will* dope this damn thing out. Both Innocent's hands clasped the gun, which now looked to Kirby like a round-mouthed gray metal snake with a crest (the front sight). Innocent's right forefinger squeezed the trigger, and the Mark VI said, "Tsk."

Neither Innocent nor Kirby could believe it. They both looked at the gun. Innocent aimed it at Kirby and pulled the trigger. "Tsk," it said.

"Shit," said Innocent.

"*Oh,* boy," said Kirby, and rolled madly away, over and over across the dusty bumpy ground. When he sat up, filthy and dizzy, he was some yards from Innocent and the Land Rover. Shaking his head, trying to focus, he saw Innocent hurry back to the vehicle, saw him reach inside it and come out with a small cardboard box, saw him fumble the box open onto the Land Rover's hood. A few cartridges rolled away across the hood and plopped onto the ground. "For God's sake, he's *reloading,*" Kirby said.

Somebody, unfortunately, had explained to Innocent how to open the cylinder. As Kirby struggled to his feet, still dizzy, and tottered across the open ground, Innocent pushed bullets business end forward into the cylinder. More cartridges rolled about and fell on the ground.

Innocent saw Kirby coming and backed hurriedly away, stumbling a bit, pushing just one more bullet home, struggling to close the half-full cylinder and scramble backwards at the same time, and all the while watching neither his hands nor the world behind him. Kirby, pursuing, cried, "Innocent, why? *Why?*"

"You killed her," Innocent said, and slammed the cylinder shut, pinching one finger nastily in the process. He put that finger in his mouth and pointed the gun at Kirby.

Who had stopped a few paces away, too bewildered to be either scared or smart. "Killed? Who?"

"Wallawa Weeng," Innocent said.

"*Who?*"

Innocent took his finger from his mouth. "Valerie Greene," he said, "and you're going to *die* for it!"

"Tsk," said the Mark VI, as Kirby threw his arms up to protect his head.

"God damned *bastard!*" Innocent cried.

"I didn't!" Kirby yelled. "Innocent, I'm innocent!"

"Tsk."

"*Shit!* Where *are* they?"

"I didn't *do* it!"

"Boom," said the shotgun in Manny's hands in the doorway of the house, and a number of leaf bits and twig mulch pattered down onto the tableau of Innocent and Kirby.

Innocent, wide-eyed, looked over at Manny who, untroubled by recoil, was lowering the shotgun barrel from his aim at the tree branches to a new sighting on Innocent's torso. This piece of armament was a Ted Williams over-and-under shotgun with 28-inch barrels, 48 inches overall, weight seven and a quarter pounds, firing either two and three-quarter or three inch standard or magnum shells in 12 gauge, available at Sears stores. Manny's finger had already moved from the front trigger, which had just fired the modified choke lower barrel, to the rear trigger, which at any instant could unleash the contents of the full choke upper barrel.

Having no idea what Manny planned to do next, hoping against hope he wasn't running into a blast of shotgun pellets, Kirby dashed forward, grabbed the Mark VI out of Innocent's slack hands, and ran away holding the gun in both *his* hands, yelling, "Don't shoot! Don't shoot!"

Innocent stared after him in frustration and aggravation: "How can I shoot? You took my gun!"

"Manny!" Kirby yelled in explanation. "Manny, don't shoot!"

Manny came out of the house, the Ted Williams butt still nestled into his shoulder, cheek still lying against the hand-checkered walnut stock, right eye sighting down the ventilated rib, directly at Innocent. Estelle came out after him, looking stern, in her right hand the cleaver she used for quartering chickens. A couple of the dogs came out and trotted over to Innocent, sniffing him in search of the tastiest parts. A few children came out and arrayed themselves to one side, as audience. Innocent looked pained.

Kirby, at a safe distance from everybody, looked at the weapon of destruction lying across his palms. He turned it around, held it in his right hand like people in the movies, and pointed it down at the ground. He squeezed the trigger. "Bang!" it said, and the recoil slammed up into his arm bones hard enough to jolt his whole skeleton. "Jesus," he whispered. One *tsk* from eternity.

Innocent was now looking merely weary, rumpled, and resigned. Kirby glanced at him, and walked toward the house. He passed Manny, who said, "Kirby? What do you need?"

"A drink," Kirby said. His right shoulder hurt.

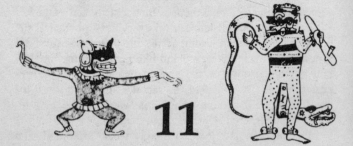

11

THE MYSTERY OF THE TEMPLE

The Indians didn't expect the plane, Valerie could tell that from their reaction when it buzzed low over the village late in the afternoon. They loved it, of course; they seemed to love everything Kirby Galway did. They came scampering out of their huts and, driven by curiosity, every last one of them went hurrying out of town and up and over that nearby scruffy hill to meet Galway where he'd be landing. Driven by her own curiosity, Valerie followed, keeping some distance behind.

She had never been up this way before. The Indians had told her how dry and lifeless the land was over here, fit for nothing but an airstrip, and she'd noticed they themselves never came up this way except that one earlier time to

272

meet Galway. Now, she labored up the hill and it wasn't until she reached the top and looked down the other side at the plane taxiing across the flat land in this direction that she suddenly realized where she was.

It had to be, had to be. She and the kidnapper/driver had come in from that direction, way over there. The airplane had been parked exactly where Galway was now parking it. Her confrontation with him had taken place down there below the right flank of the hill. So this place, *this* place, had to be . . .

. . . the temple?

Valerie gazed about herself, wide-eyed, open-mouthed, bewildered. This was no temple. This was merely an arid brown hill, covered with a stubble of dead brush and dying stunted trees.

Could this ever have been a temple? Unlike the Egyptian pyramids, which had been actual buildings filled with rooms and spaces, the Mayan temples had been mere stone skins veneered onto existing hills, so, in the few short days after she'd first seen this place, could Galway possibly have stripped it completely, every stone and every stela, every corbel arch, every wall, every terrace and stair?

No.

Having done that one impossibility, could Galway then have gone on to remove every trace of what he'd done, every mark and indentation, every touch of the ancient Mayan builders' hands?

Again, no.

Impossible. In fact, absurd.

"But . . ." Valerie said aloud, and continued to stare this way and that in total befuddlement. She had *seen* the temple, with her own eyes. She had stood down there, and looked up here, and had gazed upon an undoubted temple. Exactly where the computers had said it would be. Exactly where she had *known* it would be. And Kirby Galway had been so upset at her finding his secret temple that he'd gone absolutely berserk, threatening her with a machete, hopping up and down, throwing his hat on the—

Movement down by the plane attracted her attention. Kirby Galway himself had climbed out and was talking and gesticulating with Tommy Watson and Luz Coco and Rosita while the other villagers stood around watching, wondering as much as Valerie what was going on. But now a second person was clambering awkwardly out of the plane, making his way to the ground with the help of several Indians. Valerie's breath caught. It was Innocent St. Michael!

She stared, forgetting the mystery of the temple. The ringleader himself, *here*. Ducking low, she watched through the fronds of dead foliage as the talk went on down there, Tommy and Luz now explaining some sort of situation to the other Indians, Kirby explaining, even Innocent St. Michael explaining. People started to point at Valerie.

Well, not at Valerie, but certainly uphill. Toward the village, it must be, because the whole group, still talking and explaining, set out en masse, moving in this direction.

What should she do? Crouched on her hilltop, watching the Indians and the villains climb the slope, she wondered what would be best. Hide in one of the huts, or stay away from the village until after Galway and St. Michael had gone?

They were getting closer, their voices rising toward her. Clear on the afternoon air came the sound of Kirby Galway's voice. Unmistakably she heard him pronounce one word:

"Sheena."

Betrayed! By whom? It didn't matter. But now Valerie understood why Galway and St. Michael were here; they had come to finish the job their minions had started, there could be no doubt about *that*. Like the startled deer she was, Valerie rose and ran.

Downhill, fleet as the wind. Hoping Rosita wasn't her

betrayer, hoping none of the Indians she had come to like and admire in the last nine days had done this terrible thing, Valerie scrambled down the back side of the non-temple. Nervously missing her footing here and there, she hurried on, fright bringing bile to her throat.

The huts were ahead. There was no help now, not even from the villagers, who were somehow or other in Kirby Galway's thrall. Every man's hand, it seemed, was turned against Valerie Greene, yes, and every woman's too, and probably most of the children.

The village was deserted. There was no place to hide, no sense trying to stay. The prospect of wandering in the wilderness once more was daunting, but not as daunting as the inexorable approach of Kirby Galway and Innocent St. Michael. She had to run for it; that's all she could do.

Rosita had been making tortillas outside her hut, now cooling on a flat stone. Grabbing them up—who knew when she'd find food again—Valerie tucked them inside her repaired blouse, leaped the little stream, and plunged into the woods.

12

IT HAPPENED ONE AFTERNOON

Innocent sat on a flat stone, catching his breath. All about him, the Indians were in fevered motion, running in and out of huts, splashing through the stream, yelling at one another, slapping their children, kicking their dogs. Kirby Galway paced back and forth like a pirate captain on his bridge, shouting orders, barking commands, pointing this way and that, and being mostly ignored. The two men and one woman in the village who spoke English stood in the middle of it all arguing at the tops of their voices, though not in English, so it didn't help.

Long before the finish, Innocent knew how it would end. The question was, when it happened would he believe it?

On the other hand, what was there at all to believe about this day? Himself, to begin with, he found utterly incredible. He had committed—or had attempted to commit—physical violence. He, Innocent St. Michael, a man who had always prided himself on his subtlety, a man who let his brains do his fighting and let his money hire what physical labor had to be done. He had committed—or had attempted to commit—a major felony, and *not for personal profit*. He had committed—or had attempted to commit—a crime of *passion*! Him! Innocent St. Michael! *Passion*!

Attempted; attempted; attempted; hadn't even done the job right. Ten times he had fired at Kirby Galway and ten times he had missed. Well, nine and a half. One little scratch on the shoulder that Kirby carried on about as though he'd been crippled for life, before finally calming down and swearing all over again that he had absolutely, positively not killed Valerie Greene.

There were reasons at least to believe that last part, which Kirby had elucidated for him in several repetitive shouted sentences. First, if he had murdered Valerie Greene and Innocent had found him out, there was absolutely no reason why he shouldn't now go ahead and murder Innocent as well. Second, even if he'd had time to plot a murder with Innocent's driver, the fellow was still *Innocent's* driver and Kirby would have been crazy to trust him with such a dangerous request. And third, Kirby now believed that Valerie Greene wasn't dead after all but was living in an Indian village under the name Sheena, Queen of the Jungle.

So hither they had come, hope and skepticism fighting in Innocent's breast, to be surrounded by bright-eyed curious villagers, to be assured that yes, Sheena was living with them, she was right over the hill there—Kirby's hill, Innocent had noted, wondering if it meant anything—and on to the village they had come, for the onset of pandemonium. Once the running and shouting and general disarray started Innocent had merely sat down on a flat stone outside one of the huts to catch his breath, knowing how it would end and wondering if he would believe it when it happened.

Which at last it did. The village had grown quieter, and here was Kirby standing spraddle-legged before him, the very icon of frustrated generalship. "She's gone," he said.

Innocent looked up at him; he had mostly regained his breath by now. "The question is," he said, "do I believe it?"

Kirby looked exasperated to the point of violence. "And just when, goddam it," he said, "was I supposed to have set up *this* one?"

"Your gun-toting pal Manny," Innocent suggested. "He has a radio there at that house. He got on it as soon as we took off, he called here—"

"There's no radio here," Kirby said, and waved his arms extravagantly. "Search the goddam place yourself, Innocent. We never put a radio in because we didn't want to attract attention."

A fact—if it was a fact—that Innocent stowed away in his brain for later consideration. "There are other radios in this world," he said. "Perhaps only half a mile from here, some friend of yours. Manny called him, told him to pass on the story he'd heard you tell me, about the white woman living in an Indian village, and the villagers calling her Sheena, Queen of the Jungle, and— Kirby, many people would not believe that story."

"They'd all be wrong," Kirby said.

"Let me ask you something," Innocent said. "You were here the day before yesterday, they told you about Sheena living with them in their village, and *you didn't go look at her*."

"I didn't believe it," Kirby said.

"So why should I?"

"Because I saw a white woman after, when I flew over. I *told* you that, Innocent. I wasn't sure then, but now you tell me Valerie Greene disappeared, and the degenerate *you* gave her to has skipped the country, and—"

"All right, Kirby, all right." Innocent felt very tired, rather sad, oddly ineffectual. "But all at once she's gone. She was here, but not now. Why?"

"She don't trust *you*," the English-speaking Indian—Rosita—said, suddenly with them, pointing a sharp-boned finger at Kirby. "She told me all about how you cheated Wintrop Cartwright."

Kirby blinked. "Who?"

"The man she was gonna marry," Rosita said.

Innocent lifted his head at that, and looked at this sharp-featured skinny girl. "She was going to marry someone?"

"Wintrop Cartwright." Rosita smiled at Innocent, apparently finding something pleasing there. "He's a rich man like her papa, but old. That's why she run away. She's a pilot, you know."

Innocent shook his head. "This is ridiculous," he told Kirby. "If the woman does exist, she's the wrong woman."

"Wait a minute," Kirby said, and turned to Rosita. "Listen," he said, "you people just called her Sheena as a nickname, right?"

"It was Tommy's idea," she said. "He's the reader."

"So what was her real name?"

Rosita thought a second: "Valerie."

Innocent looked at her, trying to see inside that narrow head.

Kirby said, "What was her last name?"

"How do I know? I just called her Sheena. She liked it."

"But her real name," Kirby insisted, "was Valerie."

"And she told me all about *you*," Rosita said. "How

you don't really have no crazy wife in an asylum anywheres, you're just taking advantage of me."

Innocent frowned deeply at this new development. "A crazy wife? *What* crazy wife?"

"Never mind," Kirby said hastily. "The point is, Innocent, her name is Valerie, and she took off either because she's afraid of you or she's afraid of me. Any case, she saw us coming."

"She has no reason to be afraid of *me*," Innocent said.

Rosita said, "Maybe she thought you were here to take her back to her papa, make her marry Wintrop."

Kirby said, "Wait a second, light is beginning to dawn. Valerie was on the run—probably from that driver of yours, Innocent—and she was afraid to tell the truth, didn't know who she could trust, so she told these clowns the old runaway heiress plot, and they bought it."

"That's just what she is!" Rosita said, happy to confirm the truth. "She didn't want to marry that Wintrop, so she got in her plane and flew away, but then she got in a storm and crashed in the Maya Mountains over there and walked and walked and walked for *days* and then we found her. And she made us swear we wouldn't tell, and then she told us the truth."

"The truth," Kirby said. "The runaway heiress story."

"Too many stories going around," Innocent said.

Rosita looked off westward, toward the blue-shouldered Maya Mountains. "We'll find her pretty soon, I think," she said.

Innocent sat up straighter. "You do? Why's that?"

"Stand up a second," she told him.

Innocent frowned at Kirby, who shrugged. So Innocent shrugged, and stood up, and Rosita looked at the flat stone where he'd been sitting and said, "Yeah, they're gone."

Innocent looked at the flat stone, at Kirby, and at Rosita. He said, "May I sit down?"

"Sure."

"What's gone?" Kirby said.

"Sheena's got this throat problem or lungs or something," Rosita explained, "so she can't smoke, so if we turn on sometimes she can't join in, you know?"

"And?" said Kirby, while Innocent reflected that for Kirby a crazy wife would be redundant.

Rosita said, "So I promised I'd make her some pot tortillas, but I never got around to it till today. They're pretty strong, you know."

"You made pot tortillas today?" Kirby asked.

"Yeah, and put them on that rock and now they're gone. Sheena must of took them." Rosita looked westward again, toward where the shadows lengthened on the steep faces of the mountains. "She won't get very far," she said.

13

SOME ASPECTS OF
PHARMACOLOGICAL EXPERIENCE

"Vaaaallll-erie! Oh, *Vaaaa-llll*-erie!''

"Sing,'' Valerie sang, under her breath, beneath her breath, down among the mushrooms of her mind. "Sing to me, and sing to me, and then I'll run away. Oop!''

Down again. Another scratch on the same knee. Not treating this model well at *all*, take it into the shop they'll say, Jeepers, lady, where you been driving this model? Mountaintops and bellyflops, a poor white convertible upside down with its whitewalls spinning, upholstery all muddy, scratches on the fenders, this is a *dent*, lady.

"Vaaaallll-erie! It's Ro-*zeee*-ta! It's oh-*kaaaayyyy*!''

"Vrrooommm,'' Valerie said, giggling at the idea of

having the idea of being a car, and from somewhere above and behind her left shoulder she watched herself go up the jungly slope on all fours. Mud, dirt, roots, dangling branches. Little buggies scuttling out of the way of her Donald Duck hands. Wflap! Wflap! Big webbed hands out of the sky.

Still light in the sky, *dark* blue light, sun gone away to the other side of the mountain, waiting over there for Valerie. Vaaaallll-erie, I'm waiting. Here I come, here I come, here I come.

Ridge. Downslope. Climb a tree trunk to verticality, vertiginous verticality, the ground darker than the sky, her feet way far down there in the pool of darkness, puddles of night all around her feet. The calling voices were fainter, but could still be heard, the beacon behind her that gave her direction. Keep the voices between her shoulderblades, hurry the opposite way.

Splop. Splash-splop. Stream; water. Chuckles down from the right, scurries on off to the left, white rabbits down the hideyhole. Follow? No, go the other way. Where'd those rabbits come from? Hide with Mister Rabbit at home.

Splush, splush, splush. Water cold and nice on the cuts, running around her shins, ribbons in a wind tunnel. Stop a minute, kneel in the water, get her hands and arms all clean, throw water on her heated face. Sssss, steam from her heated face—just kidding. Stones on the bottom of the stream, though, *that's* no joke. Up again, *up up up up up*. On.

Siiiiii-lence. Oh, *siiiiii*-lence. How long has it been? Very very dark. No stream, no light. Reach out and touch a telephone pole. Step. Reach out; step.

Are there stars out tonight? Oh, gosh, oh-oh, don't look up, it's *awfully* dizzy up there!

Hungry all the time for some reason. Must be all this exercise. Pig out. Only three tortillas left between her blouse and her flesh, beneath her breasts. Munch and munch. A little dry and tough, but tasty. Satisfying.

A path. Yes? Yes. A narrow path angling downward, slightly to the left. Pitch black, can't see your face in front of your head. Walk down the path, swing the arms, the last two tortillas stuck to her skin.

Ow! Tripped right *over* that log, fell on a man! A man? Roll away—not with *me* you don't, buster!

Flashlights came on, men's voices, they'd been asleep or resting or what, Valerie gaped around at them, her little pin-prick eyes staring in the flashlights, seeing the camouflage uniforms on the chunky little bodies, the weapons, the bush hats. Soldiers, British, Gurkhas. Gurkha patrol, is that a song? "Rescued!" Valerie said in cheerful surprise, and smiled happily, and her eyes rolled back in her head.

14

"SAME AGAIN ALL ROUND!"

For a moment after he switched off the van's engine, Vernon sat on in darkness, staring at the wall of the Fort George Hotel directly in front of himself and willing himself to be calm. He was going to do this, he was going to come out the other side, it was all going to be all right. All of it. All right. The chicken and rice he'd eaten for dinner at J.B.'s on the way down from Belmopan sat like an auto accident in his stomach, unmoving.

If only the village had not already been selected—the one the journalists would be visiting tomorrow. Vernon had done his best, but he'd been too late. The village had been selected, and it was not the one the Colonel had insisted the journalists must see.

What choice had he had? He was racing across a tight-rope, high above the rocks with no net, already off balance, running forward as fast as he could because it was the only way not to fall. The other side, the other side, sooner or later he had to reach the other side. In the meantime, he could only keep running, keep improvising, try not to miss his step.

The wrong village. With great difficulty Vernon had arranged to be made the driver for tomorrow's expedition. Then, using the absent Innocent St. Michael's authority, he had also arranged to be ordered to come to Belize City tonight, ahead of time, staying at the Fort George along with the journalists, ostensibly so they could begin early tomorrow morning but actually so that Vernon would be beyond any countermanding orders. *He* would be the driver, and that's all.

And he would make a mistake. An honest mistake. He would take the journalists to a different village, not the one the government had selected but very similar. A simple mistake that anyone might make. And then it would all be over, he would have reached the other side of the abyss, no more tightrope, firm ground at last.

Vernon whimpered, a little mewling sound. Behind him, the dozen empty seats of the van were filled with the ghosts of wrong turnings. He shuddered, and took the key from the ignition and his overnight bag from the floor space between the front seats, and got out onto the blacktop.

The desk clerk was both cold and obsequious; obsequious because Vernon's room was being paid for by a government department, suggesting power and authority, and cold because Vernon himself was so clearly nothing but a minor clerk. When I'm rich, Vernon thought, but this time

the thought wouldn't complete itself. Where was his
rage? Sighing, he filled out the registration form, then
showed his list to the desk clerk, saying, "These are
journalists staying here, I must see them in the morning,
you'll—"

"I believe they are in the bar," the desk clerk said,
coldly and obsequiously.

So Vernon went to his room and unpacked, and went to
the bathroom, and washed his hands and face and the back
of his neck, and went to the bathroom, and took some
antacid pills, and went to the bathroom, and changed his
shirt, and combed his hair, and went to the bathroom, and
washed his face, and turned out the light, and went down
to the bar, where two of the large round black formica
tables were occupied. The four silent gloomy beer-drinking
fellows at one table with their big red faces and big red
knees jutting from both ends of their short-trousered British Army uniforms were certainly not journalists, whereas
the seven oddly assorted people clustered around the other
table, all talking at once, nobody listening, certainly were.
Vernon went over and stood beside that group, waiting for
a simultaneous pause in all seven monologues, or for
someone to notice him.

Someone noticed him; a skinny sharp-nosed gray-faced
man in a safari shirt and bush jacket and U.S. Army
fatigue trousers and Hush Puppies, who looked up, saw
Vernon, and in an East London accent said, "Right. Same
again all round, then."

"I'm not a waiter," Vernon said.

"No? Then be off with you." The man turned back to
his chattering companions.

"I'm your driver," Vernon said.

"The hell you say." The man looked him up and down.
"And where am I going, then?"

"Requena," Vernon said. The settlement was called

that because it was the last name of the majority of the settlers.

"That's tomorrow," the man said. By now, two of the others, including the group's lone woman, had also stopped talking and were looking at Vernon, wondering what entertainment or news value he might possess.

"I am here tonight," Vernon told them. "I am introducing myself, and I will spend the night in the hotel, so we can get an early start tomorrow."

"Well, good fellow!" the sharp-nosed man said. "Johnny on the spot, that's the ticket. Introducing yourself, are you?"

"My name is Vernon."

"And how do you do, Vernon? You'll find that I am Scottie. This ravishing lady to my left is Morgan Lassiter, a world-class lesbian and ace repor—"

"Just because *you* never got any," Morgan Lassiter told him, but calmly, as though she were used to him—or possibly to his type. Her accent was anonymously Midlantic, as though she'd learned English from machines, on Mars. She nodded in a businesslike way at Vernon and said, "Nice to see you."

"And you, Ma'am."

"This lot," Scottie said, and interrupted himself to bang his whisky glass on the table, crying, "Shut up, you berks! Vernon's here to introduce himself. And *here* he is, our driver, Vernon. Bright and early on the morrow he shall whisk us from this hellhole here out to the other hellhole over there, and then back again. Back again is included, am I right, Vernon?"

"Yes," said Vernon.

Scottie gestured this way and that. "Over there is Tom, a fine American photojournalist, just chockablock with all the latest American photojournalist technological advances, isn't that right, Tommy?"

"Fuck you in the ass," Tommy said.

"Chahming," Scottie said. "Next to him is Nigel, the dregs of humanity, not only an Australian but an Australian *newspaperman*, until he forgot himself once, told the truth, and was exiled to Edinburgh."

"What Tommy said," said Nigel.

"Never does his own research," Scottie commented. "Here beside me we have Colin, the demon scribbler of Fleet Street, and beside him is Ralph Waldo Eckstein, who won't tell anybody why the *Wall Street Journal* fired him, and—"

"What Tommy said."

"Yes, yes. Now, Vernon, lad, you've probably been told we are a party of six, is that not right?"

"That's right," Vernon said.

"But here we are, as you can plainly see, a party of seven. Did Morgan give birth? Perish the thought. In fact, perish the little perisher. No, what has happened is that even here in this pit of nullity, this farthest outpost of Empire which Aldous Huxley quite rightly said was on the way from nowhere and to nowhere, journalists seek one another out, come together for comfort and liquor and the latest lies. That gentleman over there, with the truly wonderful moustache, is one Hiram Farley, an *editor* if you please with a most famous American magazine called *Trash*. No, I beg your pardon; *Trend*."

Hiram Farley leaned forward with his meaty forearms crossed on the table and looked unsmilingly at Vernon. He said nothing. He seemed to be exploring Vernon's eyes, looking for something, traces of something. A cold finger touched Vernon's spine. *He knows*, he thought. But he can't know, get hold of yourself. Vernon blinked.

Scottie said, "Mr. Farley would very much like to come

along with us tomorrow, if he may. Busman's holiday and all that, the old fire company horse hearing the bell. Please say yes.''

''Yes,'' said Vernon.

15

DEVIL DANCE

Twenty little devil-gods stood on the rattan mat, knees turned out to the sides and deeply bent, arms flung wide to show their bat webs, eyes glittering with evil, mouths stretched back in a violent smirk out of which forked tongues curled, poised to strike. In the flickering candlelight, the massed group of 20 demons seemed to move, shimmer, almost to dance, their eyes staring back at Kirby, who blinked, cleared his throat, and said, "Fine, Tommy. Very effective."

"They get to you, don't they?" Tommy held the candle lower, the movement causing the creatures to alter their knee bends and roll their eyes, while their shadows magnified and swooped on the far wall of the hut.

"They're real good, Tommy," Kirby said. Behind him, outside, a low-key party was under way, partly in hospitality at the presence of Kirby and Innocent and partly a vigil, waiting for word of Valerie Greene. Rosita and a couple of the others were still out there in the darkness somewhere, occasionally calling, but everyone knew they wouldn't find their Jungle Queen tonight. At first light they'd look again, hoping nothing bad had happened to her, reeling around stoned and lost in the darkness.

Innocent was in another hut right now, being shown some of the blankets and dress material the villagers had made and dyed themselves, so Tommy had taken the opportunity to bring Kirby here and show him he'd actually been at work making the promised Zotzes.

Zotzilaha Chimalman, replicated 20 times, danced in the candlelight on the rattan mat. Each figure was about 10 inches high, seven inches wide, formed from clay, hollowed out as an incense burner. Buried and dug up again, all of them had been knocked together a bit to simulate age and rough treatment, each one subtly different, showing the specific touches of the half-dozen artisans who had worked on them.

Fakes. Mockeries. Tiny clay imitations of an ancient long-dead superstition, but still brimming with the potency of dread. Zotzilaha Chimalman hated mankind and had the power and the genius to do something about it. Kirby had never been a Maya, but nevertheless he felt uneasy in the presence of this naked malevolence. He could understand why it was so hard for Tommy to turn his hand to the creation of such a being, and even more so for the other villagers, whose straightforward relationship with life and the spirits and their ancestors had never been corrupted by exile to the outer world.

Over the candle flame, Tommy's eyes gleamed at Kirby almost as gleefully as the demons': "Had enough, Kimosabe?"

"They're fine, Tommy," Kirby said, calm and dignified. "Thanks. And, uh, let's get the hell out of here."

Tommy chuckled, and they went outside to a clear night full of stars, with a moon about seven months pregnant. The villagers liked to party, but were troubled by the disappearance of their Sheena, and therefore merely sat in groups, murmuring together. The little plastic radio had been turned off; no salsa music from Guatemala tonight. A horizontal scrim of marijuana smoke hung at nose level. Jars of homebrew clinked against stone. The mountains that had swallowed Valerie Greene were black against the western sky.

Innocent was no longer admiring materials but sitting on them. A bulky old mahogany armchair had been brought out of one of the huts and set near the largest fire, then draped with colorful cloths; black-and-white zigzags over red or rust or orange, bright red and deep blue diamonds in alternating patterns, representations of flora and fauna so stylized by centuries of repetition as to have lost all hint of their original realistic nature. Upon this soft throne sat Innocent, smiling upon the fire and the shyly smiling villagers, in his left hand a large Hellman's Mayonnaise jar mostly full of what to drink.

Crossing toward him, Kirby thought at first it was merely the ambiguity of the firelight that made Innocent's face look so much softer and less guileful than usual, but when he got closer he saw it was more than that. "Innocent?" he said.

Innocent turned his smiling face. He wasn't drunk, and he wasn't participating in the gage that was being passed around. It seemed as though he was just, well, happy. "How are you, Kirby?" he said.

"I'm fine." Kirby looked around for something to sit on, found nothing, and sat on the ground beside Innocent's left knee, half turned away from the fire so he could continue the conversation. "How are you, Innocent?"

"I'm all right," Innocent said, with a strange kind of dawdling emphasis. "I've had a very strange day, Kirby."

Kirby ruefully touched his shoulder, where Innocent's bullet had kissed him. "Haven't we all," he said. Around them, the Indians conducted their own conversations in their own language, nodding or smiling at Kirby and Innocent in hospitable incomprehension from time to time. Tommy and Luz were at some other fire, waiting for Rosita to give up and come home.

"This morning," Innocent said, "I was in despair. Would you believe that, Kirby?"

"You seemed a little hot under the collar."

"That, too. But it was mostly despair. When I got out of bed this morning, Kirby, I was prepared to throw my entire life away."

"Not to mention mine."

"*Mine*, Kirby," Innocent insisted, but still with that same new languid manner. "I didn't take my laps in the pool this morning," he said. "Can you imagine that?"

"I guess not."

"I *never* skip my laps in the pool. I didn't eat breakfast. I didn't eat lunch."

"Okay," Kirby said. "That's a couple of things I can't imagine."

"It was love that did it to me, Kirby. At my age, after all these years, I fell in love."

"With Valerie Greene?"

"Strange thing," Innocent said, "until just now I couldn't even use the word. *Love*. I could say I missed her, I was angry about her loss, I liked the idea of her, but I couldn't use the word *love*. I could plan to shoot you because of it, but I couldn't say it. Plan to throw my entire life away without ever saying that word."

"My God, Innocent," Kirby said, "you've had an epiphany."

"Is that what it is? Feels pretty good." Innocent smiled and sipped a bit from the jar.

"But," Kirby said, hesitating, not wanting to spoil Innocent's good mood or changed personality or whatever the hell this was, "but, Innocent, are you *sure*? I mean, how well did you know Valerie Greene?"

"How well do I have to know her? Kirby, if I knew her better, would it make me love her more?"

"It wouldn't me," Kirby said, remembering his own less than satisfactory last sight of Valerie Greene.

"I spent one afternoon with her," Innocent said. "Just Platonic, you know."

"You didn't have to say that, Innocent," Kirby said comfortably.

Innocent chuckled. "I suppose I didn't. Anyway, I expected to see her again, and it didn't happen. I was thirsty, and the water went away."

"You're a wonder, Innocent," Kirby said. "I never knew you were a romantic."

"I never *was* a romantic. Sitting here now, thinking about it, I think maybe that's what was wrong. I was never a romantic, never once in my life. Do you know why I married my wife?"

"No."

"Her father had the money I needed to buy a certain piece of land."

"Come on, Innocent, there must have been more to it than that. There were other girls with fathers with money."

"There were two other potential buyers for the land," Innocent said. "I didn't have time to fool around."

"So why Valerie Greene?"

"Because," Innocent said, "there was nothing in it for anybody concerned. She's an honest girl, Kirby, she's the most completely honest girl I ever met in my life. And *smart*. And *earnest*. And something more than just out for a good time. But the main thing is, no matter what she does, where she is, what's going on, she's always one hundred percent honest.''

"You know a lot about somebody you spent one afternoon with," Kirby pointed out.

"I do, that's right." Innocent smiled, remembering something or other. "She wants to give happiness and receive happiness," he said. "She's not out to buy or sell anything. She doesn't try to get an *edge*."

"You've got it bad," Kirby told him.

"I've got it *good*," Innocent said. "And now that I believe you and these people here, now that I'm in this nowhere little nothing village and I know for sure Valerie's out there, not far, not *dead*, now that I know she's not dead, it's just fine, isn't it?''

"If you say so."

"She'll be back," Innocent said. "Some time tomorrow she'll be found, these eyes will look at her, this mouth will say, 'Hello, Valerie.' " He beamed in anticipated pleasure.

"Innocent," Kirby said, with wonder in his eyes and in his voice, "you've regained your innocence."

Innocent pleasantly laughed. "I suppose I have. Never knew I had one to lose. Kirby, maybe this would have happened anyway, maybe it's that man's change of life thing, but it needed somebody *good* to bring it out, and that was Valerie. This is a whole new person you're looking at, Kirby."

"I believe you," Kirby said.

"He was tucked away inside me all the time, I never knew it."

"The love of a good woman, huh?"

"Go ahead and laugh, Kirby, that's okay."

"I'm not laughing, Innocent," Kirby told him, in almost total sincerity. "I think it's great. So this is the Innocent I'll be seeing around Belize City from now on, is it?''

Innocent's smile was sleepy, comfortable, self-confident. "I know better than that, Kirby," he said.

"You mean it won't last?"

Innocent said, "Kirby, did you ever visit someplace that was really nice, a place that made you happy, so you started to think maybe you'd like to just stay there forever?"

"Sure."

"But then after a while you realize it isn't *your* place, you don't fit in except as a visitor, you don't belong there and you never will. So you go home, where you do belong, and where you're happy most of the time because it's the right place where you ought to be."

"Okay, Innocent."

"From time to time," Innocent said, "you remember that other place, and how nice it was to visit, but you don't make the mistake of thinking you can go back and *live* there. So that's what's happening now, Kirby. I'm visiting some other me, a real nice me that I never knew before." That lazy smile softened Innocent's features once more. "But don't worry about it," he said. "I'll go home to the real me when the time comes."

"In that case," Kirby said, now completely sincere, "I'm glad I was here to meet the other fella."

16

PILLOW TALK

Voices. Murmuring voices.

Valerie opened her right eye and followed the progress of an ant as it tottered along the dark damp ground, carrying a big piece of chewed-off leaf above itself like a green sail. Her left cheek was pressed against that ground, so her left eye remained closed, while her right eye tracked the ant and her right ear received the input of those murmuring voices without attempting to decipher.

Mouth: dry. Body: extremely stiff. Head: painful. Knees: stinging. Hair: matted. Brain: semiconscious.

Her right arm was bent up at some little distance from her face, lying on the ground, leaving a miniature arena in which that ant-sail bobbed as though on a dark brown lake.

Valerie watched the pale green triangle until it reached her thumb, reversed, turned right, reached the knuckle at the base of her thumb, reversed, turned left, and carried on out of sight, into the great large ocean of the world.

Human beings—much larger than ants—went by. Valerie's working eye swiveled upward, sighted over her hulking shoulder, and glimpsed the two men moving away, talking. Camouflage uniforms. Curved knives in black leather sheaths at their waists. Gurkhas.

It was coming back, slowly and erratically. The eye swivel had been unexpectedly painful, so Valerie shut the lid, retired into darkness, and permitted memory to work its will upon her.

Indian village. Airplane with Kirby Galway *and* Innocent St. Michael. Flight, with tortillas. Great confusion as darkness settled, her mind adrift—what *had* that all been about? Had terror unhinged her? But she didn't remember feeling that frightened, certainly not after she'd gotten some distance from the village. She'd even paused beside a stream, she remembered, sitting there a few minutes to catch her breath and drink water to wash down her first tortilla. After that . . .

After that, wandering in darkness, much of it mere confused imagery in her mind. *Had* she been laughing uproariously, pretending to be an automobile, talking out loud like Donald Duck? Surely memory was wrong. Or had there been something in the stream? "Don't drink the water," isn't that what they say?

But then— Rescue! A Gurkha patrol, bivouacked for the night, and she had literally fallen among them. So now, after all the perils and dangers of the last weeks, finally she was safe, amid her rescuers, whose murmuring voices were all around her. Not speaking English, of course. What would it be? Something Asian. Nepalese, was that right, for people from Nepal?

". . . kill . . ."

Weariness spread through her body, a kind of outflowing unconsciousness, padding all around her aches and sores, moving toward her brain.

". . . attack the village . . ."

Awake too early, wrong to be conscious before her body had knit up its wounds. Soothing, soothing sleep. The darkness flowed.

". . . take no prisoners . . ."

Strange. Understanding their words, but not in English. She'd never understood Nepalese before.

". . . kill them all . . ."

Valerie's right eye shot open. *Kekchi!* She could understand them because they were speaking Kekchi! Not the dialect she'd originally learned, nor the somewhat muddier version they spoke back in South Abilene, but some other sharper version, more guttural and glottal, but comprehensible nevertheless.

Why would Gurkha soldiers speak Kekchi to one another?

"When do we kill the woman?"

Valerie's entire body clenched. Her open eye stared at her wrist, her ear dilated.

"When we get there."

A slight unclenching, but eye and ear both still wide.

"Why not shoot her now? She'll slow us down."

"No shooting. What if somebody hears and comes to look?"

"I could cut her with this knife."

"And if she screams?"

(Oh, I'd scream, yes, I would.)

"I know you. You're just in such a hurry to kill her because she scared you so much last night."

"Me? Who had to change his pants? Was that me, or was that you?"

"Yeah, I thought *you* were gonna drop dead, you were so scared. You thought a real old-time devil came to get you."

"I didn't go run and hide in the woods like some people."

They discussed this further, bristling a bit, each accusing the other of being more superstitious, more prey to fears connected with the old Mayan gods and devils, while Valerie lay silent and unmoving, taking little pleasure in the irony: *They* had been afraid of *her*.

Then at last they got back to it, one of them saying, "So what do we do about the woman?"

"She thinks we're Gurkhas, taking her back to camp. So she'll come along, no trouble. When we get to the village, we gag her, wait till the people come out from the city. When we shoot the villagers, we shoot her, too."

"What about the people from the city?"

"We kill the driver. We wound one white man, it doesn't matter which one."

"Why don't we kill them all?"

"Because they're the people who write the stories." (There is no word for *reporter* in Kekchi.) "When they go home, they'll write all about how the Gurkhas killed all the people in the village."

"Then we go back across the border?"

"And the Colonel gives us our money."

Valerie continued to lie there, feigning sleep, while the false Gurkhas continued to talk. They discussed for some time whether to rape her, finally deciding not to do so yet but wait till they got to the village and then play it by ear. (The idioms are somewhat different in Kekchi.) Then one of them said something about how they should get started soon, the village was a good hour's hike north of here, and Valerie decided it was time to wake up. She made a moaning sound, stretched, rolled over, sat up, looked around wide-eyed at the group of men seated and standing all about her, and said, "Oh, my gosh!"

They looked at her. One of them said, in Kekchi, "Smile at her. Show her we're friendly."

A cluster of ghastly smiles were beamed her way. Valerie smiled back and said, "You rescued me!" Her performance was based on Judy Garland in *The Wizard of Oz*.

They nodded and smiled. Apparently, none of them spoke English.

With some difficulty, Valerie struggled to her feet. The dozen men watched her, smiles still pasted on their faces. Looking around, she said, "Where can I wash up?"

"What does she want?"

"Food, maybe."

Valerie made hand-washing gestures and face-washing gestures.

"She wants the stream."

"She wants to piss and wash her face."

Three or four of them pointed past some trees at the edge of the clearing.

"Oh, thanks," Valerie said, her own ghastly smile still firmly in place, and turned away.

"I say we definitely rape her."

"Not before we get to the village."

Valerie paused at the first trees to look back, smiling and wagging her finger. "Don't peek now," she said.

17

THE SECRET ROAD

Vernon couldn't eat. He pushed the fruit around in the bowl and looked gloomily at the coffee, while over at another table the seven journalists wolfed down everything in sight, Scottie going so far as to pretend to bite the waitress's arm. She offered him a professional smile, refilled his coffee cup, and came over to ask Vernon if everything was all right.

"Fine," Vernon said.

Vernon was at a small table to one side of the large dining room at the Fort George, with the ravenous correspondents in front of him and the view of the timeless sea beneath a timeless sun off to his right. (The black freighter still stood at anchor in the offing, the paperwork on its eventual auction suffering the usual timeless bureaucratic delay.)

What is going to happen in the village?

I didn't ask that question, Vernon told himself. I don't want to know the answer. I only want to survive to the other end of the tightrope. I don't want to know what links together the Colonel's various demands of me.

Refugee settlements.

Photos of Gurkhas.

The refugees flee Guatemala, flee the Colonel and the government he serves. They become lost to the Colonel, protected by borders, by international law, by the British, by the wandering Gurkha patrols. The refugees come to trust the Gurkhas, short dark men who come from so far away but who look so like themselves. British intelligence in this part of the world is excellent, mostly because the refugees and the other Indians will tell things to the Gurkhas that they won't tell any normal Brit. (When, in 1979, Guatemala started a secret road westward through the jungle into southern Belize, it was the Indians who told the Gurkhas, and the Gurkhas who advanced through the jungle and stopped the road.) Faith and trust in the Gurkhas emboldens the refugees, protects the refugees, swells the tide of refugees, and at the same time increases the embarrassment and frustration of the government the Colonel serves.

The journalists at last had finished their breakfasts, were rising. Vernon put a piece of papaya in his mouth, but couldn't chew it. The fruit was cool at first, but warmed slowly in his mouth.

The correspondents streamed by, talking at one another. The American photojournalist named Tom stopped to say, "Give us ten minutes and we'll be ready."

"Mm," Vernon said, nodding his head with the papaya in it.

"Your vehicle's out front?"

"Mm." More nodding.

"See you there."

"Mm."

Scottie went by with the extra man, the editor from *Trend* named Hiram Farley. Scottie was saying, "Tell me now, Hiram, old son, we've known each other all these many hours, what do you think of me, eh? Eh?"

Farley, with a judicious expression, said, "I would describe you as tiresomely witty."

"By God, that's succinct! Don't pay by the word over on *Trend*, I'll bet!" Scottie said, and clapped Farley on the back with a sound like a gunshot. Vernon blinked, and swallowed his papaya.

18

THE HARMONICA PLAYER

The letter read:

Hiram,

You've gone away, you bad boy, without tell-
ing us a <u>thing</u>, and now we have this very <u>inter-
esting</u> cable from Kirby Galway, which we've
enclosed. Well, of course we cabled him right
back that the answer is <u>yes</u>, and we're on our
way to sunny Flo at this very mo, <u>with</u> cassettes.
And <u>this</u> time, believe us, <u>nothing</u> will go <u>wrong</u>.
We may even get some actual Mayan treasures
for you to photograph, wouldn't you like that?
We'll be home by Monday, so call us as soon as

you return from wherever you've gadded, and we'll certainly have <u>good news</u> for the old news-hound.

Love and kisses,
Alan and Gerry

"A very dry Tanqueray Gibson on the rocks, please," Gerry said.

"Gerry," Alan said warningly.

"Just *one*," Gerry said.

The stewardess said, "I think the only gin we have is Gordon's."

"Oh, well," Gerry said. "All right, I suppose."

"So that's one martini," the stewardess said.

"Gibson."

"The onions didn't come aboard this trip."

"Oh, well. All right, I suppose." Sadly, Gerry turned away and gazed out at cloudtops; they looked dirty.

"Sir?" the stew said, turning her acrylic attention on Alan, in the middle seat.

"The same," Alan said. "Whatever it was."

With a thin smile, the stew turned to the curator from Duluth, Whitman Lemuel, in the aisle seat: "Sir?"

"A Bloody Mary."

The stew beamed her appreciation at a man who under-stood airline drinking, and turned away. Shortly she turned back, the tray tables were lowered to a position just above knees, drinks were exchanged for cash, and they were left in peace, each in his own narrow pocket in the egg carton flying them Floridaward.

Lemuel raised his glass of red foulness: "Confusion to our enemies."

"Oh, my, *yes*," said Gerry.

"I'll drink to that," said Alan, and they did, and Alan made a face. "Swill," he said.

"Better than nothing," Gerry told him, and took another tiny sip of his own drink.

The truth was—and Gerry would go to his grave without revealing this to *anyone*—the truth was, Gerry had no real sensitivity to the tastes of alcohol. If something were really very sweet, like Kahlua, or very bitter, like Campari, he could tell the difference, but in the range of gin drinks and vodka drinks and all of that he was very little aware of distinctions of taste, so this prepackaged martini here with the defrosted pimento olive was about the same to him as the finest ever Tanqueray Gibson on the rocks which a superb Upper East Side bartender would have prepared without even slightly bruising the gin. But one was expected to know the right things to drink, and *appreciate* them, and so on, and one of the ways to show that sort of sophistication was to say, "A very dry Tanqueray Gibson on the rocks, please," so that's what Gerry said whenever the subject came up, and everything worked out fine.

He wondered sometimes if Alan *really* knew or cared about the distinctions in booze. Impossible to ask, of course.

As for Whitman Lemuel and his Bloody Mary, there must be something so *liberating* about being a provincial, not having to keep up a front of sophistication.

What an odd alliance theirs was, after all. Brought together inadvertently by Kirby Galway, they'd had just scads of lies and deliberate confusions to clear out of the way before they could begin to understand one another, but then they'd realized at *once* what a golden opportunity lay before them. From what Lemuel had said about his encounter with the apparently quite frightening Innocent St. Michael, it wasn't Galway after all who'd stolen the tapes, so they were probably safe in going ahead with the original arrangements. As for the legality, morality, all that, Lemuel had explained to them at passionate length that it was practically their *duty* to buy Kirby Galway's loot and see it got proper homes in the United States among people of refinement and taste, people who could *appreciate* and *preserve* such irreplaceable treasures.

Much better than playing Woodward and Bernstein for Hiram. And more profitable, too.

Gerry had been rather surprised and thoroughly delighted when the conversation with Lemuel had shown that Alan also was more than ready to forget *Trend* and actually deal with Galway.

But cautiously, cautiously. That Galway had been engaging to deal with both of them, behind one another's backs, and undoubtedly planned later to use each other's existence to create a bidding situation for the more valuable pieces, showed the sort of slippery customer he was, as if they needed any further proof. Besides which, there was surely still more to the goings-on in Belize than any of them knew. Who could guess what intricacies, what wheels within wheels, might exist even further below the surface?

That was why they'd left that letter for Hiram; in case there was any trouble at all with the law—an idea that made Gerry's heart flutter in his breast—the letter and the cable would prove that Gerry and Alan had had *no* intention of actually becoming accomplices of smugglers. On the other hand, if everything went well, Lemuel would take away the first shipment from Galway, Alan and Gerry would arrange to pick up the second shipment and then return to New York, and when they next saw Hiram they would tell him Galway had never shown up and they'd decided to abandon the whole project.

How oddly things worked out. But that, Gerry thought with some self-satisfaction as he sipped his premixed Gordon's martini, is another mark of sophistication: the ability to deal with truly complex patterns, whether in art or in life. A simpler person like Whitman Lemuel, for instance, no matter how dedicated he might be to the preservation of pre-Columbian artifacts, was still essentially—

A man walked down the aisle. He was about 40, not very tall but barrel-bodied and bull-necked, his large head stubbled with a gray crewcut, his face mean and disgruntled-looking, with down-turned thick lips and cold piggy eyes. A brown string tie hung down on a yellow shirt tight across his chest. He was so muscular he seemed to have trouble walking, his thick shoulders working massively back and forth. His tan jacket was too small for him, hanging open, with strain creases around the armpits.

What made Gerry notice this creature was that he was *staring at Gerry*. He looked mean and angry, as though something about Gerry just simply enraged him. Helpless to look away, Gerry sat open-mouthed and watched the man go by, their eyes locked as though with Krazy Glue. Gerry's head turned like a ventriloquist's dummy until at last the man removed his own glare to face forward, and as Gerry looked to his left, over Alan's head, still compulsively staring, that open jacket swung out and back and something glinted inside it at chest level, and then the man was gone.

Something glinted.

A badge.

A policeman.

They *know*.

"Ohh," said Gerry faintly.

Alan gave him a look: "What now?"

"I'm going"—Gerry swallowed loudly—"to be sick."

Alan glared. *Sotto voce*, he hissed, "I can't take you *anywhere*."

"I don't want to go anywhere. I want to be home."

The man went by again, in the opposite direction, giving Gerry one withering glance before continuing on, his jacket taut across his back.

"You *had* to sit by the window," Alan said. Turning

away, jawline eloquent with rejection, he icily explained
to Whitman Lemuel that they would *all* have to get *up* so
Gerry could be *sick*.

"Ho—" Gerry said. "Unk— Ho-ome."

Still, everything might have been all right if the lavatories hadn't all been occupied.

19

THE ROLE OF THE ANTI-HERO IN
POSTWAR AMERICAN FICTION

Kirby spent a few minutes watching the Indians wrap Zotzes in *Beacons* and then went back outside to a sunny day and a stormy Innocent, who rose from his mahogany throne to say, "Well, Kirby?"

"Well, what?"

"Aren't you ready yet to give it up?"

Kirby frowned at him. "Give what up?"

"I don't see any Valerie, you know." Innocent put his hands on his ample hips and gazed around at the timeless morning scene: Indians squatting over fires in front of their huts, nursing their hangovers. Rosita's distant unremitting call of "*Vaaaallll*-erie," sounded from time to time across the sunny clean air like the cry of some local bird.

"They'll find her," Kirby said, somewhat impatiently. Last night's Innocent had been a lot easier to get along with.

"It's almost noon," Innocent said. "She won't be back, and we both know it. Stop the playacting, Kirby."

"You believed me last night, Innocent, you said so yourself."

"I talked a *lot* of nonsense last night."

"You had an epiphany."

"I *believe* what I had," Innocent said, "was the shortest nervous breakdown on record. The disappearance of a fine young woman looked like what caused it, but it was really brought on by overwork, male meno-whatever-it-is—"

"Pause."

"That's my problem, I never did. Just work work work, I thought I was tough enough to go on forever." He looked angry when he said all this, and Kirby was gradually coming to the realization that Innocent was partly angry at himself.

But not entirely; there was plenty left for Kirby. Glowering at him, Innocent said, "And smart fellas like you, Kirby, coming along all the time, looking for that edge, trying to put something over on me."

Betraying a bit of his grudge, Kirby said, "The way I put over that land deal on you, right?"

"What have you been *doing* with that land, Kirby?" Innocent stared at him round-eyed, leaning forward, alive with curiosity and frustration. "That's what caused this whole thing! That land up there"—he flung his hand toward the barren hill in question, just visible from the village—"isn't worth *shit*, Kirby!"

"That's not the way you talked when you sold it to me."

"What are you *doing* with it? What is all this goddam *temple* about?"

Kirby took a step back, head cocked, giving Innocent a wary look. "Temple, Innocent? Which temple is that?"

"That's what *I* want to know, dammit! You bring all these Americans down, give them some song and dance about a temple, there *isn't* any temple!"

"That's right."

"Valerie comes down, comes to *me*, Kirby, says she has computers up in New York tell her there's a temple on your land. Wants to go out to see it. That's where it all starts, Kirby. I wanted to know what you were up to."

"So you sent Valerie Greene out to see."

"She was coming anyway, that isn't the point."

"No," Kirby said, seeing it. "The point is, you made that creep of yours her driver."

"I regret that, Kirby," Innocent said. "I regret it bitterly. But I blame you as much as me."

"What? You turned that girl over to that hoodlum, and it's *my* fault?"

"I had to know what was going on," Innocent said. "What you were up to. That was the only driver I could trust."

"Some trust."

"Kirby," Innocent said, coming a step closer, calming himself by an obvious effort of will. "It's time to tell the truth, Kirby," he said.

"Go ahead."

"Time for *you*. I know you didn't kill Valerie Greene, just as surely as I know poor Valerie is dead. I know my own driver killed her and then ran away, so you don't have to put on this game any more."

"No game, Innocent," Kirby said, trying to look sincere. "Honest."

"Don't use words you don't understand, Kirby. I'm not even mad at you anymore. All you have to do is give up all the playacting, admit this is just one more of your cons, and we can go home."

"But it isn't. Valerie Greene actually was here, but now she's gone."

"If I know anything for certain in all of this, Kirby," Innocent said, "it is that you're lying."

Kirby paused, thought things over, and then said, "All right, Innocent, I have a deal for you."

Innocent's agitated face suddenly cleared, as though a storm over a pond had gone, leaving the surface smooth and blank. Even his eyes showed nothing as he said, "A deal, Kirby? What sort of deal?"

"Buy that land back," Kirby said.

"Why?"

"Buy it back for exactly what I paid you, and I'll tell you the full honest truth about Valerie Greene *and* the temple."

"Lava Sxir Yt."

"Oh, you know its name, do you?" Kirby said, and smiled his admiration.

Very faintly Innocent frowned. "That's not a deal," he decided.

"It is if we shake on it."

Innocent considered. He glanced over at the blighted hilltop. He studied Kirby. He said, "The truth, Kirby? How much of the truth?"

"I'll answer every question you ask, as long as you keep asking."

"Then I'll have the land *and* your con, whatever it is, and the truth about Valerie."

"That's right."

Again Innocent considered. "There were some expenses involved in the land transfer," he said.

"You eat them."

"Hmmm." Innocent brooded, and then faintly smiled. "I'll never know what the trick is until I say yes, will I?"

"It's up to you, Innocent." Kirby maintained a poker face, tried not to even *think* about anything. The instant

Innocent had mentioned the temple, Kirby had known the scam was doomed, it was about to become necessary to move on to something else. But here was a way to get out of it whole, get his money back and get rid of that scabrous hill, trade it all for a live girl and a dead racket. Not bad. Only don't think about it yet, don't let it cross your mind. It wouldn't surprise Kirby if Innocent were telepathic.

At last Innocent nodded. "All right," he said. "You have a deal." He put his hand out.

"Fine." Permitting himself only the tiniest of smiles, Kirby took Innocent's hand and they both squeezed down hard to seal the pact.

"*You!*" cried a familiar voice.

They turned, hands separating, and watched Valerie Greene leap with unconscious grace across the stream and come running toward them. Flushed, out of breath, quite dirty, somewhat ripped and torn, hair a mare's nest, she was rather astonishingly beautiful. Stopping in front of Kirby, chest heaving, hands on hips, she cried, "I know how bad you are, I know you're a terrible person, but nevertheless you're the only one I can turn to. Innocent people are going to be massacred, and *you* have to *help*!"

"Sure, lady," Kirby said.

Valerie Greene turned to frown in bewilderment at Innocent. Still on his feet though sagging, open-mouthed, glassy-eyed, shallow of breath, he seemed to be doing a Raggedy Andy imitation. "What's the matter with *him*?" she said.

"He just bought the farm," Kirby told her.

20

INSIDE THE JUNGLE THE LAND IS RICH

Inside the jungle the land is rich, almost black, fed over thousands of years of growth and decay, well-watered and fertilized. The lower slopes of the mountains are so lushly overgrown that a man with a machete is lucky to make five miles a day through its tangle, and each day the jungle grows in again behind him, so that a week or a month later he would still need his machete to follow his path back out.

The Espejo and Alpuche families had once lived in Chimaltenango Province, west of Guatemala City, but that became in the 70s one of the hottest areas of the revolution and the counterrevolution and the death squads and the army raids, so when the owner of the land where they sometimes harvested crops offered them a new life far to the east in the peaceful Peten, they accepted. They were sorry to leave their people and their land, but life was too frightening now in Chimaltenango, so they got on the trucks along with nearly a hundred other Quiché Indians, entire family groups, and drove for days over the rough roads, northeast above Guatemala City, through Salama and north through Coban into Peten Province, where they would live from now on.

None of them had ever had any formal schooling, but from time to time they had heard speeches on the radio about Belice, the province just to the east of the Peten. Belice was the Lost Province of Guatemala, stolen a long time ago by the British but some day to be recaptured by the brave young men of Guatemala. In the meantime, a state of not-quite-war existed between Belice and the rest of Guatemala, though the Indians imported from the west into the Peten were never actually aware of it.

The war they were aware of was the war they thought they'd left. The landowners had tried to get away from the revolution by moving into the underutilized and almost unpopulated Peten, a plateau of good plains land just waiting for the plow, but when they had imported workers from the west they'd imported the revolution as well. After a while, some of the Indians disappeared into the bush. Tourist buses heading up to the Mayan ruins at Tikal were attacked. Some Army jeeps were blown up and some soldiers ambushed and killed. Soon the death squads were roaming the area by night, as in Chimaltenango, savaging the innocent stay-at-homes since they couldn't find the actual revolutionaries.

Within four years, it had all turned very bad for the Espejo and Alpuche families. There were so few of them to service the owner's land that they were worked harder than at home. They were given no cash money, and less time than before to work their own plots of land for food.

They were separated from the support systems of their families and their tribe. They were away from their ancestral land, on some alien land they didn't know or understand. They were worse off than before they'd moved.

One day the owner made everybody come listen to a speech by an Army colonel who told them he intended to crush the revolution and slaughter every last revolutionary. He told them that if any of them were even suspected of aiding the revolutionaries they could expect no mercy. He told them to go on working for the owner, to never complain, to keep silent, and to do their duty and they would be safe. He told them that if any of them was thinking of running away to Belice they should forget it because they would be shot down and left in the jungle to rot if they tried it. Don't even think about running away to Belice, he told them.

On a clouded night two weeks later the 27 members of the Espejo and Alpuche families, 12 males and 15 females ranging in age from 53 years to three months, left their two one-room clapboard shacks and turned their faces east.

A 27-year-old woman who had always been sickly died along the way. They buried her.

They ate fruit, nuts, berries, roots, flowers, sometimes fish, less often birds or iguana or coati-mundi. They moved from the Peten plain into the Maya Mountains, traveling as far as they could each day, always frightened and always exhausted. They had no idea when they would leave the Peten and be in Belice, so they just kept going. On the 24th day they found a road ahead of them, crossing from north to south. While the rest of the family waited, two of the young men—an 11-year-old Espejo and a nine-year-old Alpuche—made their way to the two-lane blacktop road and hid beside it. Soon a truck came by. Its license plate was black with white numbers preceded by a large *A* and along the bottom it said *Belize*. Both young men were illiterate, but the 11-year-old had seen "Belice" on maps and remembered it.

Three automobiles went by over the next half hour, all with license plates having black lettering on a white ground, starting with the letter *C* and with the word *Belize* along the bottom. The man and woman in the third automobile, well dressed and laughing together, were quite obviously black people, which was the final proof: in Guatemala, black people are not encouraged. The scouts went back and reported their conclusion: they were in Belice.

The families retreated a bit farther from the road, found a fairly level place in the jungle, and cleared a small patch of land. The trunks and branches and fronds they cleared away were used to make three huts. More land was cleared and the seeds they'd brought with them were planted: corn, yams, beans.

Four months after arrival they were a going village, 28 people strong, two of the women having made the trip pregnant. They were harvesting crops, they were hunting successfully. Having found a few similar tiny settlements around them in the jungle, they had done some trading and now had two piglets, one male and one female, which were guarded with great care.

One day a pair of strangers came in from the road, bouncing in a Land Rover up the rough trail the people had made. They were a man and woman who spoke a crisp kind of Spanish, hard to understand, and who said they were from the government of Belize. Seeing the fright this caused, they promised not to make any trouble, but said they had come only to find out if the people needed help in any way. No, the people said, they needed no help. Well, if they ever needed anything, the man and woman told them, medical help, for instance, anything like that, all they had to do was go out to the road, turn right, and about 11 miles south they would find a town with a police station. "The police don't have guns, and they aren't mad at you," the woman said, smiling.

The people didn't believe the man and woman, but on the other hand these strangers seemed to have no ulterior motive, so they smiled and nodded and thanked them for the information. The man and woman said the town also had a weekend market if they ever had excess produce to sell, and had a Roman Catholic church, if the villagers were interested. (They were.) And a school for the children. (Maybe later.)

Cautiously, after that, the people broadened their contacts with this new land. A few occasionally went to the Catholic church, though they weren't yet ready to talk to the priest, who was nothing they'd ever seen before, being neither Indian nor black nor Spanish. A sale of yams in the market had produced cash; crumpled pale-green Belizean dollars with Queen Elizabeth II on them and frail-seeming Belizean coins, which they kept in a sack in one of the huts, not sure yet what to use them for.

The man and woman, in the meantime, having returned to the capital at Belmopan, had entered this new settlement of refugees onto a map. The two families by chance happening to be of equal strength there, the man and woman named the settlement Espejo-Alpuche.

21

ZOTZ

"Valerie," Innocent said, "what do you expect *us* to do about it?"

The false Gurkhas, irritated and uneasy at the disappearance of the tall American woman, hacked their way northward through the jungle.

"There isn't *time* to radio for help!" Valerie cried.

No one in the van noticed Vernon moaning and shaking his head and punching his thighs as he drove, because Scottie was telling a story involving female Siamese twins, an Israeli Nazi-hunter and a one-kilo package of uncut cocaine in a box marked *Baking Soda*.

Kirby stood frowning westward, thinking hard, brooding at those tumbled dark mountains. "It's worth a try," he said.

The false Gurkhas came to a gravel road and boldly crossed it. A British Army jeep went by as they did so, bluish gray, and the two uniformed Brits inside it waved as they passed, the false Gurkhas waving back.

"Tell me what to do," Valerie said.
Kirby said, "I need thin cloth, cotton, the thinner the better, and a lot of it."

Tom, the American photojournalist, called out, "Vernon, how the hell much farther is this damn place?"
"Oh, twenty-twenty-twenty minutes, no more," Vernon told him, showing an agonized smile in the rearview mirror.

Innocent stared at the dancing leering Zotzes: "What *are* those things?"

"Devils," Tommy told him.

Halfway up the slope, Kirby stopped to look back. Valerie and Rosita and Luz Coco were cutting and hacking the sheets into squares or rectangles or ovals, a foot and a half or two feet across. None of them were making the circles he'd asked for, but it didn't really matter. Half the village was running in and out of huts, looking for string. Tommy and Innocent came together out of one of the huts, each carrying a cardboard carton; they started this way.

Kirby nodded, and hurried on over the hill to start Cynthia.

One of the young men of the village came into the clearing. "Soldiers coming," he announced.

Everyone stopped what they were doing to stare at him or move closer to him or ask, "Who? Which soldiers? What kind of soldiers?"

"Gurruhs," said the young man, which was as close as they'd come so far to the word *Gurkha*.

Twice in the last several months Gurkha patrols had moved through here, short black-haired men who held their shoulders proudly and handled their strange severe weapons confidently and yet smiled with amazingly bright teeth. The Gurkhas were a different kind of soldier, without the sullenness and fear and cruelty and tendency toward petty crime—and sometimes major crime—of the soldiers of their previous world. When the young man said, "Gurruhs," they all smiled and relaxed. *That* kind of soldier. Fine.

Valerie, her arms billowing with cloth, came over the barren hilltop and saw Kirby Galway just getting into his plane. Innocent and Tommy were partway down the slope, carrying their cartons. Rosita and Luz followed Valerie with the rest of the cloth, and a half dozen villagers straggled up the slope in their wake, carrying bits of string, cord, twine and rope.

Is this going to work? Valerie frowned, thinking of the innocent villagers about to be slaughtered. Against murderers and machine guns, *this?* But what else is there to do?

She hurried down the farther slope.

Crouched on the blacktop in front of the van, Vernon shook open the map, holding it by its very edge with his fingertips as he guided it to the ground. It slipped from his grasp; he slapped at it. Just out of sight in the brush, Scottie had found a hollow log to piss resoundingly against. Across the road Morgan Lassiter, the woman journalist, was out of both sight and hearing for the moment, having gone discreetly away with a handful of Kleenex. The other news gatherers strolled around the empty road, yawning and stretching. Hiram Farley, the *Trend* editor, came over to place his Frye boots beside the map and say, "You know where this place is, do you?"

"Oh, yes," Vernon said, looking up at him, squinting as though he stared into the too-bright sun. Farley's face showed nothing, his eyes were level and patient. Why do I feel he knows my soul? But that's just foolishness; if he knew the truth, he'd stop me.

There was some wistfulness in that idea.

"Everything's fine," Vernon said.

Innocent said, "Kirby, this is a crazy idea." With some difficulty he had climbed up on the wing and was leaning in at the plane's open door so he could talk to Kirby above the engine noise. Wind whipped at his clothing, and the plane trembled all over. "A *crazy* idea," he said, more loudly.

Kirby, studying his instrument panel, gave Innocent an impatient look: "Do you have a better one?"

"Radio the police. Radio the British soldiers at Holdfast," meaning the small British Army detachment out near the Guatemalan border.

"I'll do that, once we're airborne, but it won't do much good. If Valerie's right, there isn't time to send for help. At the very worst, maybe we can slow them down."

Innocent looked past Kirby at Valerie in the other front seat. She was riding with him because she was the only one with a hope of leading him back to where she'd been. Now, her head was bent forward, she was busily tying strings to cloth. Her profile rang like a gong in Innocent's soul. "By God, she's alive," he said.

"And our deal still holds," Kirby told him.

Was there something underhanded about the deal if Valerie were not dead? No; nothing you could put your finger on. Innocent sighed. "I suppose it does," he said.

The false Gurkhas entered the village.

Valerie looked up from her knot-tying as the plane suddenly jolted forward. She looked at Kirby, then out at the Indians backing away from the plane. Innocent St. Michael was out there, waving, offering her a kind of sad smile. She hesitated, then smiled and waved back.

Had she been wrong about him? Was Innocent *not* the archvillain? His almost pathetic pleasure in seeing her alive—she was sure for just one second she had seen a tear in his eye—could not possibly have been pretense. The plane taxied forward, and Innocent was left behind, out of sight. But if Vernon and the skinny black man had not been obeying Innocent's orders, then whose? Who *was* the mastermind behind the plot?

This man Kirby, coming so promptly to the rescue of poor endangered Indians he'd never even met, couldn't be the ringleader. All you had to do was look at him when he wasn't waving a sword in your face to see he wasn't the type.

Who, then?

There came into her memory again the last words she had heard between Vernon and the skinny black man in that filthy shack where they'd been holding her prisoner. The skinny black man had said, "Say it out, Vernon. Say what you want." There had been a pause, and then Vernon had said, so low she could barely hear it, "She has to die."

It had been his order.

Vernon was the ringleader? He'd certainly been the one to make that particular decision, but somehow the idea of Vernon as Mister Big . . .

The plane had swung about, and now it suddenly raced madly out across the dry and bumpy ground, shaking itself to pieces. The angle of the plane was such that from inside it they couldn't see the ground out the windshield but only the sky; how could Kirby be sure there was nothing in front of them?

The roar, the speed, all were so much more *present* than in a big sensible airliner, and then all at once the trembling

328 *Donald E. Westlake*

stopped, the roar grew somehow less frantic, and out the side window Valerie could see the ground falling away below.

"Tie knots!" Kirby yelled.

"Oh! Yes, sorry." She bent her head, tied knots, then paused to look at his profile. He was reaching for the microphone, turning dials on the instrument panel. She leaned toward him: "Do you know someone named Vernon?"

He frowned at her. "Vernon What?"

"Never mind," she said, and went back to tying knots. He gave her an irritable confused look, then started talking into the microphone in his cupped hand.

"It will be along here," Vernon said, the van moving slowly as he watched the right-hand verge. The jungle was deep and green and moist, tumbled and piled up high on the right. Behind him, the journalists started gathering their paraphernalia.

"Yes, there it is."

Vernon braked to a stop, then turned the van very slowly off the road and onto an up-tilted patch of eroded rutted ground, cleared barely as wide as the vehicle, with stones and dirt and roots under its wheels. Engine roaring, the van struggled up the slope, branches and vines scraping both sides. Vernon clutched hard to the steering wheel, as boulders tried to deflect the wheels and drive him into tree trunks or ditches. Even at two or three miles an hour, the van jounced so badly that everybody in it had to hold on.

Too narrow; too steep; impossible. Vernon stopped the van, switched off the engine. In the sudden humming silence, he said, "We have to walk from here."

"Hold on, chum," Scottie called. "The idea was, this place is *accessible*."

"It's just up ahead there," Vernon said, pointing out the windshield. "We just walk up to it."

"Accessible by *vehicle*, old son."

"Not past here."

Tom, the American photojournalist, leaned forward to look past Vernon's shoulder, saying, "A Land Rover would make it."

"Too many of us for a Land Rover." Vernon's eyelids were fluttering, he was aware of black-and-white pinwheels at the extreme edges of his peripheral vision.

Scottie, all jollity gone, called, "There's no villages easier to get to than *this*?"

"Oh, come along, Scottie," Morgan Lassiter said. "Work some of that lard off your gut." And she slid open the van door to climb out.

That did it. With a woman to lead the way, the men all sheepishly followed, climbing down out of the van, pushing past the leaves and branches, hanging their canvas bags of equipment on their shoulders.

"This way," Vernon said. His legs were trembling, his knees were jelly, but none of it showed. "This way," he said. Soon it will be over. "This way." He started up the hill.

Why am I doing this? Kirby wondered. Of all the brainless things I have ever done in my life, this has to rank right up there among the best of them. Buying Innocent's land, for instance; this could conceivably be even dumber than that.

In the first place, there's no reason on Earth for this stunt to work.

In the second place, the woman I'm helping, this Valerie Greene riding along with me on this rescue mission, is the primary cause of all my recent trouble, and is someone I dislike so intensely I'm amazed I'm not at this moment shoving her out of the plane.

In the third place, whether the stunt works or not, the end result of trying it must be that the temple scam is blown permanently and forever. Innocent already knows too much about it, Valerie Greene is going to figure things out any minute now, and even the people on the *ground* are likely to catch on, once the fun is over.

In the fourth place, some of those people on the ground have machine guns and could possibly even shoot Cynthia out of the sky.

In the fifth place, it isn't my fight.

Valerie, busily tying knots, said, "I really appreciate this, Mr. Galway. I don't know how to thank you."

"It's nothing," Kirby said.

The Quiché Indians of western Guatemala are not among the tribes who speak some variant of Kekchi. It was in a different language entirely—mixed with some Spanish— that the people welcomed the Gurruh soldiers, smiling at them, nodding, gesturing for them to sit a moment, offering them water.

The Gurruh looked around, not seeming to know what to do. They talked to one another in their incomprehensible tongue, they smiled rather meaninglessly at the people, and they wandered around the outsides of the three huts, gazing at things. One of them picked up the female piglet and held it high with one hand around its neck, the piglet squeaking and its pink hoofs thrashing the air as the Gurruh said something to the other soldiers and laughed. Then he put the piglet down again.

There was some strangeness about these Gurruh, all the people sensed it. They weren't like the first two groups, they didn't exude the same air of self-sufficiency and disinterested amiability. One of them went into a hut uninvited, picked up an orange without asking, and came out eating it.

A young man of the village, an Alpuche, had been looking toward the trail that led down to the road. "Someone else is coming," he said.

"Can you circle just once more!" Valerie Greene asked. She was tying nooses now.

Kirby, a bit annoyed, banked Cynthia hard and made a gliding swooping turn over the tumbled land below. "You're the one says it's urgent."

"I just want to be sure." Noose in hand, she peered down at that disorderly maze of greens and browns. "Yes! There's the stream where I— That's the stream from this morning. See it?"

Kirby rolled Cynthia over and came back, while Valerie clung open-mouthed to her seat. "Got it," he said. "Due north from there they said?"

"One—" Silence.

Kirby looked over and saw her distress. "Sorry," he said, and turned Cynthia right side up. "One hour north," he said. "On foot."

"Yes," Valerie said.

The false Gurkhas saw the people looking toward the trail up from the road, and unlimbered their Sterling submachine guns. The villagers, already sensing something wrong about these soldiers, now drew back, wide-eyed, and everybody in the small clearing grew silent, except the female piglet, still squealing and shrilling about the indignity that had been done her.

High above, the sky was clear and blue. Thick brush and great trees surrounded the clearing, arching high overhead, and smaller trees had been left to stand beside the huts for shade. Except in the very center, where steady sunlight shone on their plantings, the settlement was dappled with rays reaching through the trees, angling down to touch with creamy light this person, that hut, that finger resting gently on a trigger. At the narrow end of the clearing, a patch of hotter, brighter light backed by fuzzy greens and yellows showed the top of the trail up from the road.

An Espejo girl, eight years old, picked up the piglet and cradled it in her arms. Her thudding heartbeat calmed the piglet, which grew quiet.

A straggling group of eight people, hot and sweaty and sun-dazzled, appeared at the end of the silent clearing and came slowly in, looking around themselves.

Vernon saw the Gurkhas, saw them holding the machine guns, and moaned as he dropped to his knees, unaware of the journalists staring at him in astonishment. "No," he said, too late.

"The last one," Valerie said, tightening the final noose on the final neck.

"Good."

The hurried work finished, Valerie for the first time had a chance to actually *look* at these things. She held a small statue in each hand, the identical little evil creatures capering there with the nooses around their necks. "These—" she said, and frowned. "Are you sure these are real?"

"Van parked there, in from the blacktop road. See it?"

She saw it, partway into the green jungle, white roof gleaming, front of the vehicle pointed west, away from the road. "This must be it!"

"And the visitors are here already."

Valerie clutched tightly to the Zotzilaha Chimalmans as the plane banked and dropped low to the ground.

The sound of a passing plane was drowned by the chatter. Nine-millimeter bullets stuttered across the clearing, chopping Scottie's legs out from under him and punching Vernon's stomach three times, in a line just above his belt. People screamed and ran, and three villagers fell bleeding.

The plane was louder, not passing after all. Disturbed at their work, the false Gurkhas looked up as the plane roared through the clearing, sideways, right wingtip pointing down at them as though to say, "You. I see you."

"Throw them!" Kirby yelled. "Throw them!"

Valerie was too busy to answer. She was lying on her side, against the side wall of the plane, elbow on the fixed part of the window. As quickly as she could, she pushed the little statues one at a time through the window flap.

Zotzilaha Chimalman. Out of the plane he fell, time after time, swathed in cotton material, the cloth pulling away in the breeze of his falling. The noose around his neck was made of four strings, tied to four edges of the cloth; enough of a parachute for such a little devil.

Two false Gurkhas lifted their Sterlings, but the plane was already through the clearing and gone, circling. The people were running into the jungle, the journalists lay flat in the sunlight. Creatures floated down out of the sky.

Cynthia made a hard, tight circle through the air, left wing straight up and right wing straight down, and once more she crashed through the clearing. More demons plummeted from her side.

A false Gurkha aimed his Sterling at one of the things parachuting toward him. He peered through the metal arch of the foresight protector, focusing on the gray-brown figure in the air. He recognized it. A great fright struck him and he stared, forgetting to shoot.

Vernon, curled in a tight ball around the agony in his stomach, wept, and blamed the Colonel for everything.

A false Gurkha clutched a statue out of the air, held it in his hand, stared at it in disbelief. Dirt clung to it, as though it had just come from the grave; some of the dirt was now on his hand. Suddenly, he flung the thing away. He thought his hand was burning. Stepping back, his foot rolled on a statue on the ground; it tried to trip him, bite him, bring him down. He shrieked, threw away his Sterling, and ran.

"There aren't any more!" Valerie cried.

Kirby lifted Cynthia up and away. Valerie tried to see back to the village. "Wait! What's happening back there?"

"Give them a minute to think about it. Then we'll go back and see."

What was this airplane? How had it come to be exactly where the false Gurkhas were, exactly at the moment when they were starting their work? Had they been betrayed? Were other enemies on the way?

These were the rational problems, the sensible questions, the meaningful dilemmas. They were as nothing beside the creatures hanging in the sky.

Twenty Zotzilahas floating down through the dappled air, falling one by one to the ground, gathering their cotton cloaks about themselves, grimacing and winking and grinning at the false Gurkhas, three more of whom flung away their guns and ran for the jungle.

"Come back!" the leader shouted, and fired after them, missing.

Another, backing away from the devils, saw the leader turn eyes and gun in his direction and he fired first, killing the leader 11 times.

Two more murderers in Gurkha uniform ran away into the jungle, these keeping their weapons.

Valerie stared back at the anonymous green. She wanted to *see*. Fretfully, she said, "Could they be that afraid of clay?"

"Their ancestors were."

The false Gurkhas had been brought up in Christian homes. They had been taught to know and to love God and the Blessed Virgin Mary and all the saints. They had been taught to despise Satan and all his works. They had risen above such education, and struck out to live their own lives by their own rules.

No one had ever told them they had to believe in the Mayan gods and the Mayan devils. Those beings were there in the stories, that's all, there in the drawings and the cloth designs and the carvings, there in the rites and ceremonies that a minority of their older relatives sometimes engaged in. Nobody had ever told them they *had* to believe in Zotzilaha Chimalman, and yet none of them had ever in his heart doubted that the cave of bats existed, the forked road to eternity existed, the evil hater of mankind was there in the darkness just waiting the *opportunity* to drag them down to eternal death.

He flies, Zotzilaha, he comes out of the sky like a bat. He is full of tricks and malevolence. If he catches you when your heart is black, you're doomed.

When the sound of the plane was heard again in the clearing, there were only five false Gurkhas left in it, four living and their leader, who was dead. The dead one lay surrounded by images of Zotzilaha Chimalman.

When the silence in the clearing ended, filled up instead by the growing buzz of the airplane, the last four of the false Gurkhas faded away into the jungle.

The plane roared overhead again, and gone, and Vernon opened his eyes. Through his pain and tears he could see the villagers clustered around their three fallen relatives, the journalists gathering around Scottie. Hiram Farley, separate from both groups, bent to pick up one of the figures that had fallen from the plane.

Vernon closed his eyes. Everything he saw was red. The pain in his stomach was duller and his brain seemed to move more slowly.

When he opened his eyes again, Hiram Farley was

standing over him, hefting the little statue in his hand. "Well, Vernon," Farley said.

Vernon slowly blinked. With his mouth open to breathe, dirt was filtering in, coating his tongue and teeth.

"Now why, Vernon," Farley said, "would Asian soldiers be afraid of a Central American devil? Something tells me you can answer that question."

Vernon looked at Farley's dusty boots. He mumbled something.

"What was that, Vernon?"

" 'They didn't even kill me,' I said."

22

CHICKEN ESTELLE (SERVES FOUR)

"*That* isn't South Abilene,"
Valerie said.

Kirby Galway turned the little plane in a long slow parabola, out and around, while down below a man and woman chased goats from the long green field surrounded by forest. At one end of the field was a squat brown house with several additions, and behind it patches of cultivation.
"No, it isn't," Galway said.

She gave his bland profile an extremely suspicious look. "What is it, then?"

"Where I live."

"Why are we going there?" After all she'd been through, must she now defend herself from *this* man's attentions?

Galway made minor adjustments with the plane's controls; its nose was aimed now at that long field, with the tiny house and the tiny people at the far end and the goats all cleared away. He said, "I want to talk to you before you talk to Innocent."

"Why?"

"I'll tell you when we're on the ground."

She watched him, but he had nothing else to say. But wasn't what he'd already said significant, didn't it mean once and for all that Kirby Galway was *not* in league with Innocent St. Michael? If there was some secret he wanted to keep from Innocent—and what else could he be planning?—it meant they weren't partners in crime after all.

So which one was the criminal?

And what was the crime?

It was all too confusing. She had seen the temple, exactly where it was supposed to be, where she and the computers had both predicted it would be, and then two weeks later, at the precise same spot, it was *gone*. She had seen Kirby Galway with Whitman Lemuel from that museum and had *known* it meant they were stealing rare Mayan treasures and smuggling them out of the country, but when she'd at last held several of those treasures in her hands she'd found herself doubting they were real. She had thought Vernon was working for Galway or Innocent or possibly both of them, and now it *seemed* to turn out he'd been working only for himself. And what had Vernon been trying to do? Get his hands on the (fake) treasures of the (nonexistent) temple? She shook her head, and spoke her frustration aloud: "What is everybody *up* to?"

He laughed. "I'm actually going to tell you," he said, and the plane bounced on the uneven turf, bounced again, landed, settled, and slowed to a sedate roll as they neared the house, where the man and woman stood waiting, smiling.

"I'm beginning to remember," Valerie said slowly, "that you're a very bad man. You are, aren't you?"

"Extremely bad," he said, and the plane turned toward a copse of trees on the right.

"Except when you're rescuing people," she acknowledged.

"My one saving grace," he said, and the plane stopped in tree shadow. Galway switched off the engine, and the silence flowed in like a wave.

There was no door on her side. She had to wait while he unstrapped and climbed out, then follow him, crawling across his seat and accepting his hand to balance her as she made it down to the ground.

The air here was very warm and heavy after so long in the plane, and she found herself stiff and sore when she tried to walk. The couple had come over to greet them— the man short, the woman much shorter—and Galway led Valerie around the wing to make the introductions: "Estelle Cruz, Manny Cruz, this is Valerie Greene."

"How do you do?"

"Hello, hello, hello."

When Manny Cruz smiled, he had many more spaces for teeth than he had teeth, but somehow that merely made his smile look happier. And for such a gnarled little woman, Estelle Cruz's smile was surprisingly shy and girlish.

Galway removed both those smiles by then saying, "Miss Greene is an extemely annoying woman who has absolutely loused up everything I've been doing here."

Estelle glared at Valerie, who gaped at her accuser in shock. Manny said, "This is Sheena! So she *is* alive." He didn't sound happy about it.

"That's right," Galway said. "The temple scam is dead, everything's gone to hell in a handbasket, and I'll probably have to move out of this country."

The Cruzes were both terribly shocked. Estelle looked

as though she might leap on Valerie and claw her to death, while Manny said, "Move from this *house*, Kirby?"

"It isn't her fault, Manny," Galway said. "She didn't do it on purpose; she's just stupid and ignorant."

"Now, wait a minute," Valerie said.

"She thought she was doing right," Galway went smoothly on, "so I don't blame her. And now she can help me in one little way, and that's why I brought her here, to tell her the whole story, and I'm sure she's going to want to help out."

Valerie looked at them all suspiciously, even Estelle, whose manner was just as mistrustful as her own. "I won't commit any crimes," she said.

Galway gave her an enigmatic look: "If I were going to commit a crime, Miss Greene," he said, "you're about the *last* person I'd ask to be my accomplice."

If that was an insult—and it did seem to have been intended as such—it had to be one of the strangest insults in history. Feeling mulish and put-upon, Valerie said, "That's all right, then."

Manny said, "Whadaya want her to do, Kirby?"

"Let's talk over lunch," Galway said. "I'm starved." Looking at Valerie, he said, "How about you?"

Dear God! Her stomach! In all the excitement and activity and confusion, she hadn't even noticed, but all of a sudden her stomach gave her such a *hunger pang* she actually gasped from it. Food? When was the last time she'd eaten? Nothing at all today, nothing since last night, on the run, when she'd eaten those tortillas.

The very thought made her head swim.

"Right," Galway said, correctly reading her expression. "We'll just wash up and then eat out here, Estelle, okay?"

Estelle nodded, tentatively smiling again, waving at the outdoor table beside the house.

Galway said, "Kids all in school? Just the four of us? What are we having?"

"Escabeche," said Estelle.

ESCABECHE (Ess-ka-*bet*-che)

One hen.
Two large onions.
Spices.

Kill, pluck and separate the hen. Stew in water one hour, adding cloves, pepper, and chopped-up chilis to taste.

While hen is stewing, prepare tortillas in usual manner, and thinly slice onions.

Add onions to stew for the last 15 minutes.

Serve stew in large bowls. Place napkin in bottom of basket, place tortillas in basket, close napkin across top, place in center of table.

Place small bottle of Pineridge Hot Pepper Sauce on table.

Open four bottles of Belikin beer, place on table.

Stand back.

"Oh, my, this is good," Valerie said.

"There's more," Estelle told her, beaming from wrinkled ear to wrinkled ear.

"More beer?" Manny asked. "Kirby? Valerie?"

"Oh, yes," everybody said, and Valerie was surprised to find herself smiling at Kirby, who grinned back and reached for another tortilla.

Kirby. Valerie. They were on a first-name basis now, ever since he had shown her into his surprisingly neat and Spartan apartment to clean up before lunch and she'd said, "Which door is the bathroom, Mister Galway?" and he had looked at her and said, "I don't like to be called

Mister Galway except by the police, and I refuse to call you Miss Greene any more, so what shall we call each other? Shall I call you Fido, and you call me Spot?'' So that was that.

Sunlight gleamed on the yellow hair on Kirby Galway's arm as he raised his spoon and ate. She kept glancing at him, thinking he had a good laugh and an easy self-confident manner, and it was too bad really that he was such a villain. If, in fact, he was a villain.

Was he not a villain? At his most furious with her, when he was waving that sword about, he hadn't actually *used* it on her. A villain—and Valerie had met some villains now—would certainly have sliced her head off at that point, and thought no more about it.

Nor was he even a vile seducer. The contrast between this lunch and the eating of conch with Innocent that time was so extreme it almost made her laugh out loud. Innocent had been so smooth and so accomplished, and had just *filled* her mind with thoughts of sex. Kirby Galway laughed and told jokes and ate his escabeche and didn't try to manipulate her at all, made not the slightest effort to fill her mind with thoughts of sex.

And if her mind *was* filled with thoughts of sex, quite suddenly and unexpectedly, making her blush—they'll think it's the hot sauce, and it almost is—she knew enough psychology to know it was merely a normal reaction to being in safety after a period of extreme danger and extended physical stress.

And, of course, the sun gleaming on the yellow hair on Kirby's arm.

He looked up and caught her eye and grinned, and she looked down at her bowl, suddenly flustered. Then, afraid she'd given herself away, she looked over at him again and he was frowning slightly at his own bowl, thinking about something.

Time to change the subject. "Listen, Kirby," she said. "You wanted to tell me something."

"Right." He nodded at her, his brow clearing. "You're right, Valerie," he said. "It's time I told you what's been going on."

"Good," she said, and went on eating while he talked.

23

HOW TO MAKE MONEY IN
REAL ESTATE

Kirby told her the truth, almost every last little bit of it. "My big mistake," he started, "was when I bought some land from Innocent," and then he went on to tell her about the land, his finances, his meeting with Tommy Watson and the other Indians, his invention of the temple and the Indians faking the artifacts under Tommy's direction, and Kirby himself going off to find his suckers in America to buy the fakes. "*They* think they're breaking the law, so they don't tell anybody about it."

"So what I saw," Valerie said, with a wondering expression, "was your fake temple."

"A little bit of it, from a distance."

"It was very good."

"That was mostly Tommy's doing. Anyway, when I first met *you*," and he went on to describe Valerie's inadvertent foiling of his first attempt to snare Whitman Lemuel, mentioning it with hardly any visible resentment at all, and then went on to tell her about the Indians dismantling the fake temple just as soon as she'd seen it, because everybody knew she was on her way back to Belmopan to report her discovery.

At that point, Valerie took over briefly, and told Kirby about her experiences with Vernon and the skinny black man and her wanderings in the wilderness, all of which had apparently been very difficult and frightening, though she was brave about it in the recital.

Kirby then took over again, saying, "Well, anyway, you were lost, and Innocent kept going back and forth between believing you were alive and believing you were dead, and if you were dead then he was sure I was pulling some con to persuade him you were alive for some reason, and back and forth like that. Also, he was going crazy about that hill and is there or isn't there a temple."

"We were *all* going crazy, Kirby."

"Well," Kirby said, "I offered him a deal. Buy the damn land back from me at the same price I paid for it, and I'd tell him the absolute truth about you *and* the temple, whether you were alive or not, and what the temple scam was."

Valerie looked quite interested: "Did he say yes?"

"He did."

"Well, that was very sweet," she said, looking doe-eyed. "That Innocent would worry about me that much."

"Sure," Kirby said. "But that's why I didn't take you back there just now. Innocent and I no sooner shook hands on the deal when you showed up alive, so he already has that part. That's half my deal gone already. Now, with what you already knew about my land and the people in

South Abilene, and with what Innocent already knew, he
could have put together for himself what I was doing with
my temple scam, not needing to pay me to tell him about
it, and that's the other half. So why does he need *me* any
more?''

"Oh," Valerie said.

"If I know Innocent—and I do—at that point he would
have found some way to weasel out of buying back the
land.''

"So you don't want me to talk to him," Valerie said,
"until *he* has the land and *you* have your money.''

"That's right.''

Her expression was extremely enigmatic: "Do you mean
I've been kidnapped again?''

Feeling a bit uncomfortable, Kirby said, "I was hoping,
after I explained the whole thing, you'd sort of see it my
way and agree to wait a little while. Not long. I mean,
nobody's pinning your arms down or anything.''

"Mmm," she said, and folded her arms across her
breasts to sort of pat her own biceps.

"It would just be for a day or two," Kirby assured her.

"Mmm," she said again, and then she yawned, covering her mouth with her hand. "I'm too tired to think now,
Kirby," she said. Raising her arms over her head, she
arched her back and *strrrretched*. She was, Kirby noticed,
very interesting when she stretched. "Lunch was delicious," she told Estelle lazily, "but it made me so *sleepy*.''

"That's good," Estelle said. "You just sit, I clean up.''

Looking over at Kirby, her eyes round and guileless,
Valerie said, "Your little apartment looked *so* cool and
comfortable. Maybe I could just go there and take a nap.''

"Sure," Kirby said, getting up from the table. "I'll
walk you over.''

She smiled, looking up at him from under her lashes as
she rose.

Sex. How about that? If he and Valerie Greene got a

little something on together, maybe she'd be more on his side in re: Innocent. He had no idea where that idea came from, it was just suddenly there, just sort of popped up into his mind.

He ignored Estelle's giggle as he escorted Valerie around the corner of the house.

24

PRESENT IMPERFECT

Saturday morning and Innocent sat in his office in Belmopan, his old self again, playing the telephone like a virtuoso, taking care of business he'd let go all to hell, covering his ass in every conceivable direction, and primarily seeing to it that none of the mud from the Vernon affair would stick to his own voluminous skirts.

Vernon. Who would have guessed? "I trusted that boy," Innocent muttered aloud, yet even as he said it he knew that wasn't the really accurate way to describe the situation. Innocent hadn't exactly *trusted* Vernon, it wasn't in Innocent's character or training to throw something like *trust* around with a lavish hand, but what he had done was something that had the exact same effect as misplaced trust: he had underestimated Vernon. Patronized him, condescended to him, assumed that Vernon had no importance.

"And all along he was selling me out."

Selling out his nation, too, of course, but that was secondary. He had betrayed *Innocent*, which meant Innocent had been unwary enough to get into a position where betrayal was possible. Now, among all the other things he was taking care of today, Innocent was going through Vernon's desk and correspondence files, seeing what other unpleasant surprises might be in store, while down in Belize City Hospital Vernon was busily spilling what guts he had left, telling everything he knew about everything, naming every name.

"He could hurt me, that boy, if I'm not quick."

"Talking to yourself, Innocent?"

Innocent looked up, frowning, not liking to believe he was the sort of person who talked to himself, certainly not wanting to be caught at it, and there was Kirby, grinning in the doorway, dressed for flying business in his open-neck shirt and khaki slacks and sturdy boots. "Well, Kirby," Innocent growled, seeing nothing in *that* doorway that pleased him, "and what the hell happened to you yesterday?"

"Saved a village," Kirby told him, grinning. "Went home to rest."

"And what about Valerie?"

"Here she is." Kirby stepped into the office then, and Valerie followed, looking happy and healthy and just a bit sheepish.

That son of a gun took her to bed, Innocent thought. There was pain in the thought, but also release. One of the things he'd been trying not to think about ever since Kirby and Valerie and the plane had all flown away yesterday from South Abilene was what he would feel—and what Valerie would feel—the next time they saw one another. The gradual suspicion had been forming inside him that the great life-changing love he had felt for Valerie was perhaps easier to maintain when she was dead or disappeared, a great mythic figure, than when she was an actual flesh-and-blood girl. The epiphany that Kirby had claimed Innocent was having the night before last in South Abilene had been a great shaking and cleansing of his system, long overdue he now believed, but it probably wouldn't have been possible if Valerie had not been both (1) good, and (2) unobtainable.

So what should their relationship be, now that she was no longer among the missing and he'd already had his apotheosis? To go on being obsessed by her when she was *present* would be kind of silly, but what was the alternative?

On the other hand, even if she were no longer a goddess on earth but merely a woman, she was still quite an intriguing woman, and that pleasant afternoon spent in Vernon's house—Vernon! by God, he knows so *much*! —was something Innocent would not at all mind repeating. Just how long would it take to get used to and bored with this great big tall girl with her happy enjoyments? It would be fun to find out.

But it was not to be. One look at Valerie, and a second look at Kirby, confirmed it, and a moment of sadness and nostalgia and regret passed over Innocent, like the final tremor when you're getting over the flu. But then it was washed away by a sudden flood of relief: He would not have to follow through on his protestations of love after all. He would not have to behave toward Valerie present as he had sworn he wanted to when she was Valerie absent. He could have his epiphany, and get away with it!

"Well, come on in, you two," he said, rising from behind his desk, beaming at them, coming all over avuncular. "Looks to me like you've buried the hatchet."

"We straightened out one or two things," Kirby agreed.

"We talked it all out," Valerie said, smiling softly, "and we understand one another now."

"But what we're here for, Innocent," Kirby said, "I want to make good on our deal. You already know about Valerie, but I promised to tell you about the temple."

"Oh, you don't have to, Kirby," Innocent said, just as smiling and open and friendly as anything. "What I saw in South Abilene, and talking with Tommy Watson, I've got it pretty well figured out by now."

"Hmm," said Kirby. He didn't seem pleased.

"And then the tape, that helped," Innocent said. "But you haven't heard the tape, have you?"

"What tape?"

So Innocent got the tape out of the locked desk drawer and put it in the cassette player, and once again those sounds and words filled his office: "This way, gentlemen. Watch out for snakes." *Throk.* "The noise keeps them in their holes."

Valerie just looked bewildered, but Kirby stared at the cassette player as though it were *his* ancestors' form of Zotzilaha Chimalman. The words and the sound effects went on, and Kirby just stood there and stared and listened until his own voice said, "Do you know how many people there are in New Jersey?" and that other voice said, "No one *I* know."

"Witcher and Feldspan!"

Innocent hit the STOP button. "They recorded every conversation with you, Kirby."

"Holy Christ! *Those* two?"

"Never underestimate people," Innocent said: *Vernon.*

"But— They're legitimate antique dealers!"

"That's right. Doing undercover reporter work for a friend of theirs named Hiram Farley, editor of a big American magazine called *Trend*. Ever hear of *Trend*, Kirby?"

"Those dirty bastards."

"I managed to have them lose these tapes at the airport," Innocent said, "or otherwise you and your temple would be all over *Trend* magazine by now. You didn't know I was helping you like that, did you?"

"Didn't want me blown out of the water," Kirby said, "until you figured out what I was up to and how you could horn in on it."

"You always think the worst of me, Kirby," Innocent said, and risked a smile at Valerie, telling her, "I hope *you* won't be like that, Valerie."

"*I always* say nice things about you, Mister St. Michael," Valerie said.

Innocent almost laughed out loud. Oh, good, Kirby, you have no *idea* what you're hooked onto here. He said, "The point is, Kirby, if you think of dealing with those fellas again, just remember these tapes."

"Oh, I will," Kirby said grimly, "but the deal I most want to talk about, Innocent, is ours. We did shake hands on—"

"Kirby, Kirby, do you think I'd try to *renege*?"

Kirby frowned at him: "You won't?"

"Certainly not. It's true I know Valerie's alive without you having to tell me; there she is, as beautiful as ever."

"Thank you, sir."

"And it's true I know all about your fake temple without you telling me. But, Kirby, I'd like to think I'm an honorable man. Why, I've been doing nothing at all this morning except put together this paperwork on our transaction." And he handed over the manila folder.

Kirby, looking dubious, settled into one of the side chairs, opened the folder, and started to read. Innocent said to Valerie, "I am glad you're safe, Valerie."

"So am I," she said, smiling.

"I keep remembering that lunch we had together, and how much you liked the conch. You did like the conch, didn't you?"

She giggled, a sound Innocent would long cherish. "I liked it a lot," she said.

"Wait a minute," Kirby said. "This isn't even *half* what I paid you."

"Read on," Innocent urged him. "You'll see it makes sense."

"Not if I'm— *What?* I'm taking back a *mortgage*?"

"That's right," Innocent said, with his blandest smile.

Kirby looked outraged. "People don't give mortgages on *land*."

Innocent shrugged. "All the trouble there's been lately, I'd have a hard time right now getting my hands on that much cash. But I didn't want to let our deal fall through just because I didn't have enough cash money, and I knew you'd want to get all this settled and have *some* money to take with you when you leave, so—"

"Leave? Where am I going?"

Innocent gave Kirby a friendly but troubled look. "Don't you know what your situation right now is, Kirby?"

"I'm being shafted by you, as per usual."

"No no no. Kirby, you're a *hero*."

Valerie smiled and said, "Isn't that nice?"

"Well, yes and no," Innocent told her. "Unfortunately, Kirby's the sort of hero who would be very smart to be modest and avoid the limelight."

Kirby said, "Tell me about it."

"Your radio calls to Holdfast and the police," Innocent said, "meant help got there within thirty minutes of you breaking up the massacre. Two villagers dead, five terrorists dead, three captured and talking. Those little statues you threw out of the plane are being studied right now by a whole lot of experts. An American photojournalist on the scene managed to get some *very* dramatic shots of your plane coming through the clearing, in which your registration number is clearly visible.''

"Oh," Kirby said.

"Right now," Innocent went on, "Kirby Galway is the brave pilot who saved the defenseless village. However, I happen to know several people who are out and around Belize looking for the hero, because there's just one or two questions.''

Kirby sighed. Valerie said, "Mister St. Michael, what does this mean?''

"It means if Kirby's smart," Innocent told her, "he'll leave Belize. Just for a while, till it all blows over. Say three or four years.''

Kirby sighed again. Innocent smiled amiably and said, "That's why I worked so hard to get you just the best deal I could before you leave. A nice ten-year mortgage. And if you add up the purchase price and all the interest payments over the ten years, you'll find it comes out to *precisely* what you paid me for the land in the first place.''

"And you get to write off interest payments and . . .'' Kirby shook his head, disgusted. "You'll put the whole amount in a high-yield investment, make my payments out of the interest, and it'll never cost you a thing. *And* you'll have the land. You'll *make* money on this!''

"You'll have your purchase price back, Kirby," Innocent pointed out, and spread his hands. "That's what you wanted, isn't it?''

Kirby gave Valerie a long-suffering look. "Valerie," he said, "if you ever see me even *talking* to this fella again, run over and knock me down.''

Valerie laughed, her eyes gleaming as she watched them both, enjoying herself.

Innocent pointed to the folder. "And down in there, Kirby," he said, "you'll find a check for the first month's payment. How's that?"

"Terrific," Kirby said bitterly. Then he shook his head again, and sighed, and said, "Okay, Innocent, you win. Where do I sign?"

25

CROSSROADS OF DESTINY

Trump Glade, Florida. Route 216 south 8.4 miles from the movie house. Left at the sign reading Potchaw 12. Whitman Lemuel peered out the windshield of the rented car and there it was, a battered old metal sign, shot to death by any number of retarded louts but still discernibly reading, "Potchaw 12." And the odometer showed exactly eight point four miles since he'd passed the movie house in Trump Glade.

The Potchaw sign included an arrow, which pointed off to the right, where a blacktop road ran away between orange groves, but Kirby Galway's directions said to go the other way, so Lemuel spun the wheel and the rental turned left onto the dirt road meandering out across the flatness of Florida's scrub.

Now it was supposed to be 15.2 miles on to where he would find a red ribbon on a barbed wire fence. Turning up the air conditioning slightly, Lemuel relaxed a bit against the seat, and drove slowly but steadily toward his meeting with Kirby Galway.

Of course Galway expected those two New York merchants, Witcher and Feldspan, but he would certainly be willing to make his arrangements with Lemuel instead, once he understood that Witcher and Feldspan were now out of the picture completely.

The memory of Feldspan on that airplane, and the revolting horror he'd created up and down those aisles, came back suddenly into the forefront of Lemuel's brain, complete with sensory elements, and his lip curled in remembered disgust. It was *better* those two were out of it, much better.

Actually, Alan Witcher would have been prepared to go forward, but Gerry Feldspan was just too nervous for the job. Some other passenger had looked at him wrong and the result was absolute chaos; fortunately, Feldspan at least did manage to be sick at one point on the passenger who'd started all the trouble, apparently ruining a quite valuable harmonica.

But the upshot—well; perhaps we'll find a better word—the result of it all was that, in the Miami Airport, Feldspan absolutely *shrieked* that he was never going to commit another crime, he wanted nothing to do with smugglers, on and on and on, it was a miracle he didn't get the entire terminal arrested. Witcher, alternating between icy embarrassment and quite touching concern for his friend's wellbeing, at last agreed it was impossible for them to go forward, they would have to abandon the project forever. They would turn around at once and fly right back to New

York—"And get back that *letter* somehow," Witcher had said mysteriously—and leave the field to Lemuel.

Which they had. So here he was, driving 15.2 miles down this dirt road to his first rendezvous with Kirby Galway.

It was better for it to end this way, really. Witcher and Feldspan, apart from their rather nauseatingly blatant homosexuality, were merely merchants, the exact kind of money-grubbing art-denying dealers who had given the import of precious antiquities such a bad name, so it was just as well they wouldn't be getting their greedy little hands on any of the treasures from Galway's temple. As for Galway himself, the man was merely a thug, wasn't he, personally beneath contempt but useful as a tool in rescuing these treasures from the ignorance of the Central Americans and the venality of the likes of Witcher and Feldspan, so he could turn them over to selfless, dedicated, intelligent, learned, honest, unimpeachable scientists like himself.

He was the only truly *decent* character in the whole story, and he knew it.

And, as happened far too rarely in real life, this time the decent character was going to win. The meeting with Kirby Galway would happen in just the next few minutes, and whatever Kirby Galway was bringing to give to Witcher and Feldspan he could darn well just give to Whitman Lemuel instead.

"I deserve it," Lemuel muttered, as he drove.

The next section of barbed wire fence beyond the red ribbon had fallen in, making access easy, so Lemuel was already out on the weedy spongy field when the airplane first appeared. It circled overhead, he waved, and down it came, landing at the opposite end of the field and roaring over to come to a stop just near where Lemuel was standing.

The door opened in its side as Lemuel came around the wing, and there was Kirby Galway clambering out, seeming in an awful hurry. In fact, the engines still ran, propellers spinning, plane all atremble to be off.

Galway looked at him in surprise. (There was someone else in the plane.) "Where's Witcher and Feldspan?" he shouted, above the engine noise.

For some reason, Lemuel gestured behind himself, saying, "They went—"

"Still in the car? Okay, this is for them."

"No, they—"

Galway turned back and wrestled with something in the seat behind the pilot's, the other person helping. Lemuel stared, bewildered, and some sort of bale of hay came free at last, dropping out of the doorway, bouncing off the wing, landing on the ground at Lemuel's feet. "What—"

"Sorry you're getting it, too," Galway told him, grinning, not looking sorry at all. "Tell your pals in the car, I know all about *Trend*."

"Oh, my God. What have you—"

"Anonymous call to the DEA," Kirby told him, with nasty satisfaction.

"The what? What's that?"

"Drug Enforcement Administration," Kirby said, and climbed back up into the pilot's seat. "Sorry you're here," he called. "You should watch the company you keep."

Which was when Lemuel recognized the second person in the plane, and it was Valerie Greene. "YOU!" he cried.

She nodded and smiled, with a little wave.

"Every time I see you something terrible happens!" Lemuel shrieked, pointing at the girl. Kirby pulled his door shut and the plane moved away. "This is the third time!'' Lemuel screamed, following after, shaking his fist. "You're a *jinx*!"

The plane picked up speed, leaving him. Lemuel stopped, suddenly panting for some reason. And now that the engine roar was receding, the plane was way over there lifting into the air, Lemuel could hear another sound, behind him, far in the distance.

Sirens.

Getting closer.

He turned and looked back toward the rental car parked on the little narrow dirt road, and his eye fell on the bale Kirby had pulled from the plane.

"That isn't hay," he said aloud.

Third time lucky.

26

SAILING DIRECTIONS (EN ROUTE) FOR
THE CARIBBEAN SEA

Valerie sewed with tiny stitches. Perched naked tailor-fashion on a beach blanket bearing a picture of Mickey Mouse surfing—seated mostly on his smile—she was up from the beach just far enough to be in the dappled shade of the coconut palms. Behind her, just visible through the ring-necked trunks of the trees, was the island's only enclosed structure, a low house of unpainted concrete block with a slanted metal roof, flanked by the television satellite dish on the left and the electricity-generating windmill on the right. In front, the calm blue Caribbean folded itself time and time again on the beige sand.

Deceptively calm. The unnamed wee island on which

Valerie sat and sewed the hem of a full white cotton skirt lay deep within the perimeter of a well-known nautical hazard, the Banco Chinchorro, about 16 miles off the Yucatan coast of Mexico, due west of Chetumal Bay. At latitude 18 degrees, 23 minutes north and longitude 87 degrees, 27 minutes west, and existing mostly just below the surface of the sea, the four-mile-wide area of Banco Chinchorro is described in the United States Government publication *Sailing Directions (En Route) for the Caribbean Sea*, which Valerie had looked at shortly after arrival here, as "a dangerous steep-to shoal" with "numerous rocky heads and sand banks. The stranded wrecks which lie along the E side of the shoal were reported conspicuous both visually and by radar." This navigators' guide finishes its description with a "*Caution.*—In the vicinity of Banco Chinchorro there is usually a very strong current that sets toward its entire E side."

Commercial shipping and pleasure craft alike steer well around Banco Chinchorro. And yet, on a few of its tiny islets, the beach is wide and clean, the sea is blue and gentle and nearly transparent, the air is warm and soft with a delicious easterly breeze. If you'd like to be alone with your sweetheart, there are few better spots on earth than this.

Apart from Valerie herself, and the small house with its dish and windmill, the only other sign of human incursion on this island was Cynthia's wheelmarks on the hardpacked sand, off to Valerie's right. The first few times Kirby had flown down to San Pedro on the Belizean island of Ambergris Caye, 45 miles to the south, to pick up supplies or to be sure Innocent's check had been deposited into their account (the bank branch in San Pedro is open three mornings a week), Valerie had flown with him, telling herself she needed the change, the opportunity to shop in the hotel boutique, walk around among other people, but in fact she didn't need any of that at all. The truth was—

and she soon realized this—the truth was, if she left the island with Kirby every time he was going somewhere, it meant she was afraid he wouldn't come back, he'd strand her here. And *that* meant she didn't trust him.

And if she didn't trust him, what was she doing with him?

True, this life was a jolly and an easy one, particularly after all the running around just before they came here, but even more particularly after the total earnestness of her entire life prior to Belize. Thinking of that earlier self, of her earnest minister father and her earnest teacher brother, thinking of her own earnestness in pursuit of the dry joys of archaeology, she found it hard to believe she had spent so much time not being silly.

Not being silly.

What was the name of that book she'd read when she was a kid? *Green Mansions.* The idea inside that book had been an idea of *fun*, an idea of adventure and travel and strangeness and beauty, and what had she taken from it? In order to become Rima the bird girl, she had gone to college.

Not that college had been wrong for her, only that college had been wrong to be *everything* for her. A life circumscribed by the graves of the Mayas and the computers of UCLA is *not a full life*.

On the other hand, if she had always been too serious, Kirby had never been serious enough. They were good for one another, she felt. He took her out of herself—mm, yes, in several ways—he made her less self-consciously earnest and intense. At the same time, Valerie was leading Kirby slowly into the simpler forms and nearer waters of responsibility, showing him that a life spent in constant flight above the surface of things really isn't very satisfactory in the long run.

And that was why, about three months ago, she'd said to him one day, "I don't think I'll come along to San

Pedro this time. I want to do more digging on the other side of the island.'' (There were traces of ancient occupation buried over there, bits of rubble that might have been pots, small pieces of charred wood. Toward the end of the Mayan civilization, after their great days of temple building, they had become merchants awhile, sailing their goods up and down the east coasts of Mexico and Central America, with outposts and warehouses on various islands along the way. Had this been one? Valerie was still an archaeologist.)

Kirby had argued against her staying that first time, but she'd been adamant, and at last he'd agreed, and kissed her, and flown away. She'd watched Cynthia rise above the blue water into the paler blue sky, waggle her wings in farewell and roll away to the south, and she'd had no idea then if he would come back or not. If he did return it would mean he loved her as she loved him, they could trust one another, they were right to be together. And if he never came back, that would at least be a good thing to know.

And if he didn't come back she was sure that, sooner or later, once again she would be rescued.

But, as it turned out, she was past rescue now; Kirby had come back. Now she traveled with him perhaps one time in three, and mostly only went up in Cynthia for her flying lessons, which progressed slowly but steadily.

Valerie finished the hem, knotted the thread, bit off the end, and put the needle away in the little terracotta incense pot (fake-ancient, a gift from Tommy Watson). Standing, she shook out the skirt, looked at it, decided it was all right, and folded it over her forearm; there was a mirror in the house, she'd try it on there. She was stooping to pick up the incense pot when the buzz first became audible.

Cynthia.

She could always hear the plane some time before she saw it. Staying back in the shade, nevertheless holding one hand out above her eyes, Valerie searched the skies, and there it was, just circling by to come in from the northwest, against the easterly breeze. Cynthia disappeared briefly behind the coconut palms, then emerged again, much lower, about to touch down on the sand far to Valerie's left.

It took airplanes such an amazingly long distance to stop after they'd landed. Still moving quite briskly, Cynthia rolled down the beach past Valerie, who waved, then continued on a while farther, and at last stopped. A brief engine roar, and then the plane turned around and trundled back, wingtips bobbing slightly. Smiling, Valerie started out of the tree shade, when all at once she realized Kirby wasn't alone. There were other people in the plane.

Oh, dear; and she naked. Quickly she stepped into the skirt and fixed the snaps at its side. There was nothing she could do about her top, and it would just be too silly and childish to run away to the house. Well, she'd just have to pretend everything was perfectly normal.

Kirby had climbed down from the plane and waved to her, and now two people were getting out, a man and a woman. A brave smile on her face—I am *not* embarrassed at being bare-breasted—Valerie walked down like a proper hostess to greet her guests.

The man and woman were both under 30, and extremely unalike. The woman was a skinny little ash blonde, with dry-looking skin the color of mahogany and a very attractive but tough-looking face. The man was very tall and gawky and pale-skinned, with a layer of soft baby fat all over his body. He was very slightly bucktoothed, and looked eager and naive and innocent and well-intentioned, whereas the woman looked like somebody who'd seen everything and believed nothing.

"Valerie," Kirby said, grinning, as she arrived, "I'd like you to meet a couple people I just ran into down in

San Pedro. Ran into *again*. This is Tandy; she's a Texas girl with a rich daddy.''

"How do you do," Valerie said.

Tandy looked her up and down, taking it all in, the unusually tall girl with the all-over tan and the flowing white skirt, and she shook her head. With a crooked smile, she said, "You win."

Valerie wasn't sure what that was—a compliment?—but she knew it was meant in friendly fashion, so she smiled back and said, "I'm glad Kirby brought you."

"And this is Tandy's friend—" Kirby began.

"In a manner of speaking," Tandy said.

"Aw, Tandy," said the man, grinning and gawking.

"He's—" Kirby frowned, then leaned toward the man. "I'm sorry, I forgot your name again."

"Oh! Wull, uh, it's *Albert*."

"Albert, this is Valerie."

"How do you do?"

"Wull, this is *wonderful*. You live here, do you? On this *island*."

"For now," Valerie said.

Smiling at Valerie, Kirby said, "You'll never guess. Albert has a *great* interest in pre-Columbian art."

Valerie found herself grinning from ear to ear, enjoying Kirby's pleasure. "Is that right?" she said.

"Oh, wull, *yes*. Back in Ventura, I converted the entire west *wing* to a kind of *museum*."

"That sounds wonderful."

"You must come *see* it."

"Maybe we will," Valerie told him.

"Albert is very interested," Kirby said, "in Mayan treasures in particular. I thought we might have a nice talk about that."

"That would be fun," Valerie said.

Kirby put an arm around her shoulders, saying, "We'll unload Cynthia later. First I think we ought to go up to the house and settle in and have a drink. Tandy and Albert are gonna stay over, we'll do a little cookout, then all four of us go back to San Pedro tomorrow, have a nice sit-down restaurant dinner. What do you want? El Tulipan or The Hut?''

''Let me think about it,'' Valerie said. I'll wear this skirt, she thought.

They started up from the beach toward the house. Still with his arm around Valerie's shoulders, Kirby bent his head and gave her a quizzical look, saying, ''Don't you think you're overdressed?''

Valerie laughed.

BESTSELLING BOOKS FROM TOR